Cynthia came to consciousness with a gasp, surrounded by icy water rushing in around her. Out the smashed rear window, she could see the top of the trunk was still an inch or two above water. There was no sound other than the water rushing into the cabin. Grasping the rearview mirror, she pulled herself up and began a search for the glove compartment. The realization that Adele could already be dead panicked her.

"Adele!" she screamed. "Adele, hold on." Her fingers were growing as numb as the rest of her body as she fumbled and groped the inside walls of the glove compartment.

The car tipped forward, plunging her deeper into the cold water. She willed her hands to work faster and kept her eyes on the window, judging how long she had before she had to get out. . . .

By Echo Heron
Published by The Ballantine Publishing Group

INTENSIVE CARE: The Story of a Nurse
MERCY
CONDITION CRITICAL: The Story of a Nurse Continues
TENDING LIVES: Nurses on the Medical Front

PULSE
PANIC
PARADOX

FATAL
DIAGNOSIS

Echo Heron

BALLANTINE BOOKS • NEW YORK

A Ballantine Book
Published by The Ballantine Publishing Group
Copyright © 2000 by Echo Heron

All rights reserved under International and Pan-American Copyright Conventions. Published in the United States by The Ballantine Publishing Group, a division of Random House, Inc., New York, and simultaneously in Canada by Random House of Canada Limited, Toronto.

Ballantine and colophon are registered trademarks of Random House, Inc.

www.randomhouse.com/BB/

Library of Congress Card Number 00-190726

ISBN 0-8041-1913-9

Manufactured in the United States of America

First Edition: September 2000

10 9 8 7 6 5 4 3 2 1

In memory of Mooshie

ACKNOWLEDGMENTS

I wish to thank the following people:

Ken Holmes, coroner, for his continued support and invaluable information on law enforcement and forensics

Sgt. Laura J. Warren, for information on police procedures

Cynthia M. O'Neill, my feisty SF policewoman and backstreet guide

Darrell C. Greenhouse, for the tour through nanotechnology

Henri Bergmann, for encouraging me to get out of DOS mode and for help with the nanotech questions

Jan Voskuyl, my real-life pacemaker lady extraordinaire

Tom Meadoff, ever my complete medical encyclopedia

Simon E. Scott, my English interpreter in London

Kurt Helm, for mouthwatering tidbits of information

Glen and Jane Justice, for providing me with a space to write while in my nomadic phase of life

Terry Hand, for the medical information

Ernie Bartelson, for the plot seed and those bits and pieces of info

Nicole Leclair, for the translation

Sherry Ann Schumacher, for her research on the Middle East

Scott Jones and Kellie Moore, my San Francisco/Marin detectives and explorers of cubbyholes

Greg Ryherd, my car expert

Laura Gasparis Vonfrolio (Moose Woman), for the support and the much-needed laughter

Sue Shotridge, for giving me direction and insight into the Tlingits

Bert R. Wren, for taking the time to show a complete stranger the logistics of being locked inside the trunk of a car

Frank Langben, for bits and pieces of this and that

Mr. Anonymous, for his information on Federal Bureau of Investigation procedures

And *Colette Coutant Trembly*, for being there always. You are a true friend.

ONE

THE BODY OF FIFTY-ONE-YEAR-OLD DAISY ROTH-
schild floated above the antiseptic sheets while her mind paid
a visit to the day she discovered the plughole.

It was the first time Nanny Rita let her play unsupervised in
the massive claw-foot tub. Doofus, her yellow rubber ducky,
bobbed and dipped between the clouds of gardenia-scented
bubbles while the Bad Thing that usually hid at the back of
her toy closet hovered near the privy, waiting for a lapse in her
bravery to rear up and take shape.

A chubby balloon of babyflesh adrift on an enchanted sea,
Daisy was lost in daydreams of princesses, wish-granting
fairies, and an island where people lived in houses made of
chocolate cake and whipped cream. It had all been perfectly
pleasant until Nanny Rita came in on a blast of cold air wield-
ing the thin rough towels and told her she was going to shrivel
like an old prune if she didn't come out straightaway. Willful
and overindulged, Daisy refused, though the water had turned
cold and the porpoise had swallowed all the bubbles.

Nanny Rita, who didn't particularly like children, gave the
pull-chain a jowl-jarring tug. The white rubber stopper popped
out with a loud, sucking *Shooowack! Glug! Slurp!*

Not only was Daisy's adventure shattered, the pull-chain—a
fine string of gold beads, compliments of the Fairy Princess—
was receiving rather shabby treatment at the hands of the spiteful nanny. Daisy reacted as any spoiled four-year-old might
in such a moment of overbearing adult interference by throwing a tantrum and refusing to be removed from the draining tub.

In her own fit of rage (brought on in part by Mr. Nanny

1

having run off three weeks earlier with a woman half her age), Nanny Rita refrained from braining the ill-mannered, rotten child but left her to take chill in the drafty bath. At the same moment Nanny Rita slammed the door behind her, Doofus swam past, headed for the drain. He looked terribly alarmed, and Daisy was sure she could hear him quacking for help.

Her eyes darted to the privy—the Bad Thing had moved. She fixed her gaze on the plughole.

Slurrrrp! Glug!

Vaguely she recalled having looked down the plughole once before and feeling afraid. It was dark and bottomless; she imagined it was actually the opened jaws of a sinister eel monster, like the one Nanny Rita showed her in the London Aquarium—the one that gobbled up naughty, unruly children.

The slight tug on her toes caused her to whimper and pull her foot away from the plughole, except she couldn't get away at all—her foot slipped back. The monster was sucking her into his mouth. As the plughole jaws were about to close around his tail feathers, Doofus squawked in rubber ducky distress. Catching him at the last second, she threw him overboard. The duck hit the doorknob and landed with a squawk of gratitude somewhere near the privy.

The milky water swirled faster as the thirsty beast greedily sucked it down. All the stories Nanny Rita read from *Grimm's Fairy Tales* were true! How could she have forgotten that after monsters had their fill of water, they wanted meat? Little girl meat—tender and pink.

Now she wished she had listened to Nanny Rita and not eaten the second helping of pudding after supper. The monster on the other side of the plughole would smell it inside her and there was nothing monsters liked better than a creamy pudding center inside their little girls. It would tear her open and rip out her tummy with rows of sharp, pointed teeth.

As terror paralyzed her, the bottomless, sucking gullet got hold of her toes. How could Nanny do this to her? Had she really been such a naughty girl? She felt the first pricks of teeth as her foot slipped between its jaws. Freeing herself of the terror that had found her throat, she loosed a bloodcurdling scream that brought Nanny Rita running. Her round face pushed close to Daisy's own.

"Stop this shouting at once!" demanded a shrill voice that was not Nanny Rita's. "You will disturb the other patients."

"The plughole," Daisy whispered, gasping. "I was going down. It was eating my foot!"

Nanny Rita's face grew thinner, then went out of focus. Her jowls (the pouches in which Nanny Rita said she kept her extra supper, although Daisy suspected it was really where she hid her fangs) turned into a brilliant red-lipped mouth that smiled. Nanny Rita had never smiled as far as Daisy knew. The gray hair that was perpetually pulled back in a tight bun at the nape of Nanny Rita's neck was now jet black and fluffy.

Nanny's hooded steel eyes became the soft brown eyes of that sweet Nurse Murphy.

Daisy sighed in relief and had a thought that would have killed her mother: *Thank God for the Irish.*

"Oh. Terribly sorry. I seem to have fallen asleep. Is surgery over?" Daisy looked down at her chest but saw nothing except white sheets pulled up to her chin.

The nurse shook her head. "No. You are still in the preoperative holding area. Dr. Knowles has been detained at hospital." The nurse looked at her watch. Daisy could focus enough to see the watch was expensive. How did a nurse—an Irish nurse at that—working in London afford such a nice timepiece? Even an American nurse's salary would not permit a watch of that quality.

"He is already an hour late." The nurse was saying in an accent that Daisy didn't think sounded Irish at all, at least not when you really listened. Not Russian, but . . .

Nurse Murphy was doing something to her intravenous line. Daisy craned her neck, trying to see exactly what, but the nurse moved deliberately out of her range of vision. "I have called in Dr. Wilson to perform the biopsy."

Daisy was dismayed. "But Dr. Knowles has been my physician since I was a girl. He knows me thoroughly. I'm not at all familiar with Dr. Wilson." She tried turning onto her side so that she could see the nurse (what *was* she doing back there?)

and discovered that she was held tight to the bed by straps across her ankles, legs, and chest, and one on each wrist. It struck her as odd, though she said nothing.

"Really, though, don't you think this a storm in a teacup? All this fuss! I can just as well have the biopsy when I return to America. Certainly the physicians in California are as qualified as any medical man here.

"Why must I have these straps?" Daisy giggled faintly. "Afraid I might escape? I say, why don't we postpone this whole affair until . . . ?"

She shuddered when the man came into her circle of vision. Unsmiling, he studied her with detachment, as if she were a specimen under a slide.

"I am Dr. Wilson," the swarthy man said in an accent much heavier than Nurse Murphy's. He turned to the nurse. "You have given her the second dose?"

"Dose?" Daisy asked in as pleasant a tone as she could. "What dose? What are you giving me?"

"How much time do we have?" Nurse Murphy asked, ignoring her.

Dr. Wilson answered in a language she recognized: Arabic. One of her neighbors in California was an Arab and frequently spoke the language—most often at full volume either in early morning or late at night.

They loosened her straps and roughly turned her onto her side, facing away from them. The nurse swabbed something cold and ill smelling over her right hip and buttock. At once, Daisy felt dizzy and nauseated. It was hard keeping her eyelids open, as if she no longer had any control over them. She wanted to say she'd changed her mind and thought it best she leave, but she couldn't make her tongue and lips obey. All that came out was a soft whoosh of air.

Her feet were the first to go. A numbing tide crept slowly up her thighs, over her belly, and was having a go at her lungs. Each breath was work—she had to concentrate. *Pull in, let go. Pull in, let go.*

The panic settled in her brain as her body disconnected. *DO SOMETHING!* She let go of a silent scream. For a brief moment, she managed to force her lids open, but all she saw was the two of them standing there watching—glowering down at her like Nanny Rita used to.

For the first time she noticed Nurse Murphy certainly didn't look like any Irishwoman she'd ever seen before. And that nose! Goodness. *Nurse Murphyallah was more like it,* she thought.

Her eyes shut of their own accord and panic ignited in her temples. She should have suspected something was off when only two hours after her visit to Dr. Knowles's surgery, Nurse Murphy called to inform her that the doctor had reconsidered his advice. Suddenly it was essential that the lump he'd found in her breast be biopsied while she was still in London rather than wait until she returned home to California. Nurse Murphy said Doctor was quite insistent.

Daisy tried not to worry, although she realized that there must have been something terribly wrong with the blood samples he'd sent off to the laboratory to make him change his mind so completely. She'd spent the night in a dither, imagining all sorts of horrid things: chemotherapy, losing her hair, and having to wear one of those awful medical brassieres with the steel reinforced cups.

As if that weren't bad enough, Nurse Murphy then gave her the address of Dr. Knowles's emergency private surgery, where he practiced on Thursdays. In Lambeth, south of the river? It was preposterous. She couldn't imagine Dr. Knowles setting foot in such a place, let alone having his Thursday, Friday, or any day surgery there. He would never have stood for all those cracks and watermarks in the dingy plaster ceiling, nor the torn vinyl couch in that shabby hole they'd called the waiting room, nor the stench of rats that permeated the air.

She managed to open her eyes again, and for a brief moment she saw Nurse Murphy holding up to the light an object that appeared to be a cross between a syringe and a gun. She tapped it lightly, and disappeared out of view. There was a slight pressure on her upturned hip. Within a second or two, the numbness that had been creeping into her lungs was complete—no sensation remained except panic and fear.

Her lids closed again. In the background, Daisy heard a familiar sucking sound: *Slurrrrp! Glug, glug.*

"Open your eyes!" Dr. Wilson demanded.

With great effort, Daisy obeyed. He stood over her. She had a brief concern about the fact he was wearing a suit. And he didn't have a surgical mask?

Violently, Dr. Wilson repositioned her so that she was facing them.

"Count backward from ten," commanded Nurse Murphy.

"Ten . . ." Daisy heard the words but had no idea who was saying them. Surely it couldn't have been her voice.

". . . nine . . ." She noticed their hands. The nurse wore exam gloves, but the doctor did not. Neither had on a surgical cap or gown. Perhaps she should suggest an apron at least. *What about contamination? Hadn't they heard of Florence Nightingale and sterilization? Shouldn't they . . . ?*

". . . eight . . ." No surgical lamps? It was so dark. How could he see to . . . ?

Dr. Wilson stepped aside, and Nurse Murphy took his place. The woman pulled down the sheet and pointed to Daisy's hip.

". . . sev . . ."

My God, they're going to operate on the wrong part of my body! They've got the wrong patient. Stop!

Dr. Wilson nodded and handed Nurse Murphy a scalpel.

Nurses practicing surgery? Wait! No . . . no!

There came a low, gentle slurping, sucking sound, rather like a thick liquid being pulled down a plughole. She was too far gone to feel anything of what they were doing, but as the dark swallowed her whole, she had a last, clear thought:

Forty-seven years later and the plughole monster was going to get her after all.

TWO

ADELE MONSARRAT, R.N., CAREFULLY PLACED THE leech—no larger than her pinky—behind the sleeping patient's ear. The bloodsucking annelid remained still. She wondered if it was hungry after the red-eye flight from South Carolina, or if it was experiencing some sort of worm jet lag.

"They were fighting over a parking place at Vista Point?" Adele asked, a smile beginning at the corners of her mouth. The leech attached itself to the patient and began to feed.

With long-nosed surgical tweezers, Cynthia O'Neil, R.N., fished a second leech out of the jar and held it as far away from herself as she could. "Yep. Minnesota tourist versus *Intelligencer* reporter. Mr. Knudsen here didn't have a chance—the Coast Guard sure as hell wasn't going to wait for the press to find parking spaces while they fished a body out of the Bay."

"So exactly what happened after the reporter bulldozed Mr. Knudsen's car?"

Cynthia carefully placed the leech on a sterile square of gauze and blew back a wisp of hair that fell across her cheek. "Like any good Minnesotan, Mr. Knudsen was politely pointing out that the bumper wasn't meant to be part of his backseat, when the reporter went zerko and bit off his ear. One of the bridge workers found it and brought it in on ice. It took Dr. Wortz almost four hours to reattach it. Ears are tough, I hear." She examined the thing at the end of the tweezers and shuddered. The whole idea of using worms on fresh surgical wounds made her want to throw up.

Adele caught the younger nurse's involuntary movement. "Whatsamatter, dearie? Leechcraft too primitive for you?"

7

"Don't get me wrong—I like worms. When I was a kid, some of my best friends were worms, but here we are surrounded by ultra-advanced medical technology, and we're using worms on fresh surgical wounds? It's bizarre."

"I look at it this way." Adele placed the second leech an inch away from the first one. "Their saliva provides a local anesthetic, anticoagulant, and antibiotic. The best bioengineers in the world can't re-create the stuff. That's advanced enough for me. The only two drawbacks are that they have to be constantly supervised or they'll wander off and try to suck someone dry, and you have to kill them when they're full, which gives a whole new meaning to the term 'the Last Supper.'"

Adele straightened. "So who got pulled out of the Bay? Anybody we dislike enough that we might be considered as suspects?"

"Nah." Cynthia shrugged. "Just some old guy—probably a drunk who fell in. It was totally gross. The sharks got his head, hands, and guts. It was in the *Chronicle* today—back page, second section."

They said nothing for a while, watching the leeches feed.

"Where'd they take the body?" Adele asked.

"Since Coast Guard fished him out on the Marin side, he came to our morgue. Boxer did the postmortem. He's still downstairs waiting for someone to ID him."

"Who?" Adele asked, "Boxer or the stiff?"

The women laughed. David "Boxer" Takamoto, Marin County's chief medical examiner, was known for his precise and somewhat inelastic manner. The three of them had remained friends even after Cynthia dumped him and he'd been forced to join the growing retinue of Cynthia's ex-lovers. Adele suspected that like most of Cynthia's heartkill, Dr. Takamoto still carried a torch for the pretty green-eyed nurse. Like all the dumpees before him, David eventually came to her for the soothing of ruffled ego feathers. Adele liked to think of them as "her flock"—graduates of the Cynthia O'Neil School of Cruel Love.

Wearing her usual constipated-for-a-month expression, Grace Thompson, a.k.a. the Queen Mother, head nurse of Ellis Hospital's infamous Ward 8, a.k.a. the Catchall Ward from Hell, blocked the doorway with her squarish figure. Her silvery white hair, styled after an inverted bird's nest, was nicely festooned with a peaked nursing cap. Her mode of dress told anyone bored enough to stare exactly whom they were dealing with: white uniform, white stockings, and regulation white nursing shoes, the Queen Mother was a vision right out of a 1940s nurses' training film.

"As the two of you seem to have time for lollygagging, I've assigned the next admit to you, Adele. O'Neil, you can take the one coming up on his heels."

"Do you really think that's wise, Grace?" Adele asked, keeping her eyes on the leeches that were already changing— growing darker as they filled with blood. For the two years since Grace Thompson had replaced the ward's former head nurse, Adele refused to conform to the Brit's noncollaborative, anti-common-sense style of management. This left her an open target for Grace's postmenopausal, pre-hormone-replacement rages.

"I've got to keep a close eye on these leeches in addition to caring for the other six patients you assigned me. How about if Skip takes the new guy? He's got the lightest load."

"Nurse Muldinardo will be taking over your two patients in eight-fourteen C and D," Grace interrupted, her jowls flapping slightly. The precise British accent was heavier than usual. "The new patient is a VIP. He is . . ."

"That means he has a ton of money," Cynthia said, placing herself in front of the head nurse. "How old is he? Is he cute? Is he sexually functional and does he have hair on his back?"

Grace's graying eyebrow arched. "Mr. Penn is . . ."

"Oh my God!" Cynthia grabbed Grace's wrist—the one with the watch almost completely hidden by folds of flesh. "Sean Penn?! Oh, God, I'm going to scream. He is so outrageously awesome! He's building a house in Ross—I've been driving up there every day before work and parking outside the gates. I think I saw him drive past last Tuesday about six in the morning? I almost had an orgasm from twenty yards away!"

Grace's jaw unhinged to display a mouth full of dental

mishaps. "Good God!" She wrenched her arm away from Cynthia with a look one might give a leech. "This is not Sean Penn." Grace looked down her nose. "I wouldn't assign a dog to that dreadful excuse for a thespian. Thomas Edison Penn is the president of Pacific Gas and Electric for Northern California."

"Wow," Adele said, scrubbing her hands. "Did he get his name as part of a predestined career choice package, or is he a direct descendent of Mr. Electricity himself?"

"I believe there is a direct bloodline, so make sure this gentleman receives the best of care," Grace said. "His admitting diagnosis is possible cerebrovascular accident and a malfunctioning pacemaker. Dr. Dhery has requested that vital signs and neurological assessments be recorded every thirty minutes until Dr. Ravens arrives."

An emergency department gurney rolled toward room 800. Adele caught a glimpse of a gray face.

"Well, well, speak of the drooling devil himself," Cynthia said, moving past Grace and falling in behind the gurney.

Grace hung back to avoid any and all contact with the patient. Rumor had it that like some administrative nurses, the woman had never worked as a bedside nurse after her student clinicals. Of her own admission—made public at the Ward 8 Christmas party after three glasses of sucker's punch—Grace had an aversion to sick people.

At the door, Adele turned. "Hey, Grace," Adele said, "keep an eye on those worms, would you?"

"We followed the usual stroke protocol."

Kadeja, the new ER nurse, stood on her toes to hang the IV bag on the pole attached to the bed. "We have been trying to get him into the CAT scanner for the last forty minutes, but they can't get it going, so he's scheduled at Bellevue scanner in an hour."

"When was the onset of symptoms?" Adele asked.

"We have no way of knowing," the girl said, adjusting the clip holding back a mass of frizzy black hair. She was intense and pretty in an earthy way; her accent lent a charm to her otherwise abrupt manner.

"It made using thrombolytics out of the question. He was found wandering around Main Street in Tiburon in his pajamas an hour ago. He came into ER with a BP of one seventy-four over a hundred, in atrial fibrillation at a ventricular rate of a hundred and ten, and a temp of one hundred and one. He's complaining of a headache, and there was one episode of dizziness and vomiting. There was no trace of blood or pills or undigested food."

Mr. Penn yawned so wide, his jaw popped. Adele took the opportunity to check for signs of injury inside the mouth. "Did you find any signs of trauma or seizure activity?"

"There are a couple of fresh scrapes on his elbows, but that's all. Respiratory rate is normal with only fine rales in the lower lobes, but otherwise clear. When he first came in, he scored thirteen on the Glasgow Coma Scale, but he has come up to a fourteen now. He is oriented, but his speech is still slurred. He is hard to understand unless you listen carefully. His BP just before we left ER was one hundred thirty over eighty, pulse is still around one-ten."

Adele leaned close to the man's face and laid her hand on his arm. "Mr. Penn?"

The man stared vacantly out the window, seeming not to hear.

"Mr. Penn, look at me, please."

Slowly, he turned his gaze on her, and her assessment began. He'd followed commands, his pupils were equal and reactive, and there was a slight droop of the left side of his mouth. His breath did not smell of alcohol or acetone; his skin was intact, flushed, and dry; and there were no outward signs of trauma—no bruises, lacerations, or fractures. His respirations were unlabored, although there was a tightness about his eyes that Adele interpreted as pain.

"Mr. Penn, do you know where you are?"

His lips worked for a few seconds before any words came out. Each word took several seconds and painstaking effort to form. *"Un médecin qui parle anglais?"*

Miroslav Dvorak—"Mirek" to those nurses who played mentor to the second-year nursing student—laughed. A

Czech immigrant, Mirek reportedly knew six or seven languages and was frequently called on as an interpreter.

"What did he say?" Adele asked.

"He is speaking French." Mirek fit nasal prongs into the man's nostrils and turned the oxygen flow to five liters. "He says he wants a doctor who can speak English."

"Thomas! I *am* speaking English!" Adele said as she untied his hospital johnny and let it drop. "Are you in pain?" Her eyes were drawn to a new pink scar over the left breast. Donning a pair of exam gloves, she gingerly fingered the area and adjusted the overhead lamp so that both she and Mirek could get a closer look. The light flickered several times, went out, and then came on again. Adele sighed and hit the lamp with her hand. The light flickered back on.

"Hey, looks like you've got yourself fixed up with a new engine there, sport," Cynthia said, and hooked the monitor leads to his electrodes. An unusual amount of artifact filled the screen. Through it, Adele could make out occasional pacemaker spikes firing in a haphazard rhythm, regardless of the man's own rhythm. None of the spikes seemed to be capturing.

Mr. Penn closed his eyes, letting his head fall back against the pillow. "Headache." The word came out "heahachh."

"Do you remember when your pacemaker was put in, Mr. Penn?"

Thomas Penn mouthed a word or two and swallowed with a little difficulty. Adele made a notation on the palm of her hand: "+ swallow reflex."

"Where's the family?" Cynthia asked.

"He has a daughter living in Seattle," Kadeja replied. "Our clerk left a message for her to call the hospital."

Mr. Penn sighed. "Helen." The name was slurred but understandable.

"Is that your daughter's name?" Cynthia asked.

"Kitty," the man whispered. The word came out like "Kigghe."

Cynthia leaned closer. "You have another daughter named Kitty?"

"Here kitty-kitty." His voice broke and he coughed.

Adele opened her palm again and added "+ gag reflex." "Do you have a cat named Helen? Is that what you're trying to say?"

Mr. Penn nodded, mouthed words, and sighed again. The circles under his eyes gave him a haunted, exhausted look.

"Don't worry about your cat, we'll make sure somebody gets over there to care for it." Adele glanced at Cynthia. "Is Rymesteade still in the house?"

"Do I hear my name being taken in vain?" Rymesteade Dhery, Ellis Hospital's current doc on call, entered the room carrying a chart. On his way to the bed, he gave Cynthia an air kiss. Since the two became a couple, Dr. Dhery had blossomed the way a new bride blossoms in her first year of marriage. The original ninety-seven-pound weakling, Dr. Dhery had gone from being a nervous, circles-under-the-eyes, timid, pale wimp to being a tired, blushing regular guy—not quite Charles Atlas yet, but people had stopped kicking sand in his face.

"How's Mr. Penn?" the physician asked.

"Stroking as we speak," Adele said. "Fill me in on the history and details."

Rymesteade checked the IV bag of Lactated Ringers solution. "Sixty-five-year-old CEO of Pacific Gas and Electric with a history of atrial fibrillation was found disoriented and wandering around Tiburon.

"He's been seeing Dale Zimmer over at UC who had him controlled on Pronestyl, but a month ago while on a business trip in Berlin, Mr. Penn apparently had a syncopal episode. He was rushed to a nearby clinic in a profound bradycardia, diagnosed with sick sinus syndrome and a pacemaker was inserted posthaste. When he returned to the States, he neglected to get a follow-up with Zimmer for reasons we have yet to uncover.

"I spoke to his daughter in Seattle, who said she visited him after he got back from Europe. She didn't notice anything unusual at the time, but said he called her two nights ago complaining of exhaustion and an irregular pulse. She said her father has a history of forgetting to take his Pronestyl regularly, so she advised him to make an appointment with Zimmer right away for blood levels and to have his pacer checked.

"He told her he was going to see some doctor in San Francisco that the Berlin clinic recommended. He hasn't. . ."

The sudden earsplitting blare of catcalls, whistles, and applause caused everyone, including Mr. Penn, to cover their ears and search for the source of the disturbance. Their eyes all went to the wall-mounted TV as it crackled to life. On the screen, Oprah Winfrey was interviewing a thin young man dressed in a Carmen Miranda costume. On one bulging deltoid was the tattoo of a swastika.

Adele reached for the remote control, but the TV went blank before she touched it. As soon as she stepped back, the set clicked on again, and the call bell activated.

In the doorway, Malloy, Ward 8's swing-shift monitor tech and resident Buddhist, nodded his shaved head in the direction of the monitor. "I did some mapping and found that besides the pacer spikes being erratic, he's not capturing. Do you want me to call for an EKG?"

Dr. Dhery shook his head. "I doubt it will be any different than the one they got in ER." He reached up and unplugged the TV from the wall. "The lights kept flickering down there too, and when they got him into the scanner, it malfunctioned. Hopefully Bellevue's scanner will be working." He turned back to Adele.

"I suspect we're dealing with an occlusive stroke, but we won't know for sure until after the scan. Until then, I'd like every-fifteen-minute vitals and neuros charted."

Yawning, Mr. Penn rolled onto his side with a grunt. The lights stopped flickering, and the call bell and monitor interference ceased at once.

Adele stifled a scream by stuffing the side of her hand into her mouth.

One of the leeches had become so engorged, the body— black and huge with blood—had rolled off and was lying dormant on Mr. Knudsen's shoulder. The other was in a feeding frenzy over the patient's carotid artery.

"So much for Grace's nursing supervision," Cynthia said,

calmly picking the leech off the man's carotid and dropping it into a plastic container of rubbing alcohol.

This time it was Adele who shuddered and looked away. A tree-hugger from way back, she hated killing anything— even if it was a leech. The sight of the annelid going through its death throes triggered a memory of the time she attempted to expand on her usual vegetarian fare by cooking escargot for a gathering of her carnivorous friends. As she dumped four dozen live snails into the boiling water, she was so appalled by the uproar of tortured screams that she ran from the house and would not return until Cynthia had removed every trace of the carnage.

"Christ on a bike," Adele yelled over the noise of the sirens. "Slow down!" She willed herself not to look out the ambulance window. She didn't want to see the crash before it happened. "We're only going five miles with a perfectly stable patient. Why exchange that for three dead ones?"

Twenty-two-year-old Trevor Snipes bobbed up and down in his spring-loaded seat. At every pothole, his head hit the headliner and his hands bounced off the wheel. Grinning wildly, the young man turned to look at her. In his crew cut with the lightning bolts shaved into the sides, the three gold loops on his left ear, and the silver one through his left nostril, he looked like a happy moron on a carnival ride.

Adele hoped he had a girlfriend or a mother who loved him enough to forgive him his hair and piercings.

"You say something, babe?" Trevor yelled back over the wail of the sirens and the zydeco music turned up to max on the civilian radio.

A flash of temper lifted Adele out of the jump seat next to Mr. Penn and sent her lurching to the cabin. With a flick of the wrist, she hit the switch that turned off the sirens and snapped off the radio. "Slow down!" she screamed in the ear with the gold loops. "Before you kill us all."

Trevor's grin didn't falter as he took his foot off the gas, and the rig slowed. 84 ... 65 ... 40 ... 25. "This slow enough for ya?" Trevor's laugh sounded like Barney on methamphetamines.

Adele gave the kid a wary eye and stepped back out of the cabin. "Whatever. Just don't . . ."

The rig took a sudden sharp turn that knocked her off her feet. She bounced off the equipment cabinets, hit her head on the overhead rack, and fell next to Mr. Penn. The man opened his eyes momentarily, looked around, then closed them again as if to shut out the insanity going on around him.

Scrambling to her feet, she looked out the window just as the plastic head of Señor Taco Homeboy slid by. She estimated that the rim of his giant red sombrero missed scraping the side of the emergency vehicle by an eighth of an inch. The microphone hidden inside the plastic head clicked twice.

"Buenos días, amigos," said a voice that had no specific gender. "What'll it be?"

Trevor leaned out the window, still bobbing and grinning. "And buenos díos to you, Señor Homeboy. I'll have uno grande Coka-Cola with mucho ice-o." He glanced over his shoulder. "Yo, babe, you want anything while my Spanish is hot? How 'bout you, pop? Want a burrito or somethin'?"

Adele was speechless—almost. Picking herself up off the floor, she pulled down the skirt of her scrub dress and pushed her face into his. "Have you lost your mind? We have a patient here, and you're stopping for a Coke at a fast-food joint?"

His grin faltered a little. "Yeah, but you just said the old guy was stable and I've got me some serious throat dust balls that'd choke Death Valley. Homeboy's was like right there, you know? You ever tried their fries with huevos rancheros?"

The microphone clicked again. "Just a Coke? Whatsamatter, gringo, you on welfare? We got a special on fries today. Two for the price of one. How about it?"

Trevor's eyes slid away from the daggers she was throwing through narrowed eyes. His grin was badly wounded and limping off his face. "Ah, no. I think that's it, Señor Homeboy." He paused, looked at Adele again, and added: "In more ways than one."

* * *

It was the third time he'd offered her the extra, free bag of fries, and the third time she'd turned them down. The first bag he'd finished before they'd left the parking lot of Señor Homeboy's. She'd never seen anyone inhale food quite that way before. Maybe Nelson once, but Nelson was a dog with a brain the size of a walnut.

"You know how much longer it's going to be?" asked Trevor as he dangled several limp fries above his opened mouth. They reminded Adele somehow of the leeches. She watched fascinated as his tongue slithered out and wound itself around the fries like a trained snake. As the organ performed nimble feats, the fact that it was pierced through the middle seemed a relatively minor attraction.

"If the scanner behaves itself, we'll be out of here in another forty minutes. Why? You in a hurry?"

The boy swallowed the fries and quickly lowered another handful—greasy Christians going to the porcelain lions. She watched carefully to see if he chewed. He didn't.

"No, just wondering." Trevor looked around and then back at her. "You got cool eyes. I've never seen eyes like that before. They fake or something?"

"Fake?" Adele gave him a look.

"You know, like colored contacts or something? I've never seen gold eyes except on a cat."

"They're real," she said, picking up a used copy of the *San Francisco Chronicle*. She was used to people commenting on her eyes. Her optician told her that only one percent of the population had eyes the color of cider—or urine, depending how you wanted to look at it. The disadvantages were that they had a tendency to stick in people's memories, which made her easy to pick out of a crowd—or a lineup—again, depending on the mood of the day.

"How come it took so long setting the old guy up in the scanner? Did he get claustrophobic or something?"

"There was too much interference," she told him, looking up from the paper. "It wouldn't work until we positioned him in just a certain way. Same thing happened over at Ellis. It wasn't just the scanners either. Every time he'd move, lights started flickering, or the TV acted up. The monitors were picking up erratic tracings. It's strange."

"EMI," Trevor said, burying his face in the fries box, like a horse with a feed bag. "I read about it in *Science Journal*. Electromagnetic interference. The gomer has a pacemaker, or some kind of internal defibrillator, right?"

"Yep." Adele nodded, reconsidering her opinion of Trevor's intellect. "A malfunctioning pacemaker."

Trevor screwed up one corner of his mouth. "Only thing is, I can't imagine a pacemaker putting out enough juice to disable or affect anything like a monitor or a TV. It might be able to disable some kind of extremely sensitive scientific device, but that's about it."

Adele gazed at the portable monitor propped in the viewing window of the scanner. Mr. Penn's pacemaker continued to behave itself: the pacemaker spikes were followed in perfect synchronization by the appropriate complexes. She wondered if the pacemaker in question was different than those manufactured in the United States. Perhaps the difference that pertained to European electric currents extended to the electrical capabilities of their pacer generators. She'd have to remember to ask Wanda Percy. If there was anyone who knew everything about pacemakers and how they worked, it was Wanda.

"So much freaking random stuff going on in this place, man," Trevor said a few seconds later. A stranger to silence or calm repose, he executed a fast drumroll on the arm of his chair with his index fingers. "We had this woman a few weeks ago? Picked her up at her house in Greenbrae? There she was, you know, just lying in bed like she was sound asleep." He snapped his fingers. "Dead as a roach in a Roach Motel. It was facinorous, man. I mean, *very* facinorous. Blood *every*where. More blood than a tick festival at the local rodeo."

Trevor upended the box of fries and emptied the fragments into his mouth, tapping the box with his finger. "When we took off the covers?" He paused and glanced over to see if he was getting the right effect.

Expectantly, Adele nodded. "Yeah?"

"Both her boobs had been sliced open like ripe watermelons. Heinous to the maximum. I mean, it looked like somebody freakin' ransacked her boobs looking for treasure! You could've stored a Steinway piano inside 'em, there was so much empty space."

She handed him the *Chronicle*, pointing to the article about the headless man found in the Bay. "You by any chance transport this?"

He shook his head, showing her a nice view of both sets of lightning bolts on either side of his head. "Naw. The police meat wagon wheeled that fish in."

Neither of them spoke while Trevor beat out a rhythm on his kneecap with his index fingers. After a minute, he looked away and casually said, "You got a boyfriend or somethin'?"

For the third time in two hours, Trevor Snipes, Wonder Cowboy of the Meat Wagon Grand Prix, had rendered her almost speechless. She stared at him, the Crazy Woman laughter wanting to break free of her throat. She wondered if she could be arrested for child molestation if it was the child who did the molesting.

"Thanks, Trevor, but I'm old enough to be your mother."

He gave her a once-over from the corner of his eye. "Yeah, well, my mother sure don't have legs like that."

Adele snorted. "I'm still old enough to be your mother."

There was another long pause, until finally, he stopped drumming his caps and turned to face her straight on. "Okay then, how much do you charge per hour to baby-sit?"

"Mr. Penn has had a small embolic stroke that seems to have mainly affected his speech." Dr. Ravens told her. "I expect he'll resolve quickly without much residual."

The neurologist looked across the desk and studied the statuesque woman in scrubs. Her assured manner was that of an R.N. who knew the ropes, although he had no way of knowing what her exact station was since her name tag read simply: A. MONSARRAT—NURSING. Ever since Ellis Hospital joined the cesspool of managed care, the nurses had not been allowed to distinguish their ranks. She might have been an R.N., an L.V.N., an aide, or even an unlicensed technician—but that was the point. Under the new system of using only generic name tags, the patients wouldn't know that the person at their bedside, giving them potentially lethal drugs, was an unlicensed "helper" who'd had two hours of training.

"We'll need to get a speech therapist up in the morning to evaluate and . . ."

"No offense to your medical expertise, Doc," Adele interrupted, "but I think we need to deal with Mr. Penn's pacemaker before we do anything. It looks like either a fractured wire or the generator itself is malfunctioning."

He smiled and held out his hand. "I'm saving that for last, so as to keep your interest, Ms. . . ."

"Adele Monsarrat," she said. She noticed him studying her name tag and added, "R.N."

His huge hand engulfed hers in its warmth and held it there for a fraction of a second longer than necessary. She was glad she no longer flailed about like an idiot when under the scrutiny of an attractive man—it left her instincts free to see the person under the pretty veneer. And George Ravens was pretty. She'd heard through the greased vines of the hospital gossip network that the Native American was a competent neurologist, pro-nurse, politically savvy, and, last but not least, gorgeous. His straight black hair was slicked back from a face that was exotic and striking in its strong features.

"Adele is one of the senior R.N.s here on Ward Eight," Rymesteade said, studying her face, which was changing color. He'd never seen her blush and wondered if she had a fever.

"Mr. Penn's pacemaker is misfiring," Adele continued. "There also seems to be some sort of problem with the pacer causing interference in any electrical device within six feet of him. I've put a call in to Wanda Percy, the head of our pacer clinic, and asked her to stop by to evaluate the pacemaker."

"I heard about the electrical events," Ravens said without looking up from the chart. "I was thinking of inviting him over to my house to see if he could get my lawnmower started."

"Why don't you just take it to a fix-it person?" Adele asked. "In my limited experience of fixing lawnmowers, I doubt it would be too challenging."

Dr. Ravens rose from his seat and then rose some more. His six-foot-three-inch frame was as well done as his face. "It's a guy thing," he said. "Asking directions, taking things to the fix-it man—it's all the same. But I do agree with you about Mr. Penn—the sooner the pacer is replaced the better. Dr. Zimmer will be here later this evening. Hopefully, Mr. Penn should have a new generator by tomorrow morning.

"I spoke with Mr. Penn's daughter, too. She beat the guilt drum for ten minutes with twenty-seven excuses why she couldn't/ shouldn't leave work. I got all the details of how many people were going to suffer from her absence, and how many thousands of dollars would be lost. I told her what she wanted to hear—that there really isn't a burning need for her to rush down."

Adele opened her mouth to protest, but Ravens held up a hand. "Mr. Penn was more worried about how much it would cost her to fly than about her not being here."

The physician pointed toward Malloy. "Your holy man over there can fax Ms. Penn a consent form to sign."

Adele scribbled something on her palm and reached for Mr. Penn's chart.

Dr. Ravens took her hand and brought it nearer his face. His expression went to puzzlement. "Call Nelson and prepare him for Helen?"

"How do you feel, Mr. Penn?" Adele shined the small shaft of light into the man's pupils.

He grimaced and pulled back. "Better."

The word was slurred to sound more like "beller," but she'd been deciphering stroke-speak since nursing school.

"Helen." His voice cracked. "Worried."

"I was just thinking about Helen," Adele said. "Is there a neighbor who could take care of her or at least feed her while you're . . ."

Mr. Penn hit the bed with his fist. "No neighborsh Gah— gad—goddamn nosey bishybodies!" He hit the bed again. The veins in his forehead pulsated. "Spen-thrips! Try tah tell me how . . . live!" At the word "live," a few drops of spit flew from his mouth and landed on her cheek.

She wiped it off. "Would you like *me* to check on her? Maybe feed her or something?"

Thomas Penn instantly calmed, and his eyes welled with tears. Stroke victims were almost always emotionally labile. "Oh p-please. You take care of her?" He laid his hand on hers and began to weep. "Worried."

"Okay, don't worry. I'll take good care of her. It would be easier for me if I could bring her to my house. I live just a few miles away from here. Would that be all right with you?"

A look of panic crossed the patient's face. "H-h-houshcat. No outside!" His respirations picked up, and he was beginning to look a little dusky around the fringes.

"I promise I'll keep her safely inside. I live alone." *With a weak-minded child trapped in a dog's body.* "So, no one will mistakenly let her out or harm her." *Unless, of course, Nelson decides he needs to rearrange her ears by licking.*

"Anything special I need to know? Any quirks?" She was thinking of Nelson's peculiarities—of which there were many.

Mr. Penn nodded and smiled a one-sided smile. "Paws four times for litter box." He tapped her arm four times to demonstrate. "Food—fthee."

"Got it. Four taps for elimination, three for intake."

"Key under mat."

"Really?" Adele said pleasantly with a frozen smile. "No alarm systems?" Secretly, she was appalled that someone who lived in Belvedere would be so primitive in his mode of security. "Well, don't worry, I'll make sure I leave a few lights on in the house when I leave. Maybe turn on a radio so the house appears occupied?"

Mr. Penn frowned and mumbled something she couldn't understand. She leaned closer. "I'm sorry, I didn't hear you."

"N-no lights!" he muttered. "N-no radio. Waste electrishity. Too expensive."

She cocked her head. "I thought you were the CEO of Pacific Gas and Electric."

He stared at her blankly as if to say: "Yeah, so?"

"Sure," she said, preparing to leave. "No lights or radio. I'll just grab Helen and her food. Is there anything I can bring you?"

"Hearing aid." He was growing tired. His speech was becoming more garbled, to the point where she could barely understand him.

"Okay, and your hearing aid."

He frowned, started to say something, but stopped and closed his eyes.

She straightened the room, did a last set of vitals and neuro checks, and went out to the charting desk, where she found his admitting papers. On the inside hem of her scrub dress, Adele wrote down his address. Falling into her habit of talking to imaginary characters and inanimate objects, she whispered to Robin Leach, who suddenly appeared next to her adjusting his ascot: "Sheesh. Can you imagine? *The* most exclusive residential area in America, and he's worried about running a sixty-watt bulb and a radio?"

Misers! Robin said in that Ross Perot voice of his. *All those rich pricks skimp on the small stuff.*

"Really?" she asked, again amazed by the things her own imagination sometimes came up with.

Sure, Robin said, swinging his polo stick. *Confidentially, did you know that Steve Forbes saves used aluminum foil? Uses it three or four times before he throws it away. Trump washes out his used sandwich baggies and hangs them out on the line.*

Relieved that she wasn't the only one who did those things, Adele went on about her business with renewed respect for thrift.

Mr. Knudsen was wearing his hunting cap, the left flap with the teeth marks pulled down over his bandage. Mrs. Knudsen was wearing an identical hunting cap but with both flaps up, Minnesota hunting lodge infirmary style.

"So. Whatcha think?" Mrs. Knudsen asked in that peculiar though charming accent that belonged only to Minnesotans.

Adele washed her hands and looked over the flow sheet of vital signs, fluid balances, lab results, and descriptions of how his surgical reattachment was doing.

"Perfect," she said. "I think you'll be ready for discharge in another day, thanks to Dr. Wortz and those leeches."

A dead silence fell. Eyes round as marbles, Mr. and Mrs. Knudsen looked at each other. Mr. Knudsen cleared his throat. "Ah, did ya say leeches?" His voice cracked.

Adele paused in piggybacking the IV antibiotic into his main IV line and glanced over at the pair. Their shock was clearly registered between the flaps.

"Well, yes. Didn't Dr. Wortz tell you? We used medical leeches to help with the post-surgical swelling. We usually do with reattachments."

Mrs. Knudsen leaned toward her wearing a stricken expression. "But—but we're Lutherans!" she whispered. "I don't think that's allowed!"

Adele's Crazy Woman laughter, characteristically inappropriate and uncontrollable, exploded without warning. When she was to the point of slapping her knee and gasping for breath, Mr. Knudsen whispered to Mrs. Knudsen, "Do ya think she's havin' a fit?"

"Sure, you bet," Mrs. Knudsen said glumly, shaking her head. "Uncle Ollie used to do that for no reason, too. Ended up at Happy Horizons."

Mr. Knudsen nodded. "Yah. He was crazy, ya know."

"No, no really," Adele said, wiping her eyes of laughter tears. "I'm not crazy, it's just that . . ." She looked at their grave expressions, the hunting caps with the flaps, and the Crazy Woman laughter began all over again.

At the charting desk Mirek Dvorak and Skip Muldinardo were silently charting like mad. Mirek had student post-clinical conference in less than thirty minutes. Skip, his hair and glasses strictly from another era—like in the fifties when squares were still happy—sat with his feet up on the charting desk in direct defiance of the Queen Mother. The four nurse's aides—all from registry—stood at the far end of the hallway talking among themselves.

Sitting behind the monitors, Linda Rainer, another of the regular cadre of Ward 8 nurses, was in charge. If the test of a true nurse was the test of time, Adele and Linda were true blue. Like Adele, Linda had worked the ward from hell since the time when nursing caps, white stockings, and rising to one's feet whenever a doctor entered the room were still requirements of the job.

Adele finished reporting off and sat down to review Mirek's charting when there came the unmistakable sound of a body hitting the floor. Every nurse within hearing distance stiffened.

The Thud was one of the many sounds nurses dreaded. Like the chilling command of the Code Blue announcement, or the rattle of an obstructed airway, The Thud meant death, impending code, broken hip, concussion or, in short, a potential law suit.

Everyone was up and running toward the screams coming from room 819. Two of the four beds were presently occupied by the eighty-three-year-old Mrs. Cottrel, in for COPD, and the forty-year-old Ms. Evans, who was suffering from abdominal, chest, and facial injuries caused by a seat belt and air bag during a parking lot incident. Adele was putting money on Mrs. Cottrel and a broken hip as the source of The Thud. The old lady had probably tried to crawl over the side rails.

Bursting into the room, the first thing she saw was Mrs. Cottrel standing on her own two legs, pointing toward the bathroom. Her hands were covering her mouth, although they did nothing to muffle the continuous scream. Ms. Evans lay in the bed opposite her, oblivious to the world and snoring like a Marine sleeping off a four-day drunk. Adele made a mental note to tell the next shift's nurse to cut back on the woman's pain meds.

A thin rivulet of blood oozed out from under the bathroom door. Adele tried the knob and pushed. Whatever—or whoever—was blocking the door, was heavy. She threw her weight against it, managing to open it wide enough to stick her head through.

Cynthia lay perfectly still, her legs and hips wedged between the wall and the base of the toilet, her head against the door. The toilet paper roll was spattered with blood, as was the nurse's ash blond braid.

For an instant Adele could not make sense of the scene. She knelt next to Cynthia, touched the pale ivory cheek and drew back her hand. The skin was cool and clammy. Switching instantly into nurse mode, she checked for a pulse.

"Oh my God!" said Linda, kneeling next to Adele. "What happened?"

Adele located the rapid but steady pulse. "I don't know. She must have passed out and hit her head."

The door to the bathroom opened wider and Skip and Mirek looked in.

"Skip, have Malloy page Dr. Dhery and bring in the portable oxygen and a monitor," Adele said. "Mirek, bring me an ammonia popper then get Mrs. Cottrel out of here."

Skip returned with the oxygen tank and tubing. Gently, without moving Cynthia's head, he fitted the mask over her nose and mouth. Adele unbuttoned the top of Cynthia's scrub dress that was soaked with perspiration and tried to place electrodes on her chest, but none of them would stick to the wet skin. Grabbing a towel, she wiped Cynthia's chest dry and tried again. Two of the pads stayed on long enough to show a slightly irregular sinus tachycardia.

Mirek handed Linda an ammonia popper, which she broke and waved under Cynthia's nose. "Hey, Cyn, come on, wake up!"

Cynthia moaned. Her arm came to life, flopped around, then shot straight up, smacking Adele in the nose.

"I think she'll live to fight Mike Tyson and win," Adele said, securing the wild arm with her thigh.

Adele pinched her nose and mimicked to a T the voice of the public address system operator. "Attention all personnel. Code Blue! Ward Eight. Code Blue! Ward Eight."

Cynthia's eyes snapped open as her feet twitched in an effort at running while prone. "Wha—? Which room? Somebody grab the crash cart!"

Through a blue haze, Cynthia made out Adele's face looking down at her. That seemed odd, because she couldn't remember why she'd decided to spend an overnight. Had she and Rymesteade had an argument about his mother *again*? Had she gotten drunk? Her head was throbbing.

"God," she said finally, rubbing her eyes, "What a horrible

dream. I dreamed that I was doing CPR on a baboon that was actually Grace's child out of wedlock with . . ."

Behind Adele, Skip's black-rimmed Coke-bottle glasses appeared. Cynthia's eyes grew wide. *Jesus!* she thought, her stomach turning over. *We got drunk after work and had a threesome with Skip?*

Then before she could fully process the trauma of that possibility, over Skip's shoulder rose the round, flappy face of Grace Thompson, like a cartoon moonrise on Halloween.

Cynthia shook her head to clear it. There was no way she could ever get drunk enough for *that*! At the movement, a pain seared through her head and she winced.

"You're on the bathroom floor in eight-nineteen," Adele said, hoping to reorient her. "Did you faint?"

Cynthia closed her eyes trying to get the circuits to reconnect. "Mrs. Cottrel . . . I was giving her last dose of hydrochlorothiazide when I felt like I was going to be sick. I tried to make it to the bathroom, but I passed out before I could throw up."

"Cyn!" Dr. Dhery pushed Skip and Linda gently out of the way. "What happened, honey?" He laid his hand on the side of Cynthia's face and glanced at the portable monitor. "You're going at a hundred and twenty. Can you move your feet?"

Cynthia smiled weakly. Her eyes were on him, but didn't seem to really see him. She refocused and tried sitting up. "I'm fine, you guys. I just fainted. It's no biggie."

Adele supported Cynthia's upper body against her chest while she and Dr. Dhery quickly ran their fingers through the thick hair in search of injuries. They found the three-inch gash at the back of her head almost immediately. Adele laid her back down while Linda ran to find some absorbent bandages.

Rymesteade deftly checked over the rest of her and, relatively sure she hadn't sustained any serious injuries, helped her into the wheelchair. "I'm taking you down to ER," he said. "I want to have some blood work and X-rays done. I'll suture up that laceration and then we'll need to . . ."

Before anyone could stop her, Cynthia got out of the wheelchair, wobbling on her feet. She daubed at the sheen of perspiration covering her face and neck. "No blood work and no rays. I'm fine. You can suture me up at home or in your office. I'm not going to go to ER. That's ridiculous. I just passed out. What is the big deal? It isn't the first time I've ever passed out, you know. I do it all the time. It's a hobby of mine. Leave me alone!"

"Bleeding Christ in a wheelchair!" said Adele, rolling her eyes. "What *is* your problem, Cyn? I mean, why can't you just go with the program?"

"No!" Cynthia yelled with such vehemence, it startled them. "I told you I won't have . . ."

"Ms. O'Neil!" Grace Thompson took her arm authoritatively, although not in an unkind way. "You must go to ER at once and that's an order. It is a policy of this institution that any injured employee must be checked. I simply cannot allow you to bleed all over the patients, and if the wound should happen to became infected, the hospital will be liable."

Cynthia opened her mouth, the refusal ready on her lips.

"I won't hear it!" the head nurse cut her off. "This is not a negotiable issue, Ms. O'Neil. You must be sutured. Whether or not you allow the laboratory to take blood samples or X-rays is your affair, but you must be sutured if you wish to continue to be an employee of my ward. Do I make myself clear?"

Astonished by Grace's sudden show of command, Cynthia closed her mouth and stared, as did the others. "Return to the wheelchair now." Grace tugged at Cynthia's arm and led her to the chair. "Adele, take her to the emergency department straightaway."

"Yes, Queen Mother," Cynthia said in as sarcastic a tone as she could muster, curtseyed, and sat down.

A profound silence fell over the rest of the group. No one had ever actually called Grace "Queen Mother" to her face.

Looking at Cynthia with cool amusement, Grace Thompson puckered her mouth a few times. "You're obviously confused from your fall." Her smile went wide enough to reveal yellowed mismatched teeth. "I am accustomed to being addressed as 'Your Majesty.' "

THREE

NO MATTER HOW THEY CAJOLED OR THREATENED, no one, not even Adele, was able to convince Cynthia she needed lab work or X-rays. The ER staff gave one another knowing glances the moment Cynthia was wheeled into the department, and not just because she was being a "difficult" patient. It had more to do with the fact she was a Ward 8 R.N. Ward 8 nurses had a reputation for being a breed apart: warped—chemically or genetically unbalanced.

This was due in part to the fact that Ward 8 nurses worked on the toughest, most understaffed unit, under direction of a termagant who didn't know her ass from a sphygmomanometer. Mostly, it was due to the ward being a magnet for all kinds of trouble one associates less with a hospital than with a lockdown facility for the criminally insane.

Having a back as broad and impervious to sticks and stones as the Great Wall of China, Adele was able to disregard the stares and whispers of the ER staff. However, Cynthia's erratic behavior—one minute sniffling and needy, the next, scornful and shrew-nasty—drove her out of the exam room.

The bobbery of the ER waiting room caused her to stop halfway across the crowded room and take in what was going on. The sights, sounds, and smells of human crisis assaulted her senses. Every available chair and couch was filled. A middle-aged woman rocked, holding her head in both hands. Two construction workers held greasy rags soaked with blood—one to his hand, the other to his leg. A woman in running gear rested her obviously broken ankle on the shoulder of a man who sat on the floor in front of her. A plastic

29

sandwich bag filled with ice chips, carefully balanced on the front of the injured joint, dripped onto the carpet. Next to them was an older Mexican man with a bandage covering one eye. "Alphonso" was embroidered over his shirt pocket.

Five young Mexican children sat on a long couch, three of them vomiting into blue Wal-Mart shopping bags decorated with yellow happy faces. The other two were absorbed by an armless, naked Barbie doll. An elderly gentleman sat alongside the vomiting children, his hands firmly gripping his knees as he labored to breathe. Adele could hear him wheezing from where she stood.

Turning on her heel, she walked back into the ER. She found Chris, the nurse manager, in one of the treatment rooms irrigating the eye of a man in a UPS uniform.

"Listen," she said. "I get floated down here about six or seven times a year, so I'm not a stranger to ER. You've got a waiting room full of patients, and I've already reported off upstairs. If you want, I can help out while my difficult friend gets stitched up."

Chris studied her with a doubtful expression, the pouches under her eyes shiny with sweat—or maybe tears. "You're that detective from Ward Eight?"

"Well, I wouldn't say I'm a private eye," Adele told her, shifting on her feet. "I mean, I'm not an official investigator or anything."

The nurse was staring at Adele's eyes in the same way a child might stare at a person with physical deformities. "Are you ACLS-certified?"

"Only for about fifteen years."

Chris sighed, shut off the valve on the irrigation tubing, picked up a chart from the counter, and handed it to her. "Okay, bring the sickest in first. You'll be threatened by the ones who've been waiting for longer than four hours, so watch your back. We've already got two nurses out on disability from being assaulted by the disgruntled masses.

"As soon as you get them in here, set 'em up wherever you find a room. Clothes off, full set of vitals recorded on the in-

take sheet. Start IVs and oxygen on the ones who need it."
She turned and started out the door, then stopped.

"And if you see any of the supervisors? Hide. I don't want
the department charged for float help."

Adele nodded, heading for the lobby. "No problem."

"Oh, and Adele?"

She glanced back, pretty sure of what was coming.

"No funny stuff. This isn't Ward Eight."

She looked around the lobby again, this time using her
nurse's eye, that inborn sixth sense that told her what was
what in the world of ills. The elderly man's struggle to breathe
was noticeably more labored. She brought the wheelchair
over and helped him in.

"You're looking a little dusky around the gills, Mr. . . ."
She looked at the chart. ". . . Godfrey."

Too weak to answer, he nodded, his shoulders pumping up
and down.

Wheeling him to the automatic door, she did a final sweep
of the patients, taking account. The Mexican kids were lying
listlessly on the floor, their faces flushed, their dark eyes
burning with fever. The rocking woman had taken a cigarette
break. Everyone else was the same except for the runner with
the broken ankle.

Adele steered the wheelchair close to the couple who
looked as if they came right out of a *Runner's World* catalog.
The way his hand stroked her leg, and the aura about them—
as though they owned the world and were happy to have it
all—left no room for doubt that they were a couple. The
young woman was no longer sitting up, but now lay as best
she could on her side, head propped on the arm of the couch.
Her foot rested on the young man's lap, and they were chuckling over some private joke.

Adele's gut tightened. She leaned forward to ask the injured woman a question, when a hand landed on her shoulder.

"What are you doing down here, Ardel?"

Adele spun around.

Mattie Noel, day shift Ellis Hospital nursing supervisor,

stood before her clutching her clipboard to her chest with the ferocity of someone guarding the secret of life.

"Excuse me?" Adele said in a voice a full register lower than her normal one. She hadn't tried to make it lower, it just came out that way. Her voice, like her laughter and her tongue, had separate activating systems that were not always in full partnership with the ones in her brain.

"Why aren't you on Ward Eight?" Mattie's eye tic was going like mad, set off by the prospect of nailing one of the senior nurses to a cross. That it was one of the more troublesome Ward 8 nurses was like hitting the jackpot on double Green Stamp day.

Her decision to lie, as Adele explained later to Cynthia, was influenced by the tic.

"Because I don't work on Ward Eight. My twin sister works up there. Adele Monsarrat?"

Ms. Noel rolled her eyes, tic still pumping. "Oh, puleeeeze! Do you think I was born yesterday, Arden? What are you doing down here? I certainly hope you don't think you can just walk off your assigned ward and work anywhere you please."

"I'm afraid you've made a mistake." Adele insisted, "I'm Andie Monsarrat, Adele's tw—"

"Well!" Mattie's shoulders quivered with righteousness. "I certainly haven't made a mistake, Missy Arnel. I think I'd know what nurses work where and when. I *am* the senior nursing supervisor here."

"I'm sorry, ma'am." Adele bowed her head for effect. "But as a well-informed senior supervisor, I'm sure you were told that today is my first day. I'm still in orientation, not even on the payrolls or the schedule."

This piece of news caused Mattie to scowl. Muttering, she pulled the clipboard away from her chest with such difficulty, Adele momentarily wondered if the muscles of the supervisor's arms were becoming permanently contracted.

Mattie was on her second page of schedules and lists of nurses when Adele decided the charade had gone on too long—Mr. Godfrey was looking a bit blue around the lips.

"No offense, ma'am," Adele said, her voice dropping a few

registers. To her surprise, she'd also adopted a faint Swedish accent. "I'd like to stay and chat some more, but I have one very sick man here who needs immediate medical attention."

She pushed the wheelchair a few feet when the supervisor stepped around and blocked her way. "Hold it. What did you say your name was again?"

"Andie," she answered, skirting around her. "Andrew Monsarrat. Adele's twin brother. See, our mother thought she was having girl twins, so she used to dress us in matching dresses when were kids? I guess I got used to it, so I became a trans . . ."

Mattie smushed the clipboard so tight, her eyebrows reached her hairline, and her lips thinned into a zipper of red flesh.

". . . sexual. I wanted to be like my twin." Adele began lifting the hem of her scrub dress. "Want to see? Those docs in Sweden did a really great job. You can hardly tell . . ."

Mattie jumped back. Her tic was wilder than Adele had ever seen it before, as if her eyelid were trying to pry itself loose of her face.

"I'm not ashamed!" Adele said proudly. "Come on over here and take yourself a little look-see. It's kinda cute what they can do these days. Why, I've even got a nice little . . ."

The supervisor marched stiffly away.

In treatment room number 9, Adele placed Mr. Godfrey on oxygen, did his vitals, obtained a short medical history, and was calling for a chest film when her gut screamed and sent her running for the lobby.

Her gut was never wrong. It was only when her mind interfered that she made bad calls.

As soon as the pneumatic doors swung open, she caught sight of the young man getting to his feet, panic just dawning. He bent over the young woman, saying her name louder every time he said it. He held out his hands to Adele in a gesture of helplessness. "What?" he asked in a whisper, his eyes full of disbelief. "What's happening?"

Adele was on the woman, checking for signs of life. There was not so much as an agonal breath or a stray beat of her heart. Initiating CPR, she shouted for help as he went into a kind of shock, clutching the sides of his head.

The children paused in their retching to stare wide-eyed, while the migraine woman watched with detached horror. The mother pulled her children close, hiding as many of their faces in her large breasts as she could. The Mexican man named Alphonso slowly approached the young man who was still holding the sides of his head and chanting, "Kimberly no, Kimberly no, Kimberly no, Kimberly"—like a mantra.

Three nurses ran out, a gurney in front of them. With the help of the two injured construction workers, they managed to lift her. Before the double doors swallowed them, Adele looked back to see Alphonso put his arms around the young man and let him cry.

She grasped the image—suffering in the arms of compassion—and held on to it throughout the chaos of what came next.

Kimberly Anne Prior, 25, did not survive. Den, her husband of three months, would not believe them when they came out to give him the news. "It was only a tumble," he told them, looking first at Adele and then at Chris. "We were running on Concrete Pipe Trail and she tripped on a stupid rock and fell off the side—rolled into a tree at the bottom. She broke her ankle, is all. She hopped a mile back to the car. We were just joking about how stupid she looked. We—she—" He shook his head slowly then suddenly sat up.

"Hey, wait a minute." He grinned. "I got it. You're kidding, right? This is a huge setup. Kim sent you out here—right? It's a joke to get me back for the time I pretended to have her car stolen. Right?" He paused for two seconds. When there was only silence, his grin fell. "Right?"

"When she fell, she hurt her spleen." Adele managed to say through a throat that was constricted to the point of pain. "It was bleeding very slowly, Mr. Prior, and—and . . ."

Chris, who was used to giving the news to survivors of ER tragedies, was calmer, and less emotional, her words more businesslike and to the point. "The bleeding was contained inside the capsule around the spleen, but it became so distended it ruptured into her peritoneum." The nurse hesitated. "The organ burst, sending blood into her abdomen." She looked at him, evaluating what he was able to absorb. "Do you understand what I'm saying? Your wife went into shock. We tried everything to get her back, but we couldn't. We've contacted her parents. Do you have someone we can call to come and be with you?"

He stared at them dumbly, dry-eyed.

Chris heaved a sigh and got up, leaving Adele to deal with what was left of him.

"Den, please give me a phone number for someone who can come and be with you," Adele pleaded. "You shouldn't be alone now."

Alphonso sat down on the other side of him. The young man looked at him and then back at her. "This isn't happening," he said, real panic creeping into his voice. "Tell me this isn't happening."

She sucked in a breath and lowered her face. "I am so sorry. Please. Let me call someone."

In a shaky voice he recited a phone number, which she wrote on the palm of her hand.

"How can this be?" His eyes locked on her, as if she had an answer that would make a difference.

It was a question she'd been asked a thousand times by the survivors, all of whom looked at her in the same expectant way. It was the innocence of the question that amazed her—as if those who asked never once considered the risk involved in loving that which could be taken by death.

When he finally released the gasping sob caught in his throat, she left him to the care of the Mexican man, who held him without question.

Twenty minutes later, Adele and Cynthia rode the service elevator back up to Ward 8 in silence, each ruminating on the people closest to them and how they might feel if those people were suddenly gone. At about floor 3, they slipped an arm around each other's waist and hugged.

Adele leaned her head against Cynthia's. "Things like this always sneak up and bite you in the ass . . . like a wake-up call."

"Death can come and get you any time, can't it, Del?"

"Ayuhn," Adele answered softly, wondering how Den Prior would cope in the coming months, hoping he had good friends and family who would see him through.

"Yeah," Cynthia said sadly. "It makes me feel I should be a kind and loving person to everyone at all times."

The elevator bumped softly to a stop. After enough time had lapsed for Adele to get an adrenaline rush from her claustrophobia center, the doors finally opened on Grace Thompson.

"Well," Cynthia said after a beat, "most of the time anyway."

"I'm going to be very curious to see this baby once it comes out of there."

Wanda Percy, the pacemaker goddess of Marin County, was a good deal shorter and wider than Adele. She was one of those ageless women who, although she couldn't be described as a great beauty, made up for it with an inner beauty that drew people. Her high cheekbones were the highlight of her face, unless one wanted to count the flawless creamy brown skin and huge dark eyes that were made even bigger by the large glasses. Her lipstick was very red and glossy, which focused attention on her mouth. All in all, it was an intense, intelligent face.

Wanda never lacked attention. Her personality was outgoing yet at the same time soothing. Without trying, she had a way of making people feel good about themselves. It was beyond Adele how anyone could be so nice all the time. She doubted the woman had ever been in a bad mood in her life. Wanda was someone who woke up in the morning happy and went to bed happier. It was, Adele thought, a touch perverse.

"What do you think is going on?" Adele sat back on the overstuffed couch, keeping an eye on Cynthia, who was changing out of her scrubs.

Wanda shrugged soft round shoulders and tucked a bit of hair behind her ear. The large ornamental earrings faintly jangled. "Girlfriend, in my twenty-four years of dealing with pesky machines, I have never seen anything like this. The closest I can come to a comparison is this one bedside monitor in CCU that every time someone walks in the room, it goes blank, then comes back on. The electricians and the biomed guys have been beating their heads against the wall for years trying to figure out why. It's just one of those weird electrical phenomena.

"What I'm thinking with Mr. Penn is that his pacer was put in in Europe. Their models and brands are different than what we use here in the United States, so our programmers and interrogators aren't able to read it."

"Programmers and interrogators? Sounds like the CIA."

Wanda sat back, letting her shoulders sink into the couch. "They're nifty machines—about the size of your fist. You lay them on top of a patient's pacemaker and hook up an electrical wire to a machine that gives a monitored picture of the pacemaker, plus it will read out the microchip inside the pacer. It tells you what percentage of the day the patient uses the pacemaker, at what heart rate it's used, and all sorts of other parameters that can be printed out on a hard-copy graph with the model and serial numbers."

"I take it ours didn't work on Mr. Penn?"

"I tried." Wanda sighed. "I might as well have been using a ham hock on him."

"So what do you think happened to his pacer?"

"That's easy." Wanda flipped her hand. "When he flew back to the States, he went through the airport scanners forgetting he had a pacemaker. The security people probably waved one of those magnetic wands over him and that could have deprogrammed it or mucked it up somehow." She sipped her coffee. "I've never been able to find out why, but European and Asian airports use much stronger magnets in their wands than the U.S. Also, if he was carrying heavy baggage, or was being very physical, he could have fractured the leads that go from the generator into the heart."

"That would make sense." Adele nodded, thinking that Mr. Penn would be the type who would break his nuts carrying two fifty-pound bags rather than give up a buck tip to a porter. "Are you going to be assisting with Mr. Penn's generator replacement?"

"Sure—if I'm on duty."

"Well, what if you aren't on?" Adele pushed. "Will you come in?"

"Why? Do you want me to?"

"Yes," Adele said. "If you're in there, I know it'll get done right." She shrugged. "Plus if you're there, I'll get to know exactly what the problem was. Nobody else is going to take the time or trouble to figure it out."

The woman nodded. "If you're really that interested, I'll see if I can get you permission to scrub in as an observer." Her laughter was easy. "Lord knows everybody else does. We even had the janitor in there the other day."

"I'd love it," Adele said, surprised at her own enthusiasm.

Wanda stood, her eyes sparkling. "Great." She pulled a business card from the pocket of her lab coat and handed it over. "I live right down the road at Skylark Apartments. That's my pager number. I've had the thing surgically implanted, so it's always with me."

She stopped at the door. "Hey, girlfriend, you don't get faint in surgery, do you?"

"Not me," Adele said. "I save that for the morgue."

Adele's '78 Pontiac station wagon, a.k.a. the Beast, was parked in the back lot of Mill Valley's Jack in the Box. In stunned silence Adele watched as Cynthia downed two Sourdough Jacks, two Jumbo Jacks with extra cheese, two chocolate milk shakes, and an order of stuffed jalapeños.

For almost the entire meal Cynthia talked a blue streak. The only time she stopped was in the middle of her recollection of the day her parents brought her to a gay pride parade, then embarrassed her by heckling the participants. She was at the climax of the story about her father ripping fake breasts off a transvestite in the Castro when she exited the Beast and came back ten minutes later with four apple turnovers and two cartons of milk.

When the last syrupy glob of turnover had been licked off her fingers, Cynthia sat back with a satisfied smile and fanned herself with one of the empty burger cartons.

"Thank God *that's* over," Adele said. It was the first time she'd spoken since she asked Cynthia if she wanted to go straight home or not. "Are you ready to go home yet, or would you like to hit Round Table Pizza while you're on a roll?"

Cynthia mopped the sweat from her freckles with a ketchup-stained napkin. "Problem with you, Adele, is that you don't ever eat any real food. How do you expect to function in today's world if all you eat is make-believe food?"

Adele's eyes rolled. "Honey pie, if inhaling two hundred grams of saturated fat and eight thousand calories in one sitting is eating real food, I'll manage—at least long enough to take care of you as you lay dying of breast, colon, and stomach cancer."

Cynthia looked at something long in the distance to the right and above the horizon. "I have to keep in mind that this is coming from the same lunatic who believes that twenty years from now the FDA is going say that microwaves cause cancer of the brain." She shifted her gaze back to Adele. "Shit, Adele, you're like one of those people at the turn of the century who refused to have electricity in their houses because they thought it would make them sick."

"It does." Adele said resolutely. "If I could afford to, I'd go solar."

"Where are you going after you drop me off?" Cynthia asked, locking her seat belt with a metallic click. She had learned how to drop issues she knew would lead them into a heated, unresolvable debate.

"To Belvedere to pick up Mr. Penn's cat and bring her to my house."

"Why doesn't he just have the neighbors take care of the cat?"

Adele shook her head. "He doesn't trust anyone. He's the sort of guy who's so paranoid, he'd make himself the executor of his own will."

Cynthia looked at her watch. "Ryme doesn't get home until

eight. Can I go with? I'd love to see the inside of one of those Belvedere mansions."

"Are you sure? I mean, just two hours ago you were having a near-death experience after painting the bathroom walls of eight-nineteen with your blood. Then you devoured half a cow and a few quarts of grease, and now . . ."

From the backseat there came a sound as if someone—a very small elf perhaps—had said, "Hellloooooo yelllloooow dowwwnnnn!"

Adele's head swiveled so fast, she popped a vertebra in her neck. Simultaneously, Cynthia broke into a hard laugh that grew into a wheeze. This was accentuated by her slapping at her knees. Adele searched the floor of the backseat, looking for the child or elf who had spoken. She turned back to Cynthia, her eyes wide in question.

Cynthia wiped the laugh tears from her face. "Isn't that incredible?"

"What the hell was that?" Adele asked.

"That was my stomach!" Cynthia cried with glee. "I swear, sometimes it's like having my own ventriloquist. Or like in *The Exorcist* where the demon speaks from Linda Blair's abdomen? I've almost gotten to the point where it can say whole sentences."

Adele stared at her for a minute, then, without saying another word, started the car, looking for a back way out of the parking lot. Like most Marin County vegetarians, she was loath to have anyone see her leaving Jack's Carnivore Carnival.

Of course, just as she pulled out onto Miller Avenue, the first car that passed was driven by Detective Sergeant Tim Ritmann. He honked twice and waved. Through the windshield, she could see he was having himself a good laugh over the Fanatic Vegetarian Monsarrat turning to Carnivore Clown for something to stick to her ribs.

The Penn dwelling was one of the lesser Belvedere mansions, but it was a mansion all the same. A three-story granite beauty, it overlooked the Bay and the Golden Gate Bridge.

Just as Mr. Penn had said, the key to the house lay under the

welcome mat. Except Adele didn't really need it: the door had
been pried open. Splinters of wood littered the marble-tiled
foyer, while the brass lock hung by a screw.

"Don't touch or move anything," Adele said as she and
Cynthia stepped inside. Blindly, she searched her purse for
her cell phone and the .22 Colt. One in each hand, she cautiously glanced around the entrance hall and up the dual stair-
ways, which curved and crossed at the second-floor landing
and went on to a third floor.

For a fleeting moment, she wondered if his furniture had
been taken or if Mr. Penn was a minimalist. Considering his
penny-pinching attitude toward the consumption of electricity, she decided the lack of furniture had more to do with
the old guy subscribing to the Tightwad School of Home
Decoration—if Target or Dollar General didn't carry it, he'd
go without.

"Call the police," Cynthia whispered.

Adele shook her head and with a nod indicated that Cynthia was to stay put at the bottom of the stairway and remain
silent while she herself checked the house. Entering the room
off the right side of the entrance hall, she found what appeared to be a formal sitting room, although there wasn't a
stick of furniture in it, let alone something on which to sit.
She flicked the light switch.

The magnificent glass chandelier hanging from a sculpted
gold-leaf base produced barely enough light to see where she
was going. Of the one hundred and twenty sockets each beg-
ging for a fifteen-watt bulb, only three had been filled. She
imagined the old man at the top of a tall ladder unscrewing
the other one hundred and seventeen bulbs, thinking, *Forty-
five watts is enough for anybody to see by! Any more is a goddamned waste of electricity!*

Passing through the archway of the sitting room, she found
herself in a formal dining hall furnished with three card tables
pushed together. Eight white plastic patio chairs—the type
that sold for five dollars at Kmart—were set around it.

The gourmet kitchen ran the entire width of the house. The
west wall, the one that faced the Bay and the Golden Gate

Bridge, was one giant window, floor to ceiling. More out of curiosity than anything else, she checked the refrigerator and kitchen cabinets; they were almost devoid of anything edible. All she could find was a box of crackers with a sale sticker of fifty cents; a jar of kosher dill pickles, also marked down to a quarter; a bulging carton of unopened cottage cheese from two years before; and, in the freezer, a solitary roasting chicken.

Noting the large areas of freezer burn, she checked the expiration date and was aghast to read TO BE SOLD BY: FEB. 17/1978. No mistaking the seven for a nine or even an eight. The fowl was definitely from 1978—the year President Carter pinpointed physicians and their organized medicine to be the major obstacle to decent health care in the United States.

The old Scrooge was probably saving the bird for a special occasion. She could just imagine him standing at the head of his card tables, rubbing his hands together as he spoke to his formally attired guests: "This evening I have a special treat in store for you: a lovely seventy-eight pullet." Everyone would be ooohing and aaahhing, not suspecting for one moment he was going to serve them an underdone chicken older than most of their children and loaded with enough botulin to kill off half the world's population.

Off the opposite end of the kitchen was a duplicate of the formal dining hall except instead of card tables and plastic patio chairs, the room was occupied by three battered bean-bag chairs, all of which had been patched with silver duct tape. The next room, the one opposite the dimly lit sitting room across the foyer, was a library/study.

She blinked in astonishment at the contrast in decor. Leather-bound books lined the walls behind the grand mahogany desk, while a wingback chair upholstered in maroon velour and a matching overstuffed couch sat in front of the fireplace. Lending warmth to the room, antique prints and oil paintings of landscapes and various farm animals went well with the exquisite Persian rug.

The only disturbance she could see was that the desk had

been opened and obviously rifled. Rolodex cards and files lay scattered about the floor. In a wall cabinet Adele found a sound system that, on the black market, would have fetched a few thousand dollars. The fact it was still there made her wonder if Mr. Penn might not have broken into the house himself and made a mess of the desk while searching for something. She'd known stroke victims who had done stranger things while in a confusional state.

She walked into the entryway. "I don't think whoever broke in . . ." She stopped. Cynthia was not where she'd left her. She called softly up the stairs before taking them two at a time to the second floor. To the right was an empty room of outlandish proportion. The middle room at the top of the landing was graced only by a yoga mat and two candle-holders. Facing west, it featured the same floor-to-ceiling window as in the kitchen.

"A meditation room?" she whispered, trying to imagine Mr. Penn in a loincloth and full lotus position, clearing his mind in hopes of attaining nirvana.

Gandhi materialized in his Ben Kingsley form and held up a finger to indicate he was about to throw a little spot of wisdom her way. *To meditate is divine,* he said. *It is also free of charge.*

To the south side of the landing was a bedroom suite beautifully done in Shaker style, comfortably elegant in the simplicity of its oak and maple furniture and handmade rugs and quilts.

The third floor was a true architectural wonder. The ceiling, a wide dome designed from squares of beveled glass, projected rainbows all around, shimmering down over the walls all the way down to the entryway floor. The two doors at each side of the semicircular balcony were both closed.

Again, Adele went for the door on her right and pushed it open. The feeling in the pit of her stomach made her wish she had called the police when Cynthia told her to. Clutching the Colt in both hands, she stepped over the threshold and pressed her back to the wall, sliding a foot or so to the right.

When her eyes adjusted to the dark, the sight before her

caused her arms to drop. "Christ on a bike," she whispered in awe.

Every miser has his soft spot—the one hobby, person, or pet on which no expense is spared. Apparently, Helen was Miser Penn's soft spot. The entire room was a veritable paradise of kitty paraphernalia. Every square foot was occupied by carpeted jungle gym, cubby holes, poles, dangling mice stuffed with catnip, bright-colored balls with bells inside, fur-lined sleeping beds, four different scratching posts, cute kitty feeding bowls filled with three different kinds of kibbles, a running fountain in the shape of a black marble panther, motorized mice toys, and an automatic kitty-litter box.

She took a step away from the wall and clucked her tongue a few times. "Here, kitty kitty. Helen? Where are you, Helen?" She spied what looked like a tail hanging from one of the carpeted cubby holes and smiled. "I see you," she cooed. "Come on out, kitty girl. We're going to Auntie Adele's and Uncle Nelson's for a little taste of life in the real world. I won't hurt . . ."

The door hit her with the force of a speeding train and knocked her off her feet. She managed to hold on to the Colt, but the cell phone flew out of her hand and landed in the kitty-litter box. The automated box whirred to life and bore down on the gadget.

Crouched low, a man holding a gun came at her from the shadows, a white handkerchief covering most of his face. She coiled, prepared to deliver a kick to his kneecap. At the last second he changed course and ran into the hall.

She staggered to the door, willing her diaphragm to work. "Cynthia?" The name came out as a croak.

There was no answer. She leaned against the balustrade. At the bottom of the stairs, she caught a glimpse of the man as he disappeared out the front door.

"Cynthia, where are you?"

She stumbled to the door on the other side of the landing. It fell open under her weight. A conventional blue-and-white bedroom suite right out of Martha Stewart's homogenized and sterile imagination was bathed in the fading afternoon sun. Cynthia lay snoring on the king-sized four-poster bed.

On her chest, contentedly making biscuits, was a big, fluffy black cat.

"It's deaf, blind, and can't make noise except purring," Cynthia told her, checking Adele's ribs and face bones for any obvious breaks. Other than some swelling over the right cheekbone, she found no injuries.

"Ah," Adele said, stroking the animal who had curled up in her lap. The long fur was as soft as angora. "Thus the name Helen Keller."

"Except Helen is a boy," Cynthia added, picking up the cat's tail and pointing out the obvious. The cat sniffed her hand, licked it, and began to purr. "Typical man," she said.

Adele gingerly touched the side of her face that had been hit by the door and winced. "Well, at least now I'll have matching fractures."

Cynthia looked at her sideways. After two reconstructive surgeries from her last run-in with a psycho, Adele's nose had only just returned to looking normal. "I'm sorry, Adele. I should have stayed put at the bottom of the stairs, but I got so tired, I couldn't keep my eyes open. I wanted to see the house, and you seemed intent on what you were doing, so I . . ."

"It's okay." Adele pushed the braid that was still caked with dried blood off Cynthia's shoulder. "Who knows what the guy might have done if you'd seen him. He had a gun. He might have shot you."

Cynthia suddenly lowered her head and began to sob.

Having survived the childhood from hell, Cynthia was a tough cookie. She would have to be in it up to her nose and bleeding from all pores before she mentioned she might need some assistance. That she was blubbering girl-tears at no obvious provocation had Adele gawking.

"What the hell?"

Cynthia shook her head, and looked up, her green eyes red-rimmed. "I can't tell you."

A wave of mild panic washed through Adele. "What do you mean you can't tell me? We share everything except politics and four thousand other issues. Are you sick? Have you killed someone? Has someone hurt you? Is Rymesteade being a jerk?"

Cynthia picked up Helen and hugged him to herself. The animal hung limply over her shoulder, like a stick of soft licorice. "I can't talk about it yet. When I'm ready, I'll tell you."

Adele knew when not to push. "Okay. Just make sure you tell me first." She slapped her hands on her thighs and smiled a constrained, bright smile. "Well now, how about if we call the cops to report a break-in?"

Daisy could not get comfortable no matter what she did. All the over-the-counter anti-itch ointments hadn't worked. Nor had the four expensive prescription creams she found at the bottom of the medicine cabinets. The Chinese herb paste—guaranteed to take away any itching—made it worse, and the homeopathic elixir did nothing more than make her eyes water and her palms turn olive green.

The itching was driving her mad. In a moment of lunacy she'd actually called her mother for one of her old-fashioned home remedies. Daisy contemplated the carton of oatmeal and took another long swallow of gin. The gin she chased down with a bite of chocolate éclair.

Chewing thoughtfully, she wiped her hand on her neon pink spandex exercise pants and poured half the box of oatmeal into a bowl. To that she added warm water and stirred the gooey mixture with her finger. She considered the possibility that her mother might be going a bit off her rails. It was mad, suggesting that a bowl of porridge was going to cure what ailed her.

She drank off the tumbler of gin and finished the éclair. Weaving slightly, she peeled down the spandex, grabbed a handful of wet oatmeal, and slapped it onto her backside in the general vicinity of the trouble.

Instant relief brought a squeal of joy. Daisy giggled and heaped on another gelatinous glob. "Oh yes!" she shouted, shuffling with tiny steps to the hallway mirror.

Contorting neck and shoulders, she was barely able to see

around the large sacks of flesh that formed her body. The dark red center of the welt was now covered with oatmeal, while the outer ring of rash showed a vibrant red.

Someone cleared his throat and coughed. In her rapture, she'd forgotten that the front door was open. She gazed at herself for a moment longer—naked from waist to knees, oatmeal dripping onto the Persian rug—and raised her eyes to the screen door.

There were several things to consider, all of which Adele was mulling over while working the remaining kitty litter out of the crevices of the cell phone with her fingernail.

One: What would she tell the emergency operator?

Two: Would the responding patrolmen believe her story and not try to hassle her and Cynthia? Beat cops could be such macho assholes.

Three: Would someone from the Tiburon station notify Detective Sergeant Ritmann at the county sheriff's office once they knew it was Adele Monsarrat they were dealing with?

She punched in 911 and turned away from Cynthia. The detective was another subject the two friends could not discuss. For Adele, thoughts of the red-headed Irish Jew who had once been Cynthia's live-in lover were, to put it mildly, disquieting.

The phone rang once.

In the beginning of Cynthia and Tim's relationship, they'd been like an exclusive club of three—the happy couple and the third wheel. Within two video and popcorn get-togethers, it was apparent to all who was more suited to whom. But, as it goes with such sensitive matters of love and sex, no one said a word, and the pink elephant lived in their clubhouse for almost a year until Cynthia dumped Tim and put the obvious on a verbal plate for all to consider.

Cynthia's allegation that Adele and Timothy were true soulmates was vigorously resisted by Adele, who in turn insisted Cynthia and Tim were still in love and that Cynthia's allegation was simply a cover for her commitmentphobia.

Someday, Adele predicted, they would see the light and return to each other.

In reality, Adele knew her prediction didn't even resemble the truth, but it had helped keep the blinders on. After Cynthia and Rymesteade Dhery became an item, she could no longer use the defense of a lingering romantic tie between her best friend and the detective to steer clear of—what?

The phone rang a second time.

During the last case they'd both been involved in, she and Timothy had stumbled along, slowly revealing to each other their inner workings. They were, after all, two people who took major risks—the last of which had almost killed them.

Her mind replayed the moment in which a murderer's bullet passed through her and into him. The sight and *smell* of blood as Tim's chest opened in slow motion still fueled her worst nightmares. For the two months it took for them to heal physically, they grew closer, the way fellow survivors of a disaster often do.

By the time she realized they had developed habits and daily routines that belonged exclusively to them, it was almost too late—the man had already begun to feel like home. An overpowering fear, stronger than her desire for him, raised the battle cry of the Monty Python gang: *Run awayyyyyyyy!*

She didn't need to visit a shrink to know her avoidance of him was related to the psychological tangle of her father's death, her fear of abandonment and of losing the freedom to be herself. It was, she decided, safer to step back and let Mr. Ritmann pass. Look, Ma, no entanglements, no mess. Wash my mouth out with soap if you hear me say the R-word. Bad word. Pain word. Relationship. Relationshit.

The phone rang again.

She'd never been good at playing the game with men, at least not on the level that Tim Ritmann would require. She was more comfortable being one of the boys, not *with* one of the boys. Through the ages of her life it had been like that: jeering at the girls and their dolls and carriages from the basketball courts where she played Horse with the neighborhood boys. Later, she secretly scoffed at their obsessions with hair and weight, prom dresses and boyfriends, choosing to spend her free time hanging around the detectives at Novato PD.

Not until her second year in college did she even consider dating, and then her taste showed a definite dislike of the fratty beer bash boys and a leaning toward the artsy types. As it turned out, the artsy types were all spiritual rapists and emotional vampires. Instead of using alcohol or drugs, they seduced with original poetry and music. A few weeks after their conquering victory, they would move on, due (they said, with heavy, dramatic sighs) to a stifled spirit and a jealous muse.

Once out of college, Adele gravitated toward the intellectual-professionals, right up until she met Green Beret Gavin Wozniac. She agreed to marry him with the same sense of desperation as when she lost her virginity: that of wanting to get the event over and done with, like paying off an old debt.

No one but Cynthia fully understood what a charade the marriage had been. Gavin had been more like Adele's own personal drill sergeant than a loving partner; their one mutual desire had been that he would teach her all he'd learned as a Green Beret. She took an honorable discharge three years later when Gavin went AWOL and disappeared.

Assuming full custody of Nelson, their black Labrador retriever, she moved into the tidy brown shingled house on Baltimore Avenue in Larkspur. Since then she had gone about living her uncomplicated life.

Lonely.

She shook off the memories and, at the fourth ring, clucked her tongue and huffed.

"Sort of like the highway call boxes on our Cheap Shoe Adventure, huh?" asked Cynthia.

"Yeah." Adele laughed at the memory of the day they'd taken a drive down to Mexico to purchase some cheap running shoes. When the conditions were just right—after dark on a deserted stretch of highway—the Beast decided to pull its Going to Sleep Trick. Adele ran to the nearest call box then stood in the cold listening to it ring for an hour and a half.

When her feet went numb, she gave up and ran ten miles to the nearest exit.

According to the California Highway Patrol, all emergency call box calls went to a ten-by-ten room somewhere in central California where no more than three people at any given time were available to answer.

The phone rang again. The thought that perhaps the same three people who took the highway calls were also answering Marin County's 911 calls crossed her mind.

Someone answered.

"We need a patrol car at . . ." She paused and read the address off the inside of her hem. "I've interrupted a break-in. The perpetrator is a slender male with black hair about six feet tall. He's armed with a handgun."

The operator mumbled something incomprehensible.

"Excuse me? Could you speak slower?"

The operator spoke slower—in Spanish.

"I don't speak Spanish. Ah, *no hablo español. ¿Habla usted inglés?*"

No, the operator did not speak English.

"Un momento." Adele took a breath. *"Está nueve-uno-uno?"*

"Sí."

"Es esto emergencia teléfono para Marin County, California, los Estados Unidos?"

"Sí. Usted tiene una emergencia?"

Adele's mouth flapped. *"No comprendo. Habla usted inglés?"*

"No. Hablo español. ¿Qué pasa?"

Gently, she hung up and dialed information for the Tiburon police department.

On the fifth ring, the operator answered. *"Bonjour, sureté de police Tiburon. Puis-je vous aider?"*

Adele pulled back and looked at the phone to see if there was something written somewhere about it being a foreign language phone. "Hey, come on now," Adele said. "I need an English-speaking person."

This time, the operator hung up on her.

* * *

As soon as she heard the outgoing message on her answering machine, Adele hit the number code for room monitor and spoke to her dog.

"Hi, babycakes, it's Mommy. Are you there?" Adele still was not used to driving and talking on the phone, especially since using a phone in a '78 Pontiac station wagon created such an incongruous image. In addition, as a nurse, she knew that the survivors of car phone accidents were far outnumbered by the fatalities. She didn't need to talk to *any*body that bad—even if she was in California, where it was as basic to carry a cell phone as it was to have plastic surgery before the age of forty.

Nelson laid the six-by-five-inch square of what was left of his security blanket—once a Mickey Mouse rug—on top of the phone machine and whined.

"Oh, honey, I'm so sorry you feel that way," Adele answered in a perfect Mr. Rogers voice, "but you see, Mommy had to do a favor for a patient and then she had to talk to the bad policemen Gestapo bullies who needed to show off and do a lot of macho posturing."

Nelson howled. It was a howl that stank of dog abuse threats if she ever heard one.

"Well, I understand why you might feel that way, Nelson, but that's why you learned to go pee-pee in Mommy's toilet. Didn't I remember to leave the seat up?"

In answer, the dog gave a complicated series of whines and snorts to which Adele listened patiently.

"That's fine, but guess what? Mommy has a surprise for you!"

The black Labrador cocked his head and picked up the receiver in his teeth. He lay down with the white plastic between his paws and began to gnaw. It was his latest bad dog trick, which had recently replaced his old bad dog trick of chewing through the front door. Adele had had to replace three phones in five months and increase his visits to Dr. Nutt, the doggie shrink.

Dr. Nutt blamed Nelson's clinical depression on the disappearance of his pet rabbit, Bugs. Adele didn't think that was far off the mark. Ever since the lagomorph hopped the fence, Nelson had taken to staring out the bedroom window for hours and whining. She had thought he was keeping a watch out for Bugs, until she realized he'd been tracking Fluffy, the angora rabbit the neighbor kids kept penned in their backyard.

"Nelson! Stop chewing the phone!"

Nelson stopped, wagged his tail, and barked.

"Good boy. Now listen—I'm bringing home a guest. A kitty, Nelson. Kitty-kitty? Would you like that?"

Nelson's head jerked. A growl sneaked out followed by a bark.

"No, he's not like Queen Shredder," she said, referring to their neighbor's cat—a twenty-four-pound feline monster with a fiendish disposition. In the backseat, Helen opened her mouth in a silent miaow and pawed the back of Adele's head three—or was it four?—times.

Adele sped up.

"When I come home, Nelson, you *must* behave yourself. No chasing or biting. This is a special-needs kitty. Do you understand?"

Nelson laid his head on his Mickey rug remnant and whined.

"Okay. Good. I'll see you in . . ."

Helen pawed the back of her head again. It was definitely four times. She looked around for a hydrant or a tree, realized Helen was feline, and looked for dirt or naturally occurring kitty litter. There wasn't much dirt in downtown Mill Valley, but there was the park. Doing a U-turn around the safety island in the center of downtown, she gunned it and headed to Old Mill Park.

Helen was not smell-impaired. In fact, it was with his nose that he saw and heard everything that went on. Adele carried him from the car, leash firmly snapped on to his halter, and set him down under a thick overgrowth of a neighboring hedge. Helen sniffed the air and crept delicately toward softer ground in a nearby clump of redwood saplings.

While Helen dug a perfect hole in the dusty soil (Adele

could almost read the feline's thoughts: *Three inches wide, two inches long, and one inch deep*), Adele dialed David Takamoto's private line at the Marin County coroner's office. She would leave a message that was brief and to the point: "Hi. I want information."

"Doctor Takamoto here."

As always, someone picking up the line when she was expecting an answering device rendered her mute, her tongue paralyzed by sudden performance anxiety.

"Hello?" David said. "I hear breathing. Are you there? If this is an emergency, you'll have to dial nine-one-one."

"Don't talk to me about nine-one-one, pal. It's me, Adele. I was all set to leave you an obscene message on your machine. How are you?"

He let out a long, forlorn sigh. "Oh, you know. Surviving the county layoffs. Me and the morticians—we're truly recession-proof."

She laughed and glanced at her Timex. "Why are you there so late?"

"I have someone coming in in a few minutes to ID a body. It was the only time she could get here, so I've been mopping the floors, washing windows, putting away the bodies . . ."

"Can I stop by?"

There was a silence from the other end of the phone.

"I promise to be good," she pleaded, watching as Helen very scrupulously—almost eerily so—filled in the hole, then sniffed and patted the soil on top. "I won't, you know, like, pass out or anything. Cynthia already did that today."

She was only slightly ashamed at having brought up Cynthia—it would be sure to pique David's interest and overcome any other concerns he had about letting her visit at such a late hour. Although their romance had been over for years, David's continued obsession with Cynthia provided her more inside information than she could ever have dreamed possible short of breaking into the medical examiner's office and stealing files.

"Okay," he said wearily. "Come on over, and we'll pump each other for information."

* * *

Daisy did what she always did in those all-too-frequent embarrassing moments: she refused to acknowledge the humiliation, blocking the entire situation from her mind in a flash.

The telephone man followed her lead, speaking through the screen door in a normal tone while she breathed heavily with the labor of pulling the pink spandex up over the mountain of flesh that was her bum. The oatmeal, having been smeared as far as the reinforced steel hooks of her Super Woman bra, was soaking through the material.

"But all my phones are in tip-top working order," she insisted. "How can there be trouble with the line when I have service?"

In answer, the Pacific Bell repairman simply looked at her. He was much thinner and younger than she (weren't they all?) but he had a raw animal magnetism about him that transcended age barriers up or down.

"The main line broken," he said in an accent she found as attractive as his dark brown eyes. "I test all phones. It is only way to see problems." Hesitantly, he pulled open the screen door. "I come in?"

"Oh. Well, yes, yes, please do!" She backed up as he entered, taking a good look at the front of his pants. It was surprising the size of equipment some of these small men actually had. Unfortunately, his equipment was covered with a wide leather belt that held real tools such as hammers and a large measuring tape.

She threw back her head and laughed at the thought of asking if he had anything he wanted her to measure. He flinched at the sound—halfway between a shriek and nails going across a blackboard.

"It's really quite amusing," she prattled, twisting a platinum curl around and around her finger. "Whenever you want a telephone repair person, you can't get one for weeks. And when you least expect one—toodle-doo—there he is right at your front doorstep!"

The repairman searched the house with his eyes, taking stock of the layout.

"You show me telephones?" He pushed past her, heading for the one in the kitchen.

She followed, taking the opportunity to get in a good scratch. "May I offer you a gin and tonic? I was just about to have one. I make a rather good one if I do say so myself. You see, I coat the lip of the glass with the oils from the lime twist, then I . . ."

He unscrewed the cover of the yellow wall phone, ignoring her completely.

"I say, do you always work this late in the evening? I was under the impression the phone repair people only worked nine to four. The last time the phones went out, we couldn't get a repairman out here for days. Mr. Landor next door waited almost three weeks before . . ."

"I am special repair."

She waited until he was finished mucking about inside the phone with his screwdriver, then held up her glass. "Well, if you don't care for gin and tonic, would a nice hot toddy do?"

"No drinking on job."

Her lips formed an exaggerated pout. "Not even one teensy-weensy, itty-bitty nip? I promise I won't tell a soul."

He snapped the cover back on the phone without answering.

She poured herself a half tumbler of gin straight up and drank it down in two swallows. A sense of well-being infused her as the gin eased through her system. As she watched him, the warm surge of sexual desire caused the blood to rush to her face and neck. How long had it been? Years, she thought, if one didn't count her indiscretions with various delivery boys. She sighed heavily. It was just too unfair that Mr. Roth-schild had died the month before Viagra came on the market.

"Where are other phones?"

Daisy dropped a token ice cube into the glass, poured in the remaining gin, and stirred it with her finger. Giving him what she hoped was an inviting look, she licked the liquid from her finger then sucked on it.

In return, he stared impatiently, unaffected.

"Okay." She sighed. "Follow me."

All five phones were dismantled, checked, and put back together in an efficient manner in spite of her constant chattering and questions. Except for his name, all her questions went unanswered.

"Johnson?" she repeated, her eyebrows raised. "You don't look like a Johnson with all that black hair and that lovely olive skin." She ran a finger down his arm.

Repairman Johnson drew away. "I am done now," he announced and strode out, slamming the front door behind him.

She stared at the door, weaving slightly. "Well!" she said indignantly, "Excuuuuuse me!" At once she broke into high-pitched hysterical laughter, until the itch returned with a vengeance.

On the dissecting table, the barely recognizable body of a man lay reeking of rotting tissue. The head and hands were missing, as were the skin and muscle of the upper left arm. The abdominal cavity gaped open to reveal an absence of organs.

Leaning over the incomplete corpse was a fortyish woman with black hair that had been hennaed into mahogany straw. Dressed in a black designer suit and diamonds, she vigilantly examined the cadaver's penis while sobbing. Every few seconds she would cry out, beat her breast, wail lamentations in a foreign language, and then go back to studying the corpse's appendage.

It was probably one of the more bizarre scenes Adele had ever walked in on.

Dr. David Takamoto glanced at her and held up a finger to indicate that she needed to stay where she was. Adele almost didn't recognize him with all his clothes on.

She put down her purse and positioned herself at one of the workstations in the laboratory in order to see them better. Even from where she sat, Adele caught the scent of the woman's perfume—a variation on Lily of the Valley—that had managed to overpower the sweet, greasy smell of decomposing flesh. She couldn't see the woman's face, but she did have a perfectly good view of the rocks that weighted down her left hand.

"Christ on a bike, I'm surprised she can move her arm." Adele whispered to the imaginary Kay Scarpetta perched on the counter of the workstation.

Yes, Kay replied, *but what woman wouldn't want a stress fracture of her ring finger from too many diamonds?*

David Takamoto's mouth moved. Adele managed to catch a few words: ". . . sorry . . . must . . . positive ID . . . investigation . . ."

The woman nodded, looked away for a moment seemingly at nothing, then took the penis between her thumb and index finger. David moved the surgical lamp directly over the organ and the woman brought her face close—within a couple of inches.

"What is this?" Adele squinted. "Diamond Deb does the morgue?"

Dr. Scarpetta shot her a disapproving look. *The morgue isn't a place for the weak of stomach or Eddie Murphy, Ms. Monsarrat.*

The woman turned the penis this way and that, twisting it around as if she were building up momentum to flick it across the room. Abruptly, she dropped it, stood, and turned her back on the body. Boxer went to her side and touched her elbow. She murmured a few words Adele couldn't hear, then allowed him to lead her away from the table. They headed in her direction.

Not wanting to be caught spying, Adele calmly placed a stray slide on the microscope platform and bent over the eyepiece lens. Her thick black hair fell like curtains over each side of her face. The scrub dress let her blend into the morgue's green walls. She stayed with her eye to the scope until they passed. David spoke in a low voice while the woman whimpered and beat the invisible breastplate of her Chanel suit. Peeking over the eyepiece, Adele watched the woman sign a form, then lean on the medical examiner's arm as he led her out.

Adele decided to take a look at the remains, willing herself not to let the smell get to her this time. She matched her small steps with small breaths through her mouth, trying to adjust to the odor that always took her days to get out of her olfactory memory. Inching closer, her olfactory glands registered the smell of decomposing flesh. If they could have recoiled and screamed, they would have.

Adele considered the carnage on the stainless-steel table. The shape of the body, with its raw gray surfaces and opened middle, strongly reminded her of what hung in butchers' back rooms. She turned away, burying her nose in the fabric of her scrub dress. For the life of her, she did not understand how any civilized human could eat meat—it seemed cannibalistic at best.

"His name is Raymond Clemmons," Boxer told her as he entered the room. Fastidious to a fault, he washed his hands, dried them, and put on latex exam gloves. "The rather theatrical woman handling his genitalia was Mrs. Laila Clemmons. She has successfully identified her husband by this rather unusual pineapple-shaped mole." He held up the organ, pointing to the mole. The two-by-one-inch marking so closely resembled a pineapple in detail, Adele zoomed in to make sure it wasn't a tattoo.

"Mrs. Clemmons reported Mr. Clemmons missing on Wednesday. The Coast Guard fished him out of the Bay on Friday." The slender Japanese man, whose smiles were always brief, laughed outright, showing extraordinarily white teeth. "Today is Tuesday. What took you so long to get here?"

"Cynthia didn't tell me until yesterday, or I would have." There was a momentary pause, then she said, "Was there a toxicology report on this guy?"

"It was negative. He's clean."

Adele held her breath and positioned herself on the opposite side of the body. She pulled on the extension arm of the pie-sized magnifying glass, and brought it close to the neck, then swung it down to his abdomen and finally to his wrists.

David watched, assuming the expectant expression of a college professor observing his most promising student take on a difficult challenge.

"What do you see?" he asked after a few minutes.

Adele let out a breath and closed her eyes, remembering the vial of sample perfume in her purse. "I don't see shark bites or tearing injuries—I see deliberate amputation and decapitation." She rummaged around her oversized canvas satchel until her fingers found the small glass vial of perfume. Her hand closed around it, but did not draw it out.

"To the naked eye, the cuts appear to be precise," she continued. "I'd guess the blade to be a large scalpel, or one as sharp as that since there doesn't appear to be any hacking or sawing-type marks. If there'd been a shark or other marine predators involved, chunks would be missing and the flesh along the edges would be more jagged."

She brought out the glass tube and popped the plastic stopper. Upending the sample against her finger, she daubed a bit of the perfume under her nose. Instantly she felt better, although Opium would never be the same for her.

Dr. Takamoto nodded, took a pen from his shirt pocket, and pointed to the left arm from which there was a section of flesh missing. "And this?"

Adele brought the magnifying glass around and studied the area again.

"It's too clean to be a shark." She shook her head. "I don't know. It's pretty shallow. Could have been an accident or maybe a vaccination mark?" She looked up, raising her eyebrows in silent question.

"Not bad for an amateur forensics fan," he said. "If you could just get over this silly aversion to the smell and take a few classes, then agree to receive about half of what you make now, you'd make an A-one forensics investigator."

David lifted the man's leg. "See these deep scrapes on the heels and calves?" He pointed to the ragged lines of torn flesh. "They're linear, the skin scraped in a pattern that would be consistent with having been dragged. When I scraped them with the forceps, the debris I found deeply embedded was small bits of blacktop and gravel—substances found in your typical parking lot. Obviously, he had been mutilated and decapitated before he was dumped in the Bay, but from the lack of blood I found in the remaining organs, I'm almost convinced he'd bled out long before he got wet."

"But wouldn't he continue to leak blood into the water? I mean, how can you tell he bled out before being dumped?"

"Because cold salt water restricts bleeding by constricting the vessels." He crossed his arms over his chest and leaned back. "It would be purely speculation to say how much had been lost before he got dunked, but I found almost no blood at all in the deep veins of the legs or even in the inferior vena cava and heart. The absence of blood might have something to do with why there were no shark bites, but more so because sharks don't usually attack things that aren't swimming or moving on their own."

He walked slowly to the other side of the table. "A plausible explanation for this little piece of butchery"—he tapped the missing piece from the man's upper arm—"would be an attempt to remove all identifiable marks."

Adele cocked her head. "As in a tattoo or a vaccination mark—maybe even teeth marks?"

"All correct assumptions, but Mrs. Clemmons denies that her husband had any marks in that region of his arm. The head is obvious, as are the hands. No hands—no fingerprints. Mr. Clemmons served in the Navy, so his prints would have been on record."

"What about the abdomen and lack of viscera?"

David frowned and shook his head. "Don't know for sure. The edges of the cut don't match up. There's a strip of flesh approximately two inches wide and fifteen inches long that's missing. I would have said a tattoo belt or a scar, but Mrs. Clemmons says no such thing lived there."

He leaned against the sink. "Another point of speculation is that whoever did this had a lot of time and a fair amount of surgical knowledge. That's evident from the way the cuts were made. Another thing to think about is that there would have been a lot of blood, so the killer had to have a private place where he wouldn't be disturbed for a while. He also had to have a means of disposing of blood and body parts when he was done."

David nodded at the dead man. "As you can see for your-self, a ninety-kilogram man makes for a pretty big package. The head and hands wouldn't be that much of a problem to get rid of. I could think of a hundred ways to dispose of items that size. They're small enough to be burned in a small incin-erator unit, or concealed and discarded with the weekly garbage. Maybe they're in the center of a concrete block at the bottom of the Bay.

"There's also the tentative assumption that the brutalizing of the body over a fair amount of time suggests a murder that was planned, perhaps even ritualized. The missing parts could have been taken for trophies—or used in some sort of ceremony.

"If I were a forensic psychologist, I'd guess that the per-son or persons who did this were organized and relaxed enough to take their time. This implies a certain amount of self-confidence—almost arrogance. I doubt this was your garden variety twisted psycho fuck. I'd guess he—or they—are of above average intelligence."

David yawned. "But I'm only guessing. I leave those de-tails to the investigators. I just supply the physical facts, ma'am."

"Does the wife have any ideas who might have wanted to do this to him?"

He shook his head. "She says not. Says he's as loved as the day is long."

"How old was he?"

"Seventy," David answered, then, added before she could ask, "The Mrs. is forty-two."

Adele's eyebrows rose. "And I'll bet Raymond was one wealthy dude."

"That would be one bet you'd win," David said quietly, re-moving the latex gloves and scratching the palm of one hand. "Mr. Clemmons owned lots of prime San Francisco real es-tate. I guess he was one of those young men back in the forties who had enough forethought and family money to buy up a few prime properties and build a fortune from there. You know the Clemmons Building downtown on California Street?"

"That's him?"

David nodded. "He sold it when he retired in the late eighties—along with most of his other properties."

"All his assets go to his wife?" Adele asked.

"Probably." He gave her a sidelong glance and folded his arms across his chest. "I sincerely doubt she'd have the guy bumped off like this just to lay claim to his estate. Most everything was in her name anyway, and he didn't have any relatives to contest. If she wanted to off him, my guess is she would have found a less dramatic way to do it."

For a long moment, both of them stood staring at the mangled torso.

Her eyes wandered away from the body. "What about the woman they found a few weeks ago with the spliced breasts? Is there any way it could be related to this murder?"

David fixed her with a look. "How did you hear about that? Twin Cities PD was keeping that quiet."

"I haf my vays, dahlink," she said in a decent imitation of Marlene Dietrich. Her smile faded when his eyebrow arched in irritation, and he fastidiously, almost protectively, drew the white sheet over the remains.

"Sorry," she said quietly. Boxer Takamoto might perform autopsies in nothing but boxer shorts and a plastic apron, but she knew he took his work as seriously as a heart attack. "I heard about the case through an EMS person and I'm curious."

"You're way more than curious, Del," David said, smiling a little. "You're an A-one shit disturber." He sighed in resignation and washed his hands again. "And although you prefer to keep a low profile by calling your investigations a casual armchair hobby, it's more like a hardcore addiction." He pulled down a paper towel. "When we were an item, Cynthia told me that you subscribed to no less than ten private investigator journals, and six additional magazines that had to do with some angle of crime solving. Nothing casual about that."

He sighed, and stood next to the steel table occupied by Mr. Clemmons. "You received bad information about the Fischer case. It wasn't a few weeks ago, it was more like six weeks ago, and it wasn't bilateral—it was one breast. Actually, it looked a lot like someone practicing subcutaneous mastectomies. With the exception of a quarter inch of subcutaneous fat, all the breast tissue had been removed right down to the pectoralis fascia. The incision was quite precise around the areola and down the underside. Everything—the scene, the wound itself—was all neatly done. Not much evidence left behind. The lack of obvious sexual activity at the scene seems to go against the idea that this was a sexual crime. Again, I doubt this was a random murder by some psycho who just wandered off the street. I think it was deliberate, and well thought out by someone who was compulsively neat and organized."

Her mind danced around the information. Until this moment, she hadn't really believed Trevor's story about breasts cut open like watermelons. Suddenly, the smell coming from the body under the sheet seemed overpoweringly offensive. She leaned back, away from the steel table, feeling sick. A fantasy about the corpse under the sheet being stuffed with bread cubes and celery invaded her mind. She imagined herself sitting at a table, carving knife in hand, cutting the trusses that kept the stuffing inside. If just looking at a freshly roasted golden brown turkey made her squeamish—*this* was taking her to a new level of nausea. The whooshy whirring began—far away, but present all the same.

Dimly, David's voice filtered back in: "I'm not sure yet that the Raymond Clemmons and Zelda Fischer murders are related, although in each there is the factor of surgical knowledge and the use of a fine-bladed instrument."

"So, you don't think Fischer was a sex crime? Not even a desexing murder?"

David shook his head. "In desexing murders, usually the breasts, buttocks, and/or vagina are removed, carved, or bitten into. With the Fischer woman, the killer very precisely removed certain tissues. She hadn't been left exposed, nor had the killer arranged her body in any sexual or degrading poses. Just the opposite: he'd gone so far as to pull down the nightdress and cover her with the bedclothes."

"Was she sliced up before or after she was . . . ?" Adele trailed off.

"During the transition is my guess."

She closed her eyes and swallowed the wave of nausea that was starting just inside her throat. "What was the actual cause of death?"

David raised an eyebrow, still drying his hands on the paper towel. "Exsanguination is my guess. Both carotid arteries had a vertical slit upward. The blade used on the carotids was ser-rated—different than the one used on the breast, which was more like a scalpel." He threw the towel into the wastebasket.

"Whoever murdered her demonstrated a fair working knowl-edge of anatomy and physiology. The investigators were hot to nail some intern over at UCSF. Apparently Mrs. Fischer had an appointment in the dermatology clinic the day before. One of the interns who saw her made some suggestive com-ments so she complained to the administration."

"You didn't find anything else? Fibers or hairs? Semen? Teeth marks?"

"There was a microscopic metal fragment left on the inter-nal surface of the breast wall. It was an unusual type of metal that I thought might have been from a newly sharpened knife or a damaged scalpel, but when we put it under the scope, I changed my mind. We're not a hundred percent sure what it's from yet."

Dr. Takamoto leaned forward, looking at her intently. "Hey, Del, you still with me? You've got that expression like you're going to clean my floor with your face again."

She stumbled to her feet. Halfway across the room, she slipped in a spot of grease *(melted human fat?)*, regained her balance, and made it as far as the workstation. Sitting down heavily, she rummaged through the rubble of her purse, look-ing for the perfume sample. She settled for a peppermint candy. Her fingers shook as she unwrapped the gaily colored sweet and put it under her tongue. Within a few seconds, the whir and the faraway feeling faded.

"What the hell *is* it with me and the morgue, anyway?" She

hadn't meant to ask the question aloud, and didn't realize she had until David answered.

"It's all in your head, Del." His tone was kind. "You're a nurse. Dealing with gore and dead bodies is nothing new to you. It's the *idea* of the morgue. You've got a mind-set about it."

"It's ridiculous!" She ran her fingers through her bangs and down over the back of her neck, which was damp and cool. Underneath the bangs, her face was pale. "What happened to the insides of the Fischer woman's breast?"

"I don't know." David shrugged, reached into her purse, and picked out another peppermint, which he unwrapped and popped into his mouth. "Remember, I said there were no signs of sexual activity at the scene. But he could have taken sexual photographs. Who knows, maybe he took the tissue home and warmed it up in the microwave in order to masturbate with it."

Adele looked at him for a long moment. "That is truly disgusting, David."

"I didn't make that up, you know," he said. "There are some psychos out there who do things like that."

"Yeah," Adele said dryly. "I know all too well what people are capable of."

FOUR

IN ROOM 800, BED B, MR. PENN'S TELEVISION HAD been unplugged and the bedside cardiac monitor alarms suspended. The various lights around the bed continued to flicker, creating a blinking sign effect one might find in a cheap downtown hotel room.

Adele spooned lime Jell-O into his mouth, encouraging him to chew and swallow. So far, he hadn't drooled any of it.

"Nothing was stolen of value that I could see," she repeated. "Your stereo system was still there, and all your paintings and books, but it looked like your files and drawers of your desk had been rifled." She waited for him to swallow. "My guess is that whoever broke in was looking for something specific. Do you keep top secret documents for Pacific Gas and Electric hidden away?"

A vapid expression wandered over his face and settled in. He shook his head and continued to chew the gelatin, which no longer had substance. She wondered why old people frequently chewed things that weren't there. She also wondered why she found the way their dentures clicked so fascinating.

Mr. Penn's evening nurse came in long enough to hand Adele a medicine cup filled with pills and ask her to make sure he took them. Adele placed one of the capsules inside a spoonful of Jell-O and instructed him how to swallow on the unaffected side of his mouth and throat. It was a concept most people found difficult to grasp, let alone someone whose swallow reflex was impaired.

He picked up the cup, threw back the contents, and swallowed them without the aid of water or Jell-O.

"Okay," said Adele, eyeing the empty med cup—the wad of pills would have choked a horse. "Since you seem to be rallying, perhaps you can tell me if there was any cash hidden away that whoever was . . ."

"No ca—cash!" Mr. Penn told her, taking command of the spoon. His speech was still halting and slurred, but improving rapidly. "N—never ca—cash in house. No val—val . . ." He turned scarlet with the effort of getting the word out. Adele could just imagine him blowing another vessel in his brain.

"Valuables? You don't keep valuables in the house?" *Oh yeah, well, what about a vintage chicken? That's got to be worth a few bucks to the biological warfare people.*

He shook his head and his color returned to normal. "I lif a simble life," he said. "Don't n—need fancy gewgaws. Helen is . . . I want Helen." Mr. Penn broke into sobs.

Adele squeezed his hand reassuringly. "And Helen is such a sweet cat, Mr. Penn!" She thought of the cat curled up and purring like mad in one of her old sweatshirts in the Beast's backseat. "He's all packed up and looking forward to a new adventure at my house." *With my dog who outweighs him by eighty-five pounds.*

"Hearing aid?" he asked as she wiped the tears away from the unaffected side of his face.

"Oh damn!" Adele hit her forehead. "In all the excitement I totally forgot your hearing aid. I'll go back first thing in the morning and bring it in for you. I—"

"N—not me!" The old man shifted back to fury. "Helen! Kitty hear."

"The cat has a hearing aid?"

Mr. Penn made an exasperated gesture. "From Miracle Ear. C—cost a damn forshune!"

"I'll pick it up tomorrow," she said. "By the way, I had a lock in the car that I put on the front door as a temporary security measure. If you want, I'll have a locksmith install a new—"

Mr. Penn went scarlet. "No!" he hit the bed covers with his fist. "Goddamned shieves! I'll fixsh the lock. Leabe it."

It took her a moment to realize he was calling the lock-smiths thieves. "But aren't you afraid someone will break in again in the meantime? You've got a Cadillac sound system in there that's worth—"

"Came wif house. Don't lishen to m—music. Uses too much electrishity!"

They sat in silence while the lights flickered crazily around them. She stood and arranged herself. "Okay. I guess I'll be taking Helen home now and get him ready for bed."

"Warm milk."

"All right. I'll give him warm milk."

He reached out and tapped her on the arm then held up a shaky finger. "Got to shleep with someone. Doesn't have to be you. Just n—needs a warm b—body for comfort."

"Sounds like every boyfriend I've ever had." Adele laughed, already trying to figure out how she was going to keep Nelson off the bed and away from the cat. Even though he slept under the bed with his Mickey Mouse rug most of the time, he couldn't stand it when anyone slept in the bed with her.

Not that *that* had been a problem in recent years. Other than her stacks of investigator's handbooks, crime novels, and textbooks, and an occasional sleep-over by Cynthia, not much had slept with her since her divorce.

"Has Dr. Zimmer been in to see you yet?"

At the mention of his cardiologist's name, Thomas Penn began to hyperventilate anew. With vigor, he again punched the bedcover and scowled.

"Charlatan! Ba—ba—bbashtard! Goddamned crook. Three hundred dollars to take a—a loushy pressure. Pill-peddling son—a—blitch!"

His verbal vehemence sent a spray of spit across her chin.

"Three hundred dollars! Good flor nothing ba—ba . . ."

"You need a new pacemaker, Mr. Penn." Adele kept her voice in soothing kindergarten teacher mode as she wiped the spittle off her chin. "The one you have isn't working. Dr. Zimmer knows you. He'll be able to—"

"Quack!" He meant to punch the bed, but he missed and connected with her arm instead. "N—not get . . . one dime of my m—money. He . . . he . . ." he gasped, trying to get air. "I'll shoot goddamned bashard if he lays a hand on . . ."

"Okay, okay." Adele adjusted his oxygen up to five liters per minute. "Relax. You don't have to have Dr. Zimmer. Last thing you need to do is extend your stroke. Think of Helen. Think of how happy you'll be to see him again."

At the mention of the cat, Mr. Penn sank back into the pillows and wept like a baby.

Helen, fresh water, kibbles, and the automatic litter box locked securely in the bathroom, Adele took Nelson with her on her run. He was jubilant to be with Her in the Out where the scents were plentiful and he had numerous opportunities to legally misbehave.

On the closed gate to Natalie Coffin Greene Park hung the hand-painted sign: OPEN: SUNRISE TO SUNSET. It was long past sunset and partway into the night. The trail around Phoenix Lake glowed eerily as a veil of clouds fell away from the face of the moon. On the deserted pathway, their shadows stretched out in front of them in weird, long shapes as if they were large separate entities from another planet going along for the run.

The soothing logic in the act of running—one foot in front of the other, a step at a time—helped her to clear her mind and relax her body. At the end of the lake, where the forest grew thick, it was dark, like midnight plus two.

She closed her eyes and put her senses on automatic pilot. It always worked: putting complete faith in the powers that be to guide her feet and not let her fall. It was, she thought, like magic.

In a last attempt to rid her sinuses of the morgue/Opium smell, she inhaled through her mouth and blew out her nose. Ten yards ahead, Nelson stuck his nose into a clump of dry dandelions and sneezed twice.

"Hey, you want to hear this, Nelson?"

The dog slowed and looked back over his shoulder, his tongue lolling to one side. A noise issued from his throat that sounded like "Yep!" The response, coupled with his expression, strengthened her conviction that he would someday surprise her by talking in a small, human voice.

"I've decided to get back on the horse that threw me."

Nelson stopped, smelled around until he found the pile of rabbit pellets, whined at a sudden memory of his pet rabbit, and set off again.

"Did you hear me?" she asked, afraid his whine had been his response.

The dog barked once, then twice, in strong affirmation of her decision.

"I'm glad you approve." She switched from a sprint to toe-running up a steep hill at the end of Shaver Grade, known among the local runners as Little Motherfucker.

Kitch Heslin, her mentor in investigations, appeared above her left shoulder. *It isn't your choice, Adele. Investigations got into your system the day you walked into the station with the evidence that cinched the DeBergua murders. How the hell old were you? Seven, for Christ sake?*

"Eight. My face hadn't even caught up with my ears or nose yet."

You were a natural. I said that the first time I heard you brainstorm with the guys on the Froman case. Remember? You blew a few minds that day, gal. The other dicks thought I was nuts to let you in on the session. Thirteen years old—geeky and spooky as hell, taller than most of the guys, dressed all in black—and by Jesus if you didn't came up with the angle that shut the goddamned case.

"I've been scared, Kitch. I've been . . . afraid. The last case . . . I was—I was . . ."

Stupid. He said it for her. *We all are from time to time. You were lucky you didn't get yourself and everybody else killed.*

He leaned back in his chair and rested his forearm over his head. *But now you know better. It's good to get the shit scared outta you once in a while. This time you'll be more careful. That's how it works, Adele.*

"I miss you, Kitch," she whispered to the weathered wooden sign that read YOLANDA TRAIL.

That's part of your problem, the old man said as he began to fade like the Cheshire cat. *You're too emotional and too eager. Clouds your judgment. Make sure you get over it soon, 'cause it just might kill you someday.*

She came around a sharp curve and ran out onto the point in the trail she called her church. It was the place she came to worship the only higher power she recognized. Overlooking redwood forest, ocean, and an endless expanse of sky, the earth gave her strength.

She locked herself into the bathroom with Helen and the automatic litter box. While she gave the cat last-minute instructions on how to behave with Nelson, Helen purred, keeping a paw on Adele's throat, feeling the sounds.

When the time was right, and all scratching, whining, and heavy breathing from Nelson's side had ceased, Adele opened the door.

Instantly, Nelson's eyes grew bright and he cocked his head in extreme interest as he watched the feline smell and bump his way through his front legs. In true Mr. Magoo fashion, Helen passed underneath the dog, his long fluffy tail flipping first around Nelson's nose, then down the length of his belly.

Nelson looked to Adele, the question clearly written in his soft brown eyes.

"Blind and deaf, Nelson," she cooed. "Special needs. Must be gentle. Gentle and nice. Can you be a nice doggie to the kitty-kitty?"

Nelson barked with a whine at the end. It was his way of saying, "Yes, but I really don't want to."

Oblivious to the monumental crime he was committing, Helen stepped on Nelson's Mickey rug scrap, gave it a good smell, and promptly lay down for a nice wash and a snooze.

Nelson stood stock-still looking as though he'd just been given tragic news. He barked twice—"Oh no!"—and raised his lip in a half snarl.

"Nelson, don't you dare!" Adele warned. "Share your toys."

The dog sneaked a look at her out of the corner of his eyes without moving his head. On his belly, he crept toward the feline an inch at a time—as if She wouldn't notice. When he was close enough so that the cat's black fur moved with the rhythm of his breath, he rapidly pushed his snout under the cat and gave a shove. He clamped on to Mickey Rug with his teeth, and crept in reverse, all the while keeping his eye on Adele.

Helen, only momentarily disturbed in his toilet, propped himself into a sitting position against the wall heater. The mysterious appearance of some disgusting foreign slime had necessitated the rewash of his chest and belly.

The imaginary figure of Kate Moss, the supermodel who looked more like a Holocaust victim than fashionably slender, stood next to Adele, instilling guilt while she air-popped a quarter cup of one of her three P addictions: popcorn, that all-essential comfort food. Alongside peanut butter and potato chips, it was as close to a chemical dependency as she got.

What do you think they feed cattle? sniffed Ms. Moss. *Corn. It's pure fat and it's headed straight for your thighs.*

Adele looked down at her legs in search of cellulite and deliberated over what topping to use. Generously dousing the popped cattle feed with fake salt and a light spray of vinegar, she settled on the couch and hit the play button on her answering machine. The weird flat electronic voice, brother to the weird cyberspace voice on her e-mail server (You have mail!), announced that she had ten messages.

5:47 P.M.: A phone solicitor wanting her to participate in a survey about long-distance phone companies.

6:02 P.M.: A recording wanting to know if she was happy with her present long-distance service.

6:17 P.M.: A real person wanting to sell her a subscription to the *Pacific Intelligencer*, Marin's Republican-slanted rag.

6:18 P.M.: A recording offering a new long-distance service.

6:42 P.M.: George Ravens.

Adele sat up with a jerk, spilling several kernels on Nelson's head, and made note of Dr. Ravens's Tiburon number.

Ohhh, my my my, tittered the president of the Dateless Undesirable Old Maids' Club. Adele imagined her as the woman on a bottle of Mrs. Stewart's Liquid Bluing. *Perhaps the good doctor wants to call on you, dearie. Doctors and nurses—you know what they say.*

Adele snorted. "Nice try, Mrs. Stewart. He probably wants to know if I can fix his lawnmower."

6:47 P.M.: A phone solicitor telling her that if he called earlier to ignore the call, but that she really needed to think about changing her long-distance service.

7:34 P.M.: Her mother wanting her to call back as soon as possible: Aunt Ruth had a question about her HMO— or, as Martha Monsarrat called it, the Half as Many Options care system.

Adele groaned at the thought of having to hear another HMO horror story. Since her mother and aunt had both joined one, they seemed to delight in making her crazy with weekly reports on how the foundation was trying to kill them with non-care. Every week they'd come up with another HMO-gram: Health Minimization Operation, Half Minute is Over, and Help Mainly Optional were a few.

7:51 P.M.: Cynthia, giggling and saying, "Not now! Stop that!" to someone in the background, told her to call the second she got in and not even to take the time to pee first because she had important news, and could she please have her recipe for gazpacho as her stomach was in the mood for a little acid.

"Too late," she told Nelson who sat perfectly still watching Helen sleep.

7:52 P.M.: A solicitor for a company that put phone service, all utilities, and cable television all on one bill.

8:17 P.M.: "Hi. It's me. I've . . ."

The cattle feed went grainy in her mouth as she set down the bowl and hit the stop button. She hadn't heard Timothy Ritmann's voice for a long time, or what she perceived to be a long time—five weeks seemed like another life ago.

She took a deep breath and released the stop button: ". . . missed whumping your butt at Scrabble and Backgammon. What's the scoop? How about bringing me up to speed on the latest insanity in what you call your life? How about some Scrabble? Maybe I'll even treat you to dinner beforehand—to get your strength up. Call me. You know the numbers."

She was analyzing every nuance of his voice when the weird little announcer interrupted her thoughts to say that was the end of her messages. She hit the save button, sat back, and picked at the popcorn again. He'd been nervous. That was easy to tell from the way he laughed too many times, and how his voice shook at the ends of certain words.

He said he missed her—or did he? Did missing someone's company mean the same as missing them, the person?

Nelson, bored with watching the cat sleep, came over and laid his head on the couch, gazing up at her with huge brown eyes. The expression said, "Hi, watcha doin'? Wanna do something—like feed me again?"

Adele smiled down at her best four-legged friend, who was more like a combination spouse and child, and stroked his head. He wagged his tail, following every kernel that went from the bowl into Her mouth. She threw him a kernel that he caught in midair and, undoglike, carefully chewed like an old man whose teeth hurt.

"Should I call him back?" she asked the general audience.

Several members of the Old Maids' Club clucked their approval. Nelson yipped. Helen, however, having bumped and stumbled his way up the couch to the backrest, pawed at the side of her head four times.

* * *

Dr. Ravens answered on the first ring: "Hello, Adele Monsarrat."

"Caller ID, huh?" Adele said.

"No."

"Then you must subscribe to *Distinctive Ring*," she said, sure he would not be aware there really was such a magazine that catered to amateur snoops.

"Well, I used to," he began earnestly.

There was silence on the line while she tried to decipher whether or not he was putting her on. "Did you really?"

"Uh-huh. It had some useful information once in a while."

There was more silence in which she debated whether or not to pursue the questions forming in her mind, or just go on to business. Ignoring the fact she had started out by baiting *him*, she decided he was trying to manipulate her into a conversation, felt instant resentment, and let her voice get chilly.

"So," she began, "what's up?"

"I was wondering if you would consider coming over to fix my lawnmower. I'd compensate you for your time and any parts you needed to replace."

The Old Maids were tittering behind their lace-and-ostrich-plume fans all over the living room.

"Sure," Adele snickered. "I'll just throw on my Ms. Goodwrench belt and run right over."

"Well, how about next Thursday after work?" His tone was even. "You said you'd had some experience with fixing these things, and I thought . . ."

She hesitated then snorted. "You're serious! I mean, that's really why you're calling? To ask me to fix your lawnmower?"

"Yes. Like you said, it doesn't appear to be a very complex machine. It's not one of those types that you sit on. It's not that old either. I think I still have the owner's manual."

Adele's smirk fell off her face. "Well, sure. I mean, I guess I could give it a whirl. But I have to be honest and tell you that on principles of environment, I don't like power mowers. They're air- and noise-polluting, and they damage wildlife."

"Yes, but like all advanced tools, they save time."

"But with the time you save, wouldn't you want to spend it pushing a hand mower, listening to the birds and smelling the fresh-cut grass?"

After a pause, he said, "You have a good point. How about if I dump the power mower in the garbage and purchase a new hand mower? Then you can mow my lawn, be environmentally correct, and smell all the fresh-cut grass you want, and I can have the pleasure of watching you enjoy yourself."

"How big is your lawn?" Adele grinned.

The sound of his laughter slid back the iron bars of her reserve.

"Big."

"Well, for your information, when I was a kid I used to get ten dollars to mow and trim the neighbors' lawns. How much do you pay—I mean, factoring in inflation and the current cost of living?"

There were clicking noises in the background, then, "According to my abacus, you can charge me forty dollars, but I have to deduct the charge for the pleasure of smelling the grass. I'll give you twenty-five dollars plus a meal?"

"I'm vegetarian."

"I am aware of that. But if you think you get some kind of extra compensation for that, you're mistaken. Vegetarians in this part of the world are a dime a dozen."

"How did you know I was a vegetarian?"

"Your smell, skin, and build. Most of my colleagues think I'm nuts, but I find that vegetarians' skin has a slightly different look and texture, as well as a certain body type that's thinner in the face and not so fleshy in other parts. Their body odor is distinctly different than carnivores—subtle and earthy, rather than animal. I would guess that you have rarely, if ever, eaten meat in your life."

She said nothing for a moment, then: "You must be a vegetarian."

"No, but I wouldn't eat meat from a grocery store or what is served in restaurants. I only eat meat I hunt myself, and only certain animals and only from certain places."

Adele nodded, imagining him in a loincloth running barefoot after the buffalo in Golden Gate Park. "Why do you know about *Distinctive Ring*?"

"Short version is that I was a deputy in my village, then, when I went to med school, I paid my way by moonlighting as a private investigator—following unfaithful spouses and insurance fraud stuff." He sighed. "Sometimes, when I get called in on a head injury case at two in the morning, I wish I'd stuck with it. It was much more predictable than neurology, though not nearly as well paid." There was a pause, and then he said, "Are you intrigued enough to mow my lawn?"

"Tell you what. I'll stop by, take a look at your lawn, and have a cup of tea. The mowing and meal will have to come later. Now—what's the real reason you called?"

"That was the real reason I called, but I'm using the excuse of filling you in on Mr. Penn."

"Do you know that he refused to see Dr. Zimmer?" she asked.

"Yes, he informed me this evening he wasn't going to see the 'overpriced bashard'—his words. He insisted I call . . ." She could hear him checking through the pockets of his jacket, unfolding bits of paper and crumpled business cards. "A doctor by the name of Edward English. Penn says he was highly recommended by the clinic doctor in Berlin. Ever hear of him?"

"Not ringing any bells offhand." Adele picked up the San Francisco phone book and flipped through the thick slab of yellow pages. "Let's see if—"

"Put away the phone book. I already talked to him. He sounds competent enough, and he was aware of Penn's case. Told me this Berlin clinic has a track record for inserting malfunctioning generators. Apparently, he had contacted them about a year ago when one of his San Francisco patients ran into a similar problem. It just so happens that he speaks German, so he and the head doctor of the clinic developed a cordial working relationship. The Berlin doctor must have remembered him when he realized Penn was from this area, so he recommended that if anything went wrong, he see English. English said that on the case last year they reimbursed him triple what he could make here from insurance or Medicare. And, of course, not wanting to incur any international medical malpractice incidents, the clinic told Penn that if he had any problems at all with the pacer, he was to call English and he'd take care of whatever problem came up—gratis."

"Ah," Adele said. "There you have the magic word: free. That's the key for our own modern-day John Elwes."

"The old guy is really that tight, huh?"

"Oh, honey," Adele cackled. "This guy's so tight, I'll bet he uses his used dental floss to sew with instead of buying thread."

"If he's that tight, he doesn't buy dental floss, Adele. He flosses with the shed hairs he finds in his brush."

Bolstered by the attentions of Dr. Ravens and momentarily feeling protected from her own emotional confusion over Timothy Ritmann, she casually punched in Timothy's number, whistling a tune she made up as she went along.

As soon as he said, "Ritmann here," the sides of her protective shell crumbled. The whistled ditty dried on her lips and her gut flew into a knot, sending an overpowering message that it wanted to rid itself of any and all food it had previously been processing.

"Oops!" she said, already running for the bathroom. "Gotta go. Call you later."

Shaken, she returned to the living room and started to call him back, but was distracted by the gunk caught in the holes of the receiver's mouthpiece. It seemed like a good time to do small electronic device maintenance.

That was good for fifteen minutes. After she'd painstakingly worked out the dirt with a toothpick and wiped down the entire phone with Clorox, she found herself in front of the wall heater, cleaning the metal vent holes with Q-Tips dipped in a degreaser. Next she moved on to the crevices along the undersides of the baseboards, until she'd worked her way into the bathroom. There, she was seduced by the mechanical mysteries of the automatic kitty-litter box.

She was sound asleep in the hall when the phone rang. Jumping to her feet, she staggered forward, smashed face-first into the corner of the wall, and fell flat on her back. The Crazy Woman laughter was on her before she could get up. As she crawled on her belly toward the phone, she snorted in a breath, then let it out with another long wheeze of hard laughter. A fraction of a second before the answering machine took over, she managed to pick up the phone with hands that were weak with laughter. She snorted again and went into another wheezy howl.

"Adele?" Tim said after a few seconds. He sounded both confused and slightly amused. "Is that you?"

She tried to speak, but another contraction of laughter doubled her over.

"Are you alone?"

Nelson barked nervously, as if to explain: "She was *fine* when she fell asleep, doc, but when she woke up, she wasn't quite herself . . ."

"Yes," she managed. Then, "I'm sorry. I—the phone startled me and I ran into the wall, and knocked myself—"

At the sound of his laughter, she immediately came to her senses. "I'm sorry I didn't call you back, but I—I—ah, remembered something and had to go immediately."

It wasn't that far from the truth.

"Oh." He took in a deep breath and blew it out. It wavered, and he immediately moved the mouthpiece away. He wiped his hand on his slacks. "Well, you missed the celebration the other week."

"Which celebration was that?"

"My return to full duty with no restrictions. No more having Chernin and Cini watching over my shoulder to make sure I don't go post-traumatic and shoot somebody."

"Hey, congratulations," she said, meaning it and then suddenly feeling like she was going to cry. With her guilt tapes providing the sound track, the pictures of his chest opening when the bullet hit played on her Technicolor mind screen. The old feelings for him rolled up into her throat like a ball of burning oil.

Silence.

"Goddamn it, Adele!" he yelled suddenly. "It wasn't your fault! Shit, I'm the one who walked into that. I was thinking about what a hero I was going to be. I knew better. I should have waited for backup. I could have gotten both of us killed. It was my fucking ego. Don't you get that?"

She stared at her fingernails without seeing them, peeling them down to the quick, one at a time.

"That isn't everything, is it, Adele?"

He waited. "You and I got . . . we were . . . close. Then one day you let it go. What happened? Was it something I did?"

Again, he waded through her silence. "You've got to help me out here, Adele, because I've been going nuts trying to—"

"You didn't do anything, Tim." She struggled with herself. *Tell him! Tell him! Take the plunge.* "It's me. You're fine. I think you're . . ." *Tell him!* ". . . great. A wonderful guy. Really."

"Adele, I don't—"

"Listen," she hurried. "Can we—can't we . . ." *Can't we go back to the way it used to be?* She forced a laugh. "It's just that I've been so . . ." *lonely for you.*

". . . busy lately at work and with the nurses' union, but a game of Scrabble sounds . . ." She closed her eyes, sinking in at the middle. ". . . fine. Just . . . fine."

This time it was he who said nothing. His leg was bouncing. He looked around his office with a vague sense that he was losing ground in breaking through the barricaded doors of her identity. He rubbed the smooth scar running down the center of his chest, and opened the top drawer of his desk. Searching for the bottle of Mylanta, a page from an old *San Francisco Chronicle* stared up at him. In the photo Adele was walking from the Marin County courthouse escorted by Cynthia and Detective Chernin. It was the day of Erin Middleton's hearing. Her face was still badly bruised and swollen, but her eyes stared defiantly into the camera as if to say she would not tailor her opinions or her actions to popular trends because it was easier.

All of a sudden he wanted to tell her that even when he wasn't with her she was still there—in him. He couldn't just go off and forget. Her voice, her smell, her eyes: they were all there inside him all of the time.

"I suppose I should be fair and warn you that I worked on my game during my leave. I actually attended the first tournament of the National Scrabble Association of America."

"You're kidding!" Her glee stopped abruptly when, to her horror, she saw what she'd done to her nails. "Did you actually play in the tournament?"

"I got trounced in the first round by a ninety-year-old sex book writer from Anna Maria Island." He laughed. "She loved her Scrabble and took no hostages. At the end of the tournament, she lifted a fifth of bourbon from the Drinks on Wheels wagon and brought me back to her room. You wouldn't believe some of the tricks she showed me."

He hesitated at the feel of a death chill coming through the phone.

Adele, who'd heard "nineteen" instead of "ninety," gripped the receiver, jealousy twisting in her stomach like a pissed-off hedgehog. "Oh, really," she said coolly. "Learn much?"

Her sudden change in tone puzzled him as he drank straight from the Mylanta bottle. "Man, did I! The old broad was so good, she about busted my nuts with these—"

"Well, listen, Tim, I'd love to talk with you about your nuts and all, but I've got some important walking and chewing gum at the same time training to do for the Special Olympics coming up next—" She stopped. "Old broad?"

"Well," he began uncertainly. "There was a whole division of ninety-five and overs, but Mabel was definitely up there. I mean, after eighty-five, they all sort of blend together with that blue hair and those orthopedic shoes, don't they?"

The hedgehog mollified, Adele snorted pleasantly, as if agreeing.

"Why don't you have dinner with me tomorrow night and I'll pass on what she showed me?"

"Okay," her mouth told him without any direction whatsoever from her brain. In the echo of her acceptance, she heard the eagerness of her voice. It was as if her body had conspired and mutinied against her free will.

"I'll pick you up about seven?"

"Can you go for five?"

"Six?"

"Done," he said, feeling as if he'd scored and needed to move on to something else before she changed her mind. "So now, want to bring me up to speed on what you were doing in the middle of a crime scene over in Belvedere this evening?"

Dreams were always an adventure for her. Full-color, action-packed episodes that ranged from the normal midget-and-housewares nightmares to the old standards of being chased by dangerous men and getting lost in shadow-plagued houses with the confrontational Mysterious Woman figure so popular with Freud.

At the tender moment the Mysterious Woman was about to say, "I do" to Scant the midget, an airplane crashed in the churchyard, blowing out the stained-glass windows. Prevented from running away by the ankle-deep molasses, she was buried under the plane's cargo of several thousand medical leeches.

Her eyes flew open, revealing total blackness. "I'm blind!" she yelled, heard the muffled quality of her words, and realized that Helen had settled over her face. The cat roused himself and slid off to the hollow of her neck. One paw found its way to her ear

Bags under his eyes, Mickey Rug scrap hanging from one fang, Nelson stood at the side of the bed laying a guilt trip on her. He lay a paw on her arm and whined piteously.

She looked at her watch and groaned. "It's two-thirty in the morning, Nels. What *is* your problem?"

In answer, he stealthily climbed, a leg at a time, onto the bed and settled next to the unoccupied side of her head.

Staring at the ceiling, her head held immobile by animal headends, she sighed and went back to the wedding.

FIVE

"HEY, YOU'RE LOOKING GREAT," ADELE SAID, PLAC-
ing Mr. Knudsen's discharge packet on the side table. "You'll
be out there riding those cable cars by noon."

Uncomfortable with compliments, the Minnesotan cautiously touched the flap of his hunting cap, which was sticking straight out from the bandage over his reattached ear.
"Yah, we're gonna be needin' the trolley to get us around now
that the car's gone. We don't have those kind of parking problems in Minnesota, ya know."

Adele set her stethoscope in place. "Well, this *is* California," she said. "The state motto is 'It's different here.' Take a
deep breath."

She finished his physical assessment, charted his discharge
vitals, and gave him a white paper bag filled with antibiotics
and pain meds. "Here's an instruction sheet on how to take
care of your ear until the stitches come out. Dr. Wortz wants
to see you in seven days. In the meantime . . ."

The intercom box at the head of the bed crackled to life
with the acrimonious growl of Ward 8's ill-humored monitor
tech, Tina: "You got a call on line three."

"Who is it?" Adele asked before she could stop herself.
Tina, a Brooklyn transplant, had never lost her accent or the
New York attitude—the accent Adele thought charming, the
attitude was something to steer clear of.

"What? I'm a personal answering machine now? How
the hell should I know who it is? I'm going outta my freakin'
banana with the phones, and O'Neil being in charge not

knowin' her ass from a barbecued pork chop? And the way you people expect me to run around doing all your stupid—"

Adele clicked off the intercom and gave Mr. Knudsen an apologetic, helpless look. "Why don't you go in the bathroom and brush your teeth. When you come back, I'll take out your IV and you can get dressed and be on your way."

Mr. Knudsen nodded and shuffled off toward the bathroom. Halfway there, he stopped and, as if weighing the pros and cons, said, "Listen, do ya think that woman out there needs help?"

The question seemed to come like a stray rock out of some Minnesotan left field, until she realized he meant to offer his assistance. It was good old Midwestern American pitch-in-and-help. Deeply touched, she shook her head.

"Nah," she said. "Tina can do anything. She's Lutheran."

"Adele?"

The voice on line 3 was familiar, but she could not immediately place it.

"Yes?"

"Bedlam and anarchy are going on at your house. Do you want me to call the police?"

She placed the voice. It belonged to Deena Mae Coolidge—busybody of Baltimore Avenue East, owner of the vicious Queen Shredder, and member in good standing of the Flapping Mouth Club.

"Mrs. Coolidge?" Adele covered her free ear and turned away from the charting desk, which was full of doctors having a my-dick-is-bigger-than-your-dick discussion about what makes and models of four-by-four sports utility vehicle they each owned. "What are you talking about?"

"Well . . ." Mrs. Coolidge took a deep breath and daintily set her feet—in fuzzy pink kitty-head slippers—on the coffee table. "I was taking Queen Shredder for her morning constitutional, and as we were passing by your house, we heard the most godawful noises. It sounded exactly like there was a massacre going on inside." The woman took another breath. "Well, naturally I tried to see inside to make sure."

"Naturally," Adele said dryly.

"And I saw your doggie jumping." She gave a breathless giggle. "Imagine! He was making a terrible noise and—"

"Jumping?" Adele asked. "You mean, as in up?"

"Uh-huh." The old gossip smiled and petted Queen Shredder, who was purring on her ample lap. "Jumping high in the air, barking. I'm afraid he's knocked down your blinds, and I think there's some broken—"

"Thank you, Mrs. Coolidge." Adele cut her off before she could get out the rest of the gory details. "I'll take care of it."

"But . . ."

"Don't call the police. They have enough to do."

". . . don't you want me to go inside and try to—"

"No!" She imagined the meddler Coolidge inside her flat and shuddered: no drawer, file, or pocket would be left unviolated. "I'll take care of it."

Adele clicked on an open line and punched in her number. As soon as her machine picked up, she hit the code for room monitor. Mrs. Coolidge hadn't exaggerated. Bedlam was there, having a ball inside her home.

Through Nelson's alternating barking and whining came the click and thud of his body and nails leaving the floor and then hitting the wall. At once, she heard the crash of what she recognized as the fireplace screen. The scene came as clear in her mind as if she were there: Helen curled against the Salem chime clock on the mantle, and Curious Nelson jumping as high as he could to get a good look at what the cat was doing—just to make sure he wasn't missing out on any fun.

"Nelson!" she yelled into the phone. Behind her, the doctors stopped talking. Indeed, the entire nursing station went silent.

"Nelson, stop jumping! Leave Helen alone! He's disabled, Nelson! Nelson? Do you hear me?"

There was a long and complicated series of whines as he came closer to the phone to explain and complain.

"I don't care," she said finally, her voice stern. "He's on the mantel to get away from you! Kitty-kitty doesn't want to play. Leave him alone. Go hump your rug. Mickey Rug. Stat!"

Eavesdropping, the table of physicians gave each other sideways glances as if to say, "It's Ward Eight—what do you expect?"

She waited until she heard the slinking click of his nails and the disappointed groan as he settled down with his Mickey Mouse rug scrap before she hung up and faced the room. Disregarding the doctors' stares, she headed back to Mr. Knudsen. As she turned the corner, she walked up Mattie Noel's sensible brown oxfords and into her clipboard.

"I want to talk to you, Arden!" The supervisor stood with her arms folded across her chest, her face was flushed. The tic in her right eye was going apeshit. "Right now."

"It's the busiest time of the shift, Mrs. Noel." Adele sighed. "I'm right in the middle of seeing my patients. Can this wait?"

In answer, Mrs. Noel moved the clipboard away from her bosom and began to read the prepared statement.

"Nurse Monsarrat, you have been relieved of your duties effective immediately. You will be escorted to your car by security. Gather your things and leave peaceably, or you will be removed by force."

Adele looked around to see who else was in on the joke. They were alone except for two post-bypass patients taking their morning exercise. "What are you talking about?"

"Yesterday you left Ward Eight without signing off, thus abandoning your patients, and then worked without clearance in another department. To make matters worse, you took part in a code during which you gave medications and acted in a capacity in which you were not authorized."

"Excuse me, Mrs. Noel, but I'm part of the day shift Code Blue team. I would have responded to the code no matter where I was."

"And, when you were confronted," Mattie Noel continued, "you lied about your identity. The nursing department has met with—"

"Personally, Mrs. Noel, I don't care if the nursing department met with Bill Gates's stockbroker. You can't dismiss me without a formal hearing. You know the drill: formal grievances have to be filed through the union, and then I have to answer and we all go to court and then you'll lose the case because it has no merit whatsoever, and then you can pay me scads of money when I bring harassment charges against the administration."

She pushed herself away from the wall. "I don't have time for these mouse fart contests, Mrs. Noel. If you need to jettison some pent-up animosity, I'd suggest you join a group— Menopausal Skinheads or something. You'll be able to use all that Nazi training without interfering with people trying to do their work."

A security guard entered the hall and headed for them. Mattie Noel gestured frantically for him to hurry. "She's not complying with the administration's request to leave the premises," she told him. "Escort her out of the building."

The guard unsnapped the strap holding his baton and pulled it from its sheath. "Let's go, miss," he said, crooking his finger. In his voice was a note of warning.

For a split second, Adele considered all the things she could do with a day off and thought it might not be so bad. She started walking in front of the guard when she saw Mr. Penn through the window of his room. He was crying. Then she remembered that Mr. Minka still needed an assessment, and that she had promised Mirek he could do an IV change. She slowed and turned around to face Mrs. Noel.

"I'm not going anywhere," she said in a way that told them she really wasn't. "Except into my patients' rooms."

She pushed past them, but before she'd gone a yard, the guard hooked her arm, his fingers digging into the flesh over her wound. He swung her around so that she fell against the wall.

Testosterone stores aroused by potential violence, he pulled his gun from its holster and trained it on her. His own actions seemed to startle him, though he did not back off.

Drs. Ravens, Wortz, and Murray and Mirek, Cynthia, Skip, and Mrs. Knudsen rounded the corner and ran toward her looking like a troupe of Fellini actors. Tina sauntered at the rear of the throng, headset still in place.

"Do you want me to call a Code Pink, Adele?" asked Cynthia pushing the guard out of the way. Mirek wanted to know whether she was hurt. Skip stood back, his hands flopping nervously until they found their way to his hips. Tina muttered, "Oh my gawd," several times, lost interest when she realized there wasn't any blood involved, and returned to her post at the central monitor banks.

Dr. Ravens, being the largest person present, placed himself squarely in front of the guard and murmured something in a low, forceful tone. The veins in his forehead and temples stood out like ropes.

At once, the guard holstered his gun, held up his hands, and backed away.

Right on the edge of Crazy Woman laughter, Adele focused on the pain in her arm—until she spotted Mrs. Knudsen peering out from behind Dr. Murray.

It was the hunting cap with flaps that set her off laughing yet again.

The incident was over as quickly as it had begun. Dr. Ravens escorted Mrs. Noel and the security guard out of the ward, Dr. Wortz checked Adele over for injury, Cynthia helped her fill out two incident reports, and Tina left a message for their union representative that one of the supervisors had gone postal and attacked a nurse.

Mr. and Mrs. Knudsen sat quietly with folded hands as Adele went about the tasks of discharging him, but it was clear by the way they both sort of ducked or flinched when she came near, that they feared she might go into another one of her "fits."

It was noon before Adele caught up enough to make herself a cup of vegetable broth and visit Mr. Penn while he ate his lunch. She was pleased to see he'd been promoted from a liquid to a soft diet.

He picked up the peanut butter and jelly sandwich and took a small bite. "Helen okay?"

"He's great." *Exhausted from trying to dodge a hyperactive dog, but great.* "Slept on my neck all night." *That is, when the dog wasn't trying to sniff his butt.* "Ate a good breakfast." *On top of the refrigerator.*

"Elimination?" Mr. Penn asked, swallowing.

Adele choked on her broth. Typical of Mr. Penn's age group to be "elimination"-obsessed, even with their pets. "If the litter box machine is to be believed, then I'd say Helen is running smooth."

Satisfied, Mr. Penn sipped his milk and opened the top bedside drawer. He handed her a business card with the address 450 Sutter Street, San Francisco. Every resident of the Bay Area knew the immense building in downtown where hundreds of physicians rented office space.

"This is the doctor the Berlin clinic told you to contact?"

"He's coming t—t—morrow morning. No charge!" Mr. Penn grinned. "Socialized medicine. Only way to go."

"Have you ever seen Dr. English before?" She tried to keep the skepticism out of her voice.

He shook his head and with a trembling hand, wiped away a piece of bread that was caught on his lower lip. "B—Berlin doctor told me he's the only doctor in Califlornia who ca—can fish this pacemaber. He said I could go home same day."

A doubtful expression crossed her face. "The same day? Most hospitals like to watch a new pacemaker for at least twenty-four hours before releasing them to the wild. We have to make sure that it's firing appropri—"

"G—got to work!" His face turned stormy. "Can't loaf alound here fo—foever! Goddamned Zimmer. Bashard wants to keep me in hoshpital a week! Sish thousand bucks a day! Son of bitch ca—can stick it where th—the . . . sun don't shline!"

"Mr. Penn, listen." Adele put down her cup and leaned toward the querulous old man. "You have what is known in the business as a gold-plated insurance plan. Pacific Gas and Electric pays good money for it. You might need to stay an extra day. Why don't you—?"

"I n—need to get to work!" he said, throwing the remainder of his sandwich onto the plate. "I got bills to pay. Can't be shlacking off in here."

"You're recovering from a stroke and you have a malfunctioning pacemaker." She paused to let this sink in. Then, knowing full well she shouldn't go there, she lowered her voice. "Don't you think you owe it to Helen to make sure you're a hundred percent before you try to go back to work? You don't want to be responsible for making him an orphan, do you?"

Mr. Penn's eyes filled.

"If anything happened to you, the SPCA might not be very understanding about a disabled kitty, you know. You don't want poor Helen worrying about his daddy."

She was going to add something about how he'd be all alone in a kennel cage wondering why his daddy never came to fetch him anymore, but decided against it at the sight of Mr. Penn's quivering chin.

Mr. Walter Minka. The very name conjured up the image of someone rheumy eyed, hunched over and dentally challenged. It did not fit the nice-looking twenty-nine-year-old in room 810, bed A.

Though she did not have the time to spare, she allowed herself one minute to watch him sleep. His long body lay motionless, limbs akimbo. One hand was next to his cheek with the slender fingers slightly tangled in a spill of fine hair. The smooth skin of his forehead was beaded with perspiration. He looked innocent enough to have been a Calvin Klein poster boy, had it not been for the IV and the sickbed accoutrements.

She moved quietly about the room, gathering his medications and the IV equipment for Mirek. When she could not put it off any longer, she lay her hand on his arm. Under her fingers, his skin was hot and dry. She wiped his face and neck with a cool washcloth. He opened his eyes and stared at her uncomprehending yet unconcerned, and moved his head to see her better.

She put down the washcloth and smiled. "I'm Adele, your nurse. I need to get your vital signs and do a physical assessment."

Not fully awake, he squinted, regarding her without any change of expression. She knew he'd received a dose of morphine, but that was hours ago.

"Walter? Are you with me?"

He shook himself and sat up abruptly, running his hands through his hair. "I was dreaming about the girl I used to . . ." He took a deep breath and coughed until he was purple.

"Shit." He labored to pull in air, his ribs showing plainly through his flesh. "Still can't get used to . . ." He tried to smile and failed. "Can't get used to this disease, I guess." He reached for the glass of water. "Hey, can a dying man get an aspirin around here? I think I've got a fever again."

The other nurses thought his acknowledgment of his condition as a healthy sign of acceptance, but Adele couldn't help but notice the lack of emotion behind the verbal gestures. It seemed more bravado than a heartfelt affirmation—the sort of thing a young soldier in the trenches would say while soiling his pants as shells exploded around him.

"Is it all right with you if one of the nursing students changes your IV this afternoon?" Adele asked, opening his med cabinet. She dropped three acetaminophen into a paper med cup. "I'll be here to observe and assist him."

"Him?" Walter's eyebrows went up, then down in a frown.

Adele read his thoughts: male nurse equals gay.

"You have a problem with that?"

He looked away, embarrassed. "I don't know, I just don't want some gay guy checking me out while I'm not looking, you know?"

"What's being gay have to do with being a good nurse? Some nurses are, some aren't, and some"—thoughts of Skip jumped to mind—"are sexually ambiguous. In any case, you've been a patient long enough to know that it doesn't matter. Nurses are your lifeline, regardless." She pulled her stethoscope from around her neck. "Mirek happens to be straight and a crack shot at starting IVs. Let me take a quick listen to those lungs."

He untied the hospital gown and slipped it off completely. It was soggy with sweat, as was the waistband of his pajama bottoms. She didn't need to touch the bedclothes to know all his linens would need to be changed as well.

She began with the lower lobes, and listened to the crackles. In her mind's eye, she saw the alveolar sacs trying to open, and the cancer spreading, eating the good tissue like an evil Pac-Man head. Moving up a few inches, she skirted around the wide scar marking where the primary lesion had been found at level III. The melanoma on his upper chest, close to the neck, had been smaller and not so advanced or deep. Not that it mattered: by the time the melanoma was discovered, it had already metastasized to the lung.

He began coughing until his face went scarlet with the effort. When the fit passed, he lay back exhausted, staring out the window toward the estuary. His expression was that of a lost soul searching for some kind of peace.

Adele calculated which of her patients could go without what, and knowing she didn't have the time to spare him, sat down on the edge of his bed.

"You okay?"

"Yeah, I'm great." He was still laboring for air.

"Bullshit."

He looked past her. "Hey, what do you want?" he said evenly. "I'd rather be making tons of money climbing up some corporate ladder, hanging out with my friends, meeting ladies, drinking beer, and listening to music. This ain't exactly my idea of the perfect life."

"You sound pissed off."

He forced a smile. "Me? Hell no. It's a fucking blast wasting away and pissing into bottles. My lungs and my liver are in such bad shape they're living out of state under an assumed name. I adore having to tell somebody every time I take a shit so they can take a look and make sure I'm not bleeding to death through my gut. It's a fucking circus!" His voice was rising, and it was costing him a lot.

Embrace it, she thought. *Go through the stages and get them over with so you can get on with it.*

He looked at her fiercely, then stopped as suddenly as he began. "I don't want to disappoint you, but I can't get into the cosmic have-a-good-death routine."

"You have to," she said, "because the options aren't acceptable. Simple as that." She paused. "Death isn't a medical moment, Walter. Outside of birth, it's the second most important defining event in your life. You can choose—"

"Fuck defining event," he gasped. "It's death. I'm dead. I'm a thirty-year-old dead man." He fell back into his pillow and looked out at the estuary, giving himself time to catch his breath. Out on the water, ducks floated serenely like so many feathered vessels.

He turned back, his facial cast less fierce, but his voice, which was on the edge of cracking, was overlaid with sarcasm. "And what do you suggest I do to make the most of this 'defining event'?"

"Anything you like within your physical limitations," she said. "You're dying, but you aren't dead yet. Make it as positive as you can. See it as a freeing experience. Shit, Walter, think of all the possibilities. Go to a concert wearing a chicken suit; give all your stuff away so you can enjoy the expressions on your friend's faces when they get your Bose speakers, or your vintage nineteen sixty-eight Fender guitar. Ask the most beautiful woman you know to marry you. After that, rent the fastest, classiest red sports car you can find and take her down to Big Sur for the weekend. What the hell have you got to lose?"

"You're fucking dreaming."

"Why, Walter? Why am I fucking dreaming?"

He opened his mouth to answer, but stopped when Mirek came into the room.

His gaze returned to the water. "Fucking dreaming, that's all."

Every nurse has one skill in which she or he is proficient. Cynthia was great at efficiently cutting to the heart of any situation—no wasted words or energy. Skip, perhaps because of his own phlegmatic temperament, had a way with demanding, little old ladies whom no one else could mollify. Linda's genius ran toward organization in the face of chaos. Adele's gift was empathy—getting to the core of a patient and sensing what they were really all about.

Miroslav possessed the valuable talent of being able to start IVs anywhere, anytime, on anyone. On any color skin, in the dark, in the middle of a code or a nuclear holocaust, Mirek could access the smallest collapsed vein and get an intravenous line running. Adele had not seen anything like it since the late Nurse Marvel.

Every few moments Mirek would pause, look into Walter's eyes, and ask, "I hurt you?" When he was finished, he listened to Walter's lungs and heart at the same time as Adele, the bells of their stethoscopes side by side, while she explained each nuance of sound to both the student and the patient.

She left the two together and tended to the needs of her seven other patients. On her way to the nurse's charting desk twenty minutes later, she was surprised to find Mirek still at Walter's bedside. The student's back was to the door; Walter was listening to him with profound concentration.

She checked her watch. Mirek wouldn't have time to chart and report off and still be on time for his post-clinical conference. The sound of soft weeping made her pause at the door.

"He was my brother. Pavel was seven, I was six. They . . ." Mirek lowered his head, and Adele realized he was crying.

". . . shot him through the head for stealing bread. In the alley. He had no choice. He knew nothing but that we had hunger all the time. He was good boy. Pavel only steals bread. Bread. They leave him in the alley. I did not know what to do . . ."

Walter's arm encircled the young nurse and drew him to his chest. He let him cry as his eyes again found the refuge of the estuary.

The rash was taking a strong lead over the oatmeal. Daisy downed two more Valium and wondered how long she could hang on to her sanity. She slid the bifocals out of the beehive of ratted hair and held them to the bridge of her nose. The thermometer read 101.8 degrees.

"Bloody hell!" She slammed back the jigger of gin and tottered to the kitchen. Heaping a handful of fresh oatmeal onto the site, she held her breath, hoping for the same relief as earlier. There was a second or two of cool remission, followed by the blasted itching.

"Might as well be carrying coals to Newcastle." From the

line strung over the tub, she snatched the rubber girdle and stepped into it. Her right foot caught on the waistband. In a movement simultaneously awkward and fluid, she fell backward onto the carpet, lifted her legs, and pulled the rubberized britches up over her thighs. She caught her breath and stared at the yellow and white daisies on the wallpaper. What was it the doctor in London had told her when she woke from surgery?

She tried to recall his features, but the room had been dark, and she'd not been able to see his face, though she did remember his hands. Nurse Murphy was nowhere to be seen. When she told him (Dr. Wilson, was it?) that she was going to be sick, he'd done nothing to help her, even when she got sick all over herself. He'd made his speech and left her alone in that horrid place. How she'd managed to find her way off the gurney and out of the building on her own was still a mystery to her.

"If you have any trouble," he had said, waving a ring-laden hand in front of her eyes, "you must see this doctor and no one else. He is the only one who will understand the complicated internal stitching we've done."

He'd pushed a white business card in her face then thrown it at her.

She snapped her fingers and pulled herself to her knees.

The business card with the name of the doctor—she'd put it somewhere. What was the name? Dr. Goodall? No, no, no. That was the gorilla woman. Livingston? No, that was Stanley. Daisy shook her head, peeved with herself. Bloody hell, what *was* his name?

Her bedroom door swung open against her weight. In her closet, hangers screeched as she pushed them rapidly, one at a time, to the far end of the rack.

What had she worn that day? The pink Donna Karan dress with the yellow Express Gap velour vest? No. The pink and purple flounce skirt and yellow silk blouse? No. The pink and yellow polka-dot linen shift? Yes.

She read the name and address and clucked her tongue. Complicated stitching indeed. It wasn't complicated at all.

She'd removed the stitches herself with a pair of common nail scissors. She threw the card in the general direction of the bedside table. She'd never much cared for going to doctors. It was the way they always brought everything around to one's bowels that disturbed her.

She worked her fingers under the rubber girdle and gingerly felt around. Contact with the spot of too warm flesh brought Miss Dickenson, her former headmistress, to mind.

Every Sunday in General Assembly Chapel, the old cow would start in on a topic as remote and uninspiring as the Boer Wars, and before they knew it, she'd be racing toward the glories of Feminine Hygiene. Boer Wars notwithstanding, according to Miss Dickenson, "the most delicate and sacred of all womanly flesh" was vulnerable to a constant siege of sinister organisms lying in wait for unclean panties, contaminated probing fingers, and the Unspeakable Worse, on which to gain entry and infect those virginal petals of tissue.

Daisy could still hear the sanctimonious old spinster's warbling rising to the rafters of the drafty chapel: "Remember, ladies, heat is infection waving its victory flag! If, during your daily course of feminine hygiene, you should feel an uncommon amount of heated flesh, report to the infirmary at once."

Of course. Daisy brightened. She had a spot of infection, was all. In the medicine cabinet, her eye fell on a plastic container of antibiotics left over from a root canal she'd had the year before. She carried the bottle to kitchen where she poured a tumbler of gin. After ten minutes of struggling with the childproof cap, she threw the thing on the floor and stepped on it.

From the splintered shards of brown plastic, she picked out three tablets, toasted the Queen, and washed them down the hatch.

Parking in San Francisco, as Mr. and Mrs. Knudsen had so dramatically discovered, could be hazardous to one's health and/or the health of one's car. There were, however, a few sections that weren't as bad as the others. The Marina District was one: a place not many people could afford to live, and the ones who could had the luxury of owning a private parking garage.

Adele pulled the Beast over somewhere in the middle of the 1500 block and flicked on the hazard lights while she consulted the purloined copy of the San Francisco phone book for the late Raymond Clemmons's address. Repeating the number aloud, she rolled forward, coming even with a two-story white stucco building. In the picture window stood a fully decorated Christmas tree. Christmas was more than nine months away, but living with the constant threat of devastating earthquakes, San Francisco residents got in the habit of being prepared in advance for all events.

There wasn't any address visible on the outside of the building. Adele clenched her teeth and rolled to the next building. That Californians were adept at omitting or hiding their house and building numbers was not new to her. It was another one of those California People Irritating Traits she'd not yet learned how to let roll off her back.

Her eyes roamed under eaves, on curbs, up and down drainpipes, windows, fancy wreaths, and mail slots—all in vain. It wasn't until the middle of the next block that she was able to locate a faded number painted on the curb. It was a place to start, although she couldn't simply count off the numbers by two. That would have been too easy. So many of the buildings had been destroyed in the 1906 earthquake that the house numbers sometimes jumped by six, once in a while by two, but mostly by four.

She parked the car and hauled a duffel bag out from the backseat. Inside were apparel odds and ends for all occasions. An ankle-length black raincoat covered her scrub dress, and a pair of green heels replaced her running shoes.

Counting the buildings off by fours, she spotted a two-story rust-colored stucco with white trim. Unlike the surrounding buildings, it was set back a fair distance from the street. Beyond the locked iron gate was a walkway flanked by an overgrown English garden.

She searched for a buzzer in the grillwork of the gate. "What a warm and welcoming house," she said to the gate decoration, a fierce-looking gnome with an iron knocker through his nose.

This ain't Disneyland, sister, he said.

"I swear, it's never like it is in the movies," she said as she ran her hands along the outside of the gate frame. "You wouldn't find Schwarzenegger having to stop and look for a damned buzzer."

Schwarzenegger wouldn't have to look, said the gnome. *He'd shoot the gate open.*

The image of herself as Adele Schwarzenegger, kicking open the freshly shot gate, her M16 clasped to her breasts, made her more assertive. She stepped onto the bottom rail and pulled herself up. The buzzer was situated about six feet from the bottom railing, and painted black to blend in with the metal. She held it down for a slow count of four—just to let them know she meant it.

There was a slight movement of the blinds covering the window on the left of the doorway. A set of dark eyes appeared in the half-inch space between two slats.

Adele reached into her pocket and, fully aware of California Penal Code 146a, having to do with the impersonation of a police officer, flipped open a black leather case to reveal the deputy sheriff's badge Tim had once given her as a joke.

The ID badge was complete with a nonsmiling head shot, department seal, and the sheriff's signature. It would have taken an experienced eye to know that it wasn't genuine.

The slat snapped down, and at a count of twenty, a loud buzz signaled that the badge had lived to fool another citizen. Adele could barely suppress a satisfied smile. Little did Timothy know that his gag gift had turned into a handy tool that opened doors and loosened mouths.

A distant voice came from the other side of the front door. "Yes? Who are you? What do you want?" The woman had a voice like an overheated blender motor.

Adele tried the doorknob and found it locked. Through the lace curtain covering the thick glass door, she saw a severe black dress and that wild mahogany hair at the top of a staircase. "I'm Deputy Investigator Monsarrat from Marin PD." It wasn't the made-up title that counted, but rather the authority with which she claimed it. The fact she found it easier to lie through a door than to someone's face also helped.

"I'm sorry, but I need to ask you some more questions, Mrs. Clemmons."

She could feel the woman watching her, deciding whether or not to let her in. While she waited, her mind raced ahead to the questions she wanted to ask. The woman disappeared, and a moment later a second blast of a buzzer caused her to jump.

The pungent smells that had gathered in the narrow stairway assailed her nostrils as the heavy door was pushed open. A bouquet of onions, garlic, butter, cumin, curry, and nutmeg created a feeling of warmth and welcome. Adele shielded her eyes against the bright lamp at the top of the stairs. The woman was stationed in front of it so that she was no more than a silhouette.

"Mrs. Clemmons? Laila Clemmons?"

"Yes?" The voice was suspicious, almost curt.

"Hi. I'm—I'm Deputy Monsarrat with the Marin PD?" There was no such agency, and she hoped to Buddha Mrs. Clemmons wasn't up on her police agency names. "I need to ask you a few questions—if that's okay?"

"Come up, please." Mrs. Clemmons disappeared around the corner of the landing.

Sprinting up the stairs two at a time, Adele was surprised to see that the landing opened directly into a spacious living room painted a not so subtle shade of pinkish orange. Huge puffy valances printed with orange and blue swirls hung over the windows. The chunky overstuffed couches and multitasseled love seats were covered with the same material. There were cabinets and side tables painted gold and a glass dining table for twelve. The focal point of the room, however, was the black marble fireplace, over which hung an elaborate six-foot gilt mirror.

Overall, the room reminded her of a Nevada whorehouse she'd once had occasion to visit. The only thing missing, Adele thought as her gaze automatically traveled upward, was the . . . "Oops. Never mind," she said aloud, staring at her reflection in the mirrored ceiling.

Mrs. Clemmons turned. "Pardon?"

Adele sat down on the couch. "Oh. I said, clever find—that mirror. It looks—" *like you have a lifetime membership card to the Discount House of Bad Taste.* "—perfect there."

"Thank you," Mrs. Clemmons said, folding her hands. Her composure was so complete that Adele could barely believe this was the same woman who had been beating her breast and flicking a dead penis around only twenty-four hours before. But it could not hide the hard lines around the woman's eyes and mouth. Adele guessed hers had not always been such an easy life.

Mrs. Clemmons was staring at her pendant. So intense was the look, Adele's hand went to her throat.

"Your pendant," Mrs. Clemmons said, reaching for it. "It is beautiful. Is it a ruby?"

Adele laughed, letting the woman handle the pear-shaped burgundy stone. "No, it's a garnet. My father gave it to my mother when they were engaged. She gave it to me when I graduated from college."

At the word "garnet," all interest faded from the woman's face. She dropped the pendant and sat back.

Jewelry snob, Adele thought, opening her notebook. *Anything under $5,000 a carat doesn't count.*

"May I offer you some tea?" Mrs. Clemmons asked, surreptitiously leaning forward to get a peek at what was written inside.

Adele casually covered the page and pulled a pen from her raincoat pocket.

"No, thank you. I don't have many questions. How long were you married to Mr. Clemmons?"

"Three years last January."

"Oh," Adele said, surprised. "Was this your first marriage?"

"No." Mrs. Clemmons hesitated, as though she wasn't sure how much detail to give. "I was married once before—when I was very young. It was an arranged marriage between families." She looked up at Adele through dark lashes, embarrassed. "That is how it was in my country. The man was my mother's second cousin. Many years older than I."

"When were you divorced?"

"Oh, many years ago," she answered. "He divorced me because I was . . . damaged."

"Damaged? In what way?"

"I was only a child, you see?"

Adele wore a blank expression and shook her head.

"I was seven years old. Too young to receive a man. But this man, he was not patient, you see? He did not want to wait for my maturity. He forced himself, and he was not a clean man. He goes many times with the street boys. I get an infection, and because I was so young, I did not tell anyone until it was too late. I do not bear children because of this. To the husband, what is a wife who cannot give children except a burden? So when I am sixteen he divorce me and takes my youngest sister for a wife."

"How old was she?"

"Six," the woman said impassively. "She died at ten in childbirth."

Adele didn't say anything for a few seconds while she fought the images. "Why did you wait so long to marry again?"

Laila Clemmons drew in a breath and looked away as if to hide her true feelings. "When I am twenty-one I come to America to earn money to support my mother and sisters. I go to school. I work. You don't think about love when there are bellies to fill. And besides, a woman who cannot produce is no good to men. Like a cow without milk. What good, huh?"

"Our culture is not like that," Adele told her, knowing she shouldn't be interjecting her personal opinions. "Granted, American men can be real assholes sometimes, but I think we've managed to get beyond the prehistoric like-a-cow-without-milk stage of development."

Mrs. Clemmons clapped her hands and laughed. The dark gloom that surrounded her lifted, and Adele caught a glimpse of the young girl she had been.

"This is why I love the American women!" she said. "You

are free to say what is in your mind. Come, let me give you some coffee and baklava. I make it myself."

Over Adele's protests, Mrs. Clemmons stood and headed for the kitchen. "You are too skinny," she said over her shoulder. "Men don't like childless women, and they don't like skinny women."

Wearily, Adele rose from the orange couch and followed Mrs. Clemmons to the kitchen. "It's not a long walk from the cow-without-milk thing to the keep-'em-fat-and-pregnant thing, you know."

Mrs. Clemmons turned, wearing a puzzled expression. "I don't understand this."

Adele waved a hand and shook her head. "It's not important. Lead me to the baklava and bring on the men."

"Raymond took me to Paris a month ago for our third wedding anniversary." Laila Clemmons held out her hand and worked the ring around so the gem was visible. "He gave me this."

Adele gawked at the enormous emerald flanked by six not so small diamonds. It was probably worth about one and a half times her annual income.

"He must have loved you a great deal," she said, mainly because she couldn't think of anything else. To have said, "Oh what an ostentatious piece of clown-wear!" might have been interpreted as hostile.

Mrs. Clemmons shrugged. "Love. Who knows about love? He was a good companion. We had fun."

"Where did you meet?" Adele sipped the sweet tea that was laced with cardamom and honey.

"In the library. He saw I was taking out a book about Claude Monet and began a conversation about how much he loved Monet's work. We talked, and he asked me for coffee and that was that.

"He surprised me with a second honeymoon to Paris. We were there for four weeks." She paused, and Adele could see that her eyes were filling with tears. "We were only home for a week before . . ." The woman let out a high wail, bent over and continued keening. "Such a good man," she said, at the end of her sobs. "We were so happy. Why does he have to die such a terrible way? Like an animal." She pulled a cotton hanky out from the cuff of her blouse, and held it to her eyes.

"Did your husband have any family?" Adele asked quietly when the woman seemed calmer.

"No. I was his family."

Adele leaned closer. "Do you have any idea at all—even if it sounds ridiculous—as to who would have done this to him? Any business associates who might have had some kind of grudge against him? Maybe somebody who was jealous of his success?"

Mrs. Clemmons raised her eyes. "Who would be jealous of Raymond, huh? Everyone loves Raymond. He is retired for two years. He had no enemies. I told you he was a good man. No one hates Raymond." She looked up at Adele, her voice gone thick. "He was so good. No one could hate him this much to kill in such a terrible, terrible . . ."

Adele waited until she collected herself. "Can you remember exactly what happened that day? Any details that might give us some kind of lead?"

Mrs. Clemmons pushed a wild thatch of hair behind her ear. "He gets up at eight. We eat breakfast. He reads the paper and watches CNN for a little bit. Then he takes his exercise. He did these things every day by the clock."

"Where did he go to exercise?"

"Every day he walk to Fort Mason. The doctor say he would live to be a hundred-year-old if he walk three miles every morning, so Raymond walk four miles every morning. His health was perfect. He was strong in body."

"How long did it usually take him to do that—to walk to Fort Mason and back?"

"An hour, sometimes two. He stops to talk to many people."

"Do you remember what he wore that day?"

The woman had to stop and think. "The gray suit and the white shirt, brown tie, and the black luffers."

Adele inclined her ear forward. "Pardon? His black lovers?"

"Luffers," the woman repeated. "He had a pair of black luffers. Very expensive."

"Loafers, you mean?" Adele bit down hard on the inside of her lip.

"Yes, expensive black luffers. He had a good pair for walking."

Adele sipped her tea, swallowing down the tidal wave of Crazy Woman laughter. "And did he always wear a suit and tie to exercise?"

"Oh yes. He was particular about how he looked. Very careful in dressing and personal things for his appearance."

"Do you know whether or not any of his friends saw him that morning?"

Laila hesitated, twisting her handkerchief in her fingers. "When he did not come home, I walked the way he goes, but could not find him. I do not think he got so far."

"How about the neighbors? Did anyone see him get into a taxi or a car?"

"No. I think only one neighbor saw him walk to the corner and turn onto Laguna."

"Did he carry a lot of money, or wear expensive jewelry? Something that would attract attention?"

"Raymond, he did not like to wear jewelry. He carries only maybe a hundred dollars, but he had no reason to show this money. He was only walking."

"Okay." Adele put away her notebook and pulled her purse up onto her lap. "Here's my phone number and e-mail address," she said, handing her a card. "Call me if you think of anything else. I'd also appreciate it if you could provide me with the names of one or two of his friends in the neighborhood."

"Yes, of course, but . . ." She pointed to the rich dessert, which Adele estimated to include about a pound of butter. ". . . you did not touch your baklava."

"I'm sorry," Adele said. "But see, that baklava—as wonderful as I'm sure it is—will want to make its home on my thighs, and I just don't have any vacancies right now."

Perplexed, Mrs. Clemmons looked from Adele to the

dessert back to Adele. "Maybe next time you come you will have some?"

"Sure thing." Adele smiled and walked to the landing. "I'll see what I can do about evicting about a pound of the current tenants."

There was barely enough time to shower and dress, let alone deal with the animal sitcom going on in her living room. Helen was still on the mantel, looking (sniffing) in Nelson's direction. He wore the expression cats always had when observing dogs from a high, safe perch. Translated into human, it said, "Stupid lummox!"

The living room and hallway floors were littered with the flotsam and jetsam of their daytime follies. The bay window blinds had been knocked down; the telephone stand was on its side; two framed photographs were lying, glass cracked, ten feet from the wall they'd hung on; and the small ceramic lamp next to the phone was smashed into pieces.

Adele stood with her hands on her hips and growled at Nelson. "Bad dog!"

Nelson slunk low to the ground. A whine escaped.

"Bad, bad dog!" she growled again. "How *could* you?" She flopped down on the couch and sprang up again. From between the cushions she pulled Nelson's wind-up rabbit, which was broken into three parts. She threw it across the room and sat down again. "I am so disappointed in you, Nelson."

He placed one paw on Her shoe. She shook it off. "You're a Seeing Eye dog trainee. Don't you recognize blindness when you see it?"

Nelson whined and crawled away to a corner of the living room. That was when she noticed that his Mickey Rug scrap wasn't on him.

"Nelson? Where's your Mickey Rug?" She got to her feet.

At the mention of Mickey Rug, the dog gave a piteous howl.

She crossed the living room to his corner, concern replacing the anger. "Nelson, show Mommy your Mickey Rug."

The dog got up slowly and howled like a wounded beast.

"Go on, show Mommy your Mickey Rug."

Nelson trotted to the bathroom, pawed once at the automatic kitty-litter box, and growled.

On her hands and knees, Adele examined the contraption as the scope of the tragedy unfolded. Clinging to the blades of the motorized scooper, two or three threads of Mickey Rug were all that was left.

At her anthropomorphic best, she shared his sorrow, secretly berating herself for not buying him a new rug before the inevitable happened. Now she worried that he might refuse to eat and get sick. The loss of Mickey Rug so soon after the loss of Bugs might be too much for him to process. The thought of losing her animal soul mate drove her mind to places she did not want to go.

Desperation being the most persuasive mother of invention, she ran to the hallway storage closet. Just seconds before the doorbell rang, she found the leather harness.

The woman at the next table, dressed in a démodé acrylic pantsuit speckled with rhinestones, slumped toward her dinner companion and drank off her third glass of wine. "I mean it, Ethel, the three best things I ever did were divorce Frank, bring Louise home to live with me, and put that sliding door between my bathroom and the laundry room."

Tim and Adele stared at each other and grinned. "We always get the best seat in the monkey room," he said. "Why do you think that is, Adele?"

A flush of warmth surged through her as the merlot schmoozed with her central nervous system. "Pure luck."

Something inside him turned over at the sound of her voice. Adele had one of those voices that could drop down to where the gravel lives.

Though he had changed a little since she'd seen him last, she'd forgotten how handsome he was. The weight he lost during his recovery gave him a lean, strong look. His clear blue eyes seemed more penetrating in the thin face, his jaw and cheekbones more defined. Letting the chains down, she reached up and touched the fine hair at his temples. Judging from the reaction of her stomach as her fingers brushed against his face, she almost expected sparks to fly. "You're getting some gray at the temples, Timothy. It looks good." *Christ on a bike, I'm not going to come out of this unscathed. What the hell am I doing here?*

He smiled, his eyes never leaving her face. Her face—it never stopped being a surprise to him. He wanted to touch everything he saw: her arm, her hair, her skin. Under the table he was gripping the support board so hard his knuckles were white. "Thanks. And you, I notice, are nervous. Why?" *How the hell am I going to keep my hands off you?*

She shrugged. "I am not." *Liar.*

"Liar. Then why haven't you taken your handbag off your shoulder. It looks painful."

She let the twenty-pound purse drop to the floor, then she pulled it between her feet. "Habit. My Walther is in there. I trade off with the Colt now. I'm still a little nervous since . . ." She looked away. She didn't want to talk about *that* day. "You know."

"I do." He sipped his Perrier wondering how he was going to eat—his stomach was churning like an outboard motor. He was tempted to order a beer or a glass of wine, thought about doctor's orders, and decided against it.

"What have you been doing?" he asked. *Have you missed me? Are you sleeping alone?*

"Running." *Missing you.* "Working at the hospital. Going to physical therapy." She held up her left arm for his inspection. Automatically, he reached over and let his hand gently touch the place where the bullet had entered.

Her eyes fixed on the sight of his hand on her flesh. At once her two sides—Pro and Con Monsarrat—went to war: *Don't let go!* vs. *Let go! I won't get pulled in!*

He felt the heat of her through her blouse. *Let me in.* "Jesus, Adele." He laughed. "You've got biceps like a guy. What're you doing, lifting weights?"

The tension momentarily eased, she smiled. "As a matter of fact, I am. They got me hooked on it in physical therapy."

She drained her glass and set it on the table. Surprised by

the sight of the empty glass, she realized she couldn't remember drinking the wine, or even if it was her first or second glass. She felt a fleeting panic and pinched her lips, checking for the telltale numbness that meant slurring wasn't far behind. For her, a second glass of wine was dangerous, entering the rarely trod territories of No Common Sense and Lost Inhibitions.

"What about you?" she asked, drinking a half a glass of water. "What have you been doing?" *In love with someone?*

"Work, rehab, more work, more rehab." He paused to think then snapped his fingers. "I'm thinking of signing up for vegetarian cooking classes at College of Marin. I know you're already a great cook, but how would you like to take the class with me? It could be fun." *And that way I'd get to see you once a week. After class, we'd go to dinner, and then long walks. Then maybe—just maybe—you'll let me in, a Wednesday evening at a time, a dish at a time?*

"My cooking is beyond help." *Just say no, Adele. Don't even try to protect him from all those desperate single Marin women.*

"Other than my mom, you're the best cook I've ever . . ." *Eaten? Tasted? Oh God, how I'd love to taste you.* ". . . known."

She blushed and drank the rest of the water. *Did he have to look so . . . hungry?*

"No, I'm not. I used to think I was a great cook until I went to a vegetarian cookoff and placed two hundred and third out of two hundred. After that I realized I was nothing more than a cafeteria candidate."

"Well, all the more reason to think about it," he urged, a vague sense of disappointment beginning in his stomach. "Registration is a couple of weeks away."

The candle, fueled by a renegade drop of wax, flared bright, casting golden firelight over their faces. In that second he caught her eyes. She sat transfixed by his steady, even gaze, until she forced herself to look away.

"So, have you had any interesting cases lately?" She let out the breath she'd been holding.

The carotid pulse in her neck was visibly pulsating. Long

ago he'd come to the conclusion that for her working a case was a sensual thing. The few times they'd engaged in brainstorming a case, it was like foreplay. He shook his watch down on his wrist. "I've got the Karon case in Fairfax. The twenty-four-year-old waitress they found strangled in her home last Sunday?"

She nodded. "Cynthia told me about that. They think the husband did it?"

"We thought so at first 'cause the guy was such a prick, but it isn't him. Then we thought maybe she was a strawberry and that her supplier got out of hand and—"

"A strawberry?"

"Street term for a female who exchanges sex for drugs. But that won't hold water either. Now we're thinking it might have just been some drunk who followed her home after work." He paused. "How is Cyn by the way? Still with that doc?"

"Uh-huh." She examined him carefully, looking for any vestiges of emotional attachment. "She's finally found a man who will rub her feet for hours while she talks—and listens to every word she says. But I have to tell you, she's been really weird lately."

"What," he asked, "could she possibly do to make someone notice that she's more weird than usual? There isn't a lot of margin there."

Adele laughed. "I guess I don't see it anymore."

"How could you? You're halfway there yourself."

"Hey pal," she said, "I'm not the one who has a live-in mannequin with a first and last name, so I wouldn't be throwing any stones if I were you."

He reached over and took a slice of warm sourdough bread and dipped it into a ramekin of olive oil. He noticed she wasn't having any. Not that that wasn't normal—rarely did she partake of sugar, salt, starches, oils, or fats of any kind.

"Live a little, would you?" he said, pushing the basket of warm bread toward her. "Have some bread and oil. You're already leaner and meaner than most gold medalists. Throw caution to the wind."

"I'm here with you, aren't I?" she said dryly. "And if I 'lived a little' every time somebody put a slab of bread or a piece of cake under my nose, I'd weigh a ton inside of a month."

He worked over another piece of bread for a bit. Around them, the room was filling up. A young couple on the other side of the room was having what seemed to be a combination bachelor party/bridal shower bash. The twenty guests were already throwing bits of food, and they'd barely been seated.

"So, what do you know about the guy they pulled out of the Bay?" she asked, trying not to watch his jaw working. It was, she thought, one of the most attractive aspects of his face.

"Our Mr. Clemmons?" He leaned back, brushing crumbs off his fingers. "That's Robinson's case."

"Do you think it's related to the Fischer murder?"

"The sexual mutilation in Corte Madera?"

She stopped chewing and tilted her head. "Do you think that's what it was?"

"You don't?"

"I don't know enough about it to guess."

"But you wish you did."

She laughed. At the next table, the acrylic pantsuit was returning from a visit to the ladies' room. Still operating under the gauze of alcohol, she started to sit, missed the chair by six inches, and grabbed for the tablecloth as she went down. With the agility only a drunk possesses, she rolled under the table to avoid a shower of plates and utensils.

Timothy, ever the gentleman, assisted the woman to her chair; the waiters were already resetting the table. The maître d' wrung his hands, offering glasses of wine on the house, and praising some obscure dead saint that she wasn't hurt.

He sat down as their meals were served. "Where did we leave off?" She speared a piece of broccoli from her pasta primavera.

He cut through a generous slab of polenta smothered in onion and mushroom gravy. "You were endeavoring to divest me of some classified information."

"Okay, so what *do* you know about the Fischer case?"

"Probably about as much as you do. She's not in our jurisdiction, so I didn't pay a lot of attention. The details are being kept pretty quiet."

"Do you know who found her?"

He shook his head. "A boyfriend, or maybe it was her boss. I don't remember."

She stopped chewing, trying to imagine the shock of walking in and finding someone you loved in that condition. "Do you remember his name?"

He leveled his gaze at her, saying nothing for a minute. "Adele," he said benignly, "what are you getting at? Are you planning something?"

She waved her fork and looked down at her plate.

"Adele?"

She wagged her head. "I have to keep in practice, Timothy. I need to work on a case . . . even if it's only to develop leads in my mind."

He sighed and wiped his mouth. The polenta had survived but a few moments on his plate. "I don't remember his name, but I think he owns the Silver Circle Gallery."

Adele nodded, holding back the disappointment. There was nothing more tedious than having to pull someone up conversation hill.

She had barely opened her mouth when he said, "Isn't this where you tell me what the hell happened over at the Penn mansion yesterday?"

"You read my mind," she said, relieved by the chance to talk about something that would keep their focus off the personal.

She related the whole story, from Mr. Electricity's admission to the hospital to the moment she picked her cell phone out of the automatic kitty-litter box.

He listened with interest, swinging between laughter and concern. Maybe it was his genuine distress over her safety or the fact his laugh made her feel *so* good, but for a few minutes she allowed herself the possibility that she might let herself go with him. Let herself love him—in real time.

"God love the old fart," he said when she finished. "Thomas

Edison Penn has the largest number of unpaid parking tickets in the history of the Marin Parking Authority."

"What?" She shifted so as to be closer to him. The cotton of their shirts touched.

"Yeah," he laughed. "He has over two hundred unpaid parking tickets dating back to nineteen eighty-one."

The waiter served their decaf lattes and Tim's slice of apple pie.

"Don't they have a warrant for his arrest?" she asked, knowing how aggressive Marin County was about collecting on its tickets. Once, when she was twelve, a Novato policeman had come to their house with a warrant for her mother's arrest for an unpaid parking ticket she denied ever receiving. Martha Monsarrat, mild-mannered librarian for Marin County public libraries, responded to the arresting officer by breaking into uncontrolled laughter—no doubt the genetic precursor of her daughter's Crazy Woman laughter—and been hauled off to jail. The arresting officer, like most law enforcement, had no sense of humor.

"Nope," he said, cutting the tip off the wedge of warm pie with his fork. He brought the piece to his mouth and sniffed it distrustfully. She guessed he took his apple pie seriously. "We rang all the bells: First Belvedere PD put a Denver boot on his car. Then they sent somebody out to talk to him, but the stubborn old cuss wouldn't let the guy in the door. He maintains that Marin should have all-free parking. He tried to get it on the ballot once. The amazing thing was he managed to get about twenty-four thousand signatures." Tim laughed and admitted the pie into his mouth. "He was only fifteen hundred signatures short."

The corners of his mouth pulled down in a grimace. After a few seconds of working the pie around with his teeth, he pushed the plate toward her, bidding her to try some. "Ugh. Strange taste!"

She took a bite. "Tastes good to me. Just the right amount of nutmeg and a dash of cinnamon. What do you think is strange?"

He gagged and discreetly spit the mouthful into his napkin.

"Cinnamon and nutmeg?" he asked disbelieving. "In an apple pie?"

She looked at him curiously. "Timothy, cinnamon and nutmeg have been living in apple pies since the beginning of time."

"What are you talking about?" He vigorously wiped his tongue. "Granted, I rarely if ever order pie for dessert, but my mother has been making apple pies my whole life, and she's never put cinnamon or nutmeg in any of them."

"What does she use instead?"

"A little butter, lemon, sugar, and a dash of onion."

As they walked down Fourth Street in San Rafael, the early spring evening was just settling over Mount Tam. A few cars had their headlights on, ready for the night to begin.

They covered the whole two blocks to his Camry without speaking, though they were both hyperaware of the twenty inches of space that separated them. He knew better than to open her door for her.

On impulse, she grabbed his arm and shouted, "Hey!" A grin replaced her pensive look. "Can we forget the Scrabble for tonight?"

His heart sunk into his colon. "I guess. Is your self-esteem really that low that you can't face losing every game?"

"I need to do something. You're welcome to take part, but I have to warn you now that it's coloring outside the lines of normal."

"Normal," he repeated. "Do you even know what that is?"

She gave him a look.

He held out both hands in surrender. "Okay, okay. What do you want to do?"

Her grin changed to something devious. "Think Ricky and Lucy Ricardo."

"Oh God," he groaned, opening his door. "Why do I have a feeling I should quit while I'm ahead?"

They made a twisted-looking trio. The special-hire security person sitting at the surveillance screen did a double take and snorted out a laugh. "Hey, Stephen, come 'ere and take a look at what just walked through the doors."

Stephen Roach (as in Roach Motel), the store manager, sat at his desk working on the screenplay that was going to make him rich and famous. He glanced up from the scene where Megan, the torpedo-titted high school girl, was about to get her head sawed off in the school's boiler room by the demented janitor, Bob, and checked out the monitor.

He cocked his head slowly to the left and then the right. The redhead in the raincoat looked quasi-normal—even though he hadn't trusted redheads since he was in the second grade and Mickey O'Connor broke his nose with a candy apple. It was the tall blind woman and the black Seeing Eye dog that said something wasn't right.

First there were her shoes: the beat-up running shoes with the neon green running stripes didn't go with the black overcoat. She was proud and moved with an air of confidence, not at all like other blind people he'd seen who at all times walked like they were afraid of smacking into a pole.

But mostly it was the dog. Seeing Eye dogs were disciplined work dogs. This dog looked more like Goofy on speed.

"Keep the camera on them," he told the security guard. "It's too early for Halloween."

Unaware they were being watched, Adele held on to the leather harness and pushed Nelson in the direction of children's furniture at the back of the store.

Timothy muttered under his breath, "I cannot believe I'm doing this." He laughed, then sobered. "Is this what you do for entertainment? What are we going to do if we run into anyone we know?"

Adele bit her lip, not trusting her grip on the Crazy Woman laughter. If she gave into it, she'd never stop. "We won't. This is the only way Nelson can get into the store. He has to pick out his own rug, Timothy. He found his Mickey Mouse rug the same way. Look at him. He knows exactly where he is and why he's here."

Tim looked at the dog doubtfully. Nelson strained inside

the harness, his eye trained greedily on a squeaky toy clutched in the hands of a toddler trying out a child-sized La-Z-Boy.

"Rug, Nelson, rug!" she commanded, and pulled him over to the three-foot-high pile of rugs.

Nelson sniffed the pile and lifted his leg.

"Nelson!" she shouted, slapping down his hind leg. "Rug!"

Nelson sniffed the pile again, sneezed and looked up at Her. She pointed at the pile and flipped through the rugs at the top. It was an odd selection: the Spice Girls, the Lion King, Phil Collins, Pocahontas, Princess Di, and, she cooed, a Mickey Mouse rug. "Oh, Nelson, look." She held out the thin rug that pictured the cartoon rodent wearing a fireman's hat and sitting behind the wheel of a red fire engine. "It's Mickey Rug!"

Nelson whined dejectedly.

"May I help you with something?" Stephen approached the group smiling his unnaturally tight I-Am-the-Store-Manager-and-You-Are-a-Scumbag smile. Adele straightened, pinching Timothy through his coat.

"Ouch!" Tim glared at her, then looked back at the store manager. "No, no, we're just fine. My wife and I are shopping for a rug for our son's room."

Adele snorted, stifling back a laugh.

"How old is the child?" asked Stephen, wondering if the couple was high on drugs.

"Three," Adele said, remembered Nelson had a birthday coming up, and added, "almost four."

"And does he have a theme?"

A *theme*? they thought in unison. Both registered the same blank look.

"The *Tarzan* and *Star Wars* themes are very 'in' right now with little Marin boys."

"Oh!" Adele smiled, thinking he was probably the type of closet queen who referred to brushing his teeth and washing his face as "completing his toilet." "Well, I think he used to be into Mickey Mouse, but now . . . I think he's moving out of that theme and into something else." She gave Nelson a nudge.

Stephen stepped around Nelson and reached for the rug on the top of the pile. "Well, let's just see what we have—"

Nelson's lips pulled back from his teeth. The growl that came from his throat was downright Eocene.

Stephen was not so anal-retentive that he couldn't let out a cry and yank his hand back. "I thought Seeing Eye dogs were supposed to be gentle," he whimpered.

"He is," Adele said, delighted that Nelson was taking a protective stance toward the rugs. It was progress. "I think we can handle it from here. Thanks for your help."

"Yeah," said Timothy. "I think we'll just find a theme and get out of your hair."

Thirty minutes later, a rapturous Nelson fairly pranced across the parking lot, his new rip-and-suckle security rug clenched proudly between his teeth.

Adele sighed happily. "Well, it's going to take some getting used to," she said, still holding on to his arm. "I mean, moving on from the Mickey Mouse rug . . ."

". . . theme," they said together.

Tim shook his head and held out his hands in disbelief. "I still can't believe he went through that whole pile and actually picked one out. It's like the minute he saw it, he knew that was his rug."

"He did the same thing with his Mickey Mouse rug," she told him. "It must be a combo of the seizing and the colors." She paused, her hand on the Camry's handle shaking her head. "But it's so . . . *ugly*! I mean, at least Mickey Rug had a kind of American Dog look and feel to it."

"Oh, I don't know," Tim said. "It's all how you look it. There's one analogy about viewpoints that says, 'A woman looks out at the waves and sees the poignancy of life and love ebbing and waning. A seagull looks out over the waves and sees the Domino Pizza man delivering dinner.' "

"But Christ on a bike, Tim, a Rod Stewart rug? Somehow 'Hey, Nelson, go get Roddy Rug' just doesn't seem right."

He watched her move barefoot about her kitchen with all the ease of a dancer. Set along the back border of the L-shaped counter, a dozen or more clear glass canisters held grains and seeds of every description. It seemed unconceivable to him that only a short time before, this same room, now so warm and hospitable, had been the scene of his worst nightmare.

A cool spring night breeze came in through the window and flipped through the pages of a cookbook left open on the table. The breeze-chosen page featured a color photo of a mouth-watering array of food—none of which had been made from anything that had once had a face.

"Leaded or unleaded?" she asked, opening the narrow pantry door and pointing to the shelf filled with no fewer than thirty kinds of tea, most of whose names he couldn't pronounce.

He pointed at the middle of the tea block. "How about some Lapsang souchong for laughs."

She began preparations for the tea and sat down at the oak farmer's table. She raked her fingers along the center part of her hair with her fingers to get the bangs and sides off her face. Resting her chin in her hands, she asked point-blank, "Is it hard for you to be here—in this room?"

He leaned back in his chair feeling momentarily light-headed and took a deep breath as he looked around. Wherever the bullet had finally ended up had been filled and painted over. "I was just wondering if somewhere in this room there isn't a tiny speck of our blood."

"Nope." She shook her head in a way that said there was no possibility. "Cynthia, my mother, and my Aunt Ruth cleaned every square inch of this place ceiling to floor with Clorox and detergent. And if you knew my mom and my Aunt Ruth, you'd know this place has been cleansed of every microspore of dirt."

His lazy smile returned and he leaned back again, watching her play with her rings: the white sapphire her father had given her mother as an engagement ring; the gold "wave" band, the exact copy of which Cynthia wore; and the modest garnet he'd given her at Christmas as a sort of "survivor buddies" memento.

"Aren't you afraid she'll come back?" he asked.

Without looking at him, Adele poured hot water into the

teapot. "I don't think about it," she lied. The truth was, she thought about it all the time—not consciously, but it came up in her dreams. More than once she'd jerked awake, bathed in terror.

He clapped his hands and sat up. "How about those cooking classes?"

She removed the lid of the pot and breathed in the smoky aroma of the tea. "How badly do you want me to do this with you?"

"Bad." He nodded.

"Bad enough to promise you'll give me information when I need it and not rake me over the coals and through the blackberry bushes?"

He winced, as if the request was more than he could afford. "Well, I can give you *advice* and direction on something you might be investigating once in a while, but as far as giving out confidential information . . ."

"Then forget it." She poured the tea.

"I'll tell you what. You register for this class—" He searched for the right way to say it. "And I'll consider each request on an individual basis. If giving information to you could put either you or someone else at risk, then you'll leave it to my judgment to withhold or not." He sipped his tea, burned his lips, and set the cup down. "Deal?"

Her lips drew into two thin lines as her thoughts scattered in seven different directions, all of which came down to one point: to resist him or not. If she took the class, she'd be opening the door to possibilities.

You can just be friends, you know, said Martha Stewart, inspecting the kitchen curtains for dustballs in her perfectly anal-retentive way.

Rosie O'Donnell, sitting to Tim's left, reacted. *What, are you nuts? Ever notice your nipples whenever you get around this joker? Remember the movie* When Harry Met Sally? *Get real.*

Martha Stewart wagged a finger. *It certainly doesn't have to be like that. Let common sense be your guide, and you won't lose your head.*

Oh yeah! Rosie laughed. *Sounds like an ad for condoms.*

Take a reality check, girlfriend. Look at the guy . . . He's Mr. Sexyman.

Adele looked at the guy and had to agree, he was. But then again, she prided herself on being in total control of herself. This could be the ultimate test of strength.

"Deal!" she said, before any of the other characters living inside her imagination could say another word.

Cyberdancing did not come easily to her. Faced with a computer, she felt clumsy and stupid, like a dyslexic in an advanced aerobics class. She was always amazed when she actually connected with the site she was looking for.

At her feet, Nelson chewed happily, breaking in Roddy Rug. In just the forty-five minutes he'd been home, he'd already ripped off the fabric contents and washing instructions tags and was working on the braided edging.

Scanning through the Marin business-owners pages, she found the first-step information she was looking for and dialed the number.

Alan Bonnewitz, owner of Silver Circle Gallery in San Rafael, came across like a full-fledged twit. He was one of those people who waited until he was on the phone in order to have conversations with everyone in his range of sight.

Yes, he was Ms. Fischer's closest friend . . . ("Oh, Mona, on those paintings in the back hall, would you get them out of there, please? They've been there forever and . . . blah blah blah.")

And yes, he was the person who discovered her body, but no . . . ("Excuse me, Bill? Would you locate last month's accounting sheets and have Ivan go over them before next Tuesday? Who? Sure, tell him . . . blah blah blah.") he couldn't meet with her right now.

Maybe she could make an appointment for sometime in . . . ("Kellie, we're low on number-eighteen hangers. Would you order another box of . . .")

Adele interrupted, tersely reminding him she was with the mythical Marin PD and needed to talk to him when he could give his full attention.

According to his calendar, he could fit her in after-hours—around ten-thirty or eleven?

She looked at her watch and groaned. She'd have to find a way to stay awake.

She picked up the latest issue of *True Crime* and flipped through the articles: "Dismemberment Crimes: A body of work—Part I." "Birth to Kettle—Mothers Who Killed and Ate Their Children." "The Mid-West Murders: He Loved Them and Cleaved Them!"

Nelson put out his paw and tore the magazine from her hands as if to say, "My God, you're actually reading this trash?"

"You're right," she said, throwing the publication toward the trash can. "I should be reading something academic and wholesome like . . ." She picked up the top book on the pile next to her bed and pretended to read the title. " 'FBI Agent's Survival Guide: Fifty Ways to Leave Your Cover.' "

Nelson whined, Helen flipped over onto his back and stretched so that he looked like a long black feather boa, Adele scratched his belly, and the cat curled around her hand, purring.

"Okay," she said, snuggling down. "I'll tell the story of the day Nelson came home from the Seeing Eye Dog rejects kennel."

Nelson wagged his tail and smiled. Helen yawned. Both gave her their full attention.

"Once, a long, long time ago, when Mommy was married to weird old Uncle Gavin the cross-dresser . . ."

<u>SIX</u>

IT WAS ONE OF THOSE THINGS SHE WAS ASHAMED of, but readily admitted upon confrontation. Adele Monsarrat suffered from Driving Tourette's—the spawn of Road Rage. Anyone who'd ever been her passenger knew this about the normally civil-mouthed nurse, and most of them still had a hard time believing the transformation that took place once she was behind the wheel.

In her pedestrian state, Adele usually didn't find it necessary to go beyond the occasional benign curse. As a driver, her vocabulary went south on a truck-driver-mouth free-for-all.

On Highway 101, just three miles south of the Central San Rafael exit, a bronze Cadillac, driven by a bald man with a goatee, was getting on her nerves. Every attempt she made to move the Beast out of the right lane and into the left was thwarted by the Caddy speeding up or slowing down. He had her blocked, and other than taking an exit she did not want, there was nothing she could do short of calling the California Highway Patrol on her cell phone. She was about to take her chances with 911 again, when, as if by divine intervention, a Marin County sheriff's car pulled up behind her and flashed its lights. In her mirror she recognized Detective Peter Chernin by the outline of his large head and the square-ish Elvis hairdo.

The Richard Burton look-alike had once taken her to a movie—with stress on the word "once." Some days, when she really needed a good laugh, she would call Cynthia or her mother and describe the evening. But despite the fact Peter Chernin continued to ask her out and she continued to decline, they had managed to develop a friendship of sorts.

Adele waved, pointed to the Caddy, and made the sign of a gun being shot. Chernin got the message immediately and moved behind the offending Caddy, his flashers on.

She fell back in traffic until the Caddy was parked on the side of the road. As she passed, she gave Detective Chernin the okay sign then glanced at the Caddy's bumper. It bore a Texas plate and a jumbo red, white, and blue bumper sticker that read I AM A PROUD AMERICAN! I SUPPORT THE NRA, PRO LIFE, BOB DOLE, JESUS AND JOHN BIRCH!

"Figures," she said dryly and drove on, secure in the knowledge that another Republican was under control.

Her fantasy of having a quiet, after-hours office atmosphere in which to question him turned out to be just that: a fantasy. For Alan Bonnewitz, after-hours didn't begin until 5 A.M.

"Hope you don't mind following me around while I take a preview of the new work," he said, in a voice on the brink of intellectual snob vs. swish. "We've got a new show opening tomorrow night and I must go over last-minute details."

"Fine with me," Adele said, climbing the stairs behind him. "As long as you can answer questions while you work."

On the second floor, he went through a ritual of sorts as he took his place in front of the first mural-sized painting. With fingers that seemed impossibly long and thin, he adjusted his silver wire rims, the lenses of which were the size of quarters. He then snapped down the cuffs of his purple silk jacket, crossed his arms, and, one hand holding his chin, moved his head back and forth like a chicken.

Adele gawked at the eight-foot-by-five-foot white canvas with a single brush stroke of shit-brindle brown going through the middle.

"What command!" he said in a whispery, awed tone as he ran his spindly fingers over the dome of his shit-brindle brown hair. His ponytail rode high on the back of his head. Little thatches of hair stuck out from the elastic band. "Fabulous."

"That's it?" she asked, staring blankly at the canvas. "That's the whole painting?"

He sighed, playing with the collar of his turtleneck. "Compelling, isn't it? The simplicity of composition! The vibrancy of color. The release!"

"It's certainly a release of *some*thing," Adele said as she took a few steps forward to read the title card:

"ÂME DE BOUE" (SOUL OF MUD) $38,000

"Oh-oh," she said, a trace of a smile playing at the corners of her mouth. "Somebody made a mistake and added three zeros to the end of the price."

He checked the price then looked at her, an expression of condescension clouding his eyes behind the wire rims. "You don't appreciate art, Ms. Monsarrat?"

"Actually, I love art," she said, smiling.

He made a face as if he were sucking the heart out of an unripe lemon and moved to the next painting.

"I understand that you and Ms. Fischer were longtime friends?" she said taking out her notebook and pen.

He arched an eyebrow and tilted his head slightly to look at the four-by-four canvas done completely in yellow. In the center were four dime-sized red circles. He rolled a copy of the exhibit program into a cylinder and tapped his white linen trousers.

Adele was gratified to see that the abstract, titled "Little Dipper," was only $25,000.

"Mr. Bonnewitz?"

He cleared his throat. "Yes. Zelda and I had been friends for about twenty years. She was one of the gallery's buyers."

"I know this is difficult, but can you tell me what took place the day you found her?"

He pursed his lips and looked at his shoes before answering. "I'd gone to the house to pick her up for lunch, and when she didn't answer the door, I knew something was wrong. Zelda was punctuality-fixated. I let myself in and called for her. Nothing seemed out of place. Her favorite CD was playing. I checked the kitchen and the bathroom and then her bedroom."

He rolled the program tighter and moved to the next painting: a four-by-four carbon copy of the canvas next to it, only with the red and yellow reversed. It amused her that the price was fifteen thousand dollars more.

"BIG DIPPER" $40,000

"Do you have any idea who might have done this? A spurned boyfriend? A jealous friend?"

Alan turned away from the painting and stared at Adele. "I said this before and I'll say it again: it was that psycho doctor at UC Med Center. She was absolutely hysterical when she got home from her appointment."

"What kind of appointment?"

He played with the gold loop in his ear. "She went to the dermatology clinic about once a month. Zelda thought it was the great catholicon for all her ailments."

"And what ailments were those?"

"I don't know," he said vaguely. "Zelda had this problem with her hair." He waved his fingers over his head. "It used to fall out so that she'd have bald spots all over."

He had a tender thought and his face softened. He almost smiled. "She'd change her wigs to go with her moods. She had them custom-made by the best wigmaker in Paris. Spent a fortune on them, but they were so good that if you didn't know her, you couldn't tell."

He moved to the next painting: a canvas of lavender with geometric shapes in various pastels.

"LARES AND PENATES AT EASTER"

The canvas was, besides hideously ugly, not for sale.

"You'd do better to talk to that amoeba parading around UC as a doctor, not me." He took a pen recorder from the inside pocket of his jacket and pressed down on the clip, speaking directly into the top of the pen. "Piece number twenty-seven sold for thirty-two thou to Holmby at preview sale. No delivery date will be set until check has cleared."

"What exactly happened on the day she went to the clinic?" Adele asked, wondering at the back of her mind who Holmby was, and how she could get hold of him—she had some art she wanted to sell him.

"It was humiliating. I told Zelda she should sue the whole damned hospital." He walked past three paintings and stopped at the last one on the wall, tilting his head slightly to look at the piece. The artist must have tired of abstracts, for glued to the plain, white canvas was an old travel alarm. Adele was relieved that it was untitled and not priced. She was hoping it was a joke.

"He made several suggestive comments about her breasts in front of the other interns," Bonnewitz said. "She told me she laughed off the first couple of remarks, but he kept pushing his luck until he was just outright rude. She flew off the handle as only Zelda could, and told him he was an inappropriate asshole. He came back at her saying she needed to return the implants to the cows her plastic surgeon stole them from."

"She had implants?" She had a brief feeling of betrayal that David Takemoto had not told her as much.

His laugh was sardonic. "Oh yes, she most certainly did!"

"Are you saying they were—large?"

The gallery owner raised his eyebrows and nodded. "You could say that. Zelda never did anything with moderation."

Well, Trevor did say they were like watermelons.

Adele looked at the canvas in front of them. It was a plain white canvas with a single purple dot in the center.

"BOUTON" (PIMPLE) $27,500

"Who was her plastics man—the one who did the implants?"

"I don't know. She wouldn't tell anyone, which was kind of absurd when you think about it." He gave a tired, sad laugh. "One day she was this tiny, flat-chested lady, and the next she had these huge knockers." He closed his eyes and let his head fall back in reverie. "Oh, Zeld. You certainly knew how to get people's attention."

"When you got to the house, did you notice the door or a window that might have been forced open?"

"Zelda didn't lock her doors," he said, opening his eyes. "There was nothing unusual at all. The psycho just walked right in and killed her. She wasn't even out of bed yet."

In an instant he turned on her, his face flushed with anger. "I'm telling you—it's that doctor." He pointed a finger at her. "Why don't you people go talk to *him*?" He pushed past her, walking quickly toward the end of the gallery.

She hauled her purse up to her shoulder and put away her notebook. The sound of a door being slammed somewhere in the distance echoed throughout the building.

"I guess the interview is over," she said to the purple dot and moved toward the stairs. To her right was a marble pedestal on which sat a flat blue dish. On top of her refrigerator, holding bananas, was the exact same dish. She'd purchased it at Woolworth's for twenty-five cents in 1971 as a Mother's Day gift, and had received it back as a housewarming gift from her mother when she moved into the Larkspur house in 1992.

The card propped in front of it read:

"DISH AZURE" $1,500.

In the dish were a variety of business cards. She picked up a handful and went through them, her eyebrows rising and falling with the names. Having money, she guessed, didn't mean one had taste.

She took a last look around and yawned. She was so tired, she felt as if she could lie down and go to sleep right there in the gallery of ugly.

Tim placed one foot on an open desk drawer and tilted the swivel chair back to stare at the ceiling. It made no sense going home, because he wouldn't be able to sleep. He hadn't had a decent night's sleep in four months. After a healthy dose of humble pie, he'd learned to sympathize wholeheartedly with all those people who suffered from insomnia—an ailment he always thought was as bogus as post-traumatic stress disorder. Now he knew better on both counts.

He wondered if she could sleep at night, and decided she

probably could. She was the one who'd dropped him like a grand piano off a fifty-story building. But *why*?

His mind started down the tortuous path of possibilities. That she was in love with Somebody Else was the worst, but in his casual conversations with Cynthia, she hadn't mentioned word one about Adele seeing someone.

He got up and walked to the bookcase, making a mark in the dust with his finger. Then again, maybe she really had been busy, or just pulling back for a while until the dust of their ordeal settled.

He rubbed the ache in the center of his chest and took a deep breath, his spirit lightening. She had agreed to take this class with him, and that was a start.

Returning to his desk, he picked up the telephone and dialed Hermonicus Robinson's number. He'd find out if there'd been any developments in the Clemmons case. It wouldn't hurt anything to give her some direction.

Not that she needed any. At work in her was the kind of intuition that only the best investigators had. It made him crazy when he thought of how far she could have gone had she chosen law enforcement over nursing. Then again, if she had, she wouldn't be the person she was.

He leafed through a stack of new bulletins and the latest issue of his favorite enforcement journal, then stuffed the wad into his jacket pocket. It would provide him with reading material for the sleepless hours ahead.

When Detective Robinson's answering machine answered, he hung up feeling depressed. Insomniacs, he thought, were the loneliest people on earth.

Saad took a fresh pack of Marlboros from the glove compartment and jogged up a cigarette. Although there was really no need, he ducked down and cupped his hands around the flame of his lighter. Inhaling the smoke deep into his lungs, he sat back against the seat, one elbow resting on the open window, the other arm thrown over the back of the seat.

He was bored. This village called Sleepy Hollow was a boring neighborhood compared to the one in which he grew up. Nothing was ever boring there, especially when he stopped to consider that each day began with searching through the pockets of dead bodies in the streets, hoping he wouldn't come across anyone he'd known too well.

The large one-story house across the street was dark except for the flickering luminescence of the television playing over the ceiling and walls of the bedroom. She would be lying facedown across the bed, snoring like a pig. Every night she got like that.

He flicked the cigarette out the Buick's window and a blazing arch of orange embers rained down over the street. The anger and resentment that had been burning in him at Amar's neglect caused him to clench his teeth so that the muscles of his jaw contracted and jumped. He was worth more to them than this: being used as a baby-sitter for old men and whores.

Suddenly he was pawing through the debris on the front seat until he found the packet. He ripped it open and sat back. They did not know about the photographs—no one but he would ever know.

He had taken precautions to leave no trace of himself behind, so if there was no harm done by taking them, and if it brought him a little pleasure, what objection could there be? He relaxed enough to smile. He would enjoy them for a little longer then burn them with the negatives as he had the others.

He ran a finger over his favorite images: a richly furnished living room with a fireplace, a bathroom with a sunken tub and colorful towels, a gleaming kitchen, the freezer and refrigerator doors opened to display a surfeit of foods, a garage filled with American toys—bicycles, a gleaming new Porsche, two pairs of skis, a basketball hoop, gleaming tools.

When he tired of them, he lit another Marlboro and fell into the fantasy that was always the same:

He was the American Marlboro man on a white horse, overseeing his army of men. The adoration in their faces as they raised their guns in salute gave him such a feeling of exhilaration. He could lead them anywhere and they would follow, gladly heeding his will.

SEVEN

THE REPORTING OFF OF NIGHT SHIFT TO DAY SHIFT was always an interesting adventure. Night people provided endless entertainment as they slurred and bumbled their way through vital signs, urine outputs, and medication errors. Shift workers—the nurses who worked a month of days and then switched to a month of nights—had seriously damaged biorhythms. After a year of this schedule, their minds began to curl and warp around the edges.

Opal, a part-time nurse who worked at four different hospitals, was on the hot seat giving report on her ten patients, five of whom now belonged to Adele. By patient number four, Opal's eyelids drooped, and her dentures had begun to slip.

"Bed eight hundred B ahhh, Mrs.—no, wait . . . Mr. ahhh . . . Let me see . . ." The nurse leafed through the crumpled papers on her clipboard. She came to the page she wanted and was scanning it with finger, when her head bobbed a few times and her chin did a slow sink onto her chest. She began to slide out of her chair, snoring as she went.

Cynthia and Linda giggled. Adele took hold of her arm and shook her awake.

With remarkable ability, Opal bolted, caught her uppers before they could slide off her chest, and pushed herself back into the chair. She popped in the dentures and looked down at the paper in front of her. "Mrs. Penn. She ahhh . . ."

"*Mr.* Penn," Adele corrected.

Opal fixed Adele with a vacant look. "What about him?"

"You said Mrs. Penn."

Opal shook her head in slow motion. "I wouldn't say anything about Mrs. Penn. She's dead. Mr. Penn is a widower."

Skip, who had drawn the short straw to become charge nurse, unfolded his arms and rubbed the stubble on his chin. "Can we get on with report, please?"

Opal's head swiveled back to Skip. "That's what I was trying to do."

Adele opened her mouth to speak then snapped it shut. No sense prolonging the agony.

Opal went back to the page and again let her finger wander. First a smile crept onto her lips, and then she snorted and her shoulders shook a couple of times. "He's doing fine," she said finally. "No problems except . . ." She bit her lips and snorted again. This time the snort had a tail of laughter.

Adele peered around Opal's arm in order to read the bold script on the top of the page: *Thomas Edison Penn, 67, resolving CVA:*

> MR. PENN HAD A STROKE
> GAVE HIS MOTHER FORTY POKES,
> WHEN HE SAW WHAT HE HAD DONE,
> HE GAVE HIS FATHER FORTY-ONE

Under that was a series of stick figures configured in suggestive poses.

Adele drew back to look at Opal, who was now openly laughing, her uppers hanging cockeyed from her pink gums.

"I'm sorry," the woman was trying to say. "We get so tired at two or three in the morning that sometimes we get downright pathetic."

When the laughter died down, Opal took a deep breath and shook herself until her cheeks flapped. She flipped to the next page, filled with vital signs, medications administered, and notations on Mr. Penn's physical and neurological status. "Mr. Penn's doctor from the city—hmmmm, Dr. English—came in at 4 A.M. and wrote discharge orders. He said Mr. Penn wanted to tie up some loose ends at work and that he'd come back by Monday to have the pacer reinsertion."

Adele blinked a few times before she could get her mouth—which had fallen open—to work. "What?"

"Docs in the city do this all the time for their VIP patients," Opal said. "It drives the nurses nuts. On elective surgery patients it's okay, but—"

"This isn't an elective surgery," Adele said in disbelief. "Mr. Penn's pacemaker is malfunctioning and he's barely got a rhythm of his own. What he does have is a good chance of dropping dead!" She stood. "Does Ravens or Dhery know that this English idiot discharged him?"

Opal held up her hands. "I tried like hell to get through to them. I told both their exchanges it was important they get the message. I spoke with the doc on call for Dhery. He promised he'd pass the news along. The discharge assessment and vitals are charted and he's had his shower. All you have to do is give him his discharge meds and his instructions. He was waiting for the taxi to arrive the last time I looked in."

Adele was up and out the report room door before any of them could say "Lizzie Borden."

The Yellow Cab driver was at the clerk's desk, hanging over the counter, his feet off the floor, gawking at the monitors. His jaw worked furiously, giving his gum the workout of its career.

"Hi," Adele said, all business. "Is it possible for—"

"Man, them things are so cool." The cabby's eyes barely left the bank of monitors. "Are each one of them lines a person's heart?"

"Uh-huh. Look, I know you're here to pick up Mr. Penn, but I was wondering if you—"

"The patients all got them wire things going through their hearts?"

Adele stared at him puzzled. "Wire things?"

"Yeah, you know, like on T.V."

She thought for a minute. "Are you referring to the electrodes and leads that we put on the patient's chest to pick up the electrical impulses of the heart?"

"Yeah, them wires you see the nurses sticking into the

people's chests when they come into the hospital?" He shook his head gravely, his chewing slowed. "Man that's gotta hurt wicked. What's real spooky is you never see them yelling in pain or nothing."

Adele let a laugh escape. There was a whole world of morons—she knew that—but she never wanted to believe it even though the proof of it jumped in front of her every day and said "duh."

"Well, see, the wires don't actually penetrate the chest. They lie against the skin and pick up the electrical impulses of the cardiac muscle."

The cabby stopped chewing in order to concentrate on making sense of what she'd said, suggesting to her that he might be one of those who did indeed have trouble walking and chewing gum at the same time.

Tina came out of the kitchen with a cup of coffee and headed for her station. Adele took a few steps back from the counter. No one dared go near the shrew until after the first cup of caffeine hit her brain. From across the room, Adele could see the woman's eyes narrow at the sight of the man contaminating her territory.

"I think you'd better get away from there," Adele whispered hurriedly. "This is our clerk's desk, and she's very particular about . . ."

Tina stared at the male thing touching her possessions, spreading his germs all over her space, and stopped chewing *her* gum.

Adele could see the spittle forming in the corners of Tina's mouth. She wished she had a hearing aid she could turn off.

The cab driver chewed even faster at the sight of the Brooklynite and waved, a silly grin exposing big, slightly bucked teeth. "Hi ya," he said, and cracked his gum three times in a row.

"You escape from the reptile petting zoo or what?" Tina asked, shooing him off the counter. "Slither," she ordered him (pronouncing the word "slithah"). "Like, just slither back down whatever hole you came out of."

The cabby smiled even wider, lowering his feet to the ground and yanking up his pants. The top of his head came even with Adele's chin. He hooked a thumb in Tina's direction. "She's fulla some kinda spirit, ain't she?"

"Spirit isn't the word for it," Adele told him, nodding. "But hey, listen, I know you came to pick up Mr. Penn, but could you wait . . ."

Ignoring her completely, he turned back to Tina and again leaned over the counter, dangling a hand in front of the sour woman who was busy assembling her phone headset. Adele sucked in a breath and scanned Tina's desk for sharp objects.

"I like a girl with spirit. You married?"

Adele winced and waited for the explosion. Dumbfounded, she did a double take as one corner of Tina's mouth quivered like it was trying *really* hard to lift smile muscles that probably hadn't been used in the harridan's whole bitter, spiteful, foul life.

"Somebody send for a shovel and a pair of boots," Tina said, rolling her eyes.

"You're a doll," the driver went on, oblivious to the personal danger he was in. "You're some kind of cute."

"Sure, sure," Tina said, avoiding looking into the smooth round face grinning down at her like a golden retriever puppy. "Cute like my Aunt Tilly's butt whiskers are cute. Go on wit'-cha 'cute' and get the hell outta here."

"Hey, you got an Aunt Tilly too?" the cabby asked in mock surprise.

And then Tina did something that made Adele wish more than anything else in the world that she had a video recorder handy.

Tina, the gorgon of Ward 8, laughed. Not a dry snort, but a great belly laugh. A hint of blush came to the normally pasty white face. With her black lipstick, it looked almost nice.

Adele glanced around the ward for witnesses, but there was no one to verify the sight. Sufficiently stunned, she tapped the driver on the shoulder, speaking to the back of his head since he was still glued to Tina's presence.

"Can you wait around for a while?" she asked. "I'm not sure the patient is really ready to go yet. I mean—do you mind?"

"No problem," he said without turning around. "Mikie McCourty is there when you need him. That's my motto."

"How original," Adele said, taking one last look at the flush of Tina's cheeks and pinching herself to make sure she wasn't having one of her premenstrual hallucinations.

Mr. Penn sat innocently on the edge of his bed, hands on his knees, dangling his feet. Sitting down beside him, Adele followed his gaze to the estuary where the rowing crew from the College of Marin was gliding by, barely making a ripple, so smooth was their rhythm.

"Mr. Penn," she began, "I really think you need to reconsider this discharge. Why don't you stay and have Dr. Zimmer insert a new pacemaker? I'm afraid for you to be walking around with a malfunctioning pacemaker."

"Save your breath," Mr. Penn said. His speech was almost back to normal. "I'm going. Is my taxi here?"

She must have looked crestfallen, for in an attempt to make her feel better, he reached out to pat her on the shoulder. "Don't worry, I'll be fine. I'll be back in a couple of days to have that operation. Maybe you could bring Helen by later tonight? I'd like to fix you dinner for all your trouble. You've been very kind to me and Helen."

A wave of mild panic passed over her at the thought of eating anything from Mr. Penn's kitchen. She shifted uneasily in her seat. "You don't owe me anything. It was my pleasure to take care of him, but won't you please wait at least until Dr. Ravens or Dr. Dhery arrive? Let them check you over before you're discharged."

"No!" he said, anger creeping into his voice. "Nothing d— doing! I'm not g—going to pay those jackasses a hundred and fifty d—dollars each so they can stick their heads in the door and say 'tickle your ass with a feather.' Nothing anybody says is going to keep me here. Dr. English told me I could leave, so I'm going! I'm a busy man. I have work to do."

She leaned forward. "What if I arranged to have you work from here? Would you stay?"

He chuckled and shook his head. "You're a persistent

young woman. I ought to have you on my board of directors."
His lips pulled into a stubborn thin line. "But I said no, and I
mean no." He looked around his room and pulled himself to
his feet. "That cab should have been here by now." He indicated the Seth Thomas on the wall. "No tip for the tardy."

"He is here." Resigned, she stood and placed his bag of
discharge medications on his side table. "I asked him to wait
until I spoke to you."

She went over his discharge instructions and checked to
make sure his heparin lock had been removed. As she worked,
she could not ignore the ominous feeling nagging at her
nurse's sixth sense. She felt like a medical warrior sending
her charge off to die because he refused the protection she
needed to give.

When she returned, she found the cabby still hanging over
Tina's desk. She visually checked him for bites, stab wounds,
or bruises, and, finding no traces of Tina's bad humor, directed him to have his cab waiting at the front entrance in ten
minutes.

Reluctantly, he bid his "angel dumpling" a cheery adieu,
and told her he'd count the hours until he could hear her sweet
voice on the phone.

Tina, in keeping with her true nature, told him to eat shit,
which made him smile even wider and blow air kisses.

Not having enough sense to know when he'd gotten off
easy, the cab driver turned at the ward doors and announced,
"Hey, Angel Dumpling, whatcha say to goin' with me over to
Land of Oz after work? A couple a good shots of gin just
might kill whatever them bugs are you got up your ass. How's
about it?"

Adele ducked.

At the absence of sharp projectiles flying overhead, she
peeked over the top of the desk.

Tina flipped him the bird, at the same time delivering a
dazzling smile. "Sure, Fuckface," she replied in the chirpiest
of tones.

The second the doors closed behind the driver, the nurses'

station began filling with people. Adele knew that if she related what she'd witnessed, they'd send her to Detox. Cautiously she approached Tina's desk.

"Call around to see if Dr. Ravens or Dr. Dhery are in the house yet." She checked out the woman's pupils, searching for evidence of drug use. "If you get either one, buzz me in the report room."

Tina, restored to her familiar bad humor, told her to eat shit and die, but then she picked up the phone and rang through to the switchboard.

Adele walked away ruminating on the highly variable natures of her fellow humans. It really was more than she wanted to chew at 7:30 in the morning.

There had been another managed care budget crisis meeting between the physicians on staff and the administration, so it was after ten before any of the docs reached the ward. Irritable and frustrated, the lot of them radiated a heavy-handed chill.

For the most part, the nurses were politically savvy union people and didn't need to be told what problems had arisen. They'd been the first of the health care food chain to feel the effects of the malignant and rapidly spreading disease of corporate health care greed. Even so, the doctors were unwilling to discuss the meeting, although Dr. Ravens put it in a succinct nutshell: "They want to tell us how to practice medicine, and compensate us with less money for doing it," he said, passing the charting desk on his way to Mr. Penn's room. "And the worst of it is, we don't have a choice in the matter."

She waited a couple of seconds for him to reappear in the hall. He looked at her, holding out his hands. "Where's Mr. Penn?"

"Discharged," she said with false brightness. "Dr. English told Mr. Penn he could take a couple of days to put things in order at the office before he reinserts a new pacer. We called both you and Dr. Dhery—twice."

George Ravens groaned, running a hand through his hair. "That's insane. The man wasn't nearly ready for discharge."

"Yes, well, you don't need to tell *me* that. I did my best to keep him here until you or Rymesteade arrived, but he refused. You could try calling him. He's at his office in San Rafael."

"I'd rather talk to English," Dr. Ravens said, fishing in his inside jacket pocket. He pulled out a small electronic organizer and pressed buttons. "I vouched for this guy in order for him to get him one-time emergency privileges. He faxed the medical staff office some of the required documents. They looked fine. I don't understand why he'd do something so stupid."

Rymesteade Dhery exited room 800 with Cynthia and sat down opposite his colleague. "The old man flew?"

Dr. Ravens nodded and dialed the number on the screen of his personal organizer.

"I'll call Mr. Penn," said Rymesteade, sliding the face sheet of the chart around in order to read the phone numbers. "Maybe I can talk him into coming back in."

"Don't bother, Ryme." Adele got up. The call light went on over Walter Minka's room. "Unless you can promise him that there won't be any charges involved in putting in a new pacer, he won't come in."

"You know I can't do that."

"Then I guarantee you he won't come back for two days— if he makes it that long. All we can do is wait." She gathered her clipboard and started toward room 810. "I'm going over to his house tonight to drop off his cat. I'll do what I can."

Dr. Ravens hung up and motioned for her to wait. "The exchange took a message and said they'd page English. Do me a favor and call me after you see Mr. Penn tonight, would you?"

"Will do."

He leaned close, taking in her scent as she passed. In that split second, he saw that her hair was as black as his own and that her skin was smoother than silk. What he noticed most, though, was the depth of the gold eyes.

She could hear Walter's racking coughs from out in the hall. When she entered the room, she was surprised to see a couple standing at his bedside, their young faces pale with alarm. The woman desperately clutched the call light, repeatedly pressing the button. "He can't breathe!" she gasped, as if it were she who could not get air. "Help him! Do something, please!"

Adele turned off the bell and calmly increased the oxygen flow to the nasal canula. Placing Kleenex in his hand, she touched his back, slick with perspiration. "Walter, look at me. You have to get in charge of yourself. Try to relax through the cough and slow your breathing."

In a frenzy of anxiety, the young man standing on the other side of the bed, wrung his hands as if he were about to start screaming for help. "Shit! Can't you give him something?"

Their panic was infectious. Though he'd been down this road hundreds of times before, Walter, too, took on a wild expression, as though it had just occurred to him for the first time to be terrified.

"Christ on a bike, everybody please just relax and take some slow breaths."

The three of them measured their breaths in long, slow intervals until Walter's coughing subsided and he caught up with them. The slight wince with every inspiration did not escape her notice; he would not have been the first person to crack ribs from the force of coughing. She listened to his lungs then pulled back to look at him.

"Are you having pain?"

In his eyes, she could see him weighing the truth against the probable reaction of his guests and shook his head no.

"Where is it?"

He glared at her, his eyes pleading with her not to push the matter: *Not now, not in front of them.*

With her eyes she agreed, wondering what it was going to cost him in suffering for the remaining time of their visit. She turned to them smiling. "He's fine. Thanks for your concern."

She went to the sink to wash her hands. When she was finished, she noticed the young woman still holding Walter's hand for dear life—his.

"You doing okay, Walter?" Adele asked, drying her hands.

"Yeah, thanks. I guess that last martini went down the wrong pipe."

Tina stuck her head into the room. "Line three. A hysterical woman. Why is it the hysterical ones are always for you, Monsarrat?"

Adele took a deep breath and rolled her head wearily. "Luck, I guess."

"Hi, is this the nurse who took care of Mr. Penn?" The voice was young and scared.

At the mention of Mr. Penn, Adele's pulse picked up, at first with joy that it was not Mrs. Coolidge, then with apprehension that something had happened to the old man. "Yes? What's happened?"

"Nothing—exactly, except he looks awful. He's white as chalk and sweating." She paused briefly. "I'm sorry, this is Sharon Wells, his secretary? He was here when I came in this morning. He said his doctor told him he could come back to work, but he looks . . . Well, to be honest, he looks like death warmed over. Is there anything I should be doing for him?" She blew out a small puff of air. "Not that he'd allow me to do anything, but I thought I'd better ask in case something happens."

Adele reflected on the obstinate Mr. Penn for a moment. In the background, the PA system paged Drs. Dhery, Vienterburg, and Murray. "Well, I guess the only things I would suggest are to make sure you know CPR, remember to call nine-one-one before you start, and brush up on your Spanish."

"Selma's daughter's mother-in-law's aunt made it for me," Mrs. Goodnik said, handing Cynthia a covered baking dish filled with something that looked like white gopher guts and deer pellets. "It's already cooked, but maybe you could you throw it in the microwave for a few minutes?"

Cynthia stared at the mess through the lid, shoved the dish at Adele, covered her mouth, and ran from the room gagging.

Adele took off the cover and sniffed. Her lip automatically curled. "What is it?"

"They call it Thinking Man's Pudding." Mrs. Goodnik smiled and tapped the side of her head. "Because it's supposed to feed your brain."

"What's in it?"

"Let's see . . ." Starting with her left thumb, Mrs. Goodnik assigned each finger a name. "Sugar, Karo syrup, butter, sesame paste, clove, allspice, raisins, and pig brains."

Adele replaced the lid. "And you actually want to put this near your mouth?"

Mrs. Goodnik nodded evenly. "Absolutely. And maybe a nice cup of hot coffee to go with it?"

"Coffee and brains," Adele repeated with mock earnestness. "Comin' right up."

Mrs. Noel and Grace Thompson were huddled in the kitchen, heads bent close together. "Let me guess," Adele said upon entering. "You're discussing what bulbs to plant in the fall?"

Mattie Noel gave her a pained look, as if she were about to have diarrhea. "You shouldn't even be here," she hissed, her clipboard in full armor position crushing her breasts. "As far as the hospital is concerned, you've been suspended from service."

"Tell that to my union and my patients, Mrs. Noel. Excuse me." She indicated that she needed to get to the microwave. Both women peered into the Pyrex dish and drew back.

"Why do you insist on being contumacious?" Grace asked, sucking air through her front teeth. "Mrs. Noel has a point. Depending on the gravity of the infraction, I may be obligated to retract your schedule for the remainder of the month. Perhaps if you left now—took a leave of absence without pay—before you're officially suspended, things might go easier on you later."

"Is this your way of asking me to leave quietly by the side door?" Adele asked, amused.

"Actually, yes," said Grace.

Adele set the time and moved away from the microwave. Folding her arms across her chest, she studied the two women with suspicion. "What is it with you guys?" she asked. "Why the push to get rid of me? Is management going to try and put a big hairy one over on the nursing staff soon?"

The two women looked at each other in a way that told her she'd guessed correctly.

"You're a rabble-rouser, Arden," said Mrs. Noel. "You constantly break rules, and incite the other girls to question management's judgments."

The microwave bleeped loudly, signifying that the deadly killer waves of radiation were at an end. Adele stepped back into the kitchen and popped open the door. "The 'other girls,' as you call them, are just as capable of questioning illegal management policies and practices as I am." She removed the cover. The brains were bubbling nicely. "And even if they turned yellowbelly, there's always going to be the union, just like there will always be shelters for battered women."

"I'll not engage in a pissing contest with you, Adele," Grace said, pushing past them into the hall. "As far as I'm concerned, the whole bloody lot of you have acted disgracefully. The nurses here need to learn how to buckle down and give it their all."

"In that case," Adele suggested, "how about if you take off those white stockings and that sterile white uniform and that Nightingale-era cap and show us how it's done, Grace? I guess we've all forgotten how to care for ten or fifteen patients apiece, working nonstop for twelve hours without meal or bathroom breaks. If that isn't giving it our all, I'll bet the staff would love to see you show them what is."

By noon Adele was ahead of the race. Her patients were fed, medded, vitaled, and charted. She had ten minutes of relative freedom in which to eat lunch or collapse in the nurses' lounge. Reporting off to Mirek and Cynthia on the status of her patients, she looked at her watch and then back at the door of the Queen Mother's office.

Directly on cue, the door opened and Grace vacated her office for lunch. A slave to habit, she would take a cab to the Mayfair British Pub on San Rafael's Miracle Mile for a pint of ale and a shepherd's pie and then go shopping before she returned two hours later.

The moment the double doors closed on the starched white dress, Adele used her duplicate key to unlock the head nurse's office and slipped inside the eight-by-ten closet of a room.

She started with the first name on the list Mrs. Clemmons had made of her husband's closest friends. After four calls, it was clear that most of them were actually no more than casual social acquaintances of the murdered man. None of them had been able to give her anything more than "Raymond Clemmons was a nice guy who appeared to get on well with his wife, and oh dear, wasn't it such a horrible thing?" No, they didn't really know him *that* well, but they did see them once or twice a year around the holidays or charity benefits.

On impulse Adele called Laila Clemmons to ask for the route her husband usually walked. There was a hesitation then a tone of reluctance as she gave vague directions. The accommodating, baklava-pushing sociability was no longer in evidence.

Adele tucked the spotty directions into her bra and turned to leave when one of the files that cluttered Grace's desk caught her eye. She yanked it from the middle of the pile. Inside was a set of schedules, one for each of the remaining months of the year. On top was the June schedule. A line was drawn through her name and extended all the way to June 30. Above the line, in Grace Thompson's precise handwriting, was "TERMINATED."

"Counting our chickens before they're hatched, aren't we, Gracie?"

The framed photograph of Queen Elizabeth, hanging over the desk at eye level, spoke up in a slightly skewed Cockney accent. *Give it a rest, luv. The Queen Mum'll collar ya sooner or later. Might as well queue up down at the job centre, an' sign on for the dole. You'll be needin' a job to keep that fine dog of yours fed.*

Adele flipped to August and was stunned to see a red line through Skip's and Abby's names with the same "TERMI-

NATED" written above. In October it was Linda. December was a double whammy: both Cynthia and Tina.

"Christ on a bloody bike!" she said, imitating the Queen's Cockney. "They're going to give all the senior staff the sack."

And bring in some gumbies to replace every bloody one of ya, the Queen said, turning her gloved hand this way and that in the stiff, modified wave that was her signature. *Then won't the budget be lookin' all spiffy for the boys upstairs. Queen Mum might even get a pay rise for this one.*

Furious, Adele searched through the rest of the folder. At the back, she found a paper folded in half. It was a memo from Mattie Noel to Grace Thompson, dated three weeks before.

> *Per our phone conversation today, any and all evidence that can be used against the troublemakers should be discreetly collected. Other than the management heads, NO ONE is to be told of the restructuring plan.*
>
> *Perhaps some incentive can be given to newer staff to "pass along" things they may witness or hear about those in question. Document every infraction no matter how trivial—the slightest rule broken is a wedge.*
>
> *The Monsarrat woman should be easy as she already has a reputation for causing trouble, but be careful with that one—she's clever. Your receptionist, Tina, has all the manners of an unneutered alley cat. Abby McGowan was involved in that disgusting murder business—perhaps we can find an angle there. Linda Rainer will be the most difficult, as her employment record is flawless. Find something, even if you must create a situation. I anticipate the others—a fairy and a loose woman—will not be hard to eliminate for obvious reasons.*
>
> *Here, in the inner circles at Ellis, we take the notion that nurses can be pushed to an astounding limit. They are capable—if kept busy—of going for an entire 12-hour shift without once visiting the lounge or the cafeteria, or even sitting down! We must be creative with scheduling as well.*

Push the limits. Sixteen, perhaps even twenty patients apiece is not unrealistic. There is incredible financial advantage in this. Using fewer "high paid" staff nurses lowers our overall operating costs and weeds out the dead-wood who do not hold the interests of Ellis Hospital above all else. In the words of our own beloved Lawrence Mill-banks: "To promote top financial health of Ellis Hospital, the CEOs have determined that those holding positions unnecessary to the well-being of the customer must be elim-inated. We have further resolved that cutting up to 75% of nursing, laboratory, and radiology departments will have no deleterious effects on customer service whatsoever!"

The officers want all top-salary people eliminated by the end of the year. I have assured my superiors we will do everything in our power to make this a reality. Re-member—a financially secure corporation is a healthy corporation.

Although you may find this difficult at first, I trust your team spirit will overcome any difficulties in weeding out the tapeworms who have firmly attached themselves to the very bowels of Ellis management.

Mattie Noel

Adele could barely believe her eyes.

Better call out your union mates, the Queen said. *Your sort are two a penny, luv, and this one's a real thieving git.*

"Thieving git," Adele repeated, fitting the folder down the front of her scrub pants, and smoothing it flat across her belly. She picked up the phone again and paged Henry Williams, giv-ing Grace's private extension number. He called back within the minute.

"Williams." He sounded irritated. "You page me?"

Adele smiled. Henry was one of her favorite human be-ings. Despite his prickly exterior and an austere attitude that clung to him like a sign pinned to his forehead, she found him to be a kind and compassionate man. Although they didn't "hang," as Henry put it, there was a strong heart and soul con-nection between them.

"Big Henry, how you all doing?"

"Adele? Hey, girl, I was just up there looking for your face. Where you hiding?"

"The Queen Mother's office," she said in a low voice. "Do you still have the key to the copy room?"

"Uh-huh, sure do." In the background, she could hear Ethel Waters coming through the earphones that were lying temporarily on his collarbones.

"I need you to make me some copies of something stat. Can you meet me in the back stairwell on the fourth-story landing right now?"

There was a pause, then: "You doing something 'gainst the man?"

"The man" was Henry's way of referring to the hospital administration and the police.

"That," Adele said, "all depends on which whipping post you're tied to."

Daisy came out of Nordstrom's feeling better than when she went in. She always felt better when she spent her late husband's money. Lance Rothschild, the great patron of the arts in Marin, had been made of the money generously trickled down from his father and his father before him. The pink sequined stretchy dress and matching pumps were exactly perfect for the Art League party on Friday.

In the window of Papyrus, she gave her hair an admiring glance. Lisa, her hairdresser at Shy Locks, had given her the most extraordinary champagne color and then arranged it in delicious, large ringlets, one layer upon another to five inches above her scalp. It *did* make her look tall and slim, exactly as the girl had assured her it would. She patted the top with her new set of pink acrylic nails and checked her watch. It was lunchtime. She frowned. No, she wasn't going to eat lunch. She was going on a diet and that was that.

Daisy zigzagged across the walkway, delighting in the variety of clothes and finery on display. She was engaging in a fantasy in which she and the beautiful male mannequin in the window of Barcelino's were dancing like professionals in a ballroom filled with all her envious friends, when she caught sight of his reflection.

He stood not ten yards behind her, pretending to look interested in the toddler wear in the Gymboree window. She'd seen him earlier that morning in the San Rafael post office and, later, two cars behind hers in Greenbrae.

At first, she'd mistaken him for the telephone man, but realized soon enough that this man was slighter and his features more angular, though not at all unpleasant.

She changed direction and headed across the path to Liz Claiborne, concentrating on his reflection. A moment later, he appeared, watching her from his cover near the Belts and Buckles shack. The idea that he was following her she found incredibly titillating. Curious whether he would follow, she walked across the path and into Brookstone.

The establishment seemed to specialize in all kinds of gadgets, most of which she did not understand. At the rear of the store, a starched, matronly woman in a light coat and carrying a serious-looking bumbershoot, was asking one of the clerks about a recording machine. Daisy moved closer as the clerk—a young man with an unfortunate complexion and hair cut shorter on one side—explained about the machine's unique features.

"It's capable of recording conversations at fairly large distances," he said, "You'll be able to hear what people say about you. These machines"—he tapped the box. His thumbnails were over an inch long—"have been selling like hotcakes."

"Like hotcakes," Daisy echoed faintly.

"As a matter of fact, this being the last one in the store, it has the extra bonus of being on sale. And . . ." Smiling down at them, he held up a finger. Daisy followed it, lips parted slightly in fascination. "This machine is so effective in monitoring private conversations, the U.S. government outlawed them. Said they were against the Constitution so the company isn't allowed to manufacture them anymore!"

Daisy lusted after the recorder. It would be perfect: she could set it up at the party and hear for herself what people were saying about her. She heaved an audible sigh of relief when the matron stepped away from the set. Daisy's fingers had settled on the machine's black plastic case when the woman grabbed it out from under her hand.

"I beg your pardon!" she huffed, her jowls jiggling. "I believe that's mine."

"Excuse me, but I had it first!" Daisy exclaimed, reaching to take it out of the woman's clutch. She hated how childish her voice sounded. "My hand was already on it. It belongs to me."

Thinking that her accent was being mimicked, the matron bridled. "Don't be absurd," she said in the same voice Daisy's mother frequently used on her. "That machine is mine, and I shall have it! Keep your distance!"

"Well!" Daisy said, starting after her, her ringlets bouncing. One escaped its pins and fell across her face like a sprung coil. "How dare you assume that you own—"

The device clasped tightly in her hand, the woman turned and gave her one of those blue-blood stares that always froze her heart. "Fat tart!" she spit under her breath. "Piss off."

Tears stung Daisy's eyes as she ran from the store to her car. At the first stoplight, she remembered the dark man and searched for him in the rearview mirror. Her anguish abated instantly at the sight of him several cars back. He was still interested—still wanted her enough to follow her.

She gave herself a desperate smile in the visor mirror, wiping away the black mascara trails left by her tears. Everything would be right, now. *He* didn't think she was an absurd fat tart at all.

Fifteen minutes later, Adele replaced the file folder, hoisted the thick stack of copies Henry made for her, and opened the door of Grace's office. Peeking through the slim crack, she had a clear view of the main hall and the double doors leading into the ward. She pulled the door open at the same second Grace stepped through the double doors and, in formal military marching style, headed straight for her. Her keys were in one hand, a shopping bag from Brookstone in the other.

Adele closed the door and froze, wildly looking around the

tiny (and growing smaller by the second) room for a place to hide. There were only two choices open to her. One was the sixteen-inch-wide closet that was already crammed with rubber boots, umbrellas, the odd file or two, six packages of English biscuits, four cans of peanut brittle, and a carton of Lipton Flo-Thru tea bags.

The other was behind the door.

When Grace came in, she'd take off her coat, and when she turned around to hang it on the coatrack, she'd see Adele, have a heart attack, and die.

Flattening herself against the wall behind the door, Adele watched the doorknob. Footsteps slowed and then stopped. Through the door she could hear the older woman's wheezy breathing.

The old girl's asthma's kicking up, Queen Elizabeth said from the wall. *Acacia trees gonna be the death of her.*

The sound of a key in the lock made her mind spin out. *Oh shit. Let me get through this one, dear Buddha, and I promise I'll never have another unkind thought about the Queen Mother again.*

The doorknob turned. Buddha's answer: *Not good enough.*

She squared her shoulders, ready for the shocked expression on Grace's face, and then the clutching of her chest and the final thud. Another panicky thought came as the door began to open: would she have to initiate CPR right away, or could she wait a bit—maybe sneak out and close the door and forget about the whole damned thing?

More footsteps. "Excuse me, Ms. Thompson?" The shy voice belonged to a new hireling named Pamela. The doorknob stopped. Through the crack, Adele could see Grace's blue-veined, age-spotted hand resting on the handle.

The young nurse lowered her voice to the point where Adele had to strain to hear her. "Remember what you told me about telling you anything that the senior nurses did that was maybe not exactly the way things are usually done around the ward?"

"Yes?"

"Adele did something with my patient in eight-fifteen when I was at lunch that I think you should check out."

There was a rustling of the plastic shopping bag and a sigh. "Oh, bloody hell. Very well. Let me put away my parcels." The door opened halfway. Adele stopped breathing and moved a hand over her heart to muffle the racket.

With great care, Grace placed the white-and-blue Brookstone bag and her umbrella on the desk, removed her coat, and went out, closing the door behind her.

Adele breathed. "Christ on a bike in Hell," she whispered as she put her ear to the door. When the two sets of footsteps had faded sufficiently, she opened the door, peeked out, and stepped into the hallway. As she was about to close the door, the Brookstone bag caught her attention.

Go on, luvie, Queen Elizabeth graciously invited. *Ain't no crime to have yourself a little look. Never can tell—might be something bloody important.*

Wondering if she might really be teetering off the edge of sanity, Adele calmly stepped back, opened the bag as if it belonged to her, and looked inside.

There were several packages of micro tapes and a glossy cardboard box with red and black lettering: INVISIBLE TAPE-CORDER. MAGNIFY AND RECORD CONVERSATIONS FROM UP TO 100 FEET AWAY! VOICE ACTIVATED. STICKS ANYWHERE! 120 MINUTES OF RECORDING TIME!

In the distance, she heard footsteps. Closing the bag, she took one giant step backward and pulled the door closed. She'd just released the handle when Grace Thompson reappeared around the corner.

Pretending not to see her, Adele knocked on the door. "Grace? Grace, are you in there?"

"I'm right here, Miss Monsarrat." Grace seemed more prunish and irritated than ever. "What are you getting up to now?"

"I was wondering if you'd be interested in a copy of the California Nurses' Association's latest achievements in the nurse and patient protection laws?" She held up one of the copies of Mattie Noel's memo and waved it—printed side turned away.

"It has a wonderful explanation of Assembly Bill three ninety-four and how it will allow the nurse at the bedside to—"

"Oh, put a sock in it!" Grace grumbled, and slammed the door in her face.

"Whew," Adele sighed. "I was hoping you'd say that."

The third-ever emergency meeting of Ward 8 staff was to take place in the nurses' lounge immediately after Grace Thompson left the premises. Henry Williams was to escort the head nurse to her car, spurring her desire to escape with nonstop talk about the majesty of Hoagy Carmichael and Buddy Bolden. The moment her license plate had cleared the hospital exit, he would page Adele, sprint to nursing administration, then shadow Mattie Noel until she either went home or called the crisis unit to have him taken away.

Over the course of the day, Tina, Adele, and Cynthia secretly contacted every staff member of Ward 8 and told them to show up—no ifs, ands, or buts about it. If anyone so much as attempted to decline, they were threatened with the prospect of having Tina drive out to track them down and bring them in tied to one of her fenders.

At zero hour, 90 percent of Ward 8's nurses and monitor techs were crammed into the lounge. The other 10 percent were watching over the patients.

"Okay, guys and gals," Adele said, holding up her hands. "Here's the deal. I'll make it fast. In the packet of papers Tina gave you is a copy of a memo from Mrs. Noel to the Queen Mother and the schedules to the end of the year."

There came the sounds of papers shuffling. Adele gave them a few minutes to read. There were a few cries of outrage and protest. Some nurses shook their heads, others took on expressions of disgust. A nurse by the name of Rupert yelled, "Death to management assholes," which was followed by general applause, hoots, and hollers.

The shy new hire timidly raised her hand then stood so as to be heard over the commotion of papers rustling. "Hi, I'm Pamela, one of the new hires?" she said in the springy, question-laden cadence that belonged to the California born and bred. "And you know, Mrs. Thompson really did tell us to report everything to her? But today? I brought her in to show her how when I got behind, Adele came in without being asked and did Mr. Puccini's dressing change and his vital signs for me?"

The blond nurse tittered and bit daintily at the skin around her thumbnail. "She looked at me like I'd just told her Prince Charles had sodomized Eddie Murphy and sold the video for a hundred dollars."

There was more laughter.

"I mean really, she told me that wasn't the kind of information she had in mind, and that if I wanted to continue on in the ward, I'd have to come up with information about the senior nurses that was incriminating. When I asked her why, she explained that the ward needed a transfusion of new, untainted blood, and that we had to try to bleed off the old bad blood."

"God," Cynthia said from her place on the couch. "I'm feeling anemic."

"Yeah, sounds like vampires to me," Tina said. "I'm gonna start wearing my garlic and carrying a cross."

Adele held up a hand to quiet the laughter. "Seriously, people, this is a problem. Management means to turn us against each other. We're really going to have to watch ourselves and each other's backs. We have to be very tight. No backstabbing, no complaining about each other. Loose lips sink ships. We can't afford to give administration anything to use against us. Tina, you're going to have to bypass whatever genetic memory came with being a New Yorker and be as nice as you can to everyone—on the phone and in person. You may have to have someone teach you how to smile and say 'good morning' like you mean it."

Tina rolled her eyes. "Gawd!" she huffed. "I never had to be nice my whole life, how the hell do you expect me to start now?"

"I don't care how, but learn fast. Skip? You've got to stop whining and complaining about everything and everybody."

There was an outburst of cheers and "Hear! Hear!"

". . . and take your OFD medication or something, will you?"

This time, the hoots turned to whistles and catcalls. In addition to all his other challenges, Skip suffered from OFD: Open Fly Disorder. At least twice a shift, one of his colleagues would have to remind him that the barn door was open, or that the trouser worm was about to escape. Grace had written him up numerous times, and once he'd even been sent to Jeffrey Lavine, the staff shrink, for counseling.

"Let me give you an example of what management will do with something as harmless as this. First they'll terminate Skip on grounds of sexual perversion, exposing himself, solicitation, and unsanitary behavior around the staff and patients."

People were still laughing when she raised her voice and held up a hand. "I'm serious, folks; these people mean business. It sounds ridiculous here in this room, but put this stuff in the mouths of the thousand-dollar-an-hour attorneys who work for the big CEOs, and the jury will want not only to fire us and take away our licenses, but to use us as examples to the rest of the world of what bad and perverted people nurses are in general. The public won't think of us as angels of mercy— we'll be made to look like the Charles Ngs and Aileen Woronos of health care."

The room went silent as the reality of the threat hit each one present.

"It's like a witch-hunt," Abby McGowan said finally.

Adele nodded. "Yes, that's exactly what it is."

"But why is this?" asked Mirek, who was missing post-clinicals at the college in order to be there.

Linda reached across him to pick up her cup of coffee. "They want to get rid of the higher-paid nurses, Mirek."

Mirek nodded, still looking puzzled.

"Then they can replace those nurses with low-paid, nonmedical workers," Adele continued. "The hospital administrators— like our own Mr. Millbanks—think they can save money, which will go to pay the CEOs' salaries. Mr. Millbanks's tax returns for last year stated his yearly income as two point seven million dollars. Last year, Mr. Crowder, the head of Pacific Health Growth, which is the corporation that owns Ellis Hospital, was compensated with sixteen and a half million dollars as his yearly salary. At the same time, thirty percent of the R.N. staff was cut. As soon as the R.N.s were let go, mortality rates soared due to inadequate staffing."

She read the disbelief in their faces. "Check it out if you don't believe me. It's all a matter of public record."

"Okay," said Linda, standing up. "Now that everyone is sufficiently depressed, make sure you take this memo home and tack it up on your refrigerator or your bathroom mirror. Read it over a few times before you come to work."

"Today," Adele continued, speaking above the hum of voices, "Grace purchased a tape recorder that's designed to record people's private conversations. I can only guess at where she'll put it, so we're going to have to keep our political or personal views to ourselves until we're out of the hospital."

"Maybe we should praise each other a lot," suggested Linda. "We could all walk around saying things like, 'Say, isn't that Tina a sweet, even-tempered, polite young lady?' "

"Hey, fuck you," Tina said, fighting back a smirk.

"Or we could have a code just between ourselves," volunteered Cynthia. "Like, 'Hey, Tina's being a real PITA today. Pain in the ass.'"

The normally serene and Zen-like Malloy called out, "Or, 'Yes, QM is here, B-U-N-D-Y—but unfortunately not dead yet.'"

The collective howl almost drowned out the ring of Adele's cell phone. The minute she answered, Henry said: "Them tanks is headed your way, boss, and they is loaded for bear. Head for the hills down the back stairwell or join the ranks of the unemployed."

Adele yelled over the din of the crowd. "Everybody out the back stairwell, STAT! Mattie Noel is on her way up."

Smooth as a grade-school fire drill, they silently filed down the main hall of Ward 8 and out the back exit. As the door closed behind the last nurse, Mattie Noel entered the double doors looking for trouble.

All she found were nurses trying as best they could to practice the art of healing.

According to Dr. Nutt, Nelson was a sensitive dog. Separation anxiety was one of the canine's main (but not only) psychological problems. One of the most important ways the responsible pet owner could keep neuroses at a minimum level, the licensed pet psychologist suggested, was to bring consistency and tranquility to all potentially upsetting situations.

It was for this reason that Adele took the time to explain that kitty-kitty had to go back home, because his daddy missed him. Nelson listened patiently, his brown eyes nervously going between her and the cat. Several times, when he couldn't stand it any longer, he put his paw on the arm holding Helen and tried to pull it away.

It wasn't until Adele put the cat into the travel carrier that Nelson lost it and tried to lay a righteous guilt trip on her. Piteous whines and groans of protest were followed by barks of outrage.

"Say goodbye, Nelson," Adele said in a firm tone. "Helen will come back for a visit in a few days."

Nelson pulled out all the stops and retaliated by using a trick he instinctively knew she hated. Bravely laying his Rod Stewart rug on her feet, he went and sat protectively in front of the carrier. His message was clear: "My rug for the cat."

It was, she realized, the ultimate sacrifice. The ploy had the desired effect and guilt set in like an avalanche.

In the end, when all traces of Helen had been collected and packed into the Beast, Nelson shoved his head under Roddy Rug and cried himself to sleep.

From the end of the driveway, she saw three lights were on in the mansion, all in different areas: the study, the foyer, and the top-story bedroom. Mr. Penn was of the Depression generation, as was her mother, and more than likely had been raised on the phrase, "Turn off the lights when you leave a room!" So Adele found it odd he would have three rooms lit at once.

She put her ear against the front door and pressed the door-bell. Her finger met with resistance. Squinting in the dark, she saw that the bell had been taped over with duct tape and an index card tacked above. She dug out her penlight and aimed the beam. The message was faded so that she had to squint:

SAVE ELECTRICITY!
KNOCK THE OLD-FASHIONED WAY
OR USE KNOCKER
THAT'S WHY IT'S THERE

She knocked, then used the knocker, then pounded on the door until it occurred to her he might be in the shower or the bathroom. When she'd called, he told her he was going to clean up before starting dinner. She looked at her watch. That had been an hour ago.

A bad feeling began in her gut. She pulled the Colt from the waistband of her jeans and tried the door. It opened easily. Slipping her way inside, she set the carrier down in the foyer. Helen moved restlessly, opening his mouth in silent meows as he pawed at the cage door.

"Mr. Penn?" she called in a forced cheerful voice. "Thomas? Helen is home. Where are you?"

Glass crunched under her shoes. Pieces of an ordinary water tumbler were scattered over the foyer floor.

"Mr. Penn?" She glanced through the office doorway. Finding it empty, she inched up the staircase toward the lit bedroom. If the old guy was still in the bathroom—well, okay. She was a nurse; there wasn't much she hadn't seen.

She knocked on the frame of the open bedroom door. "Mr. Penn, you in here?" A beige suit jacket lay neatly folded on the bed. Next to it lay the pants still on their hanger.

Her eyes went immediately to the closed door of the bath-room. She crossed the room and peered through the keyhole. All she could see was a corner of the sink and an empty towel rack. There was no water running, no newspaper or magazine sounds. She knocked louder. "Hey, Mr. Penn, you in there?"

The silence sent all sorts of things through her mind—like the fact that the majority of aneurysm deaths took place while people were on the toilet. Then there were all the police scene photos she'd seen of dead people on bathroom floors.

"I'm coming in!" she warned in earnest, turning the handle. "Here I come!"

She really hadn't expected him to be there, so that when her eyes fell on his long white leg hanging over the rim of the tub, it took a few seconds to register in her mind. Dazed, she reached down and touched his chest and face. He was cold and clammy, and the only part of him that was not dusky gray was the dark pink scar over his pacer site. The hope that he was only sleeping seemed dim—not only because of his color but also because sitting in one inch of ice-cold water didn't seem conducive to relaxation.

Snapping into Code Blue mode, she felt for his carotid and femoral pulses, then listened for air exchange. His breathing was so shallow that it was almost worthless for getting oxygen into him, but the quality of his pulse scared her more. Thready and barely palpable, it was irregular, achieving a rate of no greater than thirty beats per minute. She looked at the depth of the tub, and remembered his weight was close to 80 kilograms—more than she could lift. She opened the drain and slid him down so that his head rested flat on the bottom of the tub. Propping his feet on the rim under the handles, she ran to the phone, silently pleading with higher powers for an English-speaking 911 person.

An old-fashioned fountain pen and Dr. English's card lay next to a pink Princess phone right out of the sixties. She dialed 911 and turned the card over. Written in the archaic Spencerian method of handwriting was the notation:

4 MS tablets now. Crush. Take w/water.

Amongst a clutter of clipped grocery store coupons she found the bag of discharge medications still stapled shut with the pharmacy bill dangling from one staple. Next to that lay a manila medication envelope with the flap pulled out. MS-

CONTIN 200 MG. #6 was printed on the front. She counted the number of pills remaining: two. If the note was to be believed, he'd taken 800 milligrams of morphine and crushed the tablets as well, which meant the old man got a bolus of the drug. It was enough to kill him. She put it together like a complicated equation: Overdose + elderly + hypoventilation = lowered blood pressure → decreased oxygen flow to heart → increased degree of heart block to complete block = a self-feeding cycle to the grave.

"Limping Christ on a—"

The operator answered on the second ring—in English.

Adele asked for an ambulance stat and gave the address and the location of the unconscious man. The phone just stretched as far as the bathroom. Barely controlling her breathing, she did another pulse check and covered him with the bedspread off his bed. Keeping a finger on his pulse, she dialed Ellis Hospital and asked for the emergency room. When the clerk answered, she explained who she was and said it was an emergency and that she needed to speak to the ER doctor STAT.

To her surprise, Dr. Graham Mead came on the line almost at once. He was snickering. "What's the matter, Monsarrat, get your nose stuck someplace where it shouldn't have been?"

Adele rolled her eyes, feeling slightly affronted. It was discouraging how far her reputation had spread. "Graham, listen. The paramedics should be here any minute. We're bringing in Thomas Penn again. His pacer isn't working and he's got a heart rate of thirty. His BP has to be dragging in the sixties somewhere. I think he's got eight hundred milligrams of crushed MS-Contin tabs on board. Don't know how long ago he—"

The sound of glass being crunched underfoot reached her ears. She opened her mouth to scream "Upstairs!" when she felt a sudden pull in her stomach. There'd been no sirens, and she knew from experience that paramedics would come in with plenty of noise. The sound replayed in her head a few times until she matched it with the right image: the broken tumbler accidentally kicked.

"Call one of the cardiologists," she whispered. "We're going to need to get a pacer in him stat. I think he's in third-degree block."

Dr. Mead pressed the phone closer to his ear. "Why are you whispering?" he chuckled. "Is the murderer there?"

"Gotta go," Adele said and stood. With her free hand, she took the Colt out of her waistband. The strange juxtaposition of one hand on an instrument of destruction and one hand in a pose of healing did not escape her.

She let go of Mr. Penn's wrist and in three strides was across the bedroom. Crouched low behind the door, she peered through the crack and saw nothing. For an instant she thought perhaps Helen had escaped the carrier, then recalled the steel bolt that held the cage closed.

Adele tightened her grip on the Colt and tried to slow her breathing. She took a step backward, and flattened herself against the wall. With her gun held in front of her, she peered out to the landing. Nothing. She took a deep, shuddery breath.

I think you're taking this cops and robbers stuff a little too seriously, Monsarrat, said a dour Alex Cross.

She relaxed the muscles in her shoulders and neck. "You're right. I'm being crazy."

A groan came from the bathroom as some part of Mr. Penn's anatomy hit the tub. She ran back and took his pulse again. It might have been her imagination, but it seemed stronger, though more erratic.

On a wave of medical warrior frenzy, she cursed the paramedics under her breath. It had been almost five minutes since she placed the call. The thought came to her that the house was hard to find in the dark, and she ran for the stairs. At the bottom she heard the thin wail of the sirens in the distance.

The bank of light switches next to the entryway were all in the off position. In one sweep, she flipped all of them on. The front of the house, the yard, and the foyer blazed with light. She hoped to Buddha Mr. Penn stayed unconscious until after he was on his way to the hospital: if he saw the amount of electricity being used, he'd have another stroke.

* * *

She gave report while starting the IV. The paramedics were thrilled to deal with a medical professional instead of hysterical or chemically altered family members. On her part, Adele was pleased at the amount of interest they showed in what she had to say, and Mr. Penn—although he wasn't aware of it—benefited from their combined expertise. The only hitch was that no matter which way they turned him or what lead they used, the monitor could not register any kind of readable rhythm through the interference.

The appearance of Trevor Snipes dressed in the blue uniform of a paramedic trainee surprised her. With the change of uniforms, and the absence of his body-piercing ornaments, he was no longer the living testicular melodrama he'd been as a medical transport ambulance driver; he had been magically transformed into a serious professional. Of course, there was nothing he could do about the lightning bolts shaved into the side of his head, but no one seemed to notice.

The second the door to the rig closed, she ran back into the house, retrieved Helen, and turned off the lights. She was about to get into the Beast when she remembered the card and medications next to the phone.

She stared incredulous at the empty surface of the bedside table, then got on her hands and knees to search. She had been with the paramedics the entire time they were there—she would have known if someone had taken them. Desperately, she tried to remember if the medication had been there as the paramedics were carrying Mr. Penn out of the bathroom. She was almost sure it had been.

The chill of new fear ran through her. Every fiber of her was alert and aware of the room—the house. She turned off the light, leaving herself enveloped in dark as she made her way to the stairs. Halfway down she distinctly heard a footfall to her left and up. The third-floor landing.

There was someone there: she knew it in her gut as sure as she knew her name. "I know you're there," she said in a normal voice. "I don't know what you want, but leave the old man alone."

Insulated by an extra layer of insanity, she walked calmly to the door and went out.

Helen was using his self-cleaning litter pan in the Beast's cargo end when the voice of Wanda Percy came over the cell phone. Adele swerved back into her lane, lapsed into her Driving Tourette's, and sped up.

"Well!" Wanda laughed. "The same to you, Ms. Potty Mouth."

"Uh, sorry, Wanda. It's Adele. Don't mind me, I'm driving. Mr. Penn is on his way to Ellis via ambulance. I found him unconscious at home. I'm sure they're going to do an emergency pacer replacement as soon as they can get ahold of either Dr. Tessler or Dr. Zimmer to come in and do it. Can you be there?"

Wanda stole a glance at her date, who was making himself at home in front of her TV. He was getting cozy with the remote. She'd been politely trying to get rid of him since dinner was over an hour ago. "A state of emergency?" she said in a voice loud enough to get the man's attention.

"Well, I don't—" Adele started.

"How many lives are at stake?" Wanda boomed.

"Ah, Wanda? What the hell are you—?"

"And you need me STAT?" Wanda Percy's date looked at her, his face an essay on disappointment. He put down the remote and laid a hand on his jacket.

"I'll be there immediately," the nurse continued. "Meet you in the OR locker."

Despite the adrenaline running a marathon inside her body, Adele snickered. "You have a guest you don't want, huh?"

"Like a stubborn case of measles, girlfriend. Feels bad, looks bad, but there isn't a damned thing I can do about it."

EIGHT

ELLIS HOSPITAL ER WAS BUSY FOR A MOONLESS Tuesday night. As was the norm, the department was understaffed with the minimum number of nurses required by law.

In a perverse sense of order, two doses of .04 milligrams of IV Narcan brought the somnolent Mr. Penn out of his stupor, so that they could put him back to sleep in OR. The twelve-lead EKG confirmed that he was in third-degree heart block and that the pacemaker wasn't firing—which could be viewed as a blessing if one considered what damage could be done by a random electrical charge setting off a lethal rhythm.

The ER's external pacemaker was missing, much to Adele's and the charge nurse's consternation. One of the volunteers was dispatched to the coronary care unit for a loaner replacement, but in the meantime, it felt as if they were walking a tightrope without a safety net.

Dr. Tessler, the tall, stoop-shouldered senior partner in the Marin cardiology cartel, sat at the doctor's dictation desk going over Mr. Penn's medical records. Adele filled him in on details that might not have been clearly stated in the chart—like the fact that the mysterious Dr. English seemed to be practicing some strange and misguided medicine.

The normally reserved cardiologist pushed his reading glasses up the bridge of a nose too small for his face and read the progress notes. "What was his pulse when you found him?"

"About thirty, weak and thready."

He scratched at a patch of white hair over his left temple. "Sounds like an accurate description of my eldest son," he

161

said dryly, then added, "Do you know if he got his gram of Ancef yet?"

"They gave it right after the Narcan." Adele's attention was drawn to the door of the ER lounge through which Kadeja was just arriving, flushed and out of breath. She pulled off her sweater and took her stethoscope from her purse in a way that made Adele think she was late for work.

"Do you know this guy well?" Dr. Tessler asked. "Was he trying to do himself in?"

"I don't think he's the type. I think—" She glanced back at him. "It's my opinion that someone directed him to take those pills."

The physician frowned over the tops of his glasses. "And who, in your opinion, would have done that?"

Adele shrugged. "I think we should ask Mr. Penn that question as soon as he's a little more with it."

Kadeja pulled her long black hair into a ponytail and snapped a wide pink barrette around the base. She glanced rapidly around the department as if searching for something. When she saw Adele, she quickly averted her eyes and moved in the direction of the treatment rooms.

"I've asked Dr. Wortz if I could observe," Adele said, stretching. Her neck cracked twice. "I'll see you down there."

Dr. Tessler yawned and closed the Penn chart. "Okay. I'm waiting for a call from Zimmer. Do me a favor and tell Dr. Wortz I'm on my way."

Adele made a detour to see Mr. Penn, who was being prepped for surgery. Through the window, she saw Kadeja speaking close to his ear.

"Hey, Kadeja, how's our troublemaker?"

"You found him at home?" she asked.

"Ayuhn. He was out like a light, weren't you, Thomas?" She moved to his side, relieved to see the external pacer was working properly.

"Uh-huh." The man was still fuzzy, but able to keep his eyes open. "I was going to take a bath before . . ." He focused on her, his head weaving slightly. "How did you like my chicken?"

"We didn't get that far, Mr. Penn." *Thank Buddha for small favors.*

"We didn't?"

She shook her head. "Nope. You got as far as the bath and called it a night."

He looked around the ER then back at her. "You didn't leave the lights burning, did you?"

She held up a hand. "Everything is off, I swear."

He visibly relaxed into the pillow.

"Are they taking him to surgery now?" Kadeja studied the potentially lethal rhythm plod across the monitor, concern etching furrows in her brow.

"Right away." Adele wished the surgery tech would hurry. Wanda was waiting for her and she still needed to change and scrub in, yet she was unwilling to leave him.

As if powered by her thoughts, the door opened and the OR tech came in pulling the surgical transport gurney. Dr. Tessler and one of the volunteers trailed in behind.

"Ready to go, Thomas?" Dr. Tessler shouted.

"I'm not deaf!" Mr. Penn flared. "You see a little gray hair and some bald spots and you automatically peg a man as deaf, toothless, and addle-brained! Goddamned doctors think you know it all." Mr. Penn shook his fist, his color going from gray to scarlet. "Put a man in the poorhouse with your goddamned fees!"

Eyes flashing, he craned his neck to look at the physician. "The whole goddamned, money-grubbing lot of you can go to hell!"

"There, there, Thomas." Dr. Tessler smiled, patting the man's arm in a patronizing manner. "We're going to swap that old clunker of a pacemaker with a Rolls-Royce." In a fit of un-characteristic physician buffoonery, the doctor made the sound of a revving engine then squealing tires.

Mr. Penn practically choked with rage, and for a second, Adele thought he was going to take a swing at the doctor.

Clueless as to the patient's state of vexation, Dr. Tessler went closer. "Are you allergic to any medications?" he shouted.

Mr. Penn screamed, "NO, you dumb ass! And I don't want

you giving me any of that dope that makes people crazy. I can take any pain you've got to dish out."

The physician nodded, his mind elsewhere. "Good, good, good. Don't you worry, we'll give you the best nap money can buy."

Eyebrows raised, Adele peered at Dr. Tessler to see if he was purposely trying to goad the man. His pale green eyes said he was fighting to keep from laughing.

"Well," he said, on his way out the door, "at least I got the old guy's pressure up."

In the OR, the cast was assembled and ready. Dr. Tessler was expected to administer the anesthesia and monitor vital signs; Dr. Wortz played the role of surgeon; Wanda was pacemaker nurse extraordinare; the scrub nurse, played by a lively redhead named Rusty, was there to assist Dr. Wortz. Standing to one side was Medtronic's pacemaker representative with his bag of goodies: a brand-new sterile generator and compatible leads. The star of the show lay on the table, a blue paper drape hung to shield his head from the rest of his body.

Wanda motioned for Adele to come and stand closer to the table. "Get over here." The paper mask covering her nose and mouth crunched up and down with each word. "There's plenty of room for a stick like you."

Unaccustomed to sterile fields as large as a room, Adele inched across the room, hyperaware of her body as a potential donor of bacteria. Through her head ran useless LED banner messages that had been implanted there during her OR rotation in nursing school:

> DON'T TOUCH ANYTHING BELOW THE LEVEL OF THE TABLE . . . SURGEONS HAVE TEMPER TANTRUMS . . . WATCH FOR FLYING INSTRUMENTS AND DUCK . . . KEEP YOUR HANDS TO YOURSELF . . .

"Helen?" The feeble voice came from the head side of the paper drape. Mr. Penn struggled weakly to sit up.

Adele moved around to where Dr. Tessler was setting up a

bottle of Brevitol. "It's okay, Thomas," she said, wishing she could at least give him a reassuring pat on the shoulder. "Helen is fine. He's all tucked in for the night. You just relax and we'll have you back in your room in a half hour. There's nothing to worry about."

"Is Dr. English here?"

"On his way." . . . *out of the country.* "Don't worry about anything. Just close your eyes and go to sleep."

"I did what he told me." His eyes closed.

Dr. Tessler started the Brevitol, singing to himself.

"I took all the medicine. He said he was com—"

"Sleep tight," Dr. Tessler said with a wink and flushed the IV. Assured his patient was soundly asleep, he immediately broke into his repertoire of one-verse OR songs. "You're Nobody until Somebody Gloves You," "Gonna Take a Sentimental Gurney," Ol' Man Liver, "It Had to Be Flu," and "Some Implanted Evening" had them snorting behind their masks by the time Dr. Wortz was ready to begin.

Adele watched from behind Wanda as Dr. Wortz made the incision directly over the old one. A metal generator, the size of a bulky matchbook, was just under the skin. Unscrewing the generator from its leads, the surgeon lifted it out, examined it briefly under the lamp, and dropped it quickly into a basin.

"Yowzah!" the surgeon said, shaking his hand. "That thing is hot."

Adele pressed her fingers around the piece and yanked them away. He hadn't lied.

They all looked at the square of metal for a minute, though no one said a word about the obvious deep scrape in the metal casing. The rest of the operation went without incident. Five minutes after Dr. Wortz closed, Mr. Penn was awake and asking for Helen.

"What happens now to the old generator?" Adele leaned against the lockers and pulled the shoe covers off her running shoes.

"The cleanup guys throw it into the recycle bin for batteries," Wanda said, removing her hair cover.

"You don't have to send them away to some pacemaker agency or anything?"

"No, why? Do you want it?"

"Absolutely!" Adele said, rushing to retie her shoes. "I was hoping we could figure out what was wrong with it."

Wanda fluffed out her hair and then rubbed at the marks left across her forehead from the band of the hair cover. "Not a bad idea. I wouldn't mind taking a closer look at that case."

"Do you know how they're built inside?" Adele asked. "I mean, if we opened it, would you be able to tell what was wrong with it?"

"I think so." Wanda yanked at the mask hanging from her neck and threw it into the garbage bin. "I used to be pacer rep, so I could probably figure it out."

They arrived at OR suite 3 at the same time as the cleanup crew was going in. Wanda rushed ahead of them and found the basin Dr. Wortz had used for the pacemaker.

She held it out to Adele. It was empty except for a few smears of blood across the bottom.

Wanda turned to the two men wiping down the gurney with bactericidal solution. "Hey, did you guys already discard that generator that was in here?"

Both shook their heads.

The nurses donned gloves and began searching the room. When every waste bucket, shelf, and sink had been investigated, they went to the nurses' lounge. June, one of the circulating nurses, was sitting with her feet up, reading a mangled copy of *People*.

"Hey, June, where's that generator we took out of Mr. Penn?" Wanda asked.

June lowered the magazine. "Wow, if I'd have known how popular that thing was going to be, I would have taken it myself. You're the third person to ask in the last ten minutes."

"Who else has been looking for it?" Adele asked.

"The Medtronic rep and then some doc I've never seen before."

"Did the doc say what his name was?" asked Wanda.

"Dr. . . ." June bowed her head to think. "Pepper! Dr. Pepper. That was it."

"Dr. Pepper?" Wanda said, an uncertain smile beginning at the corners of her mouth.

"This guy told you his name was Dr. Pepper," Adele said, not wanting to believe anyone could be that gullible, "and you believed him?"

"Well . . ." June looked down at the magazine, then back at them. "Yeah. I mean, what's wrong with Dr. Pepp—" Her hand went to her mouth. "Oh, I get it." She laughed. "Dr. Pepper . . . like the soda? Oh my God. How stupid."

"Right," Adele said, her voice level. "What did this guy look like?"

"Tall and dark. Some kind of foreigner," June said. "Kind of handsome."

"Are you sure he was a doctor?" Wanda asked.

"Yeah. Well, I mean, he looked and talked like a doctor. Smelled like one too."

"*Smelled* like a doctor?" Wanda asked. "What the hell does a doctor smell like?"

"You know," said the nurse. "Like hundred-dollar bills that have been wiped off with alcohol swabs."

"I can't believe it disappeared," muttered Wanda on their way back to the lounge. "Usually we have to pay somebody to take the damned things off our hands."

"I want to know who this Dr. Pepper is," Adele said. "I like his sense of . . ."

The door to the doctors' lounge opened and Drs. Wortz and Tessler emerged just as Dr. Wortz was delivering a punch line: ". . . and so the surgeon says: 'Hell, that's no tumor, that's my lawyer!' "

Seeing the nurses, Dr. Wortz raised his hand in greeting. Under the overhead lights, there was glint of metal. Without taking the time to edit her actions, Adele grabbed the surgeon's hand and turned it over. The identifying scratch lay face up.

"Christ on a bike, Dr. Wortz," Adele said in a scolding whine. "We've just spent thirty minutes looking for this thing."

Wanda reached over and took the pacemaker from him, authority written all over her. "I'm sorry, Dr. Wortz, but this one has to be sent to the research department for tests. Whatever were you thinking? Didn't you notice that it was scratched?"

Sheepish guilt replaced the surgeon's smile. "Sorry, I was going to give it to my granddaughter for her careers project in school. If I'd have known . . ."

Wanda smiled in that way that made people want to propose to or legally adopt her. "That's okay. We'll find you a better one for your granddaughter—this one's beat up. We don't want those future doctors and nurses of America thinking we implant damaged equipment in our patients, now, do we?"

"How about tomorrow night at my house?" Adele said as they ascended the back stairs. "I'll make dinner."

Wanda beamed. "Wow. All this and dinner too? You're on, girlfriend. What time?"

"Seven?" Adele said, already thinking she would have to lock Helen and Nelson in the back room. She didn't want the word getting around that she was starting a Weird Animals Home.

Wanda gave her a high five. "I'll bring my appetite and my tools."

At the next landing, Wanda pointed at the door with the blue "3" painted on the outside. "This is where I get off," she said and stopped. "I've never been able to just pop into this place and leave. I have a compelling need to check in at my office. My mom thinks I'm obsessed with my job."

"Yeah," Adele said, continuing up the stairs. "Same here."

"Hey, wait. You're taking the *stairs* to the top floor?" Wanda stared after her, disbelieving.

Adele fished the pacemaker out of her Jogbra and held it up. "It's my insurance against ever needing one of these."

She'd just reached the fifth floor when a door opened and closed below. Sharp, snarling tones of anger caused her to stop and silently retrace her steps. On the landing below, a man and woman were arguing in a language she did not recognize. Leaning over the railing as far as she dared, she could see a pair of scrub pants and a woman's elbow.

Suddenly a masculine hand reached out and roughly grabbed the woman's arm, jerking her out of view. A cry, followed by the unmistakable sound of an open palm meeting flesh, echoed through the stairwell.

Adele had just taken the first step on her way toward the couple when the top of the woman's head came into full view, then it was yanked back again. The sound of the landing door opening and closing was followed by silence.

At the seventh-floor landing, Adele remembered where she'd seen the pink plastic barrette.

Adele's days off were marked on her calendar with stars. They were the only time she allowed herself to sleep in. Sometimes her body took advantage of the reprieve, sometimes it didn't. It was one of those mornings that no matter what she did to stop it, her body was wide awake and raring to go at 4 A.M.

She groaned and turned onto her back. If she was having a dream that was particularly entertaining, she could get her mind to go back inside the brain theater to see how it ended. No such luck today. Today, her mind had conspired with her body, and together they wanted her out of the sack and vertical.

Hugging her knees to her chest, she rocked back and forth until she got enough momentum to kick upward, arch, and land on her feet. It was an acrobatic habit leftover from her marriage to Gavin.

Circus material, said Melinda, the most critical of her imaginary friends. *You're going to break your back someday doing that. And what man is going to want to wake up and know he's spent the night with one of the Flying Wallendas?*

"No need to worry about that," Adele said, pulling on her running shorts. "With my luck, the guy would *be* one of the Flying Wallendas."

Nelson lifted his head from Roddy Rug and yawned, careful not to disturb Helen, who was sleeping soundly against his belly.

Why do you try to scare them away, Adele? Melinda was starting to sound like Linda Tripp.

"I don't try." Adele worked her breasts into a snug Jogbra. "It just happens."

Bullshit, Adele.

She finished tying her shoes and nodded once. "You're right. I try."

Perhaps you should look at that, dear. Perhaps a therapist might help. What about a visit to your friend Dr. Lavine?

Adele stretched, combed through her hair with her fingers, and headed out the door. "I'm not Woody Allen. If I start analyzing every single thing I do, I'll go nuts—like Woody Allen. Now go away."

When she reached the end of the block, paranoia caused her to go back and lock her doors and windows.

Adele drove without incident—unless one considered the fact that she could not remember anything about the drive as an incident—and parked the Beast a block away from the Clemmons Building, behind a car sporting a homemade bumper sticker: ONE MORE WHORE AND WE GET GORE.

She strapped on her fanny pack and began walking the route that Mr. Clemmons had taken the morning of his disappearance. West to Laguna. Two blocks north. The people she thought might be regulars—those folks who looked comfortable in their surroundings, or those who waved and greeted each other as they walked—were her first targets.

The elderly Chinese woman hunched over her cane looked a long while at the newspaper photo of Mr. Clemmons. Finally, she shook her head and moved on.

West on Bay for one block.

The Clover Dairy man was new on the route and didn't know anyone by sight; the middle-aged couple were tourists; the runner didn't slow his pace as he glanced at the photo then shook his head.

Buchanan for two blocks.

The barber said he didn't look out the windows much, because he had to pay attention when working with the scissors.

On Marina Boulevard, she showed the picture to seven joggers, three runners, ten walkers, four people practicing tai chi, six bay-and-bridge gazers (all tourists), and four kite flyers. The last of the Marina crowd were two elderly men playing chess on a bench.

"I seen him around here," said the white-bearded gentleman who gave his name as Bernard. Duffy, the stouter and more grizzled of the two, took the photo and nodded. "Sure. We seen him plenty a times down here. He's one of the walkers."

"Do you remember the last time you saw him?" Adele sat on her haunches.

Bernard took a cherrywood pipe from his pocket. Holding the bowl with stiff, arthritic fingers, he packed the tobacco down with his thumb. "What day was it, Duff, that you messed up a King's Gambit against the Giuoco Piano to knight defense?"

Duffy rubbed the stubble of his chin and glanced over at the Golden Gate as if the answer might be there. "Thursday morning," he said finally. "You yelled at me to stick with the Vienna."

"That's right," Bernard said, the unlit pipe clenched between his back teeth. "Must have been about ten-thirty. Seemed a little later than he's usually down here."

"You didn't see him here Friday morning?" she asked.

"No," Bernard said, a small smile starting. "And we definitely would have seen him that day."

"Yeah," Duffy said. "It was a stinker of a game Friday. We were both playing like the L.A. Rams."

Both men chuckled and watched a young woman runner dressed in a well-filled-out Jogbra and a pair of spandex shorts shoot by.

"Was he with anyone on Thursday? Did you notice him talking with anyone?"

Bernard lit his pipe, and Adele leaned closer. The smell of pipe tobacco always brought the memory of her father vividly alive. Both men shook their heads in unison.

"He sat over there for a long time," Bernard said, pointing the mouthpiece of the pipe at a bench across the path and down about ten yards.

"Yeah," Duffy said. "That wasn't like him to sit down. He didn't look so good neither, now that I think of it."

Bernard nodded. "True. Peaked. He looked peaked."

Adele thanked them and turned down their offer of a game. On the return trip, she covered the opposite side of the streets, stopping in at the little coffee shops and bakeries. Three people had seen Raymond Clemmons, but no one could remember which day.

The mom-and-pop grocery was the last commercial establishment before the neighborhood went strictly residential. A loud buzzer greeted her ears when she opened the door. No one was behind the small counter. Glancing around, she made her way down one of the three tiny aisles to the dairy and cold beverage cooler at the back of the store.

"Hello? Anybody here?"

The front door to the shop opened, and a Chinese man wearing a red apron and a white butcher's cap came in looking for her. "I help you find something?"

"I hope so." She held out the newspaper photo. "This man—have you ever seen him before?"

His eyes did not move from her face. "You police?" he asked.

The question took her off guard. "I'm a deputy investigator with the Marin County sheriff's department." The title rolled so easily off her tongue, she had a fleeting thought that she was beginning to believe it herself.

"You have ID?"

The fact that he never took his eyes off her face and his self-assured demeanor made her wonder if he were an undercover cop or just a street-smart guy who knew how to handle himself.

She produced the leather case from her pack and flipped it open. She was getting better at this maneuver; at least it didn't fly out of her hand anymore.

He studied the printed information carefully, finally looking from the picture to her, double-checking the likeness. When he was satisfied, he nodded and slipped his hands back into the wide pocket of his apron.

"Yes, I know this man. Raymond. I not see him since Friday. He in trouble?"

"He's dead." She said it as an apology. "He was murdered."

The shop owner registered his dismay by sucking in a breath. "This is sad," he said. "He was friend to many people here. Always happy. Who did this?"

"That's what we're trying to find out. You said you saw him Friday. Do you remember what time? Did he say anything to you?"

"He walk by with Haresh about ten o'clock maybe." The man suddenly drew his hand from his apron and held it out to her. "My name Kim Fong."

She shook his hand and waited for him to finish.

He took another deep breath. "They walked slow that day. I thought they would come in store. Sometimes they come in, buy water or juice—take it with them. Sometimes, when business slow, we go outside and talk. On Friday—"

The buzzer went off. A tough-looking boy entered the shop wearing a black leather jacket covered with silver studs, and Nike cross-trainers with neon orange laces. Under his arm he clasped a white motorcycle helmet with silver stripes. At the counter, he reached into his back pocket for his wallet.

Kim Fong hurried past her to the small cubby that housed the cash register. The biker mumbled something she could not hear and jutted his chin toward the cartons of cigarettes locked behind an iron grille. Before the shopkeeper could ask to see his ID, the biker removed his license and held it up.

Mr. Fong took it out of the man's hand and studied it with the same concentration he'd given hers. Impatient for his smokes, the biker rolled his head.

"Ah, come on, man," he whined. "You do this to me every fucking time I come in here. Don't you know me by now?"

Unruffled, Mr. Fong handed the man his license and unlocked the door to the cabinet. "You think all Chinese look alike? I think all punks look alike. I sell to two hundred people a day—they all look like you. How you expect me to keep track?"

The biker mumbled and pocketed his wallet.

While she waited, Adele studied the display of postcards: The Crookedest Street in the World, The Golden Gate Bridge at night, Coit Tower, the Transamerica Building, and naked babes riding cable cars. Some things would stay the same forever.

"Punks," the shopkeeper said, jerking his thumb in the direction of the door as he came out from behind the counter. "We leave Chinatown because of them. But," he said with a resigned sigh, "it just as bad here. The punks steal me blind."

Adele pursed her lips and nodded solemnly in commiseration. "Okay, so you saw Raymond last Friday about ten."

He nodded, and his hands went back into the apron pocket. "Yes. On Friday I thought they would come in, but they don't. The beer came at the same time, so I don't go out to say hello. Many times if we don't talk on way down, they stop on way back. Friday they no stop either way. I wondered why."

"Did you see anyone else with them, or someone who pulled up in a car to talk?"

He shook his head. "I did not pay so close attention. I was busy with beer delivery. Get all my beer on Fridays."

"Do you know this Haresh person?"

Kim smiled. "Ah yes. Haresh first customer when I come here. We are both lovers of tea. We trade samples. I get special Chinese tea only for Chinese. He go to India and bring many kind of tea from India and Africa. I give him rare pear jasmine dragon phoenix, he bring me Ceylon silvertip endare." He frowned. "I have not seen Haresh since Friday. Very unusual. He is not injured or . . . ?"

"No," Adele said quickly, then, "At least not that I know of. You wouldn't have Haresh's phone or address, would you? I'd like to talk to him."

Ducking behind the counter, he pulled out a tattered notebook, each page covered with numbers and Chinese writing. He laid it on the counter between them and set his finger hunting through the pages. "I make joke and call him Mr. Green," Mr. Fong said. "Ah, here: Haresh Shahani. He lives Ivy Alley. I write phone number for you."

When he handed her the number, Adele shook hands again and gave him her card. "If you think of anything else, you can contact me either by phone, cell phone, or e-mail. It's all on that card."

He tacked it to the corkboard behind the cash register and walked with her outside.

"How Raymond murdered?" he asked. From the hesitation in his voice, it was plain he'd been debating whether or not to ask.

"Mr. Fong," Adele said, meeting his eyes, "did you like this man?"

"Yes. He was . . ." Kim Fong waited for a bus to go by. ". . . kind. He had much honor."

"In that case, I don't think you really want to know."

Haresh Shahani lived only a mile or two from the Clemmons Building, but in a city as financially diverse as San Francisco, a mile could house five different tax brackets. Ivy Alley was definitely in one of the lower brackets.

Adele was careful not to touch anything as she walked down the alleyway looking for a green door. Grapefruit rinds, spotted with velvet green mold, lay scattered in the street, giving off smells not unlike those in the morgue. Dented galvanized garbage cans overflowed with black and white plastic bags hanging over the sides. The rats had left so many frayed-edged holes that if she squinted, the bags took on the appearance of lace.

San Francisco rats were worthy of some substantial thought. While she was attending San Francisco State, she had lived in the city. Late at night when she sat in her window perch studying, she'd see them scurrying through the streets, large as unneutered alley cats and twice as vicious.

A plastic bag shifted and dumped an empty can of black beans, a wad of eggshells, and half an onion covered in coffee grounds on the street in front of her, causing her to pick up her pace. Four or five buildings down, the garbage cans changed into neat, undented specimens, all nicely tucked inside bins painted with landscapes and street scenes. Windows held planter boxes instead of bars, and lace curtains covered the windows instead of ripped shades.

The lime green door was a study in scuff marks and smudgy fingerprints. She squinted and stepped back, framing it between her fingers. She could picture it hanging in the Silver Circle Gallery with a $45,000 price tag.

Inside her hand frame, the door yawned open to reveal a smallish Indian man wearing a Nehru jacket the same color as the door. His brown cherubic face seemed to rest, like a bowl on a table, atop the high collar of the jacket. They stood there looking at one another for a moment before anyone spoke.

"Mr. Shahani?"

"Yes. That is me." He spoke in a rapid, choppy cadence with a gentle upswing to the end of the last word of every sentence. "Who are you please?"

"I'm Adele Monsarrat. I called from Mr. Fong's grocery store?"

"Ah, yes. I am sorry. I did not expect someone so young. Please. Come in."

Though dark and small, the room was cozy. Sparsely furnished, it contained a couch covered by a green Indian bedspread in a paisley design that was so popular in the early seventies. Next to a beaded doorway was an ornate brass stand, on which lay a stack of books and an incense burner. The rich smell of sandalwood permeated the air.

"Please. Sit down." The man held his hand out toward one corner of the room, where there were a wooden table and two chairs—all painted green. "Would you like some tea? I have a pot of very nice tea brewing."

"Thank you," she said, and sat down under a framed rendering of Jesus. His pierced hand was held up in what she knew as the peace sign, He looked down at her from the green wall. He appeared to be suffering, but then again He *did* have a crown of thorns both on His head and around His visibly glowing, blood-dripping heart. From the look of His coronary arteries, she figured Him for at least a triple vessel bypass.

Mr. Shahani returned with a tray holding cups, sugar, and a pot. Except for the sugar, all were green. She breathed in the aromatic streamers of steam coming off the tea.

"Mr. Shahani—"

"Please." He held up two fingers in an exact imitation of the Jesus above her head. "Call me Haresh."

"Okay. Haresh, were you a good friend of Mr. Raymond Clemmons?"

All traces of the smile faded, and his face seemed to lose its shine. "Yes," he replied, bowing his head. "It is very sad. I miss him."

"Mr. Fong said that you frequently walked with him in the mornings?"

He nodded. "This is true. He was a very good walker. Every morning we walked to St. Francis Yacht Club."

"Did you walk with Mr. Clemmons last Friday morning?"

"Yes and no." He looked into his tea. "He had been away in Europe on a vacation, but he called early that morning to say he would meet me at the corner of Laguna and Francisco. When I arrived, Raymond was not there so I walked to meet him. I found him around the corner from his house. He was leaning against a building. His face was white. He was holding his stomach like this . . ."

Haresh stood, and with a dramatic air worthy of Anthony Hopkins, transformed his face into a grimace of pain, bent in at the middle, and hobbled to the beaded curtain. It was a convincing performance of what Adele recognized as the post-op shuffle.

Haresh sat back down. "I told my friend he must go to the doctor. He said his wife insists that he must go to her doctor. But Raymond hates her doctor. He said he is going to see a different doctor but he does not want his wife to know, so that is why he leaves the house as if he is taking his usual walk. You see? He was going to see this doctor."

Adele stopped writing. "Did he tell you what was wrong?"

Haresh shook his head. "Not too much. I think he has something wrong in his stomach. He touches it a lot. I tell him, 'You must come to my house. I will drive you to the doctor.' He says no, he will take a taxi."

"Did he mention the doctor's name?"

"Yes." Haresh said, "Dr. Flanagan on Van Ness."

"Did Mr. Clemmons ever talk to you about any trouble he had with anyone?"

"No," Haresh said, then added thoughtfully, "Except his wife."

Adele stared at him. "He had trouble with Mrs. Clemmons?"

"Oh yes." He nodded enthusiastically. "She is very bad to him."

"Why do you say that?"

Haresh laced his hands together. "She was nagging at Raymond all the time. She wants this, she wants that. First it is remodeling of the home, next she wants big expensive ring of many jewels. Then it is a trip to Europe. Raymond, he was very, very sad because he loved her but . . ." Haresh raised his eyebrows with his shoulders in a combo eyebrow-shoulder shrug. "Still she is not happy. I think to myself that he is sick in his stomach because she tells him many times that he is old and fat and she will find another man."

"Mr. Clemmons told you this?" She was having a hard time putting the grieving Mrs. Clemmons into the picture Haresh was painting.

"Oh yes." Haresh nodded. "He talked about this to me many, many times. It makes him sad."

"May I see your phone book?"

He went to the couch and dropped to his knees. For a split second, she thought he was going to pray for one. Instead, he pulled the thick directory out from underneath.

She made note of Dr. Flanagan's address and gave Haresh her card.

At the door he handed her a small package of tea. "Which end of alley did you come in?" he asked.

She pointed in the direction where the Beast was parked.

"Oh, that is very bad," he said gravely, shaking his head. "Rats come in that end. Very, very big rats that will attack you." He pointed in the opposite direction. "Go the long way so you live to enjoy the tea."

The Beast did not like the wear and tear on its brake pads that the hills of San Francisco required of all vehicles traveling its streets. Under the influence of the evil demon that inhabited its nasty, motorized soul, the Beast waited until it got to the head of a long line of cars on the Powell Street hill before performing its Going to Sleep trick. "Trick," Adele liked to explain, because no mechanic who'd ever crawled under its hood had been able to pinpoint the problem.

Adele guessed that the spaced-out mechanic in Sausalito came closest to the truth when he said the problem was congenital, and that the car had probably been custom-built for Satan.

The only other theory that sounded halfway plausible was that aliens had tried to clone an earthling car with a mind of its own. But, like Frankenstein's monster, the wrong mind had been installed—and oh, what an evil mind it was.

The cars behind her could pass only by moving into the oncoming traffic lane. As they went by, each driver threw her evil glances and gestures that made clear the terrible fate they wished upon her and her heap of junk.

A band of skateboarders stopped to ask if they could help. Before she could say, "No, that won't be necessary, I'm going to commit suicide right here," two of the grease-monkey wannabes were swarming under the hood, while the others jumped on rear and front bumpers, rocking the mechanical canker sore like a seesaw.

After the skateboarding mechanics went away defeated, and when she was sufficiently hardened against the various maledictions and middle-finger salutes from other motorists, she locked the doors, kicked the miserable thing in what she thought might be its balls, and headed north, looking for an auto dismantling shop.

She was five yards into her journey, when the Beast started all by itself.

For all its demonics, Adele got the distinct feeling the Beast had a deep fear of abandonment.

The inside of Dr. Flanagan's office was old San Francisco, just like the pre-1906 building that housed it: mahogany paneling, dark brown and gray terrazzo floors, and uncomfortable wood chairs that hurt your butt. They reminded Adele of the chairs the nuns made the bad kids sit in during catechism.

In a bizarre variation on the Employee of the Month plaque, hanging on the wall was a photograph of a bloody human organ lying on a blue sterile towel. The card underneath read:

GALL BLADDER OF THE MONTH: MRS. CHARLEMAGNE "TUPPER" GROGAN.

She'd stepped up to the reception counter with her fake ID badge held out like a cross. Like the receptionists in most Bay Area doctors' offices, the two women behind the counter were of the officious, self-appointed watchdog persuasion. Snappish and impolite, they shielded "The Doctor" against all patients—especially the female ones—as doggedly as a jealous wife guards her husband at a party of Playboy Bunnies.

"What is it you need to ask Dr. Flanagan about?" asked the tall blonde with the Drew Barrymore chin.

"That's confidential police information," Adele answered. "But it shouldn't take more than a few minutes."

"Is this about one of The Doctor's patients?" The older woman was one of those people who talked with her eyelids partly closed and fluttering. Adele was fascinated by the combination of eggshell-blue eyeshadow on the right eyelid and violet on the left.

"I'm sorry," Adele said in an absurdly pleasant voice. "That's still confidential department information."

"Well, is it medical, personal, or financial information you're after?" The Chin asked.

Adele's head cocked to one side. "I can't divulge that information," she said slowly, but with an edge. "Is the doctor available to speak with me?"

Eyes and The Chin glanced at one another and then back at her. Simultaneously, Eyes said yes and Chin said no.

A man stepped into the reception area to ask if there'd been any calls from his wife. Over the breast pocket of his lab coat "Scott Flanagan, M.D." was embroidered in red. Instantly, both Chin and Eyes moved together as if to shield the physician from Adele's dreadful rays.

Adele waved her ID over their heads. "Deputy Investigator Monsarrat here. I need a few minutes of your time, Doctor."

"Oh," Dr. Flanagan said, mildly surprised. "Okay. Come on back to my office."

"But, Dr. Flanagan, you have an eleven o'clock," Eyes protested bitterly.

"She doesn't have an appointment, Doctor," Chin threw in with a resentful tilt of her most prominent feature.

"That's okay, ladies, she's police." The bespectacled, balding man opened the door and motioned for her to come in. "I've always got time for the police, especially when they're pretty."

Under hostile, icy glares, Adele sailed past the dogs, issuing a little bark over her shoulder as she went.

"I have a few questions about Raymond Clemmons," Adele said, once they were in his office with the door closed.

The physician frowned. "Raymond Clemmons? That's not a familiar name. Are you sure he's one of my patients?" He reached for the phone.

"I believe he—"

He held up a finger and spoke into the receiver. "Tammy, will you please locate a patient file on Raymond Clemmons?"

"He had some kind of stomach trouble," she continued. "He called your office Friday morning and made an appointment for later that morning."

"Oh yes!" Dr. Flanagan nodded. "I remember. He wasn't really my patient, but he didn't want to go to his regular doctor and asked if—"

The phone rang. Again, he held up a finger and picked up the receiver. He listened for five seconds, thanked Tammy, and hung up.

"I spoke with him briefly about his problem and suggested he come in right away. He never showed up."

"And exactly what was his problem?"

Dr. Flanagan sat back in his chair. "I'm afraid that's confidential patient information. I wouldn't be able to release that to the police unless there's a court . . ."

"Dr. Flanagan," Adele said, leaning forward, "I'm sorry if I didn't make the situation clear—this is a homicide investigation. Mr. Clemmons was murdered last Friday. We've traced his movements right up to the point he got into a taxi to come to *this* office."

As the information sunk in, Adele noticed his hands went still and the tight smile around his mouth came to an abrupt halt. She guessed he was thinking about his attorney.

He sat up again. "Well, if you put it that way . . ."

Adele nodded. "So what did he tell you?"

Dr. Flanagan tapped his pen nervously on his desk blotter. "He said he had a rash across his abdomen and that he'd broken the skin from scratching at it. He described the area as being hot to the touch with some yellowish drainage, and a low-grade fever. It sounded infected. I asked him why he didn't make an appointment with his own doctor, and he said he couldn't get an appointment fast enough, but I had a feeling there was more to it than that."

"Did he give you the name of his physician?"

The phone rang again. "Yes, Tammy?" He sighed, sounding like a henpecked husband. "Yes, Tammy, I know what time it is, thank you." To Adele he replied, "I didn't ask: It was less than a four-minute conversation. I told him to come in, but he never showed up."

"Do you remember what time he called?"

He thought for a minute. "It had to be around ten-thirty, because I had an opening at eleven."

Adele thanked him. On her way out, she endured the glares of Chin and Eyes, wondering how the hell Mr. Clemmons had managed to get past them on his first try.

Instead of the Silent Treatment, the Beast was giving her the Mysterious Noise Treatment as a way of punishing her for their prolonged stay in the city. The sudden appearance of clanks, pings, and metallic rubbing sounds coming from various parts of the Beast's anatomy usually gave rise to panicky visions of engine parts and wheels flying off the car as she traveled the congested highways.

The faint *ping ping brong!* from the left side of the motor began as she turned south onto Van Ness Avenue. Heading toward the heart of the city, rather than toward Marin, pushed the Beast beyond its limit. Now it was going to hit below the fan belt and strike up the band of distress noises. The ping ping went to a flat-out grind and finished off with a *roombah ding!* But, like the boy who cried wolf, the Beast ceased to affect her. Adele tuned out the shandrydan's whining complaints and continued on to the Sutter-Stockton parking garage. She took her ticket and drove to the top floor, making sure to park nose out—just in case the Beast wasn't faking.

The lobby of 450 Sutter was crowded with people vacating the building for lunch. Many of them were dressed in lab coats and wore the bored, dismal expressions of those involved in the health care system.

The office directory listed nothing for the office of Dr. Edward English. Dr. France and Dr. German, yes, but no Dr. English. The security station facing the elevators consisted of a desk, a chair, and an obese baby-faced man dressed in a khaki-colored uniform faintly reminiscent of the California Highway Patrol. Prominently displayed on his hip were his gun and baton. Leaning back in the chair so that its front two legs came high off the ground, he gazed at the crowd impassively, arms crossed over his chest. She imagined he'd done the same thing throughout his school years as a little act of rebellion against the teachers who told him not to.

"Excuse me," Adele smiled, "but I was wondering if you know where the office of Dr. Edward English is located? I don't see it on the directory."

The man glanced at her briefly and looked away, giving no indication he'd heard her.

She stepped in front of him, speaking louder. "Hi. Can you tell me where Dr. Edward English's office is? I don't see it on—"

"No," he said without looking at her.

"This is four-fifty Sutter Street?"

"You're going to have to move out of my way so I can see the lobby," he said, keeping his eyes focused on the crowd.

A very old woman with a cane and thick glasses hobbled up to the desk. The ghostly white of her face was set off by the bright red lipstick that had bled into the wrinkles around her mouth. Blue veins were visible through the translucent skin. It was, Adele thought, a very patriotic look.

"Excuse me, young man, but where is the pharmacy?" she warbled in a voice as wobbly as her legs. "It's supposed to be in this lobby. I can't see much with these old peepers, and—"

"Don't know." The security officer jerked a pudgy hand in front of them to motion them out of the way.

"What?" the relic shouted. "Got to speak up. I'm deaf too."

The officer leveled cold eyes on the four-foot, eight-inch woman. "I don't know," he mumbled, so that even Adele had to strain to hear him.

The old woman shook her head, looking helpless. "I can't hear you, son. Can you please—"

Adele put an arm around the woman's shoulders and walked her across the lobby to the doors of the pharmacy. When she returned to the desk, a smug, triumphant expression had settled over his face.

"Let's try this again," she said in a razor-blade tone. "Do you know if Dr. English has an office in this building?"

He ignored her, although his neck and jowls were beginning to flush pink.

She made sure his badge and sleeve insignia said "Security Force" before pulling out her badge. Her eyes narrowed. "You need to change professions, my friend. You don't seem cut out for public service."

He glanced at the ID and then at her. From the looks of him, she guessed his blood pressure to be about 230 over 150. She put the badge away and got out her notebook. "How long have you worked in this building?"

"What's your problem, lady?" The surly expression said he was going to make it as difficult as possible.

"This is a homicide investigation," she replied evenly. She didn't want to get into any control issues with him. "We're trying to locate a physician by the name of Edward English who allegedly had an office in this building."

"Somebody's pulling your leg," the man sneered in an unhappy, bitter guy way.

"What's that supposed to mean?" she asked impatiently.

"Dr. Edward English is the name of a local punk-rock band."

"Exactly," she said, not missing a beat—she wasn't going to let him have any fun at all. "This is the man they named the band after. He saved the drummer's life."

His face went through a couple of changes, growing more scarlet as it did so.

"Nobody by that name ever had an office in this building," he said, his foot beginning to bounce, "or I'd know about it."

"Other than too long, how long have you been here?"

He had to think about the statement for a second before he got it. "Five years."

"Thanks." She closed the notebook and put it away. "Do me a favor and don't abuse the old ladies anymore, okay? Go home and beat up your pillow or something."

His eyes bored into her. "And why don't you go fuck yourself?" he said, taking a step toward her.

Not wanting to incite an incident, she turned and headed across the lobby, only half confident she wouldn't get a bullet in the back of her head. California was the Right to Go Postal State, after all.

Like a horse that finds new energy once it knows it's going back to the barn, the Beast raced through the rainbow tunnels toward Larkspur more smoothly than she could ever remember. There wasn't a single ping to be heard.

Once in Marin, she promised herself she'd go straight home and start cooking. She told herself that Ward 8 could get along without her for one twenty-four-hour period. Her patients were all fine, and nobody was dying because she wasn't there. She promised herself all the way through the lobby and up the stairs to the eighth floor and through the double doors.

Malloy nodded. "Ms. Monsarrat. May joy and peace surround you this lovely evening."

"Tell that to my car," she said, sitting beside him and simultaneously poking his ticklish spot with her forefinger. Malloy jumped a couple of inches off his seat and giggled.

She tapped the monitor screen. Under her finger ran the rhythm that belonged to Mr. Penn. "How's he doing?"

"Fine. His new generator is firing and capturing appropriately. They've checked it with the programmer, and it's all set. I just delivered his second dose of Ancef to his nurse."

The monitor tech looked her in the eye—something Malloy

rarely did with anyone. "Do you have a hard time breaking attachments and believing that things will take their own path without your help?"

If it was a rare occurrence for Malloy to look her in the eye, it was exceptional for him to be so direct and personal.

"Well, I, ah, I just like to—I mean, I was going right past the hospital and . . . I . . . thought . . . I'd—"

He held up a hand, two fingers in the V position. He looked, absent the bleeding heart and thorns, a lot like the portrait of Jesus on Mr. Shahani's wall. "I'm sorry," he said, bowing his shaved Buddhist skull. "Don't answer that. It's none of my business."

"No, it's okay, Malloy," Adele said quietly. "I do have a hard time letting things unfold. I can't stand suspense." She chuckled. "I even read books end to beginning because I have to know how they turn out."

He smiled. "You do?"

"Ayuhn." She sighed and got up. "It's not easy reading a book that way."

"Then I probably shouldn't tell you about the person who called here looking for you after you left last night," Malloy said.

"Who was it?"

"I don't know; she wouldn't leave a name or a message."

"What did she say, exactly?"

"She wanted to know if you'd gone home. I told her you had, then she asked how long ago and if she could have your home phone number. I told her I couldn't give out that information, so then she wanted to know where you lived. I told her I couldn't give out that information either, and she hung up."

"Maybe it was Mr. Penn's daughter."

A page for Dr. Sneade came over the PA system. In the background of the switchboard office, a woman cackled: "You're so bad, baby! Oh, you're so bad!"

Malloy shook his head. "Mr. Penn's offspring called here last night and spoke to Dr. Wortz. If she'd wanted to talk to you, I think she'd have asked for you then, and besides, I would have recognized her voice."

"I'm going to surprise you on this one, Malloy," Adele

said, moving toward Mr. Penn's room. "I'm going to let this little mystery go and not dwell on it. I'll let the mystery reveal itself to me in its own time. I can do this."

She got all the way to Mr. Penn's room before she turned around.

"Malloy? You *sure* there wasn't anything else she said?"

"How are you feeling, sport?" Adele asked, glad for the absence of flickering lights.

Mr. Penn smiled. "Ready to go back to work."

Adele groaned. "Give your body a day or two to heal, would you, please?"

"I want to thank you for being so good to me and Helen," he said, his eyes growing moist. "You saved my life."

They sat holding hands.

"Is Helen . . . ?"

"Fine," Adele said. "All settled in."

She searched around for an appropriate opening, found none, and shifted in her seat. "Mr. Penn, do you remember anything about what happened before you blacked out?"

He looked at her in surprise. "I've been lying here trying to recall that very thing," he said. "I remember coming home feeling punk, so I called Dr. English. He called right back and said to take the pills they gave me at the clinic." The man's face changed, and some of the old fury sneaked back into his voice. "You won't find any of these robbers over here calling you back so quick. SOBs make you wait for hours until they get off the goddamned golf course. You could be dying and they wouldn't—"

"Do you remember how many he told you to take?" Adele cut him off before the cavalry was called out.

"Not offhand. I think I wrote it down. I don't know, he might have said to take three or four. I asked him twice because it seemed like a lot. They were big."

"Did you tell him exactly how you'd been feeling?"

He glared at her. "Of course. I'm not an idiot, young lady. He said he'd come right over. I went downstairs to unlock the door and that just about did me in. I dropped a glass of water on the way back up and was so plum tuckered out that I didn't have the strength to clean it up." He chuckled and shook his head. "It took me some time to get back upstairs, but I took the pills like the doctor said and got in the bath to relax. That's all I remember until I got to the hospital."

Rymesteade Dhery waved at them from the door. "How're you doing, Mr. Penn?"

"How much is this little howdy-do going to cost me?" Mr. Penn glowered.

"Free of charge." Dr. Dhery held up his hands. "I just came in to say hi and steal Ms. Monsarrat away for a few minutes."

"Don't you keep her too long," Mr. Penn said. "Helen is going to be wanting his dinner."

Adele rose and patted the man's leg. "See you tomorrow, Mr. Penn. Sleep tight."

Mr. Penn motioned her to come close. "Just one more thing," he whispered, his mouth close to her ear. "If Helen has any trouble, you know, with his elimination?"

Adele bit the inside of her cheek. "Mmmm?"

"Mash up some soaked prunes and put them in his food." He winked. "Works like magic."

Outside in the hall, Rymesteade faced her, arms crossed over his chest. He looked as if he hadn't slept.

"What's the haps?" Adele asked, crossing her own arms. She and Rymesteade looked like a pair of Jack Bennys about to give a monologue.

"Have you talked to Cynthia lately?"

"Yeah, why?"

"I don't want you to break any confidences or anything, but she's driving me mad and I can't get to what the problem is. She won't talk to me."

The physician became wildly animated, pacing a few steps back and forth and talking with his hands. "One minute we'll be sitting there, as normal as Cynthia can be, and the next minute she's telling me to go F myself. Then we'll be having a nice conversation about something like the new postman, or the price of milk, and she starts to cry and won't tell me what's wrong. Okay, so I think maybe she's having some hormonal changes, and it will pass, but then I think, this has been going on for several weeks, so it isn't PMS. And here's the wild one: this morning I woke up at two-thirty and found her kneeling next to my side of the bed, staring at my nose. When I asked what she was doing, she slapped me and stormed into the kitchen.

"So I'm thinking, 'Well, maybe her job is getting to be too much and she needs a vacation, or maybe I left one of the towels on the floor in the bathroom. So, I haul myself out of bed and go out to sit with her, thinking maybe we can have a cup of tea and talk things over. I walk into the kitchen and she's frying up a chicken and reading the directions on a chocolate cake mix. She refused to talk to me—acted like I was invisible. For the next three hours, she cooked everything in the freezer, including the frozen vegetables, wrapped it all up, and put it back into the freezer.

"Then she started on the fruit. She either fried or pureed every piece of fruit we had in the apartment, wrapped that up with the chocolate cake, and put *those* in the freezer too. The pasta was next and then the canned goods. There isn't one morsel of uncooked food in the house!"

He put his hands on his hips. "So what the hell is going on with her? If you know, tell me, Del, or I'm going to start thinking about having her psychiatrically evaluated. With the way her mind works, we'd never get her out of Unit A."

"She won't talk to me either," Adele said. "But I'll try again if you want."

"That's scary." Rymesteade shook his head. "If she won't talk to you, that's bad."

For a while they stared at their shoes.

"I'll see if I can get her to talk," Adele said finally. "I'll invite her over for something that isn't frozen."

"That would be terrific," the physician said gratefully. "If you can just find out what's set her off."

Adele watched him walk away, worried that he had let himself get too involved. Cynthia was not the type of woman to stay with one man for very long, and she knew from the symptoms he described that Rymesteade was running out of time.

NINE

ADELE LIKED TO COOK, BUT EVEN SO, SHE OFTEN set about preparing a meal weighing the time spent cooking (hours) against the time spent eating (seconds to minutes, depending), and how appreciative the diners might be (disdainful to ecstatic). Wanda Percy looked like someone who loved food no matter whether it had a face or not.

Wanda sipped a glass of chilled chardonnay as Adele glided around the kitchen preparing spring greens soup, endive with warm goat cheese hors d'oeuvres, and tofu hummus with hot sourdough bread.

Alternately solemn over their single-woman woes, and then choked by peals of hard laughter over Geek Dates from Hell that went terribly wrong, they went as far as making analogies between themselves and the sourdough: hard and crispy outside and melt-in-the-mouth soft on the inside.

Wanda took a gray cloth bag out of her purse and set about unknotting the drawstring that held it closed. Adele retrieved the pacemaker from the pocket of a winter coat she kept in the hall closet.

"Insertion, removal, and now exploratory surgery," Wanda said, setting her instruments out on the table. "Let's give this baby a good going over." She brought the jeweler's eyepiece so close to the metal that it actually touched it.

Presently, she handed Adele a strong magnifying glass and, with a pair of small pickups, pointed to the seam around the generator. "See where the gouge is?"

"You mean the thing that looks like the Grand Canyon?"

"Look above it—all along there: do you see the smaller marks?"

Adele pursed her lips. "Looks like somebody was trying to pry the seam apart."

"Which tells me there's been tampering with the insides." Wanda sat back and pushed the eyepiece up so that it sat in the middle of her forehead, like the stump of a horn. "There usually aren't any markings on the case except the name of the company that manufactured it. Another thing: pacemakers are always encased in cadmium steel. I don't know what this is, but it sure isn't that." Wanda gripped the case in both hands and exerted enough pressure to make the muscles in her forearms distend with the effort. There was a muffled snap, and the case came open. She studied the mechanism for several minutes before picking up a small surgical clamp, called a mosquito. She moved a few things around with all the care one might give an infant's brain during neurosurgery.

"Hello, Dr. Watson. What have we here?" Wanda readjusted the lamp, studying the generator from different angles.

"What is it?"

Wanda pointed to a quarter-inch square no more than an eighth of an inch thick with metal contacts around the edges. The plastic was black, with an iridescence of purple and blue. "You got me, girlfriend," Wanda said. "Looks like it might house a computer chip of some kind, but whatever it is, it sure doesn't belong inside that pacemaker."

She snapped the pacemaker together and put it into a plastic biohazard envelope. "My sister has a friend who's a computer guru in Silicon Valley. This guy knows everything there is to know about computer technology. He's at work now, but I'll call him tomorrow and see if he can look at it."

"Great." Adele yawned. Wanda followed suit. Both jaws popped at the same time.

The mild spring night was conducive to nurse stories. Adele meant only to walk Wanda to her car, but the nurse mentioned the fact that the pacer clinic had lost three nurses to downsizing, and they were off. At some point they'd started walking, so that by the time they made the transition from nursing politics (Adele referred to them more appropriately as "politricks") to favorite patient stories, they found themselves at Rulli's picking at a plate of nonfat biscotti.

At the table next to theirs, a group of teenage boys were alternately boisterous and subdued. For a time the two women listened with concealed amusement to the Notorious Breakers of Rules bray and brag about their conquests with girls and sports as they pushed spilled sugar around the marble tabletop with their fingers, making pornographic images.

"I remember when I was working in Acute CCU a hundred years ago." Wanda bit into her second biscotti. "I took care of one of the Forty-Niners. This guy was the biggest man I'd ever seen in my life!"

"Six-foot-seven and two hundred and ninety pounds?"

Wanda pulled back to look at her. "Who said anything about tall?" She brushed crumbs off her blouse and leaned forward, lowering her voice. "Girlfriend, this man was down to his knees, and may I be struck by lightning this minute if that ain't the truth."

Adele was horrified. "His knees?"

"His knees," Wanda said, at the same time making eye contact with a nice-looking gentleman standing at the counter. The man smiled and waved, then adjusted the yellow ascot blooming in the V of his beige sweater. The size and number of rings he wore brought the word "Mafia" to Adele's mind.

Wanda sipped her wine and returned the man's smile. "I dated that Forty-Niner for two years. A fine man he was."

"What happened?"

"He got too greedy. Wanted me all to himself. And," she shrugged, "my parts couldn't take the wear and tear anymore."

Adele looked at her friend in wonder. "How do you do it? I mean, what do you do to make men fall over you?"

"Nothing, honey. That's what they like. The less I fuss, the more they like me. It gets to be a real drawback. Now take this fox over there by the counter."

Adele glanced at the man, who was watching them with more interest than if he'd been looking at a couple of naked showgirls. She checked to make sure her breasts hadn't some-how worked their way out of her Jogbra and into the open.

"That boy over there been checkin' us out, girlfriend," Wanda said, her smile going sexy and crafty at the same time. "He's got something on his mind, and I can tell you right now, it ain't coffee." Wanda leaned forward on her elbows and wet her lips, letting her tongue drag slowly over both upper and lower lips. The gesture was positively X-rated. "Now, some young girl who doesn't know any better might go running over there to stake her claim," Wanda continued. "But if you just lay back and act like you could care less, they start think-ing that whatever you got must be pretty hot stuff."

Adele shook her head and chuckled. "You ever married?"

Wanda glared, held up two fingers in the sign of a cross, and hissed like a cat. "No way! For me marriage would be like a sore-assed duck sitting in a salt pond." She shivered and hugged herself. "Uh, uh, uh. Don't even say that word. What about you? You ever married?"

"For about three years," Adele said. "He was . . ." *A cross-dresser?* ". . . a former Green Beret. Disappeared one day to . . ." *To search for the perfect brassiere and size 11 pumps.* ". . . find himself. We divorced right after that. He's married now and lives in the city. We're friends." *Even though I won't let him borrow my skirts.*

As Wanda predicted, the man at the counter sauntered over to their table, cappuccino in hand. His cologne, a musky sandal-wood, preceded him like a brick wall. "Do you mind if I sit with you lovely ladies," he asked with a slight accent, looking at Wanda and glancing briefly at Adele. His eyes went back to Wanda.

Adele and Wanda glanced at each other. The silent mes-sage sent and received, they moved their chairs closer to-gether so that he might pull up a chair.

"I hope I'm not being too forward." The man was about two inches taller than Adele, husky but not fat, and had good muscle definition. He had black hair, a straight wide nose, and the blue-black shadow of a beard.

"My name is Pierre Pandett. You are Americans?" He glanced from one to the other.

Wanda laughed. "As apple pie, but if you have to ask, you obviously aren't."

He looked into his cup, a self-conscious smile at the corners of his mouth. "No. I am from Belgium. My English is not good. I am sorry."

"Your English is great," Wanda said, holding out her hand. "I'm Wanda Percy, but most people call me Wanda . . . or sometimes Wonder." She laughed. "And this is Adele Monsarrat. You here on vacation?"

"Yes. I am visiting my brother in Larkspur, California."

Wanda gave him a look. "You're *in* Larkspur, California."

"Yes," Pierre said. "And you are from Larkspur, California, as well?"

"Adele is. I live in Greenbrae."

"And you are friends for a long time." It was more a statement than a question.

"We've worked in the same hospital for many years," Wanda said, "but we're just now getting around to being friends. I've discovered Adele is a fantastic cook, so she's going to have a hard time getting rid of me."

"You don't cook so good?" He seemed disappointed.

"I cook fine," Wanda said, quick to reassure him. "Adele just puts a little more gourmet into it than I do. I'm your basic barbecued ribs, cornbread, and meat drippings kinda girl."

He sipped his coffee, never taking his eyes off her.

Adele was feeling the heat.

"You are both doctors?"

"Don't wish that on us," Adele said under her breath.

"We're nurses," Wanda told him. "Adele works in the trenches. I work with pacemaker patients."

"I know about pacemakers," Pierre said, brightening considerably. "I have a cousin with the pacemaker. They are small, but they do much."

Adele nodded. "Sometimes they can even act as a remote control for your TV and lights."

"Yes? You have a pacemaker that can do this?"

"She's kidding," Wanda said. Cupping her chin, she leaned closer. "So tell me, Pierre, does your wife like Larkspur too?"

Adele was amazed at the sensuous intimacy that was created by such a simple move.

The man held her gaze. "I don't have my wife anymore," he said in a way that sounded as if he was talking about his '57 Chevy.

Adele drank off her cafe latte and faked a yawn. No one else in the cafe yawned, which again proved her theory that only genuine yawns begat yawns. "I'm going to walk back to the house," she said, and got up.

Pierre stood immediately. "Will you allow me to escort you home?"

Adele laughed in her "have you lost your mind?" way. "Ah, no, really, that's okay, It's only a couple of blocks away. You and Wanda hang loose."

She patted Wanda's shoulder and had started to leave when he took her hand and kissed it.

Adele sighed. She'd liked him right up until that moment.

Adele walked in on them in the act. Which was a good thing, because if she hadn't seen it with her own eyes, she wouldn't have believed it. She was just sorry there wasn't anyone she could call who would.

Nelson, with his brand-new Roddy Rug hanging stiffly from his mouth, pranced happily around the couch, up and down the hall, and through the kitchen. Attached to the dog's tail by his teeth, Helen lay on his side as she was dragged along, purring.

From the way Helen's fur had been worn away, Adele figured the two had been engaged in the activity for hours.

Tim jerked bolt upright in bed, spilling hot chocolate everywhere. His grip tightened on the journal as he read the three-paragraph article for a third time.

He looked at his watch, started to dial her number, then hung up. It was late, and she might think he was being pushy—now that he had half a shoelace in the door, he didn't want to blow it.

He read the bulletin once more and dressed. He would put it in an envelope and drop it in her mailbox with a note. But then she might wonder what he was doing sneaking on her porch, putting things in her mailbox at weird hours of the night.

He sat back down on the bed and ran his hands through his hair. Monique Arrowsmith, his sexy, flaxen-haired manne-quin, looked on in glassy-eyed disinterest.

What a miserable pussy, he thought. Scared to pick up the phone and give a woman a call?

Instantly, he picked up the phone and hit redial with a vengeance.

Somehow he was not surprised at the animation in her voice when she said hello. Before he could speak, he heard her wheezy laughter and knew she was having a Crazy Woman fit. He smiled—he loved it when she did that.

"I'm really sorry for calling this late, but I've found—"

"You won't believe this, Timothy . . ." she wheezed out an-other gale of laughter.

He looked at his watch and wondered what could have come up at ten-thirty at night that she would have found so funny.

Five minutes later, as his own laughter died down, she wiped away the last tear and took a shuddery, deep breath. "I'm okay now. Sorry. I'm glad you called when you did, be-cause I had to share that with someone."

He coughed. She cleared her throat and glanced at her watch. Her stomach went cold. Like the pretelephone atti-tudes toward Western Union telegrams, a call after ten at night meant only one thing: tragic news.

"What's wrong?" she asked, as the panic rose in her throat like a pincushion. It had to be Cynthia or her mother. In true nurse form, she was already thinking of which doctors or fu-neral parlors would be best.

"Nothing's wrong. I was lying here catching up on my of-fice reading, and I found something in an FBI bulletin that I thought you'd want to hear."

"Shoot."

"In the last eight months, there have been several mutila-tion murders, two in New York, one in D.C., and one in Los Angeles. Three have enough similarities to the Fischer case to make it suspicious. All the victims were middle- to upper-class straight-and-narrows. Real Joe Shit the Ragman types."

"Joe shit what?"

"Cop-speak for normal, everyday folk. It breaks the monotony of John Q. Citizen."

"Joe Shit the Ragman?" she repeated, making a face. "Am I a Joe Shit the Ragman to you?"

He hesitated. Gender was a sensitive area for her. "Well, no. You'd be Josephine Shit the Ragwoman."

"Oh," Adele said, deadpan. "How lovely. What else?"

"It appears that all the victims were killed by vertical cuts to the carotids, and two of the females are missing breasts. The female in L.A. had her ovaries and uterus removed, her feet amputated, and one of her breasts had the inside tissue removed."

"Christ on a bike," Adele whispered. "Just like Zelda Fischer."

"That's what I said right after I said yuck. It reminded me of the cat we used to have when I was a kid."

"Somebody gutted your cat?"

"No, but she used to catch female mice and then very carefully remove their uterus and whatever babies were in there, and eat the rest of the mouse."

"Obviously an early pro-abortion activist. Was there anything about a serrated blade being used on the carotids?"

He wondered how she knew about that detail and decided he didn't want to know. What the woman did to get her information was best not to think about.

"No, but I'm going to call the agent tomorrow for updates and do some comparing."

"Can you wait a half a day before you do that? I'd like to be there."

It was her tone that said she wasn't joking. He opened his mouth to say, "Hey, this is department business," realized to whom he was speaking, and said instead, "I've got to tell Hermonicus, Adele. It's his case."

"Great. Share with Herm, but could you pretend you never found the article until I can get to your office?"

"It's not my case, Adele, I can't—"

"You can't tell me that if you tell Herm you read an article and made a few calls, he wouldn't appreciate the effort."

He looked at Monique and remembered the day Adele met her. It was the first time she'd ever been to his apartment, a couple of days before the shooting.

"I don't—"

"Good," she said cheerfully from the other end. "I'll come up as soon as I get off the chain gang."

His glance shifted to his crotch. His erection stood at attention, ready to salute. He groaned. It was going to be another sleepless night.

TEN

THE BELL OF THE STETHOSCOPE HAD JUST touched Walter's chest when Tina's muffled voice came through saying the new admit was waiting for her.

"What admit?" Adele asked, looking up. "Nobody told me about any admit. I've got nine patients already and can barely manage as it is."

"Oh, you're killing me with pity," Tina said from the doorway, looking bored. "Here, let me go get my hanky. Queen Ma said you were taking the new one." Tina lowered her voice so that Adele had to strain to hear. "You gotta get a load of this chick. You'd think the docs never took anatomy the way they're all gawking."

"Okay," Adele sighed, "I'll bite. Who or what is the patient?"

Tina pouted her lips and grabbed her breasts. After the fashion of a North Beach strip joint barker, she boomed: "Come one, come all! Is she real or is she fake? Watch Miss Flame Desire give it a shake!"

"Flame Desire?"

Tina walked away. "Congratulations, you have passed the audio portion of your hearing test. Now please get this sideshow out of my face or I'm gonna stick a pushpin into that chest to see if she blows away."

Adele had never seen so many doctors at the nurses' station at one time—and all of them so quiet and well behaved. From time to time, one or another would peek at the woman lying on the gurney, as if they thought no one was looking. The smirking nurses and the men's furtive glances fostered in

199

Adele an overwhelming pity for the woman who had made a travesty of her body. With Mirek's help, she pushed the gurney into the empty space of 811, bed A.

Miss Flame Desire, stated age thirty but in truth closer to forty-five, was, as Tina indicated, really something to see.

Platinum blond hair extenders, woven with bright colored beads into a Bo Derek cornrow do, hung to her waist. With the help of a butcher and lots of silicone, the woman had been remodeled with lips the size of bananas and cheekbones so high they blocked her peripheral vision. Her breasts made Zelda Fischer's look like nubile nubs. The overall look was that of a blowup doll with exaggerated features.

Streaked with purple and blue veins, stretch marks, and the finishing touch of silver tassels hanging from loops that pierced each nipple, the woman's breasts seemed more related to hot-air balloons than human anatomy. No hospital gown made would have been big enough to fit over the woman's chest.

Necessity being the mother of invention, Adele cut a hole in the center of a sheet and fit it over Ms. Desire like a poncho. A pair of obstetrical panties just made it over the woman's buttocks, which had been lifted and enhanced with silicone pads.

Mirek took the patient's vital signs and started an IV while Adele studied the admission notes starting with the diagnosis: Cellulitis/rule out sepsis. Dr. Murray noted that the original source for the infection was the multiple piercings of her labia and clitoris recently done with unsterilized needles. For two weeks, Flame Desire had been suffering from chills and fever, vomiting and diarrhea, but had not sought medical care because she could not take time off from work as a dancer/hostess for the Starlight Club, a low-end all nude/love act joint on the edge of the Tenderloin. Adele could only guess what the job description might entail.

"Her temperature is one hundred and four point eight!" Mirek whispered in alarm, and handed her the bag of premixed Ancef.

Adele hung the IV bag and inserted it into a free port of the maintenance IV. "Call Henry and have him bring up the cooling blanket. Bring back a copy of the order sheet so we can figure out when the next blood culture is to be drawn, and when they're going to drain this abscess."

Adele sat next to the woman, who had not opened her eyes or spoken. "Flame?"

Flame whimpered and moved her head, sending the cornrows clicking against each other like a bead curtain.

"Flame, I'm Adele, your nurse. Can you open your eyes?" The eyelids flickered a little.

"Okay. I understand," Adele said softly. "You're a pretty sick lady right now. You've got a fever, so I'm going to give you some antibiotics through your IV. If you think you can hold it down, I want you to take some ibuprofen. Mirek is going to put you on a cooling blanket. It's cold and uncomfortable, and you're going to hate it, but we need to bring down your temp, so try to hang in there."

There was a rustle of the sheets as Flame's fingers, with two-inch fire engine red nails, slid out, found her arm, and attempted a weak squeeze. The heat from the woman's hand shocked her.

"Please." The pale blue eyes pleaded like a child. Despite everything else, they gave her face an extraordinary beauty. Tears rolled off the ledges of her cheekbones. "Adele, honey, am I going to die?" Although she spoke in barely a whisper, her accent could be heard, as thick and Southern as a pecan pie.

"We're not going to let that happen," Adele said. "I promise." She attached the automatic blood pressure cuff around the woman's arm and set it to do an automatic read every thirty minutes. She did a thorough admission profile while Mirek set up the cooling blanket. Softly keening, Flame vomited into a kidney basin then apologized for making a mess.

"You're going to be okay," Adele said, blotting the woman's face with a warm washcloth.

"Call me Dawn. Flame is my professional name. My real name's Dawn Joy."

* * *

"I'm baaaack." Adele stopped short.

A broad-shouldered man in a suit stood next to the bed holding Mr. Penn's hand. When he turned, Adele was shocked to realize that it wasn't a man at all. Small round eyes looked over the gold rims of her glasses, piercing and cold in their gaze. For the size of the woman's head and neck, her features appeared much too small. Her salt-and-pepper hair, worn closely cropped, lent no softness to the severe face.

"This is my daughter, Dylan Thomas Penn," Mr. Penn said, gesturing for her to come closer. "Dylan, meet Adele, my nurse."

Dylan Penn gripped Adele's hand in an overly firm handshake. Relieved that the woman hadn't broken into verse with a Welsh accent, Adele prepared a dressing change tray. "I understand you live in Washington."

"Yes," Dylan said, watching Adele's every move. "I'm a senior systems analyst for Citibank in Seattle."

Adele nodded, depositing the supplies on the side table. She had no idea what a systems analyst did, but from the crisp suit, tie, and starched Brooks Brothers shirt, she was sure it was a precise business having to do with computer systems and lots of math.

She untied Mr. Penn's gown, ready to remove the gauze bandage over his surgical site, when his daughter pushed herself back from the bed in a panic.

"Wait! Wait!" She held a protective hand in front of her eyes. "You aren't going to take off that bandage right now, are you?"

"Well, yes. I was—I mean, it's only a small . . ."

"My daughter can't stand the sight of anything having to do with surgery or blood." Mr. Penn chuckled. "I'm surprised she even came into the hospital—the smell makes her nauseous."

"Is there a cafeteria I can visit while you're doing this?" Dylan asked, her eyes still covered.

"Down in the basement," Adele said. "Take a left out of the elevator."

Dylan Penn thanked her and bounded to the door.

"Whatever you do," Adele called after her, "don't take a right. That's the morgue."

Adele examined Mr. Penn's surgical wound, pleased that it was healing so well. She applied a ribbon of Polysporin ointment to the site and covered it with a clean square of gauze.

"I'm sorry for being such an ornery cuss," Mr. Penn said suddenly. "I know everybody was just trying to help—even though it's a business designed to sucker every last penny out of the patient."

"It will surprise you to know, Mr. Penn, that I feel the same way about our health care system as you do."

"You do?"

"Sure. I pay for my own insurance. I know the exchange rate is far from fair." She finished taping the gauze. "When two Tylenol cost twenty dollars, I get upset."

His neck flushed. "Did you say twenty dollars for two goddamned—?"

She cut him off at the pass. "Can you remember anything about the clinic in Berlin?"

His lips flapped for a few seconds, still heading in the direction of a tirade. "One thing I know for sure is that they never charged me a goddamned penny for—"

"Can you remember who recommended you go there?"

"Nobody," he grumbled. "I passed out in the lobby of my hotel, and when I came to, they'd already cut me open and fixed me up."

"Did someone at the hotel call the ambulance?"

He rubbed the stubble of his chin, reminding her she needed to find a razor and shaving soap: electricity being as expensive as it was, he'd never use an electric shaver.

"Must have, but I wouldn't know for sure. The hotel was an inexpensive place, but clean. I don't need more than just a bed and a place to wash myself. The company would pay for it—it's not a question of that. God knows the other CEOs take advantage of every perk they can lay their hands on. Not me. I refuse to stay in one of those four-star rip-off hotels that charge five hundred a goddamned night to put a five-cent chocolate mint on your pillow. I—"

"Do you remember the name of the hotel?"

He stopped to think. "That's a strange thing too. When I went home from the hospital, I looked through the files that were rifled. This year's tax file was gone. I had receipts from the hotel and the clinic in there." He looked at her. "What the hell anybody would want with them is beyond me."

"Can you remember any of the names or addresses without the receipts?"

"I'm sorry, dear." He laughed. "It's terrible getting old. Your memory goes to hell. I don't think I could find the place again even if I was standing right in front of it."

Adele retied his gown. "How long did you stay at that clinic?"

"Overnight. They drove me back to the hotel next morning and put me to bed. I left for home two days later."

"They didn't give you any papers? Something that explained what type of pacemaker they put in, or anything documenting your third-degree heart block?"

He shook his head. "No, and I wondered about that. All they gave me were some pills—the ones I took the other night—and that Dr. English's card with instructions to call him if anything went wrong."

"Was there anything else while you were at the clinic or the hotel that seemed unusual?"

The man played with the hem of the sheet. "You'll think I've gone around the bend." He half smiled.

"No," she shook her head solemnly, "I won't."

"Thing is," he said, a V of doubt between his eyes, "it sounds kinda nutty."

"Nothing you tell me is going to sound crazy at this point."

"All right." He took a breath. "There were a couple of things that were peculiar. I think I woke up during the operation. I could hear them talking, but it wasn't German. I don't know what it was. I was three sheets to the wind." He looked at her from under white brows to gauge her reaction. "I know I wasn't dreaming because I could see the blood on the doctor's hands, but the rest of it wasn't right somehow."

"How's that?"

"They didn't have those blue gowns on, for one, and there wasn't any medical equipment or green tile walls. It was . . ." He paused. "Well, I'll just tell you out straight—there were stacks of rolled-up carpets."

"Carpets?" She pulled back to look at him. Anesthesia sometimes had disastrous, lasting affects on the mentation of older adults. "You're sure they were carpets?"

He nodded. "And there were men holding guns. There was a gun pointed at the guy doing the cutting."

"Okay," Adele said, not entirely sure what to make out of it. "Anything else?"

"Dr. English was there," he said dully. "I recognized him when he came in the other night. He wasn't the one doing the operation, but he was there."

"Did you ask him if he was there?"

Mr. Penn nodded. "He said I must have been dreaming."

"But you still think it was him?"

Mr. Penn glanced down at the gnarled blue veins on the backs of his hands then back at her. "You think I'm demented."

She opened her mouth to protest, but he stopped her. "You can go ahead and think that all you want, but I'm still with it enough to recognize a man who stood over me holding a gun to someone else's head."

Adele felt as if she was committing a crime, which, of course, she was. To knowingly wake a night-shift person from sleep was cruel—the equivalent of slapping babies and puppies around for the fun of it. Her only excuse was that with nine patients to care for, five of whom were acute, there wouldn't be another chance to call.

Sitting on the toilet, she tapped in Opal's home number. The ringing seemed inordinately loud. Raspy cat tongues of guilt licked her brain as she imagined the woman fighting her way up through the layers of consciousness, her body and mind exhausted beyond the limits of endurance.

Instead of the muffled, sleep-slurred greeting Adele expected, the voice that answered was cheerful and upbeat. In the background, KFOG was blaring a number by Rhoid

Rogers and the Whirling Butt Cherries. Adele was instantly relieved, almost glad someone was going to protect Opal from her.

"Hi, I'm really, really sorry, but is Opal awake?"

"You got her. Who's this and why are you so sorry?"

"It's Adele. How come you aren't asleep?"

"Tonight's my night off. I never go to bed before noon anyway. Only the wimpettes have to go to bed as soon as they get off. Me? I take a ten-minute nap then get up and do my errands. What's up?"

"I was wondering about the other night when Dr. English came in to see Mr. Penn?"

"Gee, you still going on about that?"

"Yep," she said. "You know me—can't let anything go."

"You ever seen anybody about obsessive-compulsive disorder?" Opal asked, then: "Hold on a minute, will ya?"

There was a pause while Opal turned down the radio. When she came back on, she was crunching on something that sounded like rocks. "What were you wondering?"

"What did he look like, for starters?"

Opal crunched while she thought. "Hmmm, maybe six feet, dark coloring, black hair. Nice suit, expensive jewelry—lots of it."

"Like what?"

"A big gold watch with diamonds around the face, gold cuff links, and matching tie tack." She paused in her chewing. "He had on two big gold rings. One was set with a diamond that was at least two and a half carats, and the other one was just a plain round face." Opal hesitated, "Well, not plain—it had a design like a wavy division sign with two dots on either side."

"Was there anything that struck you as kinda off about him?"

"Oh yeah," Opal said, happy that someone had asked. "One thing was that he didn't know what t.i.d. meant. Dhery wrote an order to check the patient's neuro status t.i.d. I had to explain that it meant three times a day. I thought that was totally off, not to mention the fact that he discharged the guy to go back to work. I mean, I know I said the docs in the city do it all the time, but Mr. Penn being in the condition he was, it was a stretch. Another thing—when I gave the doc a strip of the old man's latest rhythm, he read it upside down. I thought it must have been some sort of trick they taught him in whatever home study med school he went through."

There was renewed crunching. "I remember I told him that Penn's potassium was down to two point seven, and he just nodded. Finally I asked him if he wanted Penn to have some extra potassium, and he told me to give the old guy whatever I thought was right." The nurse laughed. "It's been a while since I've heard that out of a doc's mouth."

Someone came into the nurses' lounge and called out a hello. Adele cringed at the British accent and quickly lifted her feet onto the rim of the toilet.

"I can't really think of anything else," Opal continued. "The guy was arrogant enough to be a doctor, but he was too—oh, I don't know—he just didn't seem comfortable being in the hospital. He was staring at the equipment in awe, like he'd never seen anything like it before."

Through the crack of the stall door, Adele watched as Grace pulled the tape recorder from her purse and searched for a place to hide it. She settled on the least imaginative spot: under the table that held the coffee machine.

"Adele?" Opal stopped chewing. "I can hear you breathing—what are you doing?"

Adele waited until the lounge door closed before she spoke. "Sorry. Grace just came in and hid the tape recorder under the coffee machine in the lounge."

"Oh, good," Opal said. "Let the games begin."

By the end of the shift, word had been passed by mouth, phone, and e-mail to every staff member about the exact location of the recorder. Dialogue was already being written, the only problem being that no one could keep from laughing long enough to get through an entire script.

* * *

Besides Walter, Flame Desire, Mr. Penn, her two congestive heart failures, one confused stroke needing total care,
one rule-out MI, one fever of unknown origin, and the post-
surgical transurethral resection of the prostate, Grace assigned Adele yet another new admission, much to the
incredulity of the other nurses.

Chanting, "One for all, all for one," Skip and Cynthia took
over two of her patients completely, while Linda tended to the
others.

The way Adele had it figured, Grace Thompson was going to try to force her out by working her to death. And if that
didn't work, she'd overload her, hoping sooner or later she'd
make that one fatal error and lose her license.

Lagunitas was a town where time dropped in during the
sixties and seventies, smoked some heavy dope, went paranoid, and dropped out. If towns could be categorized with human personalities, Lagunitas was the hippie child of Marin
County who was still stoned.

Adele looked at the address Dr. Ravens had given her and
then back at the number on the rusted mailbox lying half-
sunk in the mud. Leaving the Beast on solid ground, she
started down the muddy driveway. A few steps in, she was
glad to be wearing her oldest running shoes, whose toes were
cut out for expansion of her ever-growing feet.

The stone house was built into the curve of a creek in a
manner that blended in with the natural surroundings. The
lawn surrounding it was indeed large. She rang the bell, waited
for a polite amount of time, then followed the wraparound
porch to a backyard festooned with flowering plants, a gazebo,
and a swimming pool. The clear water lapping the tiles of the
pool called to her by name.

Later, she decided it really wasn't a question of not having
impulse control, but more like having the pool exert its power
over her. She dropped her purse into one of the lounge chairs,
removed her running shoes, and jumped in.

When George Ravens arrived, she was practicing holding
her breath under water—a childhood challenge that she still

liked to take on. Without any more than a hello, he removed all but his briefs and dove off the side.

"It was," she blurted, pulling herself out of the pool, "one of those spontaneous choices."

His eyes ran over her figure, plainly visible through the wet scrub dress. "Spontaneity," he called out as he began swimming. "Isn't that one of the seven secret virtues rarely seen in Caucasians?"

"Yeah," she laughed. "It's just ahead of natural rhythm and intuition."

The sun-warmed terra-cotta tiles felt good against her body. She propped her chin on the back of her hands, feeling relaxed.

"What tribe are you from?" she asked, circling an ant with her finger. The insect momentarily went into a frenzy, unwilling to cross the dark circle of water.

He swam to the edge of the pool and lifted himself out. His hair was smoothed back tight against his head, glistening. "Tlingit. We're a southeastern Alaskan tribe."

"Is Ravens your real name?"

He shook his head. "A Tlingit belongs to either the Raven moiety or the Eagle moiety. Many different clans fall under those two. For example, I am Raven and my clan is Sea Tern. The raven in Tlingit is a cultural hero with a dual personality. He is a transformer for good, but he is also a trickster driven to outlandish adventures."

"And you chose this name because it suits you?"

"Yes, and because Tlingit is a tone language with twenty-four sounds not found in English. No whites would be able to pronounce my real Tlingit name."

They both looked out over the pool with the navy blue bottom. It was so much more peaceful, she thought, than the eggshell blue of most pools. After a while she said, "Well, I've had a swim in your pool and evaluated your lawn, so may I call you George?"

"How about Raven?"

"Raven it is, then." She flung her hair back and got to her feet. Her scrub dress was still wet, but not dripping.

"If you'll come in, I can throw that dress in the dryer. I think I have a robe that would fit you."

The house was built around a courtyard with a giant redwood growing in the middle. Inside, what wasn't made of natural wood was of the same smooth river stone that covered the façade of the house. Collections of totems and carved masks dominated the walls and corners.

"Are these carved by your clan?" she asked, studying one of the more ornate masks.

He closed the dryer door and hit the start button. The metal snaps of her dress clicked against the insides of the tub, creating a rhythmic sound she found comforting.

"My mother's brother is a Tlingit carver," he said, retying the belt of his terry-cloth robe. "His work is well known in the region. My brother was given the talent to carry on the tradition, so he trained with my uncle. I was guided to the shaman's path."

"Why didn't you return home when you finished your residency?"

He shook his head, avoiding her eyes.

"Why?"

He said nothing for several minutes while he set out glasses and cut lemon wedges.

She was examining one of the masks when he said, "I killed a man. A Tlingit. I was working as a deputy sheriff at the time. He was drunk and I was trying to reason with him. I wanted him to go home to his wife and children so I would not have to arrest him. He pulled a gun and I shot him. There was nothing else I could do. I go back to visit my family, but I could never live there again." He paused to pour iced tea into the glasses. "It is my choice."

Sensing his discomfort, she dropped the subject and continued studying the artwork. "Do the symbols in the design of the masks and totems have meanings?"

He shook his head. "They are simply elements of the native designs. There are clans who have certain animal clan designs, such as the owl, whale, frog, salmon, that are worn only by the clan members as part of their identity."

She found her purse and pulled out the paper with Opal's drawing. "Have you ever seen a symbol like this before?"

He studied the drawing for a long time before handing it back to her. "In the modern world, it could mean almost anything, but in the Tlingit culture, it isn't anything I'm familiar with." He added ice to each glass and handed her one.

"Traditionally, the circle inside a circle is a sign of divine power. The waving line I don't know. Water? Balance? It might be in the symbol encyclopedia, but I doubt it. Sometimes groups will frequently take shapes and assign their own meanings to them." He pointed to the wall. "Take this mask, for instance. My uncle carved this, but these markings have no meaning outside the Raven clan."

They drank their tea. Raven took the paper and looked at it again. "Does this have anything to do with Mr. Penn?" he asked finally.

Adele stared, wondering how he'd made the jump. Uneasiness flitted through her. "I don't know. Why do you ask?"

"Because I know of your reputation, and I know about the circumstances under which you found Mr. Penn last night. It's only logical you'd be tracking something having to do with that. It's in your nature." He went to the dryer chuckling. "If you were a Native American your name would be something like Woman Who Tracks Invisible Bear." Static snapped at the hair on his arms as he shook the garment free of wrinkles and handed it to her.

"What have you decided about my lawn?" he asked. "Will you come back and mow it?"

She held out the dress studying it hard. She thought about Timothy and wondered why she felt as if she were betraying him. The two men were so different: Tim, down to earth and comfortable; Raven, mysterious and exotic.

"Who is this man who requires so much of your consideration?" he asked.

"I'll mow your lawn," she said, ignoring his question. "I just don't know when."

He considered this and nodded, saying without words that

this would suffice. She suspected he knew exactly what she meant—the way he could read her mind and all.

"The papers on English were forgeries," he called out as she walked to the bathroom to change into her dress.

"I figured as much. Are you in trouble because you vouched for him?"

"Not yet. English did nothing more than discharge Mr. Penn too early. If he'd done a procedure or prescribed a drug that had caused the old man harm while he was still hospitalized, it would be a different story. As far as the hospital is concerned, the man caused Penn no direct harm."

She checked herself in the bathroom mirror, then saw the razor, shaving cream, and other male toiletries. Suddenly she felt like someone who had awakened after a long, hard drunk and found herself in bed with a stranger. She hastily picked up her purse and checked her watch. "I have an appointment at the sheriff's office. I should have been there five minutes ago. Traffic is going to be—"

"Fly," he said, opening the door. "Come back and mow my lawn when you want. I'll still be here."

She flew to the Beast and let herself in. Behind the wheel, she took a deep breath, feeling as though she'd had a narrow escape. She looked back at the path to his house. "What the hell was that all about?"

It's hormones, Adele, Dr. Ruth said in her cheery voice from the backseat. *The whole world runs on hormones. He is an attractive man—you are an attractive voman. Vhat do you expect?*

Maybe, Adele thought, as she blinked Dr. Ruth out of her mind, *just maybe I'm the one who needs to see Jeffrey.*

The smell in the hall outside her apartment was of frying onions and garlic. Wanda fit the key into her lock, unconsciously noticing the other smell just under the onions and garlic. A sweeter smell. Cloying. It reminded her of—what? Who?

The key turned freely. She frowned, sighed, and shook her head. She'd forgotten to lock the door again. Every woman she knew over forty was losing her memory. She was sure it had something to do with air pollution, or the water. The atmosphere was killing their memories slowly but surely.

She threw her car keys onto the kitchen counter and opened the refrigerator door. While she stood gazing at the contents, she slipped off her shoes and kicked them toward the hall closet, then pulled off her lab coat and then her uniform.

Milk or cranberry juice? A black plum or a handful of seedless Thompsons?

She hummed a generic blues song while unhooking her bra then let it dangle loosely from her shoulders. Doing a small bump-and-grind step, she reached for the cranberry juice and stopped, hand on the cold glass neck of the bottle.

She sniffed. The perfume smell was back again. Stronger. Her head was turning to locate the source when an arm came around her neck with unreal speed. In that split second before shock set in, her hands automatically went up to her throat to pull away the hard rock pressing on her windpipe, got tangled in her bra, and struggled uselessly to free themselves.

When she felt her eyeballs beginning to bulge out of their sockets, Wanda remembered the source of the smell.

The Blue Roof Motel, a.k.a. the Marin County Civic Center, was a sprawling Frank Lloyd Wright monument that housed the county courts and offices, including the sheriff's department. In this virtual maze of buildings and offices, Adele was relieved that the sheriff's department was on the ground level and easy to find. Locating any of the other offices or courtrooms required several trips to the profusion of "You are HERE!" maps posted throughout the buildings. Just reporting for jury duty could be an all-day adventure in and of itself.

"Do I smell law and order in here?" she asked from the doorway of Detective Sergeant Ritmann's office. He was on the phone, but hadn't said anything in the two minutes she'd stood watching him.

He looked up from his desk blotter where he'd been drawing cartoon faces with big noses and small, buggy eyes. His breath caught at the sight of her dressed in running shorts and a black T-shirt. She had legs like a lovely long stretch of road leading to a slim-hipped hard body that he liked.

"Come in." He covered the mouthpiece, motioning her to one of the two chairs facing his desk. "I'm on hold."

She ignored the offered chair, dropping her purse into it instead, and wandered around the office. Not much had changed, except the banner "Welcome Back Sarge!" over his door, and the dead silver balloons hanging by their necks from the ceiling that read "It's a Boy!" in baby blue lettering.

Missing from the wall was the photograph of him and Cynthia on the Ellis Hospital whitewater rafting trip. In its place was a photo of the infamous Monique Arrowsmith dressed in a police uniform. Detectives Cini and Chernin stood on either side of her, their arms draped over her shoulder, a hand covering each perfect plaster breast. Their wild grins made her laugh.

Outside the window, a crow landed on the ledge and inched closer, looking in at them with one eye. When another minute had passed, he said a few words to the person on the other end of the line and hung up.

"Are you trying to give the boys in the department heart attacks?" He pointed to her legs.

She frowned. "If I were a guy, nobody would think twice about my legs."

"They'd better not," he said. "Or we'd have to ship them over to San Francisco."

"The idea of menstrual huts and club swinging isn't quite over for you macho guys, is it, dear?"

Although she was smiling, he knew when to keep his mouth shut and swim back to shore. He got up and closed the door. "Take a look at these," he said, deciding against delivering the standard this-is-confidential-I-could-get-fired-for-this-you-know lecture. It had to be as boring for her to hear it for the millionth time as it was for him to say it.

While she read the journal articles and the FBI notices regarding the mutilation murders, he leafed through the dog-eared Fischer case file for the fourth time. Sometimes he paused to study a page and take notes. After he found the page he wanted, he spread out the file.

She flinched at the scene photos, put them aside, read the reports and statements, then went back to the scene photos, studying them until the shock wore off. It was, she thought, like seeing *The Texas Chainsaw Massacre* and all its sequels— the senses could only take so much heinousness before they quit reacting.

The woman's remaining breast looked to be approximately a thousand-cc implant. "A total of two thousand cc's," she said. "Can you imagine that little person having to lug two liters around?" She glanced up at him and saw he didn't understand. "It'd be like a five-foot-two guy having testicles the size of basketballs, weighing a couple of pounds each."

"Yeah, except they wouldn't look nearly as nice in a low-cut dress," he said, refusing to imagine having four pounds of testicles. The very idea made him ache.

"What son of a butcher would do that to someone?" she asked, looking for the medical records. "I can't imagine any legitimate plastics man agreeing to it—no matter what she offered to pay."

"I can," Tim said, sitting in the chair next to hers. "Hell, look at Michael Jackson's plastic surgeon. He took a normal-looking black dude and created a white monster who has to wear scarves over his face so as not to scare the little boys he's trying to molest. I'd love to know what Jackson paid for being made into a Liza Minnelli look-alike."

"Whatever it was, was too much," she said, working her way through thirty pages of Zelda Fischer's medical complaints. The woman's multitudinous physical complaints were in the category of ailments that usually affected women who had too much time on their hands and used it to worry about themselves. The majority of Mrs. Fischer's time seemed to be spent in doctors' offices. Her ailments included psoriasis, chronic dermatitis, chronic fatigue syndrome, carpal tunnel syndrome, migraines, fibromyalgia, chronic back pain, chronic tendinitis, neuralgia, hemorrhoids, alopecia areata, chronic cystitis, chronic vaginitis, and ovarian cysts.

By the time she found what she was looking for on the last page of the patient information sheet from the UC dermatology clinic, Adele could well imagine how a physician would have lost patience with the woman. No matter what treatment or medication was prescribed, it was never the right one.

> Pt. seen for intralesional injection of 5mg triamcinalone. Four new areas.

Here there was a drawing of the top of the patient's head with four small circles drawn in. Inside each circle was the size of the area in centimeters.

> Usual advice given re: reducing stress, biofeedback, vitamins, St. John's wort, and reducing time of wig wear. Sig. Changes: Breast augmentation five months ago. Implants est. 1000 to 1200 cc's.
> Also treated for 5 cm by 7 cm area, R. breast. Inflamed . . .

She turned the page, but instead of the rest of the doctor's notes, she found an interview with Ms. Fischer's cleaning woman. "There's a page missing from the UC report," Adele said, checking through the file again.

"That's everything we got right there, kiddo."

"Are you sure a page didn't fall out?"

He pointed to the binder. "Doubt it." We're careful with case files around here. It's one of those things we'd run into a burning house to rescue."

"And after the case files, you go back in for the kids?"

"No, after the case files, it's the framed photo of Old Shep the police dog, and *then* the kids."

He sat in the high-back swivel chair and picked up the phone. "Ready?" he asked, punching in a number, his leg bouncing rapidly. She could feel the vibrations of it through the legs of her chair.

Abruptly the bouncing leg stopped. "Special Agent in Charge, Corey Onorato?" Tim hesitated, then laughed. "Well, I always believe in being polite to a Bureau man. This is Detective Sergeant Tim Ritmann with the Marin County Sheriff's Office out here in beautiful San Rafael, California. I was just looking over your flyer number twenty-eight ninety-three outlining these mutilation cases you've got in New York and elsewhere?"

Tim paused, glanced at her, and chuckled. "Yeah, that's it. Listen, we've got two open cases here that sound enough like yours to make me suspicious. Up till now, we've been thinking these were random murders committed by psychos. But I'd like to go over some of the particulars from all our cases and yours and see if we can link these."

He wrote something down and nodded. "Sure." He picked up the Fischer file. "Our first case is a forty-eight-year-old female found at home in bed with one breast cut open and all the inside tissue removed. The medical examiner's report said the cuts to the breast may have possibly been made with a scalpel and that they suggested a subcutaneous mastectomy. In addition, both carotid arteries were cut with a blunt serrated blade in vertical upward slices. There were no overt signs of any sexual motivations.

"She'd been dead approximately six hours, which puts the time of the murder around six a.m. The scene was absolutely pristine. The psycho didn't leave so much as a fiber for us."

Tim paused and chuckled. "Exactly," he said and laughed harder. "The only noteworthy event was that the day before she reportedly got into a verbal altercation with a physician at a clinic in San Francisco, but the guy had an airtight alibi.

"Second case is a seventy-year-old decapitated male found floating in San Francisco Bay. Hands amputated and most organs in the abdominal cavity had been removed. According to our ME, all cuts appeared to have been done with surgical precision. It's his opinion that the body probably exsanguinated before it was dumped in the Bay. The wife reported him missing three days before. She IDed the torso on the basis of a mole on the guy's penis."

Tim paused and then laughed in that way guys did when sharing a penis joke. "You got that right," he said, finally, avoiding Adele's eyes. "Both victims were John Q. Citizens who were financially more secure than I am."

He laughed again: "Yeah, ain't it the truth?"

Adele was beginning to think Special Agent Onorato moonlighted as a stand-up comic. She inched closer to the other phone on his desk and rested her hand on the receiver. Tim shot her a stern look—arched eyebrows over wide eyes—which arrested further action on her part. She smiled. He frowned and wagged a finger.

"Anyway, when I saw your flyer, I figured it was worth a call. There might not be any connection, but we don't have a whole lot to go with out here, and I thought maybe you could take a look at ours and see if they fit with yours."

Tim listened for a minute, nodding and taking notes as he went. She moved around to his side of the desk and put her ear close to the earpiece. He tried to swivel away, but she stuck like glue, grabbing him by the arm.

He glanced quickly into his lap and then at his jacket, which was hanging on the coatrack by the door. He prayed Big One Eye and the Twins would behave.

Prying the earpiece half an inch away from Tim's ear, Adele could barely hear the agent on the other end of the line: ". . . got this on the wire all over the country. All victims have the same vertical cuts to the carotids. Our first victim floated up out of Belvedere Lake in Central Park ten months ago. Of course nobody paid any attention to it at the time. I mean, if New York reported on every thirty-four-year-old female who turned up with her boobs or twat carved up, we'd . . ."

Tim automatically yanked the earpiece away, as if to protect her from hearing the rest of the homicide details. In reality, it was more to protect Agent Onorato from having his eardrums assaulted by a woman prone to instant tirades over any derogatory comments about women.

Adele glared at him and made as if to pick up the extension. Instantly, he turned back to let her listen in.

". . . nothing surgically precise about it. No sign of rape, but NYPD still figured it for a sex crime. She had a good job with Chase Manhattan as a securities officer. Happily married with one kid. She wasn't fooling around, no drugs. No suspects either.

"Four weeks later, there was a similar murder in Sag Harbor of a . . ." There came the sound of shuffling papers. ". . . fifty-nine-year-old high society dame. Recent widow, four adult children, quiet type, nothing loopy about her personal life. She was found in the trunk of her Mercedes in the parking lot of a restaurant about twenty minutes from her front door. It was the same deal as the New York victim: vertically sliced carotids, but this one had been scalped and had one ear and part of the face removed along with most of her left buttock. Again, nobody's coming up with any suspects on this one.

"Third victim turned up five weeks after that. A forty-eight-year-old male, owner of a multimillion-dollar advertising agency in D.C., was found floating in his pool without his scalp. It appeared to be the same style of cut on the carotids. District cops originally thought it was a jealous boyfriend—the guy was queer as a three-dollar bill and twice as faggy as a frilly skirt."

The pause, in which Timothy did not laugh, was as pregnant as they got.

"Oops, sorry," Onorato said. "I forgot—you're San Francisco. The victim was involved with lots of different low-profile queens on the D.C. political society scene. He had a live-in boyfriend who regularly beat the shit out of him. The night of the murder, the boyfriend was at the White House, having his picture taken with the First Lady, so that took care of the main suspect. The fourth victim is one you'll find particularly interesting."

Adele pulled the phone closer to her own ear.

". . . turned up five weeks after the D.C. victim in a Dumpster outside an abandoned factory in east L.A. A twenty-eight-year-old actress employed as a stripper. Same carotid cuts, one breast scooped out, a chunk of the left buttock missing, and . . ." Onorato paused. "The ME's report said that a complete hysterectomy had been performed—and I quote here—'in a manner that suggests a knowledge of surgical procedure.' Oh, another weird touch: her feet were amputated. LAPD found a room inside the factory that appeared to be the scene of the murder. None of the missing parts have been found, and all five of the victim's boyfriends checked out clean."

Corey Onorato took a deep breath. Through it, they heard the shuffling of more paper. "Three more similars have shown up since the flyer came out. One each in Denver, Miami, and Houston. So far the Denver victim is almost a certain: a forty-six-year-old Mercedes dealer. Similar carotid cuts, scalped, and part of the right buttock missing.

"Miami was another male: sixty-five, owner of a golf course—missing a buttock and his entire unit, and I mean everything—scrotum, penis . . . everything. No immediate suspects, although his greens fees were exorbitant enough to piss off quite a few of the customers.

"The latest is the Houston victim, a fifty-two-year-old scalped female with a buttock and half her face missing. She was the wife of a Texas oil man, so you can be assured Houston is going to find suspects even if they have to pay for them."

"So we've got some possible connections here," Tim said.

"I'd say so," Onorato said. "Close in timing, vertical carotid cuts, upper-middle-class citizens who live in or near a major city. Whoever this guy is, the bastard is as thorough as I've ever seen about not leaving a trail. There hasn't been one print or fiber left behind. Every scene is immaculate, and I don't need to tell you there aren't many psychos who are that clean."

Agent Onorato covered the mouthpiece, then came back on, excused himself, and put them on hold.

Adele's back cracked as she stretched and perched on the edge of his desk. "Ask if any of the victims—"

Tim put a finger to his lips, and she immediately crouched again to listen.

"Sorry about that," said Onorato, "but I've got to fly out of here in a second. Why don't you fax me your files, and I'll fax you what I've got. I'll include the phone numbers for the guys in charge of the other investigations."

"Sounds good," Tim said, ignoring the note Adele was writing in big bold letters.

The two men exchanged several phone numbers and e-mail addresses and hung up.

"Why didn't you ask him my question?" she asked after he'd hung up. "It's a key piece that would have put a bunch of things together."

"Don't take it personally, Adele," he said. "First phone call between agencies about a case like this, you don't cover a whole lot more than physical evidence and trauma to the victims. After I get the reports and go over them with my people, then we move on to the detail questions."

Her exasperation cut short, she took on the sobered expression of one who realizes she's been mistaken. "Oh."

"What was the question?" he said, reaching for the piece of paper.

She pulled it out of his reach, folded it, and stuck it in her purse. "I'll hold on to it. It'll be an incentive for you to let me see their files when you get them."

She walked to his bookcase, pretending interest in the titles. "I've uncovered a few pieces of information that nobody else has tapped into yet, Tim. I don't know where they fit in, but I think it's important."

He tapped his pen a couple of times. "Okay, so share."

"Not yet," she said, picking up a bright yellow softcover book entitled *Crime Investigation for Dummies*.

Instant temper—that terrible affliction that plagued red-heads the earth over—flared, taking with it all the frustration he felt about her . . . about them. "You can't do this again to me." He stared at her with accusing eyes that had turned a paler shade of blue. "This withholding act of yours really pisses me off. Amateurs who play around with investigations are dangerous, Adele. It's deadly. You collect information and then withhold it, and you can't do that in this business. It puts you in danger, it puts—"

She opened her mouth to protest, but he stopped her. "I

don't want to hear it. I'm not fucking around anymore with you on this stuff. I can't stop you from nosing around—which, I don't need to tell you is illegal as hell, and which you will get busted for someday—but I can make everything in this department and the coroner's office off-limits."

He let the red haze of fury clear from his mind. When he spoke again, it was in a milder tone. "This isn't the movies. A homicide investigation isn't a one-man show—it's a team effort. You can't own a case. You're dealing with psychos who do sick things. Sometimes they're very smart. You've got to have people watching your back."

He stopped and, like a man peeking out of his storm cellar after a tornado, evaluated the damage done. She was standing rigid looking at him in a way he did not know how to interpret. It might have been shock or anger. Slowly, she closed the book and put it back on his shelf without raising her eyes. The silence between them was stifling.

"Adele, I'm sorry," he said, letting out a long breath and sitting down. "I didn't mean to dump on you. It's my temper." He made a halfhearted attempt at laugher and pointed to his hair. "Redheads. You know how we—"

"It's okay," she said, holding the indecipherable expression. "You're right about some things . . ." She picked up her purse and opened the door, still not looking at him. "But not everything."

He made it to the door before she could step into the hall. Reaching around her, he pulled the door closed. "Don't you dare leave this office without talking to me," he said, his eyes reading disappointment. "Is that what you do when somebody confronts you? Run away? I didn't think Adele Monsarrat ran away from anything."

"I don't," Adele squared her chin. "But when somebody I care about unloads on me like that, I have to have time out to think. You made some valid points, but some of it was your own bullshit."

"Okay. Okay." He was relieved she was responding. "Talk to me."

She remained silent while she mulled over what he'd said.

"I don't blame you, really, for being pissed, but you sell me short. You forget how well I know the danger behind this business, Timothy."

She went over to the window overlooking the civic center grounds. On the ledge, the crow had been replaced by a sleeping gull, his beak tucked under his wing. From the offices around them, she could hear phones ringing. Somewhere a man laughed.

"I'm well acquainted with the psychopath's work. My mind is never more than a centimeter away from Douglas Collier's eyes, or Ellen Mack's face." She turned to him, her words picking up speed. "I see every victim—Chloe, Aaron, Sonja, Helen Marval . . . you—in my nightmares every night. There isn't a second I'm not hyperaware that some crazy's bullet is looking for the back of my head."

She began pacing, then stopped. "I take chances like everybody else—you take a chance getting out of bed in the morning—you take a chance if you stay in bed. The thing is, Tim, I can think on my feet. There's a method to my madness that even I don't understand sometimes, so I follow my gut. When I don't tell you everything, it's usually because I want to make absolutely sure of my facts, or because my gut tells me it's the wrong thing to do. And like you said, I'm *not* part of the department. I'm just a Josephine Shit the Ragwoman-nurse who has an interest in unsolved crimes."

He played the imaginary violin until a smile broke.

"I'm still not willing to just hand over what I've found and get cut out of the rest of the action. However, if you want to brainstorm with me some day and pool all our information, I'll be glad to spill everything I have up to that point, whether it's correct or not—just as long as I get information in return."

"You pick the night," he said. "I'll pick the place."

"Okay, how about—"

The buzz of a cell phone sent her to her purse and him to his suit jacket. In a contest to see who could locate, flip open the mouthpiece, and press the right button the fastest, they both fumbled, dropped their phones, and picked them up.

"Hello?" they said in unison.

"Tim? What are you doing answering Adele's phone?"

"Cynthia?" he said, momentarily confused.

"Yeah. I'm calling Adele."

"Oh—sorry, we must have gotten our phones mixed." He handed Adele her phone. "It's Cyn."

"What's up?" Adele said.

"Bad news, Del."

Instinctively, she sat down. "What is it?"

"Brenda from ER called here looking for you. Rescue Fifty brought Wanda into ER. Somebody's beat her up really bad. She's got a bunch of fractures and a huge subdural. They've got an emergency call out to Zaritsky and Horrocks. They're getting her ready for surgery now. She's asking for you."

Adele closed her eyes. *It puts others in danger* . . . "Do they know who did it?"

"I don't know. Brenda didn't tell me anything else except to find you and tell you to get to the hospital STAT!"

"Okay, thanks," she said, already at a run. "Do me a favor and call Brenda back and tell her to tell Wanda I'll be there in ten minutes."

"What's wrong?" Tim asked, running after her.

"A nurse," she called back over her shoulder. "A friend of mine. We had dinner last night. Somebody beat her. They're taking her to surgery but she wants to talk to me. I'm afraid—I think I know . . . There was this man who . . ."

He grabbed her arm, but she pulled out of his grip. "Adele! Let me drive you. I can use the lights and sirens. It's still rush hour."

"But my car . . ."

"Leave your keys here and I'll have Chernin drive it to El-lis later."

She stopped, torn between the practicality of his offer and the need to keep moving. "Hurry up," she called to him as he ran back to get his jacket and keys. "This isn't going to wait."

The usual ER smells of alcohol wipes and blood seemed to bother her more than usual—probably because the blood belonged to someone she knew. Approaching the gurney, which was surrounded by people and equipment, she was astonished at the amount of blood smeared all over the floor. The EKG tech was checking the twelve-lead EKG tracing, while a lab tech finished drawing several tubes of blood. As soon as the lab tech left, Adele slipped into the spot to the right of Wanda's body.

She checked the IV solutions and, steeling herself, looked down. The face that had been shining with humor at her kitchen table less than twenty-four hours before was mangled almost beyond recognition. Both eyes were swollen shut, although one appeared much worse than the other. The bridge of her nose and left nostril were split open, and the lips were splayed to reveal missing teeth.

She covered Wanda's hand with her own. It was like a block of ice. "Wanda? It's Adele." The room went silent except for the bleeps of the cardiac monitor. The ER doctor, wearing a splatter guard, leaned over Wanda's head, pried open the grossly swollen lids, and shined a penlight into one pupil.

"She's been waiting for you or her sister to arrive. She's pretty much out of it," the doctor said, then brought her mouth close to Wanda's right ear—the one that was still intact.

"Wanda!" she shouted. "Dr. Zaritsky and Dr. Horrocks are upstairs scrubbing into OR. Your sister is on her way, and Adele is right here. If you want to tell her something, do it now."

Wanda's mouth moved, and the doctor motioned Adele closer.

Adele put her ear next to Wanda's mouth. The stench of dried blood made her hold her breath. "Talk to me, Wanda," she said. "Tell me who did this to you."

Air whistled in and out of the bloody hole as it worked to produce words. The issuing sound was horrible, made without the clarifying benefit of lips or teeth, and with an impaired tongue.

"Hihgg ache aker."

Adele frantically worked the sounds over in her mind. "Hide pacemaker?"

"Hat shisher how."

Adele rubbed the woman's icy hand. "At Shisher House?" *What the hell was Shisher House? A halfway house? A local historical monument?* "At your sister's house?"

"We've got to get her upstairs now," the doctor cut in, then added with a weary smile, "You know how those neurosurgeons and plastics people get when they're kept waiting."

"One more." Adele looked back at the brutalized face. "Wanda, was it the man we met last night who did this to you?"

Wanda was so still that for an instant Adele thought she'd gone unconscious. But then the hole moved and made a supreme effort to produce the single word: "Yeah."

The ER doctor locked the side rails and unlocked the wheels. Adele placed the portable monitor at the end of the bed and helped steered the gurney toward the door. "Was he trying to get the pacemaker?" Adele asked, bending close to Wanda's ear. "Wanda?" Adele touched the woman's shoulder. "Wanda?"

The lack of a response caused both the ER doc and Adele to push the gurney at a run.

Twin Cities PD was on Adele before Wanda could be wheeled into the patient elevator. In typical macho-cop fashion, the two young officers treated her as though she was a suspect rather than a friendly witness. Why policemen always had to take the attitude of the ugly aggressor she couldn't be sure, but she attributed it to gender insecurity. Still, having to deal with their accusatory tones and thinly veiled insinuations without losing her temper took a major effort.

What, they demanded to know, had the victim told her? How long had she known the victim and what, exactly, was the nature of their relationship? Were they "just" friends, or was there "more" to the story?

No matter what she told them, they kept bringing the questions back to the "nature" of her and Wanda's friendship. Nei-

ther of them pursued information about the man they'd met at
Rulli's, neglecting even to take down his name, preferring instead to hammer her over the head with questions that served
no purpose, except perhaps to fuel locker-room talk down at
the station.

In the end, she told them virtually nothing—which, of
course, only made them more suspicious. What she correctly
surmised was that, without a doubt, if Wanda's assailant were
found, it wouldn't be due to Twin City's efforts.

For her, that fact somehow translated into a green light to
pursue her own investigation.

Mattie Noel was tired. Not only was she tired of the daily
battles with the whining, ungrateful nurses ("I can't come in
today, Mrs. Noel, because my son got run over by a truck," or
"I can't work the triple shift, Mrs. Noel, because my union
rep said it's against labor laws") but she was tired of being
just a cog in the management wheel, hugging her clipboard
and pushing paper around. She wanted to do something that
would make the CEOs—specifically Lawrence Millbanks—
take notice. Getting rid of the senior nurses was only a start.

After twelve years of being kicked around and called the
"clipboard lady," it was time she took her place as nurse ad-
ministrator. At ninety thousand a year, she could finally get
out of her cramped apartment, put her mother in a nursing
home, and live a little—maybe even take a cruise to Mexico.

And maybe, Mattie thought, her breath coming faster, just
maybe she might even get a new car. Something small and
red with lots of pep—like a Geo Storm, or a Ford Pinto.

Her tic went quiet with the thrill of power and money. Holding her poodle cut high, she stuck out her chest and waved a
hand imperiously. "Off with their heads!" Her laugh was tinged
with hysteria.

"No! You canNOT have the day off to attend your mother's
funeral." She turned to the wall on her left. "A raise? You don't
work hard enough to deserve a raise!" She turned to the wall
on her right. "Understaffed? Ha! Too bad—deal with it!"

She flung both arms out to the ceiling. "Death to the unions! Vive la management! Vive la—"

"Mrs. Noel?" Adele stepped inside the five-by-six cubicle and looked around. "Are you alone?"

Mattie startled, jumped back, and tripped over the rolling chair. In the doorway stood the worst of the lot: that she-devil Arden from Ward 8.

"You okay?" Adele asked, brows knit. "You were shouting."

"Speakerphone," Mattie said, pointing to the phone. "I was talking to Mr. Millbanks."

"How is good old Larry Banks-a'-Million Legree? He cut the budget this year, so he must be gearing up for another raise. What's his yearly salary up to now? Five million?"

The supervisor gripped her clipboard tighter, incensed that the slacker-slut was in her office making light of the only man she'd ever loved. "How dare you come in here and insult Lawrence!" she said, trying hard to control her voice. "What do you want?"

"I need to see this month's nurses' and physicians' schedules, including the on-call schedules. I also want to see the computer printouts of the doctors' sign-in board for yesterday between the hours of midnight and six a.m."

Mattie Noel gave her a blank expression. "You've gone around the bend. Those records are confidential. No one ever sees those records, not even the director of nurses is allowed—"

"Give up the sacrosanct documents act," Adele said, rolling her eyes. "You make them sound like the Roswell files. The only thing that's confidential about those records, Mrs. Noel, is whatever comments you write on them in red pencil. I need to see them."

"Well, you can't see them," Mattie said, sounding like a five-year-old not wanting to share her toys. "I have them hidden, and you can't." She shooed her. "Go away. You have no business being down here."

"I know something about Larry that no one else knows," Adele said, hating herself for playing into the juvenile game. She was impatient to get back to the ER to intercept Wanda's sister.

"You wouldn't know anything about a decent man like Lawrence Millbanks."

Adele crossed her arms and shifted her weight to her right leg. "Oh yes I do, Mattie, and it involves you."

The woman blinked, her hand dropping from the clipboard. "Me? You know something that has to do with Lawrence and me?"

Adele nodded.

Somewhere in the background came the sound of a janitor's bucket being rolled down the hall.

"I'll trade you last Wednesday's schedules and physician sign-in records for a tidbit that only I know about how Larry feels about you." She raised her eyebrows. "It's very personal."

Wordlessly, Mattie pulled a chain from the mysterious flatlands of her bosom and removed a key, which unlocked the dented olive-green filing cabinet. From a thick file, she selected several sheets of paper and pulled them out. Adele reached for them eagerly.

Mattie kept her grip firm. "What about Lawrence?"

Adele took a deep breath. She always liked to have a full load of oxygen before any major lie. "Well, do you know that song, 'My Blue Heaven'?"

Mattie began to pull the papers toward her so that Adele almost lost her hold.

"Yes?" Her voice had gone icy.

"The other day going up the back stairs to Ward Eight, I came up behind Larry and he was singing that song—except he'd changed the words to: 'Just Mattie and me, and the Jaguar makes three, oh how happy we'll be in my blue heaven.' Isn't that what he calls his office—his blue heaven?"

The corners of Mattie's mouth quivered. "He didn't really sing those words, I mean, not really?"

The papers slid back to Adele's side. "Yes, Mattie, he really did. I think old Larry has a crush on you."

Mattie was pulling at the skin of her neck, causing red splotches to appear. "Are you sure it was Mattie he said and not Molly? They sound a little alike and—"

Adele gave a strong yank, pulling the papers free. "No, it

was definitely Mattie, and you know—he looked different somehow."

Unaware the papers were gone, Mattie's fingers were still out, gripping on to nothing. "How?" she asked in a hushed, eager voice. "How did he look different?"

"Elated. You know, the way some men get when they've either made a lot of money, or they're about to ask that special woman to make a big decision."

"He really said 'Mattie and me'?" Mattie sat down at her desk, filled with emotion.

Not bothering to answer, Adele stuffed the papers in her purse and walked into the hall, closing the door behind her.

Wanda, Adele guessed, must have been the brain of the Percy family, because Marlene was definitely the beauty. Petite with almond-shaped eyes and long silky hair to her waist, the attractive twentyish woman was hard to miss. She paced the surgery waiting room barefoot, wearing a pair of loose-fitting white Capri pants and a salmon print shirt that tied at the waist. Even with the baggy clothes, it was easy to see her figure was like those found in centerfolds and in the swimsuit issue of *Sports Illustrated*.

"Are you Marlene?"

The woman stopped pacing and rushed to her, pushing up her shirtsleeves. "Is she going to be okay?"

"She's still in surgery," Adele said. "If it makes you feel any better, Dr. Horrocks is the best plastic surgeon and Dr. Zaritsky is the best neurosurgeon in the county." She held out a hand. "I'm Adele Monsarrat. I work here as an R.N."

"Hi," Marlene said, squeezing Adele's hand. "Wanda told me about your dinner last night. She came over after she left your house and raved about the food for ten minutes."

"Was she alone?" Adele asked without ceremony.

Without letting go of her hand, Marlene pulled her to a couch. "Yeah, but she met this guy at Rulli's and he was on his way to her apartment, so she was in a hurry."

"If he was on his way to her apartment, why did she stop at your house?"

"To brag." Marlene half smiled and rolled her eyes. "Wanda and I have this competition going? You know—to see who can date the cutest guy? She was really excited about this one. She said he was the most gorgeous date she'd had in months."

"Did she give you something?" Adele said. "A plastic bag with a pacemaker in it?"

The woman sensed the urgency in her voice and hesitated. "Yeah. She wanted me to give it to a friend of ours to look at."

"Where is it now?" Adele asked, trying to stay inside her skin.

"In my car. I was going to give it to Hollis today, but I forgot about it, and then the hospital called and I—"

Adele looked at her watch. "You've got about three or four more hours of waiting to do before your sister gets out of the OR. How about we walk down to your car and get that package, and then I'll buy you a cup of tea and explain why you need to give it to me."

Her heart pounded right up until the moment Marlene pulled the Baggie out from under the passenger seat and placed it in her hand. Adele took the pacer generator out and tucked it into her Jogbra. On the way to the cafeteria, she gave Marlene an outline of the events of the evening before.

"This is so crazy," Marlene said, raking her fingers through her hair. "Why would somebody try to kill my sister for a stupid broken pacemaker?"

"Good question," Adele said. "I'm hoping your computer guru friend can help figure that out."

"Sure," Marlene murmured, preoccupied with worry. Suddenly the shape of her mouth changed with her anger. "Shit! I hope the cops nail this psycho asshole."

"Yeah," Adele said. "Like, to the wall."

Hollis, Wanda's computer guru from Silicon Valley, was sitting down to dinner with his girlfriend Vicky when Adele arrived. They were ready for her—full of questions about Wanda and what had happened.

Seated at the dining room table with her cup of decaf,

Adele gave them the same basic information she'd given Marlene, while trying to ignore the food: gray meat loaf oozing clear orange globs of fat, garlic bread floating in butter, and Spaghetti-Os with small orange meatballs.

"Did Wanda talk to either of you since last night?" Adele asked.

"She called about ten this morning and asked when Hollis would be home," Vicky said. "I told her he'd come home early and turned the phone over to him."

"She said she had a pacemaker generator she wanted me to take a look at," Hollis chimed in.

Adele nodded, her eyes glued to the area between the end of his nose and the top of his lip. It had to be at least two and a half inches, if not longer. For some reason she could not fathom, he'd chosen to highlight the facial peculiarity with a thin line of sparse mustache that fringed the upper lip. The whole effect was topped off by a set of abundant eyebrows Groucho Marx would have been proud to own.

"She mentioned something about there being a component inside that didn't belong there. She thought it might be some sort of computer chip," he continued, wiping spaghetti sauce off the awning of hair above his lip.

She pulled the generator from her bra and held it up. "Can you check it out when you're done with dinner?"

"Done now," Hollis said and stood. His huge silver Budweiser belt buckle reached only a few inches above the table. Hitching up his pants, he disappeared into a room off the kitchen. He returned a few minutes later carrying a red plastic toolbox. "Where the hell did I put that clip-on work lamp, Vick?"

Vicky thought for a minute, then popped one of the marble-sized meatballs into her mouth. "I saw it last in the upstairs bathroom, I think. I was using it to pluck my eyebrows."

"Get that damned thing hot enough, Vick, and you won't have to pluck 'em. They'll burn off," Hollis said, heading upstairs, the tops of his white cotton socks stretched out and flapping over his sneakers. A minute later, he reappeared and clipped the light on to the edge of the dining room table.

While she related the details of how the device had been responsible for triggering and disabling various electrical devices, Hollis examined the outside of the case. "Electromagnetic interference," he said, pushing workings around much in the same way Wanda had. "It's when signals combine to affect devices in unpredictable ways."

He looked over the tops of his reading glasses, upper lip and eyebrows twitching, and pointed to the iridescent plastic square that had caught Wanda's eye.

"What is it?" Adele pulled herself to the edge of the chair, her elbows resting on her thighs.

"Not a hundred percent sure. Couldn't tell you what it's programmed to do without a logic analyzer."

"What's that?"

"A device that reads what the chip does—what program it's supposed to execute." He looked at it again through the magnifying glass. "You said the pacemaker itself was really hot when it came out of the patient?"

She nodded.

His lips pressed into a thin smile. "Well, it's a stretch, but this could even be a nanochip. One of the problems with nanochips is the amount of heat they produce."

"A nanochip? Is that like a microchip?"

"Much smaller. A nanometer is one-billionth of a meter. Nanotechnology refers to manipulating and building things on an atomic or molecular level."

She gave him a look that screamed skepticism.

He grinned. "That's what the scientific community has thought about it for years too—until now. All of a sudden what used to be viewed by scientists as pure sci-fi is becoming a reality. We're learning how to create things from the bottom up, atom by atom. The U.S. government has just pledged two hundred and fifty million dollars to nanotechnology as the priority new technology. If they ever get this out in the mainstream, it's going to go hog wild."

He resettled himself in his chair. "Take the F-18C jets. They have computer chips instead of pilots—planes that think and fly by means of a computer rather than a human brain. Someday, you'll be able to fly from San Francisco to Boston in under an hour and there won't be a pilot in the cockpit—just a chip. It's fascinating stuff—nanotechnology, nanotubes, buckyballs, nanobots—the combining of chemistry and engineering." He took off his glasses and hooked the tip of the earpiece into the corner of his mouth. "It'll change the world as we know it. In the morning, you can put on a dress made from computer-enhanced fabric that can change color, size, and warm or cool you automatically depending on the weather. Houses will be self-maintaining, as will cars and all computer-based equipment. Disease will be virtually wiped out. We can drink the cure for cancer in our morning orange juice and have tiny instruments that can repair internal damage with total precision. Cleaning the environment and reversing all previous bad effects of our abuse of the planet will be a piece of cake. The possibilities are endless."

"Sounds like a Ray Bradbury story," Vicky said, finishing off the last piece of garlic bread.

"Bradbury definitely had the vision." Hollis smiled, rubbing a finger back and forth through the thin fringe of his mustache. "Not bad for a guy who never even learned how to drive an automobile. And don't forget: just a few years ago people laughed at global warming and said it was some radical's idea. Now we're in the middle of it. Same with just about any progressive idea that has ever come up before its time. Nanotechnology is definitely here to stay."

"So, do you think that this chip was running the pacemaker and it came loose or something?" Adele asked.

He shook his head and returned the generator to the bag. "Nah, I doubt it. A pacemaker generator is a pretty simple mechanism—sense and impulse, sense and impulse. I wouldn't think it would need an extra chip, especially one I suspect is as complex as this, but . . ." He stuck his glasses in the pocket of his golf shirt, which bore a logo for a logo company. "Who knows what they're doing with pacemakers these days. This thing could have been programmed to defibrillate, release minute amounts of medications, clean the guy's windows, and blow him at the same time—I don't put anything past medical technology anymore. The unfortunate part of it is that sometimes one technology is so far ahead of its time, it has to be shelved until other, enabling technologies can be developed."

"Like nanotechnology?"

"Yeah. I mean the FBI and other agencies use some nanotechnology now in various ways, but it still has a long way to go. If you really want to know what this thing is, there are agencies who could probably figure it out."

"What agencies?"

"You might be able to spark some interest in the FBI. Techno-terrorism is the in thing these days. It's worth a shot anyway. If you really think what happened to Wanda was because of this thing, somebody must have wanted it pretty bad."

Thirty minutes later Adele walked to her car, surprised at the soup of thick fog that had rolled in since she arrived. Yellow streetlight filtered through the mist giving the plants and trees an eerie halo. Adele sat in the warmth of the Beast for a long time watching the way the fog moved through the branches of the redwoods. When it got too warm, she opened the window and rested her head against the frame. She liked the feel of the fog wetting her face.

"Wanda parked in front of my house," she said to the headliner (she thought of it as the inside of the Beast's skull).

If the man was playing the part of a gentleman, he would have insisted on walking her to her car, Adele, said Miss Marple from the passenger seat.

"Which means he knows where I live."

I believe you are quite correct on that point, dear, Miss Marple added.

She sat up and pulled the Colt from her purse. Sensing her purpose, the Beast turned over without argument and headed south.

The Beast crawled down Miller Avenue in Mill Valley at 25 mph, the posted—and strictly enforced—speed limit. Adele decided that if there was an empty parking place along the median strip outside Tim's fourplex, she'd pull in and go to his door. If not, she'd visit Cynthia, who lived only a few blocks away.

The right-hand ground-floor unit blazed with light, but there wasn't an empty parking place on either side of the strip. At once both disappointed and gratified, she continued on to Cynthia's.

She hadn't gone a tenth of a mile when a red convertible passed her. Behind the wheel was a young man with long blond hair and a pair of thick glasses. He had his arm around the neck of a wooden rocking horse that was snuggled close to him, like a lover. The horse's mane was the same color as the driver's. Both man and horse wore slightly deranged expressions. It was so typically Mill Valley, no one except her gave the couple a second glance.

She found a place to park in front of Baskin-Robbins and ran across the street to the gray three-story Victorian. The door of the middle flat opened immediately. A frantic-looking Rymesteade Dhery stood before her, dish towel in hand.

"Did you get my message?" he asked before she'd even said hello.

"No. What message? Where's Cynthia?"

Rymesteade groaned and pulled at his hair. "Come in. I'll make some tea with that organic water you like."

"Filtered water," Adele corrected and followed him into the tiny kitchen at the back of the apartment. "What's up?"

He filled the stainless-steel kettle from a five-gallon bottle of Alhambra water, speaking over his shoulder: "I'm getting ready to either commit her or go to a shrink myself."

He set the kettle on the stove and lit the gas burner. "We were sitting in bed eating dinner and watching some show on the Animal Channel," he explained, offering her vanilla snaps he had arranged on a flowered serving plate, "and all of a sudden she starts to hyperventilate and gets out of bed like the house is on fire and runs into the bathroom. I asked her what was wrong, and she comes out bawling like a baby, furious as hell."

They listened to the water heating for a minute, then Adele asked, "What was she pissed about?"

Rymesteade threw up his hands like a desperate man. His eyes darted around the room. "I don't know! She kept yelling: 'You don't care! You're just like all the rest!' "

He got up and brought matching cups and saucers, and set a spoon next to each saucer. He opened the refrigerator and pulled out one of four gallons of whole milk.

"Christ on a bike," Adele laughed pointing to the surplus of milk. "What'd you do, buy a cow?"

"Don't ask," he said, pouring out a small serving pitcher of milk. "It's all part of her insanity. Has she ever been like this before? I know she had psychos for parents, but have you ever seen her do this kind of acting out?"

Adele shook her head. "What about getting some blood work? Maybe something's out of whack."

He looked at her over the sugar bowl. "I've tried everything. I even—God forgive me—stuck her in her sleep. I managed to draw up about three drops of blood before she woke up and almost brained me. I slept on the window seat for a week after that."

The kettle whistled, and he finished setting out the honey and lemon wedges before pouring water into their cups and sitting down. She waited for him to realize he'd forgotten the tea.

"Did your mother teach you this?" she asked, waving a hand over the table.

He shook his head, his mouth full of cookie. "God, no. She didn't have time. She worked full-time in the local elementary school cafeteria. We were lucky to have clean clothes. I took home economics in high school. I was too small to play sports, the guys in the woodworking shops were hoods, the ones on the school paper and all the other Ivy League electives were nerds, so I took the sew-and-cook class with the girls. I used to make my own shirts and pants in med school." He laughed. "I had to hide my portable sewing machine under the bed so the guys in the dorm wouldn't think I was gay and freak out."

"So what happened after Cynthia informed you you didn't care and you're just like all the rest?"

He sipped his tea. "She got dressed and left. Slammed the door behind her. She told me not to wait up."

"How long ago was that?"

He looked at his watch, calculating. "About an hour and forty-five minutes. You think I should try the hospital?"

"Cynthia go to the hospital on her time off?" Adele shook her head. "Ludicrous."

"Yeah, I guess you're right on that," he said, rubbing the back of his neck.

She patted his arm. "She'll come home when she's ready."

"I hope so," he said mournfully. "She took my Volvo."

Adele's eyebrows shot up in surprise. Cynthia refused to drive anything other than the Blessed Virgin Mary—her blue 1965 VW Bug. She hated the idea of any car that was new, expensive, big, or American. The Volvo lost on three of the four counts.

"Wow," Adele said. "Cynthia driving a Volvo station wagon? *Now* you've got my attention."

The Camry was still in his parking slot, and the lights in his apartment still blazed. However, a mass evacuation had taken place in the forty minutes she'd spent at Cynthia's flat. The median strip was now empty save for the pickup with the miniature wood-shingled house built onto the bed, which had been parked in the same spot for at least ten years.

She parked the Beast and punched in the number for the OR. A nurse coolly informed her that Wanda was still in surgery and that her condition was only fair. She crossed Miller Avenue and hurried down the blacktop driveway to the fourplex.

If Wanda died . . . She shuddered, unable to contemplate the possibility. She didn't want something like that living with her for the rest of her life—there were already too many other ghosts crowding her closet.

Expressions of bewilderment and pleasure crossed Tim's face one after the other when he opened the door. "Wow," he said, hooking a hand around the back of his neck. "Twice in one day? I'm flattered, but more than that, I'm really glad you're here. I've been thinking about something."

"Me too," she said.

The smoke detector alarm went off behind him, and he ran toward the billows of smoke wafting up from the stove and through the living room.

The burnt tofu-onion scramble wasn't bad, Adele thought. But then again, she was partial to lots of ketchup. They worked the food around their plates with toast points—also burned.

"I think taking this cooking class may save the building from burning down." He laughed. There was a buildup of charred toast caught in the crevices of his teeth. Immediately, she vacuumed her teeth with her tongue, using high suction.

"A steady diet of carbon isn't good for you either," she said. "Causes cancer."

He took a long pull from his beer and put it down empty. "Life causes cancer, Adele. Want more scramble?" There wasn't any more left, but he figured he'd make peanut butter on toast if she was still hungry.

Adele shook her head and waited for him to start.

"After I dropped you at your car," he said, "I talked to the on-scene dicks processing the scene at your friend's apartment. They said the place looked like a bomb hit it. Every piece of furniture was sliced open or broken, the carpeting pulled up—every container except cans of food were opened and searched. Light fixtures, toaster, everything was busted apart. From the sounds of it, I hope to God she's got a good cleaning service."

"Did they find anything?"

Tim shook his head. "Scene team did it all—video, photos, dusting for latent prints, collecting blood-splatter evidence— and still came up empty-handed."

"What about the neighbors?" She licked the last of the ketchup off her fork.

"The uniform talked to all the neighbors in the building who were home. The lady in the adjoining apartment heard her come in at about three-thirty. About ten minutes later, she said Wanda's TV came on pretty loud."

"Who found her?"

"Some guy she had an early dinner date with. He said he rang her buzzer for about five minutes, decided she couldn't hear it over the television, tried the door, found it unlocked, saw the mess, and called nine-one-one. Twin Cities was still questioning him when they found Wanda's body stuffed in the bedroom closet. One look at her and he passed out at the scene. They had to take the poor bastard to ER he was so shook up."

They sat in silence while he tilted the beer bottle back and forth in his fingers, causing the remaining liquid to run up the sides then pool back on the bottom.

"I've been thinking about what you said," she said finally, "and I think there's some things you should know."

He nodded without looking up.

"But first, you've got to tell me one thing."

He raised his eyes from the brown bottle dangling from his fingers.

"Do you have any close personal friends who work for the FBI?"

While she folded and unfolded a stray sock that she found stuffed between the couch cushions, she told him about Wanda, the pacemaker, and their meeting with the overly charming man at Rulli's. She asked for a beer and drank half before telling him about her conversation with Wanda's sister and Hollis.

He kept his gaze riveted on her, his thoughts working over everything she'd given him, cutting to what seemed most important. "So chances are that Wanda told him—showed him—exactly where you live and that you had something to do with this pacemaker that he's after."

Her hand had found its way into the sock, transforming it into a faceless puppet—the heel as its forehead, and the toe as the mouth. "You're probably right about that," the sock said in a perfect Mr. Bill voice.

Ignoring her touch of rascality, he got up and went into the bathroom. He returned with his toothbrush and shaving kit in hand. "I'm inviting myself to spend the night at your house," he said.

She and the puppet shook their heads. "No way, Mr. Hand," the puppet said. "I'll protect her."

He took the sock and looked her in the eye. "I'm spending the night at your house, Adele, either inside or on your porch. If it's me you object to, then I'll have Chernin out there. And you know sure as shit he's gonna be at your door every five minutes asking if you've ever seen *Ocean's Eleven* and then reciting it line by line."

"You wouldn't do that to me," she said seriously.

"Try me," he said and got his duffel bag from the closet.

ELEVEN

GOING OVER THE MILL VALLEY–CORTE MADERA hill, she switched the Beast's beams back and forth from high to low, settling on low for the thick fog that enveloped her. Still, she was able to see only about ten feet beyond the nose of the car. It was close to eight by the time she pulled up in front of the brown-shingled house with the green trim.

She turned off the motor, already sensing something out of place. The house was dark and the front blinds drawn. The center of her went cold. She distinctly remembered leaving the porch and living room lights on for Nelson. She never closed her blinds until she was ready for bed.

For a moment she contemplated driving on, but the thought that Nelson was inside stayed her. She wanted to kick herself for talking Timothy into waiting a couple of hours before he came over. She stared at the one-story duplex, grimly contemplating what could be inside with her dog.

"I'm being ridiculous," she said finally to the empty passenger seat as she gathered her purse and lunch pail. "The fuse probably blew. The circuits get touchy in the fog."

Yeah, said McGruff the Crime Dog in his gravel voice, *and maybe the blinds just sorta pulled themselves shut. Ya gotta look at it like this, Adele: some fish, a barrel, a smoking gun— ya know what I mean?*

"My dog is in there," she said, getting out of the car. Hand curled around the Colt inside her purse, she bounded up the porch steps. The door stood ajar.

Rising panic made her temples burn as she inched her way

242

inside. Nelson was nowhere to be seen. From the back of the house came a low, eerie noise.

She held the gun in front of her with both hands. Crossing the living room to the hall she noticed a faintly familiar odor, but could not place it right away. The scratching sounds of the camellia branches hitting the kitchen windows did not cover the moans coming from her bedroom. She went toward the sound, wishing she had paid attention to whether or not there had been any unfamiliar cars parked on the street.

Her bedroom door was closed, light showing through the crack at the bottom. She took a step backward when a most piteous whine turned into a mournful howl that might have originated in the bowels of canine hell. The dual engines of her adrenals dumped a couple of loads of adrenaline into her system as she lunged at the bedroom door screaming. Whoever had caused her dog that kind of pain deserved a bullet.

On the bed lay a version of Cynthia she'd never seen. Face smashed into several pillows, her long light brown hair stuck out from the scalp, a wild tangled mess. At her side, Nelson rested his paw on one outstretched arm while he sniffed the back of Cynthia's head.

Adele stood transfixed by the sight. Cynthia was dead. Whoever attempted to kill Wanda had broken in and, mistaking Cynthia for her, murdered her.

The spell was broken when the woman on the bed turned in her direction, sucked in a long shuddery breath, and sobbed. Immediately, Nelson let out a chilling commiserating howl: he hated to see humans cry.

Helen, lying on the far side of the bed, slept soundly.

Adele sat between her two best friends and put her arm around the human one. She let Cynthia cry, amazed at the amount of heat radiating from her body. When the crying turned into shuddering hiccups, Adele left her and returned a minute later with a cool washcloth and a glass of cold cherry cider.

"Okay," she said, holding the cider to Cynthia's lips. "Start at the beginning."

Cynthia sipped, choked, sipped again, and finally drained

the glass. She blew her nose and took in a long breath. "You know how women's minds can really do some amazing things sometimes when they don't want to look at the truth?" She looked at Adele through swollen, red-rimmed eyes.

"Like what?" Adele asked.

"You know, like when a woman walks in on her husband in bed with her best friend and her mind automatically comes to a halt and starts going down all these side streets, and she thinks to herself: 'Nah, they aren't really in bed screwing. They're probably just checking out each other's moles like the dermatologist told them to. Yeah, that's it! They're just doing mole checks.' I mean your mind refuses to believe what's happening, because if it recognizes what's really going on, then it'll have to work so much harder taking care of all the other trauma that goes along with the situation: divorce, breaking up the home, telling the parents—that kind of work."

Adele shifted on the bed. "Okay," she said patiently. "So, did you find Ryme in bed with someone?"

"Oh God, I wish I had." Cynthia's voice trembled. "That would make everything so much easier."

"What are you saying, Cyn?"

Cynthia raised her eyes to hers. "I'm pregnant."

Adele overrode the shock, willing her gears to remain in neutral. "How many weeks?"

"Six, maybe eight, although it could be ten. I don't know how it happened. I'm on the pill *and* I use the sponge. I didn't even think about it until I missed my period and my breasts started changing. I took one of those home tests . . ." Cynthia shook her head. "No, I take that back. I took *three* of those home tests, three different brands, then drove to Dr. Lieberman's office to make an appointment for an abortion."

Adele sat back. "And?"

"I don't know." Cynthia's voice was small. "I found myself staring at the ceiling at three in the morning thinking about this little kid that was growing up right there in his aquatic little room, and I felt happy. I imagined us playing in the garden, and me teaching him how to race worms and make mud huts for them. After a couple of minutes I realized I was feeling something like love and I totally freaked. I always said I wouldn't be caught dead having a kid. I didn't even like kids when I was a kid."

Cynthia began to rock slightly, the words bubbling out: "Then I think of my mother and father, and I know that Ryme could never be like them, but I'm not so sure about me." She looked at Adele. "What if it's in my genes, Del? What if I'm really a child abuser and I end up doing the same things to my kid that they did to me? I couldn't stand it."

"You have control over that, I'd imagine," Adele said. "Child abuse isn't a disease you're born with. You're a long, far cry from your parents."

"But I'll never be free again. And you know my record with men—what if I wake up some morning and I don't want to be with Ryme anymore? I can't raise a kid on my own."

"Why haven't you told Ryme?"

Cynthia covered her face. "Because he's a pussycat. He'll want to get married and have six more kids. Shit, he's already got the Volvo, and he's been talking about building a house with five or six bedrooms—breeder coops I call them." She slid her hands down so that only her eyes were visible. "I couldn't stand coming home and finding him sewing up curtains with little baseballs and catching mitt designs in the fabric. He'd fill the guest room with mobiles and teddy bears and all that baby crap." There was a downward curve of her lips, then she sighed. "And, well, to be honest, I'm not a hundred percent sure it's even his."

Cynthia laid her head on top of Nelson's. Both of them looked miserable. "I've been terrible to him lately," she said absently. "I've totally avoided him. I haven't let him touch me for weeks."

"Yeah," Adele said. "I stopped by your place this afternoon and caught him eyeing the sheep in the back pasture."

Despite the tears, Cynthia snickered. "Oh God, Adele, I'm just afraid all that stability would kill me, and I'll cease to exist. I mean putting one man and one woman together for the rest of their lives? It's unnatural! Marriage to me is the loss of control over my own destiny. Why would I invite that into my life? I'm already screwed up all on my own. Plus, I hate that codependent relationship philosophy: 'He thinks, therefore I am.' " She shook her head. "And here I was getting ready to make some moves on that new guy in radiology. You know me: take lovers, leave no survivors."

Cynthia sighed and stared off into space. "Oh, I don't know, Del, some days I wake up and it just doesn't seem worth the effort of chewing through the leather straps."

Crossing the room to the antique secretary, Adele brought back a wide-toothed comb and began to work the knots out of Cynthia's hair. "What do you want me to do?"

"I want you to tell me what to do," Cynthia answered plaintively.

"That's easy." Adele smiled indulgently, separating the hair into three plaits. "First, imagine that whatever I suggested you do, you would have to do without question. Then, imagine that I told you that you're never going to find a nicer guy than Ryme, and that you have to marry him ASAP and have this baby."

Starting at the crown of Cynthia's head, she began a French braid. "After you've gauged how that feels, then try to feel how you'd react if I told you you had to have an abortion. Other than that, my sweet, the only suggestion I can give you is to take some time to think this through beginning to end. Write down the pros and cons of each course of action and decide what you can and can't live with. Whatever you decide to do, I'll support you."

"There," she said, pulling the elastic tie off the end of her own braid and securing it around Cynthia's. "You want to spend the night?"

Cynthia slid off the bed, shaking her head. "No. I have to go home; I took Ryme's car. I should return it." She bent to put on her shoes and snorted. "Want to hear the ultimate in internal conflict?"

"Uh-huh."

Cynthia took a deep breath. "When I was going over to Lieberman's office to make my appointment for the abortion,

I took the Volvo so that if I did get into an accident, the baby would have a chance at surviving."

As soon as Cynthia left, Adele called the OR to get an update on Wanda. Without a trace of optimism, the nurse told her Wanda had just come out of surgery and was being wheeled to post-anesthesia recovery.

No sooner had she hung up than the phone rang. "Can you meet me in the parking lot outside the sheriff's office in about fifteen minutes?" Tim asked.

She could tell by the phones ringing in the background he was at the department already.

She looked at her watch. "Okay. Where are we going?"

"Tell you when you get here. Bring the pacemaker and keep your antennae up. Whoever went after your friend might be waiting to check you out as well. Be careful."

With three minutes to consider clothes, she threw on a pair of faded jeans and a pale peach scooped-neck sweater. She brushed her teeth and hair and was spraying on a bit of Aliage when Melinda appeared behind her in the full-length mirror on the back of her closet door. The imaginary critic was quick to judge, and more frequently than not, those judgments were not kind.

You look cheap, Adele, she droned. *You aren't appropriately dressed for a cockfight, let alone to meet a male friend in public. Desperate fashion measures rarely ever work with a man. Show all the cleavage you want, but just remember, he'll always love Cynthia more.*

Annoyed at herself for caring what a completely fictitious character thought, Adele blew the bangs off her forehead and looked down at what there was of her cleavage. It was pretty skimpy when compared with Cynthia's voluptuous figure.

For about three seconds she toyed with the idea of stuffing her bra with the silicone falsies Cynthia gave her for her last birthday, then as quickly discarded the idea. Not only did she find she couldn't keep from fussing with them—much in the same way certain persons could not resist popping bubble wrap—but the first and only time she'd ever worn them, they were so heavy, one slipped halfway around the band of her Jog-bra. She'd spent the evening with an extra breast in the middle of her back. It had been a singularly hideous experience.

She ran out of the house, tripped over a large and solid object, and found herself airborne. On the lawn, she skidded, rolled, and came up with the Colt pointed at the dark object that was righting itself in front of her door.

Adele swore, and put the gun back in her purse. "You've got to be kidding!"

Mrs. Coolidge dusted herself off and wobbled unsteadily toward Adele. "Hello, Adele. How are you? Were you on your way out? I didn't want to disturb you, but I was wondering if you'd heard about Mrs. Ferrari."

Adele's eyes cut to the place on the porch where Mrs. Coolidge had been crouched. In the blinds that covered the glass of the door, a slat had accidentally been turned up, giving a clear view of the living room and kitchen.

"What is it with you, Mrs. Coolidge?" Adele asked, flattening the slat. "What is it that you think I do in here which compels you to indulge in Peeping Tommery?"

Mrs. Coolidge plucked at the front of her shawl. "Why, Adele, I don't know what you're talking about. I was just bending over to tie my shoe when you came out like a lightning bolt."

"Sure," Adele said, heading to the Beast. "Kind of hard to tie up fuzzy house slippers, though, don't you think?"

Mrs. Coolidge looked down at the fuzzy pink kitty heads, then back at her with an innocent half smile.

"What can I do for you? I have to be in San Rafael in five minutes."

"Well," Mrs. Coolidge said, breathing heavily as she followed her to the car. "I'd heard that Mrs. Ferrari was in the hospital again, and I was wondering if you could check on her and let me know if she's all right?" She patted down a thatch of wiry gray hair that sprang back up the second she took her fingers away. "I guess you know—well, of course everybody knows—that she does quite a bit of drinking. They say her liver is shot, and she smokes, so you just know her lungs are gone too. This is the third time she's been taken away by the ambulance, and—"

"It's none of our business what the woman does with her life, Mrs. Coolidge." Adele put the car into gear when a thought came to her. She turned. "Listen, you want to be of use?"

The woman nodded, her hands flying out like a couple of startled birds.

"Keep an eye on my house for the next few days. If you see anybody hanging around who you don't recognize, call the cops."

Mrs. Coolidge's eyes lit up. She got to play snoop legally. It was almost more than she could stand. "Who is it that's going to be hanging around? Is this a new case you're working on? Do you want me to—?"

"Just look for suspicious people in the neighborhood. Report in with me tomorrow." Adele smiled a fake smile and rolled away, leaving the woman in the middle of the street.

While he waited, Tim tapped out the rhythm to "Devil with a Blue Dress" using the steering wheel of the Camry. It was a sad commentary on the state of the modern world, he thought, that he would never be able to hear the song without thinking of Monica Lewinsky.

He watched Adele walk across the parking lot in that sultry, self-assured way she had of moving, as though she was in complete charge of her world.

As soon as they were under way, Adele called the hospital. All the post-anesthesia nurse would tell her was that Wanda had made it to ICU. Her condition was still posted as fair. That worried her more than anything. Ellis's criteria for critical, poor, fair, and good conditions were not uniform. What management called fair, was considered in the days before managed care, poor or even critical. It was just another way around having to pay an extra nurse.

"How is she?" Tim asked after she hung up.

"Not good." She turned to look out at the fog, a heaviness descending on her the way a steady rain weighed down a tent. "Where we headed?"

"Novato," he said, glancing in his rearview mirror.

"Ah, Novato," she repeated in a faraway voice. "How nice."

Novato was Marin's version of redneck country, where the men all chewed tobacco, wore Stetsons and Tony Lamas, knew how to drive a horse and ride a tractor—and the women did the same. The only visible differences between the genders were that the women wore sadistically teased, peroxided beehive hairdos and three-inch red nails—although there was an odd cowboy here and there who wore the same color polish.

They were silent until after they passed the Lucas Valley exit. "Any idea who might be interested in following you this evening?" Tim asked, glancing in his rearview mirror.

Her stomach slapped up against her throat and settled back into place. She turned to look at him. "You're kidding."

He sped up and changed lanes. "I never kid about being followed. Know anybody who drives a dark gray Buick LeSabre? A jealous boyfriend I don't know about?"

"You sure about this?"

Tim slowed down and changed lanes again, taking the main Novato exit. At the stoplight, he checked his rearview mirror again. "Pretty sure. I'll take some curlycue turns up here to see if I can shake him."

He turned several times then pulled into the public library parking lot, switched around and turned off his lights. A few seconds later, the gray Buick rolled by, spotted them, and sped out of sight.

"Son of a bitch rabbited," Tim said, pulling out of the parking lot in the same direction as the Buick.

"He what?"

"Split."

They spotted the LeSabre three cars ahead at a stoplight. As soon as the light changed, the car turned onto one of the main downtown streets and picked up speed. They were almost close enough to read the plate number when the Buick suddenly pulled out of traffic, ran a red light, and squealed onto a side street.

Tim picked up his radio. "Control, This is K thirty-two

in pursuit of a suspect car. A ninety-four, dark gray Buick LeSabre. Couldn't catch the plate. The suspect vehicle is headed eastbound on Second Street crossing Grand. I need all available units to backup or intersect."

Tim turned to her, a weird smile on his face. "Fasten your seat belt, honey, because we're going for a ride."

Adele opened her mouth to say something when Tim held up a finger.

"Just shut up, sit down, and hold on."

She did as she was told.

Heading west on Simmons Lane, the Buick picked up speed and turned north onto San Marin Drive. Already a quarter of a mile ahead of them, the car ran a light and went west to San Carlos Drive.

Tim floored the Camry and less than twenty seconds later turned onto the same street. It was deserted. Not so much as a leaf was fluttering.

They searched driveways and side streets for fifteen minutes without sighting the vehicle. Tim called in to dispatch to cancel the pursuit, made an illegal U-turn, and continued driving west through a mile or so of subdivisions toward the outlying expanse of horse ranches and landed gentry.

She was on the verge of asking where they were headed, when he slowed and pulled into a dirt road flanked by two weathered wagon wheels. How he'd found the place was beyond her, since it looked like all the other dirt roads flanked by the same two rustic wagon wheels.

The Camry's shocks got a good workout for another three-quarters of a mile until a log cabin surrounded by scrub oaks and redwood saplings came into view. The Bridal Chorus from *Lohengrin* thundered around them the moment they stepped out of the car.

Tim banged on the door until it rattled on its hinges. The abrupt decrease in volume caused the air to suddenly feel empty. A man's deep voice resonated through the door before it was opened.

"Ritmann, you sidewinding motherfucker. You've got to need something before I can get your lazy ass out here?"

Harlan Jacquot was about as far as one could get from her
idea of what a retired FBI agent looked like. Instead of a
stately, silver-haired Sean Connery, Danny DeVito with a bad
rug and a paunch stood before them. He was dressed not in the
charcoal slacks and blue oxford shirt she would have expected,
but rather in baggy jeans with shredded-out knees, gray cowboy boots, and a black sweatshirt with a Bohemian Club logo
that looked as if it'd been through the Spanish-American War.
His neck fleshed out over the crew neck of the sweatshirt, along
with stray clumps of white and gray chest hair.

His eyes, she noticed, came level with her breasts.

"Jesus, Harl," Tim said as the men bear-hugged, "since
when did you start listening to that high-class squealing?"

"Hell, I don't know." He waved a hand in the air. "I did undercover at the San Francisco Opera House one season.
Hated it at first, and then . . ." He shrugged boyishly. "It grew
on me. Gets me right in the old solar plexus, you know?" He
turned his attention to Adele. "I apologize for my friend here
who has the manners of a pig. He didn't mention he was
bringing such an attractive guest or I would have . . ." He
grappled for a second, unsure of what came next.

"Baked a cake," Tim finished for him, and made the
introductions.

Harlan shook her hand, his crystal-clear green eyes crin-
kling up at the corners. There were broken blood vessels in
his cheeks and nose.

They sat in the main room, which encompassed the kitchen,
the dining area, and an alcove that served as a small office.
Overall, the cabin was homey. There were books everywhere,
some on shelves, some in neat piles three feet tall. File folders
were stacked on a long, narrow oak table under a set of windows. An IBM laptop sat in the center of the office desk, cables
hooked to a laser printer. The walls were adorned with a number of grainy black-and-white photographs of natural landscapes and grandchildren. The only thing that seemed out of
place was a glass display cabinet filled with a wide variety of
high-powered handguns.

"So you're Adele Monsarrat," he said, his salt-and-pepper

toupee bobbing. "I believe we have a mutual friend who is an admirer of yours."

"You know my mother?" Adele asked.

"Unfortunately no," he said, laughing. "But Kitch Heslin and I go back to police academy days fourteen thousand years ago. He used to talk about you all the time. Last time I saw him, he was *still* talking about you."

"You've *seen* Kitch? In the flesh?" Adele's tone was both disbelieving and awed. "I didn't think he was in contact with any humans since he"—she refused to use the R word; retirement never seemed possible for him—"went off to play Lewis and Clark."

"It wasn't easy finding the bastard." Harlan chuckled. "I don't know why I find that funny. I was a top FBI man for twenty-five years, and finding Kitch was more difficult than finding the Unabomber. You wouldn't believe what I had to go through to get to him: bears, mountain lions, horny moose. I had to carry heavy artillery and use a special all-terrain vehicle just to get to the goddamned place."

"So I take it he's still in the Yolla Bolla Eel Wilderness?" Adele asked.

Harlan nodded. "Oh yeah. He's Mr. Mountain Man— wears bearskins for clothes and has a beard down to his navel."

Bewildered, Adele sat back. "Really?" she asked, nervously pinching the skin under her chin. She hadn't imagined that Kitch would go *that* far.

"Well, maybe not bearskins, but he hasn't shaved since the day of his retirement party. I spent four days with him. I had a case I needed his help on, and he wanted a fishing buddy. Worked out great. He gave me what I needed, and I filled his freezer with trout."

He sat back and put his hands in his lap. "I understand you're quite the detective." There was something in his expression that told her he was much more than an aging, retired FBI agent who was small and covered his severely receding hairline with carpet remnants. "Seems you saved this guy's cookies." He hooked a thumb at Tim.

"I got him into it in the first place," Adele said, looking away, though she managed to keep a note of levity in her voice. "It just so happens I have muscular arms—slows those slugs right down."

"What can I get you two to drink?" Harlan asked, heading for the kitchen.

A big orange cat came out from under one of the chairs, stretched, yawned, and rubbed himself along Adele's leg. Harlan raised his eyebrows. "Kalamazoo usually isn't that friendly with strangers. You must have some kind of pheromones."

"No," she said, bending over to stroke the cat's back. It arched its back against the inside of her hand and purred loudly. "But I do have a dog that loves cats and rabbits. I think he's advertising for a permanent playmate-slash-pet by rubbing his pheromones onto my clothes."

Harlan took a beer out of the refrigerator and handed it to Tim, who was busy studying the handgun collection. He opened the fridge door wider for her to choose what she wanted. She pointed to a bottle of Calistoga water. He handed her a glass and a slice of lime and offered ice, which she turned down.

In the living room, Harlan put a few more logs into the woodstove. "I know it doesn't seem that cold right now, but it gets colder than a well digger's ass in here by about two in the morning."

Adele, who had just taken a sip of her drink, snorted. The carbonated water shot out her nose and down the front of her blouse, fizzing as it went.

Harlan handed her a dish towel. "Tim tells me you're on to something and might need some help."

She blotted the water, looking from Harlan to Tim and then back at the agent. "What else has he told you?"

Harlan was quick to hold up his hands in innocence. "Not much. Only thing he said was that you were on to something pretty hot, and that you'd asked if he knew anybody in the agency. I told him I'd listen to whatever you had to say and see what I could do." He sat back. "To be honest with you, I'm finding retirement boring as hell. I need excitement."

The cat had settled on the floor at her feet and stretched himself out. With one paw it batted at her leg as if to say, "Hey, pay attention to *me*!"

She pulled the cat onto her lap, where it settled as though he'd been doing it for years. She ran the jumble of facts by Harlan, leaving out only that her method of interviewing people included the use of an illegal deputy investigator's ID.

She paused when she came to her recent meeting with Hollis, trying to think of how to ask for what she needed. "The computer guy who looked at this"—she handed him the Baggie containing the pacemaker—"seemed to know what he was talking about. I might be attempting to build a bridge across the Grand Canyon, but I believe whoever attempted to kill Wanda Percy and Thomas Penn did so to get to this."

The agent took the pacemaker out and held it up to the light before snapping the case open and looking inside. From his expression, she got a vague sense that he was both disturbed and excited by what she'd told him. In an instant, the friendly visit had turned business, and Harlan Jacquot's mood had gone from jovial to deadly serious.

"What do you want me to do?" he asked finally.

She took a long breath. "I'd like someone in the FBI's computer department to check it out. If it's nothing, we lose nothing. If it turns out to be something, then everybody wins."

He stared at her, tapping his fingertips together. "Could the man you saw at Penn's house be the same person you met at Rulli's?"

She shook her head emphatically. "Not unless the guy at Rulli's was wearing elevator shoes and had put on about twenty pounds. Although . . ." She paused to think, pursing her lips. "They had the same coloring. Black hair. Olive skin. Heavy shadows of facial hair. Possibly of Middle Eastern descent."

"If everything you've told me is true," he said in an even tone, "it sounds as though it might be tied into a larger picture. I doubt the guy you saw in Penn's house was waving a gun around because he thought it accessorized his outfit nicely."

"What kind of larger picture?" she asked.

"Maybe the two men you've seen are working together as part of a group, or maybe they're rivals—we don't know." He ran a hand over his chin. "Whoever they are, they want to get their hands on this thing, and I'm willing to bet it sure as hell isn't because it turns the lights on and off."

Jacquot drank his beer and leaned back in his chair. "I'll get in touch with a friend of mine in the computer crimes unit and have her take a look at it. If there's any useful information to be had, she'll find it."

"Great," Adele said, and making several contortions, all to keep from disturbing the cat, reached her purse and rummaged inside. "There's another matter I need you to take a look at."

Tim stared at her. This wasn't in the script. But then again, was she not the proverbial loose cannon? If he was going to hang with her, he had a feeling it was something he'd need to get used to.

She unfolded the piece of notepaper on which Opal had drawn the symbol and gave it to him.

His expression didn't change as he scrutinized it, although his pulse picked up. He casually rubbed the center of his chest, as if to erase the skipped beats that were going on a few inches below.

"Do you recognize it?" She peered anxiously into his eyes.

Tim went to the couch, cocking his head sideways to see the drawing.

Harlan nodded and looked at her in a way that caused the hairs on her arms to stand up. "Where did you see this?"

"I didn't," she said. "The man who claimed to be Dr. English—the one who discharged Mr. Penn—was wearing a ring with the same marking." She hesitated, then asked, "What is it?"

Harlan held his beer bottle rigid then slowly put it down, still staring at the symbol. "How about if for now I tell you that I think you're playing with some mighty powerful people."

He looked at Tim and then back to Adele. "This is over your heads—both of you. These aren't just street-variety bad guys. What you're talking about here is closer to a specialized terrorist group."

He folded the paper. "May I keep this?"

She nodded. "Specialized in what?"

Harlan shook his head, got up, and walked back and forth in the short space between the kitchen and the living room. Taking this as a sign dinner was about to be served, the cat jumped off her lap and began rubbing against Harlan's leg.

"Hard to say. I worked on a case with the Terrorist Task Force at Quantico way back when. Don't remember the case, but I learned a lot about terrorists—personality profiles, types of terrorism, motivators—you name it. One thing that always seems strange to me is how terrorist groups tend to change targets and allegiances as frequently as they change or assassinate their leaders.

"Now *this* group," Harlan shook his head once, "this group is small but powerful and has some wealthy backers. It has a history of intense anti-Western activity that was . . ." He searched for the words he wanted. ". . . insidiously malicious. None of this blowing up airports and busloads of school kids and then publicly claiming responsibility. This group was more specialized in individual covert operations using some impressively sophisticated methods—things you didn't read about in the *Times*."

"Like what?" Adele asked.

Jacquot leaned back against the kitchen counter with his legs crossed at the ankles. "They came very close to assassinating the First Family back in eighty-seven."

Tim snapped his fingers. "Damn! Who the hell was stupid enough to stop them?"

"How the hell could anyone tell they didn't?" Adele asked dryly. "One was as stiff as a corpse and the other fell asleep during the inauguration and never woke up."

Harlan chuckled, picked up the cat, put it in the sink, and turned on the tap. At once, the cat began to lap at the trickle of water. Harlan's grin faded. He leaned his forearms on the counter. "What about this Thomas Penn? Is he—?"

Tim smiled and shook his head. "Nope. An A-one Joe Shit the Ragman."

The grin disappeared completely. "What about somebody close to him?"

"Doubt it," Adele answered. "He's got one daughter—although I wouldn't swear to the gender designation unless I could take a peek for myself under that Brooks Brothers suit. She lives in Seattle. She's too straight and smarmy."

"Smarmy?" the men said in unison.

"Yeah," Adele said. "You know—smarmy—wormy—Muffy-like."

Harlan went to the desk and tore a sheet of notepaper off a pad and handed it to her. "Write her name down for me anyway."

He held it away, squinting to read. "Dylan Thomas Penn?"

"Hey," Adele said with a shrug, "He's got a male cat named Helen. What can I say?"

Tim rose from the couch and yawned. "Okay. Time to go and let you get back to your yodeling."

With the sense of being moved along with the tide, Adele gave her card to the FBI agent. "I know I'm a civilian," she said pointedly, "but get in touch with me anyway—at least to give me some idea of what's going on, okay?"

Jacquot looked right at her. "I'll give you more than an idea, Adele."

At some point between outfitting the sofa bed with clean linens, going over the instructions on how to run the temperamental shower, and setting up the Scrabble board, the phone rang. She looked at her watch.

Closing her eyes, she picked up the receiver and listened. In the background, came the sound of a PA system: "Code Blue, ICU. Dr. Zaritsky, ICU STAT!" A voice close to the phone yelled out: "Is it her again? Is it? Oh shit!"

"Hello?" Adele pressed the phone flat against her ear. "Who is this?"

"Miss Monsarrat? Adele?" There was a note of barely contained hysteria under the tone.

"Marlene?"

"Wanda's in trouble and nobody will talk to me."

"On my way," She said. "Hold tight. I'll meet you in the ICU waiting room."

Her adrenals were dumping again. She had a brief thought about how many crises she could handle before her reserve adrenaline tanks went empty. With the stresses of Ward 8, coupled with her adventures in investigations, she doubted she'd have any adrenals left by the time she reached middle age.

"Something going on at the hospital?" Tim asked.

Adele handed him a set of towels. "Wanda's circling the drain. I'll be back in a bit. Leave the bathroom door open for Helen, and don't let these two get too crazy. Before you go bed, let Nels out in the backyard for ten minutes, but don't let him go into the next-door neighbor's yard. They've got a penned rabbit back there named Fluffy—"

At the sound of the name, Nelson barked twice and ran for the side door, his tongue dangling to the side in an expression that gave him a mentally challenged look.

". . . who Nelson thinks should rightfully be his. Nelson is a firm upholder of the dog property laws: 'If I like it, it's mine, if it's in my mouth, it's mine, and, if I can take it from you, it's mine.' "

Tim looked between Nelson, the leash, and Helen. "How about if I go with you?"

In answer she set the leash on top of the towels and walked out the door.

As she was getting into the Beast, she gave the thumbs-up sign to Mrs. Coolidge, who had a pair of binoculars trained on the front of her house.

The bite-sized pastry shells filled with steak tartare and capers were too delicious. The more Daisy daintily slid into her mouth, the more ravenous she became for the rich pastry and salty meat. Out of respect for her diet, she'd tried the raw veggie plate, but it didn't assuage her hunger. Perhaps the antibiotics had something to do with her craving for salt and protein. On the spot, she decided to stop taking them.

Daisy filled her plate with the rest of the pastries and covered them with thin slices of cheese and radishes cut like flowers. Making her way through the crowded room, she settled on the brocade couch, where she worked her way through four more pastries. She was lifting the fifth to her mouth when an explosion of laughter came from the other side of the room.

A man in his mid-thirties had drawn a crowd and was moving his limbs about in preposterous poses, making comical facial gestures. There was something about the performance that caused a sick feeling to creep through her.

At the sound of an affected British accent, she stiffened. From the cadence, mixed with the words and gestures, she at once realized he was mimicking her, making her appear ridiculous. He was recounting word for word a conversation she'd had with the hostess upon her arrival, in which she'd revealed in detail how she was having a bit of trouble with itching on her bum. The man was eliciting screams of laughter as he simulated reaching around a rear end the size of a battleship in order to get in a good scratch.

Daisy put down the half-eaten plate of food and looked at it as though it were the cause of all her present misery. She needed to escape to a safe place where she could gather her wits and dignity—at least long enough to take her leave in a proper fashion.

As she rose off the couch, she felt a tug. Turning first one way and then another, she could see a gold thread from the cushion caught on one of the iridescent sequins on the back of her dress. Across the room another explosion of laughter made the blood rise to her face. Everyone would be staring, she thought. Everyone would be thinking that she *was* a fat tart without enough common sense to fill a thimble—exactly as Mum and Nanny had always told her.

She tried to get hold of the thread, which was a centimeter out of reach. The laughter rose even higher as tears spilled, causing the pink and black eye makeup to run in twin rivers down her cheeks and into the crevices of her chins.

Suddenly, he was at her side, dark and handsome, his strong hands working deftly to free her dress. The miasma of his cologne enveloped her. When he smiled down at her, the laughter on the other side of the room ceased to exist. It was exactly like a chapter out of the romance novels she so enjoyed reading in her spare time.

He had pursued her and now his chivalry had won her. Thinking she might swoon into his arms, she wiped away the mascara streaks and held out her hand—which, to her supreme delight, he took in his and kissed.

It was an inside secret that when a nurse or physician came into the hospital needing care, the staff pulled out all the stops. All the same, it was a mixed blessing that Wanda had been downgraded from fair to critical. The sad fact was that only for as long as she was in critical condition would she receive such excellent care. As soon as she stabilized, management would insist she be transferred out of ICU to the general floor.

Wanda suffered two sudden, unexplainable cardiac arrests within an hour after surgery. The first code ran only ten minutes before she was resuscitated, but the second continued for more than forty minutes as her heart refused to respond to the drugs. Dr. Tessler performed CPR while the nurses barked orders to the lab and administered intravenous drugs. Wanda would have been pleased that the crash cart was getting a good workout on her behalf.

As the war raged on, Adele tended to the walking wounded by leading Marlene down to the bad food machines for cups of the transmission fluid that passed for coffee. It wasn't until 1 A.M. when Wanda stabilized that Adele felt confident enough to leave Marlene alone to her vigil in the ICU waiting room.

She entered the stairwell fully intending to go down. That she turned and headed up toward Ward 8 made her reconsider Malloy's words about not being able to let go. Under the hostile stares of the night-shift irregulars, she skimmed both Thomas Penn's and Walter's charts. Mr. Penn was being discharged—she'd have to prepare Nelson for another loss.

In that narrow margin of decline and improvement in the terminally ill, Walter Minka was holding his own. He, too, would be discharged soon, although it really couldn't be viewed so much as a discharge as a temporary pass.

She went by Walter's room on the way to the stairwell, slowing enough to glance through the window that robbed the patients of their privacy. He was sitting in the lounger chair, staring out his window.

"Walter?" She opened his door a crack.

He looked around and waved her in. "I thought I was the only one who never slept," he said. "Even the night nurses sleep more than I do. What are you doing here?"

"A friend—a nurse, actually—ran into a little trouble after surgery. I came in to sit with her sister. How're you doing?"

"Funny thing you should ask." He folded his arms, careful of his IV, and looked out at the sky. "I was thinking about what you said the other day."

"And you've decided to order a chicken suit," she finished.

He laughed, and the sound of it eased the pain of the day's wounds. "Not the chicken suit. I sort of liked the idea of the classy red sports car, though."

They both stared out the window for a long time, listening to the mixture of sounds: crickets and call bells. Somewhere in the distance, a phone rang and a woman's voice said, "Okay, okay, hold your horses."

On an impulse, she leaned forward. "What's it like, Walter?"

He didn't move, but she saw his jaw muscles clench up. His answer was slow in coming. "Sort of scary, sort of okay," he said eventually, still not looking at her. "Mostly I feel like I'm in a place apart from everybody else. No matter how much somebody loves me, or how good the best doctor is, or how compassionate my nurse is, nobody can stop it from happening. Death terrorizes people so much, they can't even stand to see it in somebody else."

Absently, he scratched his knee. "Every once in a while you run across somebody who has been here and escaped, or somebody who's seen it close up and isn't afraid. Like Mirek, watching his brother get shot in the head and then living in fear every day. I'm a fucking coward. The really crazy part is that I'm afraid the minute I stop being scared, that's when it'll happen. It's like my fear keeps it at arm's length."

"Layered fears," she said.

He laughed until his shoulders began to shake, and she realized he wasn't laughing at all.

"I am so sorry," she said, her throat aching. "I wish I could stop it. I wish there was something I could do."

"There is."

"What?"

"Marry me and we'll ride to New Hampshire in a sports car wearing chicken suits."

"Honey," she said, "if you think you're afraid now, I'm here to tell you that marrying me would be the scariest thing you ever did in your whole life."

"Oh they all say that," he said.

Leaving him in the lounger, she turned to go. His hand slipped into hers and pulled her close.

Their kiss had nothing to do with sexual passion, and everything to do with confirming life.

This time, she saw the lump before she could trip over it again. Stationed at the front door in a canvas beach chair, Mrs. Coolidge sat snoring. There was nothing ladylike in the noise.

Feeling eyes boring into the back of her head, Adele whirled around to see Queen Shredder in Mrs. Coolidge's front window. In the streetlight, the menacing yellow eyes glowed an eerie luminescent green. She shuddered and turned back to the lump at hand.

"Mrs. Coolidge!" she said, shaking the woman.

The woman smacked her lips a few times, smiled, and mumbled: "Mmm, daddy needs a tickle?"

Adele chuckled and shook her again. "Wake up, Mrs. C. It's Adele."

The gossipmonger frowned and, crossing her arms over her chest, drew her legs up into a fetal position. Under the stress, the canvas gave way, dumping the large woman onto the porch with a thud. Looking a lot like a crab trying to right itself, Mrs. Coolidge spluttered, fought with her shawl, tried to sit up, failed, and finally rolled onto her side. She heaved her bulk into a sitting position and blinked, taking in her surroundings. At once, a torrent of words poured out of her at an impressive speed.

"Oh! Oh, my goodness. Adele, I heard them first—the hollering, I mean. It was going on and on. I thought I'd have to—"

"Hollering?"

"Uh-huh. And whooping too."

Adele nodded and said, "I see," in that syrupy, placating way psychiatrists and therapists often used with their patients when they weren't listening to a word they were saying.

"Since you said to keep an eye on the house, I thought it would be okay if I made sure everything was all right—you know, with all the hollering and—"

"Whooping," Adele finished for her.

"I looked in the window . . ." She pointed to the horizontal window that looked in on her living room. "And I saw—well, what I saw was so peculiar, I almost fell off the chair. I knew that the dog—Nelson?—I knew that the dog hasn't been quite right in the head since he was a puppy, but a grown man acting like that?" She clutched her shawl and pulled it tight around her as if to protect her from the evil mayhem inside the house.

"And what is it that they were doing, Mrs. C?"

"Jumping."

Adele cupped her ear, thinking she hadn't heard the woman correctly. "Again?"

"Yes," Mrs. Coolidge said. "That's exactly what I thought too. Not only was the dog jumping wildly around again, but that young man too! There he was, just as plain as Yankee Doodle, up on the sofa bed holding a cat, jumping up and down like there was no tomorrow. And right along with him jumping up from the floor, that dog was trying to grab the cat's tail. If that had been my cat, Adele, I'd have called the SPCA in no time. Why, I had to restrain myself from calling the nuthouse and having them come with a straitjacket."

"Did the cat seem hurt?"

Mrs. Coolidge grabbed her arm. "No—I think it was dead, though. My God, what cat in its right mind is going to allow someone to manhandle it that way and not be dead? Why, Queen Shredder would have torn the man's face off if he'd ever . . ."

Adele was unlocking the door. "If the cat seemed at peace with being," she had to think before saying it, "jumped, and everybody was having a good time, then what harm was done?"

Mrs. Coolidge took on an "Et tu Brutus?" expression. "But Adele, that's crazy. A grown man jumping on the bed?"

She stopped to consider for a moment before going inside, then stepped back to face her neighbor, who was still clutching the shawl around her. "Here's the main question," Adele said. "Was he, or was he not, wearing his shoes while he was doing all this jumping?"

"Well, no, but . . ."

Adele gave her a stupendous smile. "Well, then there you have it. We have nothing to worry about, do we?"

It was another Kodak moment, though not owning a camera, let alone one with a flash, she had to memorize the details of the scene so that she could tell him the next morning. On the sofa bed next to Tim, Nelson lay stretched out to his full length under the covers, his head resting neatly on the pillow. The man's arm was around the dog's middle, and inside the crook of the dog's paw and foreleg rested the cat.

Like the Three Stooges, the three snored in unison.

In her bedroom, she studied each of the schedules she'd bribed out of Mattie Noel. Kadeja had not been scheduled to work the evening of Mr. Penn's emergency pacemaker replacement, just as there had been no signing in of a Dr. Pepper, or any other M.D. whose name she did not recognize. In the columns of the ER schedule, Mattie had written: "Kadeja Shakir came to office to request four hours of work. Granted, with regular stipulations agreed to." Adele could just imagine what the "regular stipulations" might have been—half pay, maybe.

Before sleep came, she lay in the dark looking out the window at the lights of San Quentin in the distance, her mind burning through ideas like a dry Christmas tree set to flame. She kept leaping from the look on Harlan Jacquot's face when he saw the symbol to Wanda's face in the ER.

Turning on the light, she rummaged through her nightstand for the stack of index cards she kept on hand for recording her dreams or ideas as they came to her in her sleep. First she reproduced the symbol. Under it, in bold capital letters, she wrote:

DO NOT TROUBLE THIS HOUSE!
WHAT YOU WANT HAS BEEN TURNED OVER TO THE FBI.

To someone as sophisticated about security as she was, the note seemed simple and utterly primitive, but certainly effective. Creeping past the sleeping trio, she tacked the note to the outside of the front door. Halfway back across the living room she glanced at him. As a confirmed right-side-of-the-bed sleeper, she experienced a reassuring jolt of relief that he slept on the left.

She'd taken two more steps when Tim leapt up, his gun aimed at her head. Even in T-shirt and boxer shorts, he looked menacing.

She stepped back and raised a hand. "Peace," she croaked.

He caved in at the middle and dropped the gun to his side. "Shit, Adele, I could've killed you." He sat on the bed, where Nelson was now standing on the pillows, wagging his tail in a way that said, *Yaaaay! Let's play!*

"Sorry," Adele said, covering her mouth. "I was just—"

"It wasn't your fault," he said rubbing the back of his neck. "I forgot you were—" He stopped and stared. She was wearing a thin white cotton nightdress that had slipped down over one shoulder. In the lambent light filtering through the blinds from the street, her skin seemed to shine, as if it'd been polished.

"Adele." His voice was husky and soft. Before he was knew what he was doing, his hand was reaching for her.

Nelson looked from the male to Her and back again, his nose working. The mating smell was strong. Following instinct, he firmly took the male's arm in his teeth: *It's okay for me to sleep with you, pal, but keep your hands off Her.*

Fahad sat in the dark of the car smiling. The evening—the entire situation, for that matter—had been farcical. While studying at Oxford, he'd seen American comedies featuring the bumbling inspector who always saved the day in spite of himself. Needing to feel the power of his own command, Amar had stupidly rearranged their duties for the evening. He had taken over watch on the fat woman, while Saad was put in charge of following the nurse.

He had barely been able to keep himself from laughing at Saad's description of how he had followed her, only to find himself in the parking lot of the county sheriff's offices. And then to end up being followed by the nurse and her policeman boyfriend.

Not that things had gone any better for him. His duty was to find the pacemaker. That had turned out to be impossible without killing a few people. First there had been the young woman who drove the Volvo and had her own key to the house, then the old woman he'd found sleeping on the porch, and finally the note.

Fahad shook his head and laughed out loud. He wished he could have taken the note, although the humor of it would be lost on the rest of the group. It was so typically American to simply write a note and say, "Go away. I do not have what you want."

He still was not quite sure why the old woman was there, but he was glad she was a sound sleeper. He did not like the killing. He was a scientist, not a killer. Amar said the same about himself, but Amar liked to kill. Often, as Saad cut the victims' throats, he'd seen the way Amar's eyes lit up, glittering with rage and hate. His interest went far beyond the medical science, of that he was sure. Even Saad, in his madness to gain stature within the group, did not like to kill, although he hated the Americans as much as his brother did.

He ran a finger over the smooth scars of his face and neck. It was ironic that he did not hate the Americans. He had more reason to hate them than either Amar or Saad, but even so, he did not see them as evil, ruled by a greedy, murdering, and corrupt government. He saw instead ordinary people who were engaged only in the struggle of day-to-day living.

He had seen American children on the school grounds and playing in their yards. In them, he did not see a future of gun-carrying militia, but only children with innocence and purity of heart. Nor did their religious leaders include hatred and bloodlust in what they preached. Only in his own country had he seen that.

It was true that Americans did not care about the wars or the hate and strife that ruled the rest of the world. They cared only for their simple pleasures, their work and families. He could find no reason to hate them for what they had by circumstance of their birth. Even if he did not have these things, he could not kill them—not directly.

Eventually, of course, he would be a part of the larger thing that would kill many of them. This he knew. The sword of vengeance was merciless, and the killing would be done with or without him. He had no choice but to either be a part of the group or be killed himself.

He started the car and drove away from the brown-shingled house. He would tell Amar about the note, and advise him that this one was lost. He would advise him to pull back and let it go for good.

What he would not say was that the woman had out-witted them.

TWELVE

FOR A WEEK WARD 8 NURSES HAD FUN WITH THE concealed tape recorder. The highlight came the day that selected nurses from all three shifts stood around the coffeemaker and read from scripts written by the senior nurses whose jobs were at stake. With the exceptions of the throw pillows each held in case they should need to muffle the sounds of laughter, the assemblage resembled the cast of a live radio broadcast from the 1940s.

After checking to make sure there was enough tape, the troupe began with the usual chitchat about how each nurse felt blessed to be getting more and more patients. Adele especially waxed euphoric about her sense of ultimate professional fulfillment with the fourteen and fifteen patients she'd been assigned each shift.

"Don't tell anyone," Adele read. "I'd never want this to get back to Grace, but I was getting ready to quit. It was really boring to be assigned only six or seven patients per shift. This new workload really stretches my abilities as a nurse."

The Greek chorus all agreed that they too were bored with such puny workloads, and they loved the added responsibility of extra patients.

Skip read next. "Say, did I tell you what I overheard old Mr. Millbanks telling Mattie Noel just today?"

The Greek chorus responded, "No, what?"

Tina piped up: "I'll bet it's the same thing I overheard them discussing the day the phone wires got crossed."

"Oh, you mean the rumor about our—our—" Linda faltered, made a sour face, and continued: "our beloved head nurse?"

Abby McGowan sniffled, pretending to cry. "It's heinous what they're planning to do to that saint of a woman."

The Greek chorus called out, "What are they going to do? Tell us! Tell us!"

"Well," Skip said in a stereotypically limp-wristed tone, "I overheard Larry Millbanks and Mrs. Noel agree in secret that as soon as Grace fires all the senior nurses, the CEOs are going to . . ." There was rustling of papers as he turned to the next page and found his place. "Fire Grace, close down Ward Eight, and turn it into an executive suite for the two of them."

"That's right!" chirped Cynthia. "Everybody's talking about how our dear Grace's office is going to be the site of the executive hot slug."

There was dead silence.

"Er—I mean 'hot tub.' "

Greek chorus: "Poor Grace. Oh, we don't want to lose her, but what can we do?"

The tape ended with a series of muffled sounds that Grace Thompson would not be able to identify, no matter how many times she listened.

The late morning sun penetrated the fine holes of Daisy's pink sunbonnet, throwing pinpoints of light across the heavily madeup face. Twin ringlets, stiff with hair spray, did not obey the laws of gravity and stood straight out from either side of the hat. Whenever she scratched, they jiggled and bounced like coiled springs. The pot scrubber she'd put in between her girdle and the site of the itch helped get the most out of each scratch, although it did irritate the already inflamed flesh.

With mincing steps, she moved to the center of the lawn, closed her eyes, and willed herself to picture how the front of the house used to look: plain yellow, broken only by the dark brown trim around the windows and door. On the count of three, she opened her eyes and gasped. The seven jumbo daisies she'd painted across the front waved at her. Bright yellow and pink petals and dark green stems paid no attention to the aluminum siding or window frames, but crawled in all their glory every which way. Not one square foot of the building's façade had been spared her brush.

She pretended to pick a dandelion, then raised her eyes to the car parked across the street. Her heart skipped a beat. The idea of throwing caution to the winds and inviting him in for a drink came and went. She didn't want to end the chase. She loved the idea that he wanted to admire her from afar for a while longer. He was like a lion stalking his quarry before he moved in for the kill.

An involuntary shudder went through her in places that she thought had died after she'd married Mr. Rothschild—God bless his impotent soul. Sighing deeply, Daisy twirled the paintbrush and started back across the lawn, exaggerating the swing of her hips à la Sophia Loren.

Adele wrote the last set of vital signs on his flow sheet, closed the chart, and looked up at him as he came out of the bathroom: shaggy hair; angular, handsome face; incredible blue eyes. If it hadn't been for the sallow skin, he could have been a model. Even the slow, graceful way his body moved was like a danseur—light but masculine at the same time. His eyes caught and held her. They sparkled with the mystery known only to the dying: *I am here, but not for long. Catch me while you can.*

She smiled. "You are such a handsome fellow."

Embarrassed, he ducked the compliment as if it were a physical thing. "Sure you won't marry me and run away?"

She clapped her hands on her thighs and stood. "Sorry, I've got too much work to do before I run away."

"Yo!" Henry sauntered in behind the empty wheelchair, his earphones in place and blaring John Lee Hooker loud enough for all to hear. In one hand he carried a white pharmacy bag. "Walter, my man. I am here to set you free from the bondage of bandages and the loving attentions of this fine woman here."

Adele and Henry exchanged a high five as Walter took the bag of discharge medications and packed them in his duffel bag. "I have one last request," Walter said, taking her hand. "Will you go downstairs with me?"

It was impossible, of course. There was no way she could leave the floor and the rest of her patients. "Sure," she said, because there wasn't any way she could say no to those eyes.

At the front door he held her and kissed the top of her head. She could feel his heart pounding through his jacket and cried for no other reason than the world was going to lose him soon and there wasn't a damned thing she or anyone else could do to stop it.

After a minute, he gave her a piece of paper with his name and pager number. "Call me if you change your mind about the trip, or getting married."

She smiled and nodded then released him to an older woman she guessed was his mother, or perhaps an aunt.

They were crossing the lobby when she turned to Henry. "I'll race you to the top. The loser owes a big favor."

Henry rolled his head the way African American men did when rankled but trying to stay cool. "Girl, you gots yourself on backwards today 'cause you ain't thinking right. See now, I am an African. We got a thousand years of physical superiority over your puny-assed white race. Hell, all you got to do is check out the color of the top athletes to know that. I'd feel like I was taking advantage of your skinny white-girl ass. But," he said, slyly, "if you insist on embarrassing yourself, I'll comply. I'll even give you a one-flight lead."

The second her foot hit the landing between the first and second flight, he turned up Meade "Lux" Lewis's "Honky Tonk Train" full blast and sprang.

To his utter amazement, the race was close. It took him until the seventh flight to catch up with the skinny white girl's ass. He lost the lead on the ninth flight but picked it up again on the twelfth when they both had to sidestep Grace Thompson, who was sitting in the middle of the top stair listening to a cassette tape, a pair of headphones perched on top of her head like a tiara.

On the fifteenth flight he took a six-step lead and never lost it.

They leaned against the Ward 8 door panting for air when he pointed at her. "You good, girl."

"Oh sure," she said, feigning disappointment. "Then how come I lost?"

"You lost 'cause you didn't have the advantage of Master Meade 'Lux' Lewis cheering you on." He patted his Walkman. "I just hope you're better at writing than you are at running up stairs."

"Oh no," Adele groaned. "What's the favor?"

"Finals are coming up, and I need to concentrate on my studying, but there's one big hairy three-thousand-word medical ethics paper due in two weeks that me and the square-headed girlfriend haven't been able to pound out."

She groaned. "What topic?"

"Euthanasia."

"And where do you stand on that issue?"

"I'm of the Kevorkian mind. If they're over fifty, and they're a-sufferin', take 'em on an all-expense-paid cruise 'cross the River Jordan."

Adele nodded. "Oh. Uh-huh. So when Alva is admitted to Ward Eight again for her congestive heart failure, according to you it's okay if we let her go?"

"I didn't say that rule included my mama," Henry said. "Or anybody else in the Williams family." He stopped to think for a second. "That is, 'cept maybe my Uncle Lamont."

The sounds, sights, and smells of the ICU never changed: the whoosh-click of the ventilators, bleeps of alarms and IV pumps, jungles of blue and clear plastic tubing, damaged bodies in various states of repair, and the battle between the odors of alcohol and benzoin, blood and human waste. The constant atmosphere of adrenaline and crisis, victories and losses was what nourished the nurses who worked there, and made the nurses who didn't work there wish they did.

In the Stepdown Unit, the head of Wanda's bed had been cranked to a forty-degree angle, as prescribed by Dr. Zaritsky. In general, Wanda looked smaller under the bandages and casts. Her robust and healthy glow had been replaced by a sunken, ashen pallor. Her left leg and right arm were in full casts; her head was completely bandaged, as was her left eye.

Adele stood admiring Dr. Horrocks's stitching of Wanda's face. With a little luck, in a year the scars would barely be visible.

Wanda opened her eye, started to smile and winced. "Can't smile," she said. "Hurts."

"I'll make sure I don't break into any Monty Python routines."

"Marlene said you took the pacemaker," Wanda said on a sigh.

Adele nodded. "I gave it to the FBI."

Wanda stared. "You're kidding."

"No. Whatever is in that thing is valuable to somebody."

"Do they know who attacked me?" Wanda asked earnestly. "Twin Cities cops won't tell me anything."

On the acute side of the unit, a ventilator screamed for attention.

"They don't have a clue who the guy is." Adele sighed.

"Wanda, if this isn't anything you want to do, I'll understand, but do you think you could go over it once more for me?"

Wanda pressed the bed control until she was sitting straight. She looked past the end of the bed at the wall with such concentration, Adele turned to see if she'd missed something, but it was only a blank wall, painted a pukey shade of hospital green.

"I've never seen so much hate coming out of one person in my life," Wanda began. "I thought he was such a gentleman." She shook her head. "What a joke."

Adele sat down and waited.

"We talked until Rulli's closed, and then we walked back to your house. I should have known . . ." She reached for her water glass and carefully sipped through a straw. She swallowed as though it pained her. "Something was off, because he kept bringing the subject back to the pacemaker. At first he wanted to know everything about pacemakers in general, and then he narrowed it down to malfunctioning ones. I played right into it and told him about Mr. Penn. That really got him going.

What did the pacer look like? What did I think was wrong with it? Had I tried to find out what was wrong? Did I open the pacemaker? Where was it now? I made the mistake of telling him I had it at home and that I'd taken it apart. The way he was hammering on the subject was creepy, but I didn't realize how creepy it was yet." Wanda stopped and looked at her searchingly. "Do you know what I mean?"

"Sure. Been there—lots of times. It's your gut posting the 'Attention! Disaster Ahead' sign."

"By then we'd walked to my car, and I asked him to come over for coffee and cake, except I gave him directions that were way the hell out of the way." She giggled, wincing as she did so. "Shit, I had that sucker going all the way west of East Bumfuck. I wanted enough time to stop by Marlene's and drop off the pacer. I knew he'd eventually get around to asking to see it and I just didn't want to deal with it. I was in the *mood* for some live action, girlfriend, and I sure as hell didn't want to throw water on that fire by doing a 'You and Your Pacemaker' teaching routine. You know what I mean?"

Adele nodded. She remembered the X-rated looks Wanda had given him at Rulli's.

"Okay, so I get back to my place and have time to fix myself up—you know, get real comfortable in a sexy little number I wear sometimes? He shows up, and I notice he's splashed on another bottle of that cologne, so I'm thinking he means business. I poured some wine—which he didn't touch—and tried like hell to get him warmed up. Well, he didn't go for that at all. It was like the harder I tried, the more he was turned off and the more uptight he got. I started thinking that maybe he was gay or he had a problem with getting it up or something. Then I got the idea that maybe he was one of those psychos who hate their mothers and go around slashing women, so I backed off. He seemed nervous by that time, so I took him on a tour of the apartment thinking he'd relax if he saw that I didn't have leather straps attached to the bed or a selection of whips in the closet."

"Whips in the closet?"

Wanda looked at her. "If you don't know, don't ask. Anyway,

he started with the one thousand and one weird questions again."

"Like what?"

"Who were my neighbors, were they nosy, did I have a roommate, was the security of the building adequate—those kinds of questions."

"Then what?"

Wanda sighed, winced, bent her leg, and rested her foot against the cast on her other leg. "In the hall outside my kitchen, I have a poster of all the pacemakers ever made, from the first prototype to the present-day models. As soon as he saw it, he wanted to see the pacemaker I'd taken out of Mr. Penn."

Wanda stopped and looked down into her water glass. A flush was spreading over her cheeks.

"And?"

"And I blew up. I'd had more wine than was good for me, I was tired, and I didn't want to waste any more time on his pacemaker fixation. I told him I didn't bring him back to my apartment so we could discuss pacemakers and then I told him exactly what I did bring him there for—in no uncertain terms."

Wanda clenched her jaw. "Oh, he was quite the gentleman. He apologized and didn't say another word about the pace-maker. He asked me when I worked next, and what time I got home. Being the horny asshole only I can be, I gave him my schedule for the next month, thinking that maybe he was a slow starter and he was going to ask me out in the next few days. He said he'd call, and left. Kissed my hand on the way out the door."

Wanda tentatively touched her lower lip with her finger, testing for feeling. "The next day I got home about three-thirty, opened the fridge, and the next thing I know, I've got an arm across my throat choking me to death. I smelled that awful cologne and knew who it was. He kept asking me where the pacemaker was, and I told him I'd thrown it in one of the apartment Dumpsters. He knew I was lying. I had a feeling he might kill me if I didn't give it to him, but at the same time, I thought that if I told him it was at Marlene's, he'd go there and kill her too."

Wanda smiled briefly. "One of us my mother could handle. Both of us—she'd croak. I gave him a fight. I got to see his face for about a half a second." Her eye filled and her voice got husky. "It's the worst thing that has ever happened to me. I'm glad I passed out after the second or third hit."

Her eye closed until she regained herself. "There's something else I haven't told anybody," she began, hesitating. "I was scared and not thinking very clearly at the time, so I'm not a hundred percent sure of this."

"That's okay," Adele said. "Throw it out anyway."

"Well, I told you it was the guy we met the night before who beat me up? And I know for sure that the cologne was the same." She took a deep breath. "But I'm not so sure it was the same man. It looked like him, the eyes I mean, but . . ." Wanda looked down into the cup. The sun coming in from the window reflected off the water causing a half moon of silver light to dance over the walls.

"But now you aren't so sure it was him?"

Wanda shook her head. "He seemed smaller. Maybe not so tall, and maybe his eyes weren't that close together. I—I don't know for sure."

Adele got up and adjusted the blinds so that the sun wasn't shining directly onto Wanda's face. "Do you remember if the man at Rulli's touched anything the night before that might still have his prints on it?"

"No. He didn't even touch the doorknob. When I think about it, it seemed deliberate. I mean, he never touched one thing the night he was there—not even a glass." She looked at Adele. "Isn't that amazing?"

"Not really," Adele said. "He probably knew that he'd come back, and he had to make sure there were no prints anywhere. Was there anything else that might give a clue as to what he wanted with the pacemaker—or who he was?"

Wanda thought for a moment, looking at the wall again. "What did he tell us his name was? Do you remember?"

"Pierre Pandett."

"That was it. I decided he was a mixture of Arabic and maybe French, because at one point he said something in French and it sounded pretty authentic." She raised her eyebrows. "Not that I know any except *Voulez-vous coucher avec moi?* And *Avec plaisir, merci.*

"He told me he was a jeweler and that he owned a shop in Belgium. He was wearing some rings that he said he'd designed himself. I gave him a line of bullshit about what great work he did and I playfully pulled out the chain he was wearing. He'd kept it hidden all night, checking it every now and then to make sure it was still under his shirt. I thought for sure it was going to be a big diamond or something, but it was only a gold pendant with the same design in it as one of his rings.

"I asked him about it, and he got real uptight—angry almost—like I'd defiled it by asking. He said it was some religious thing, but I don't remember exactly what he said."

Adele found a pen in her purse and pulled out her notebook. "Can you draw it for me?"

With her left hand Wanda made two shaky preliminary sketches before she finally settled on one.

Without really needing to, Adele glanced down at the symbol.

The patient loads of all Ward 8 nurses had been getting lighter to the point where everyone was able to give the patients the type of quality care that was commonplace back in the 1970s and early '80s. It was a time of patient teaching and communication, healing and practicing as a real nurse instead of a body just filling in.

In the middle of her lecture on sexually transmitted diseases to Dawn Joy, in which she explained in graphic detail about signs and symptoms, outcomes of diseases left untreated, and the benefits of pre- and post-coital feminine hygiene, Adele thought she heard a distant echo of her own words. Glancing up, she could see the intercom light and realized the lecture was going out over the ward's PA system.

"Hello?" Adele said directly into the speaker. "Is everyone out there finding this interesting?"

The words bounced throughout Ward 8 like a pinball gone awry. In the distance there were bursts of laughter and applause.

Tina's voice came over the room speaker. "You gotta male visitor, Monsarrat. I told him he missed the conjugal visit day, but he still insists on seeing you. Make it snappy."

Adele sprinted down to the nurses' station and stood with hands on hips.

Skip, Abby, and two of the new hires buried their faces in their charts. Tina was suddenly engrossed in a page of Dr. Wortz's orders.

"Okay," she said, eyeing the array of guilty suspects, "Who's the wise guy?"

Mrs. Foley, her eighty-seven-year-old bypass patient, pushed her walker into Adele's back. "Say, nursie, you the one giving that special broadcast lecture?"

Adele blushed. "Yes," she sighed. "I am so sorry. That wasn't meant as a public announcement."

"You gonna finish? Me and the other girls down in eight-twenty are enjoying this very much. There's a lot of information in there that I can use when Harry and I fool around."

Skip and Abby snorted. Mrs. Foley whirled around, throwing them a piercing stare. "Stop that! You think you young ones are the only ones that get juicy?"

That did it. The nurses' station cleared out—all except for Tina who stared at the old lady, her lip curled in disgust.

Adele patted Mrs. Foley on the shoulder. "I'll answer all of your questions when I come down to do your final round of assessments and meds at two-thirty."

Mrs. Foley held up a finger. "You see to it that you do. And bring some plastic models of these things you're talking about, would you? When you get to be our age, you sort of forget how some of those parts work and you can't bend low enough to see 'em real good."

Adele looked over at Tina, who was still curling her lip like Elvis Presley singing "You ain't nothin' but a hound dog."

"What's with you?" Adele wanted to know. "You look like you swallowed some rotten deer pellets."

"All that stuff about vaginal lips and smegma? It makes me want to blow lunch."

"Maybe you should pay attention," Adele said, dryly. "I noticed you're taking a cab to work in the morning. Where's my male visitor?"

Tina hooked a thumb in the direction of the kitchen. "I sent him to the Nazi coffee machine. Looked like he needed something to wake him up."

She found Tim in the kitchen trying to get the machine to give him coffee. It was temperamental and would only produce the oily, bitter brew for just the right person. Unplugging the thing, she slapped it a few times and plugged it back in. Immediately, it began to spew out coffee.

"What news?" she asked, aware of how close they were in the tiny space. She looked into his face and had to physically restrain herself from walking into his arms. But when she studied him more closely, he did, in fact, look tired, almost on the brink of being ill. She wondered how much of his pinched look had to do with the old injuries and how much it had to do with the uncomfortable mattress on her sofa bed.

"Onorato called and left a message about an hour ago," he said, watching the way she moved. "Two more victims have been reported. Another one in Los Angeles and the other in Chicago. So far, there's enough similarities to connect them to the other murders."

The news sent a wave of urgency through her. "I get off in about two hours. Can I meet you back at your office for some of that team brainstorming?"

Hiding his pleasure, he looked at his watch. "Sounds good to me. See you at the Blue Roof in a couple of hours."

"Can you do something for me in the meantime?"

"Adele, if you're going to spill a drop of that precious information you got hoarded, I'll bungee-jump off the Golden Gate if you want me to."

She took a napkin from the red plastic holder shaped like a crescent moon and wrote down the information as she said it. "Check all the airlines for any departures out of SFO or Oakland around four or five weeks ago for Raymond and Laila

Clemmons. If there was a travel agency involved, check with them about . . ."

She hesitated, sensing him lean closer to watch as she wrote. Without reason, she straightened and stared into his eyes. They stood so close that each could feel the other's breath.

He was lost in her eyes, his arm encircling her waist, his hand resting on the small of her back. The warmth of her skin and the smell of her perfume made him feel as though he was in a dream.

Adele brought her hand to his face and instantly had two premature ventricular contractions, one after the other.

"Quit dillydallying!" Mrs. Foley said, poking the tip of her cane into Adele's shoe. The two jumped apart.

"I told you, the girls in eight-twenty are waiting to hear the penis smegma and how to have a healthy vagina stories again. We haven't got all day. One of us might drop dead before you get down there."

"Christ on a bike, Mrs. Foley, you scared the hell out of me," Adele said, clutching her chest.

The octogenarian looked first at the redhead, whose face had turned crimson, and then at her nurse. "Just in time, I'd say," she said as she hobbled out of the room.

"Penis smegma and how to have a healthy vagina stories?" he snickered, his eyebrows hovering just below the hairline. "I'd like to sit in on those myself."

She put the napkin in his jacket pocket, and hurried out of the room feeling as though she'd been saved from herself yet again.

When the last set of vital signs had been taken and the last drop of urine measured, Adele gave her report and sought out a phone that afforded privacy. Temporarily free of patients, room 805 seemed like the place. She waved to the house-keeper wiping down the bed frame, took the phone, and went into the bathroom, closing the door behind her.

It was her sixth attempt to contact Dr. Kogan at UC. The last time she'd called, the clerk had taken pity on her, telling her to call back at three.

As with any large institution, she waded through the standard four or five transfers, got sent back to the main switchboard, then was put on hold for an eternity of bad Muzak. When Dr. Kogan finally came on the line, he had the voice of a ten-year-old. It was disconcerting to say the least.

"Dr. Kogan? This is Deputy Investigator Monsarrat with Marin PD." She said it fast, letting her tongue slip over the title. "I'm working on the Zelda Fischer case. I know you've already talked with our detectives, but I need to ask one or two more questions."

"I already told you people everything I know. I'm busy trying to get out of here. I've been on for sixteen hours and . . . twenty-three minutes and I'm—"

"Please, Doctor, I only have a couple of questions."

His dramatic sigh dripped with arrogance. Not only had this guy been through Intermediate Arrogance for Physicians, she thought, he'd gone on to Advanced Prickology.

"Yeah, yeah, but make it quick. I'm very busy. Jesus, I would have thought a competent department would have the murderer locked up by now."

Adele's nostrils flared from a flash of temper. She bit down on the end of her pen. "I notice that what I assume was the last page of your progress notes of her last visit is—"

"Missing." He sighed again. "Old news. That page has been missing since the morning following her appointment. As soon as I was made aware that Ms. Fischer reported me to the administration, I wanted to go over the file again to see what I'd written. I'm the one who first brought attention to the fact it was missing."

"Do you remember what was included on that sheet?"

"Nothing important. I'm sure the sheet slipped out and was put into someone else's file. The level of incompetence in the clerical department over here is astoundingly high. Most of them can't speak English, let alone know the alphabet."

"What wasn't very important? Do you recall?"

He was getting impatient; she could tell by the way his attention seemed to wander.

"Pardon?" he said irritably.

"What was on the last page?" she asked, her voice firm, matching his own vexed tone. Making people repeat themselves was an old executive's stratagem for making others feel inferior and talked down to. It said, "You aren't worth my full attention."

"I think it was something about her lab work from that day. Her potassium was high."

"That's all?"

He didn't answer right away. In the background several doctors and the pharmacy were being paged. Two women were having a conversation about where an ER patient had gone. One said she'd look in the ladies' room, the other was going to check the smoking area outside.

"I think I wrote down the name of the clinic and the doctor who did her implants."

She held her breath. "Can you remember what they were?"

"Jesus! Do you know how many patients I see a day? How the hell am I supposed to remember something as inconsequential as that?"

"Try," she said tersely. "Unless, of course, you think you might remember better in my office."

He cursed under his breath. She wanted to slap him upside the head so bad, she had to bite the side of her hand.

"The Parisian Beauty Clinic, or something like that. I can't remember the name, but I'm sure if you called around Paris for the plastic surgeon with the most malpractice suits, you'd find him. The guy did a butcher job. It was a mess."

Adele checked her notebook. "The last thing you had written on the page was a description of an area five centimeters by seven and something that was inflamed."

"Oh yeah. She had exanthema on the upper left quadrant of that right breast that was maculopapular, almost morbilliform in character."

"Are you saying that the rash might have been something like mono or measles?"

There was a pause in which she figured he was considering that some lowly female investigator knew her medical jargon—which, of course, was against the "If it has ovaries, it doesn't have a worthy IQ" school of thought to which a few male physicians still subscribed.

"Of course not," he said haughtily. "She was having some sort of reaction. My guess was that the implant was leaking into the cavity, and it had infiltrated the tissue. From the looks of the butcher job, God knows what the implant was filled with. Could have been water they scooped out of the Parisian sewers."

"Okay," Adele said. "Thank you for your time. If I—"

Without so much as a four-letter word, he hung up in her ear.

Tim hung up and punched the blinking light on the second line, motioning Adele in from the hall. "Hey Mr. Onorato, how's things in lovely downtown D.C.?"

At mention of the name, Adele scribbled out a note and set it in front of him. He read it and made a face. She pleaded. He held up a finger.

"Oh yeah? Listen, Corey, I've got someone else here in the room who's been working these cases from the get-go. She's up to speed on most of the information. I'm going to have her pick up the extension."

Tim nodded and pointed to the phone on the other side of his desk.

"Hello, Mr. Onorato, this is Adele Monsarrat."

"We're all friends here—call me Corey. As I was about to say, the Houston, Denver, and Miami victims all seem to have the same vertical carotid cuts. Our weapons lab informs us that the cuts were made by a blade similar to the others— serrated and not consistent with any popular American-made blades.

"Of the serrated blades, there seems to be more than one since we've found irregularities in the blades. The California victims all look like the cuts were made with the same blade. The blade used on the New York, D.C., and Miami victims is different from California's. Yet a third blade appears to have been used on the Denver and maybe the Houston victims. Clemmons is the only one we can't match up to anything except the mutilations."

"Maybe the guy was trying to throw us off with Clemmons," Tim said.

"So what you're saying is that there's probably more than one guy doing nearly identical killings?" Adele said.

"That's in part why I'm calling," Corey replied. "The two new victims happened less than two hours apart, so unless our guy took a rocket—and changed blades—there's a good possibility there's more than one killer, or there's a copycat thing going on between parties who know each other."

"What are the details?" Tim asked.

"Very interesting shit. The forty-seven-year-old female in Chicago was scalped, and the L.A. gal had both breasts removed. The medical examiner says the breasts were cut like in a radical mastectomy—similar to the Fischer murder. Even the lymph nodes had been carefully removed. She was only thirty. A real beauty queen. Engaged to be married."

Tim sat back. At the same time, Adele leaned forward.

"And both women had been to Europe within the last six months, right?" Adele asked.

"The Chicago victim had been in France in February," the agent answered. "The L.A. woman was in London three months ago."

"It's a tie-in," Adele said, more to herself than to the men. "How many of the others had been abroad and to what cities?"

Agent Onorato flipped through papers, reciting. "Athens, Istanbul, Paris, Berlin, Paris, London, Istanbul."

"Both Fischer and Clemmons had been to Paris recently," Adele threw in.

"Actually," Tim broke in, "Fischer was in Paris, but Clemmons was in Istanbul."

Surprised, Adele shot him a look across the desk.

"Clemmons's wife told Adele that they'd spent several weeks in Paris and then Normandy. They were only two days in Paris then they flew to Turkey, where they spent three weeks."

There was a pause. Adele stood and turned toward the wall. "What about medical problems on these people before their murders? Maybe something they might have been treated for while they were in these countries? I'm looking specifically for skin problems."

The papers moved again. "I don't see anything here—oh wait. The D.C. victim had gone to see a doctor the day he was murdered."

"For an exanthema that was maculopapular, almost morbilliform in nature?"

"For exanthe what?"

"Don't mind me," she laughed. "It's a mild form of medical Tourette's. Does it say that he was suffering from a rash?"

"It sure does."

"This is the gay man they found in the pool with his face and scalp removed?"

"Uh-huh."

"I'll bet it says the rash was on his face and scalp."

There was a pause on the other end of the line. "Want to explain how you know that?"

"Because if you'll look at the Fischer file, you'll see she was at the dermatology clinic the day before as well, in part for treatment of a rash on her breast—the same one that was removed."

"Could be coincidence," Tim said.

"Maybe," Adele said, "but I doubt it like hell. Mr. Clemmons also had a rash and was on his way to a doctor about it when he disappeared."

It was Tim's turn to look surprised.

"I'll bet if you have your agents ask the relatives or friends of the other victims," Adele continued, "you're going to find a few more who were complaining of rashes."

"So what are you thinking?" Onorato asked.

"I don't know yet," Adele said. "But I'm working on it real hard."

The swivel chair squeaked in protest as Tim leaned back scratching a patch of stubble at the angle of his jaw. Adele finished going over the airline records and looked at him.

"Did you call the travel agent who booked this package?"

In answer, he pulled up the fax sheets and handed them over.

Running her finger down the itinerary, she stopped at the listing for the Paris hotel and wrote down the name and the number.

"I'm going to check with these people if that's . . ." She stopped. He was shaking his head. "What? Have you already done that?"

"No." He laughed.

"Then what?"

"I'll never understand why you aren't working for me."

"Honey," she said, arching an eyebrow, "if I had gone into the business, I guarantee you it wouldn't be me working for you."

Marin City: Marin's answer to the Projects. Built next to Highway 101, it was as though someone had set up rows upon rows of peach-pink dominos with dark orange tile roofs and run them up the hills overlooking Sausalito. Populated exclusively by blacks, Marin City was its own self-contained world into which few whites ever wandered—except on Saturdays and Sundays.

For as long as Adele could remember, she and her mother had meandered the rows of trash and treasure at the Marin City Flea Market every other Sunday morning while her aunt Ruth attended the First Missionary Baptist Church across the road.

But now the flea market was gone, having been recently replaced by one of the characterless plastic and stucco malls that marred cities all over America like so much graffiti. Lost in nostalgia for the old market, she drove by the standard issue of mall stores: Radio Shack, Blockbuster Video, Burger King, Payless Shoes, Ross, Best Buy, Red Boy Pizza.

Henry was waiting for her in front of the Rickshaw Chinese restaurant. He leaned against the building reading from an anatomy textbook, every once in a while checking out the young women who passed by. Several of them stopped to flirt, and were pulled away by an older sister, mother, or grandmother—Henry Williams's reputation for being a ruthless ladies' man had lingered, even though it was no longer entirely true.

"Hey, bro," Adele called out. "Come on over here and let me check you out."

Henry detached himself from the building and bounced toward her in his hightop Air Jordans. Without a word of greeting, he got in and stared straight ahead, tapping out a rhythm on the back of his wrist.

"What's a matter?" she asked. "Your reputation going to be ruined if you're seen with a honky?"

He rolled his head. "Girl, you are so uncool. For your info, I am trying to memorize the bones of the human hand and you are disturbing my train."

"Well, excuuuse me. Where to?"

Five minutes later, she stepped into Alva Williams's cozy apartment, done in blue and white early American motif. Alva enveloped her with huge, warm arms. "Look at you, girl. You just a bit of a thing. Gonna disappear on me. Come on and have some of my nice butterscotch pie. Just come outta the oven."

Henry raised his hands. "That's my mama. Walk in the door and she feeds you. Sometimes it's like the City Mission around here—my mama, she drag in any old thing that's got jaws and ain't too drunk to chew."

Adele couldn't have been more pleased. Butterscotch was, besides her three P addictions, one flavor Adele never turned down. It could have been butterscotch-flavored glue and she would have tried it. During the first piece of pie, the two women chatted about Alva's health, and how she'd been managing her chronic hypertension. Over the second piece, Adele asked Henry how he had come to be fluent in French.

"Summertimes I spent with my granddaddy in New Orleans," he explained. "He spoke Creole, and passed it on down to me." Henry grinned. "I really messed with their heads in high school. You should've seen them suckers—they couldn't figure out what this Marin City nigger wanted to take French with the white college-material boys for. But their equal opportunity quota was pretty low for blacks graduating with foreign languages, so they let me in thinking I was gonna flunk out in the first week. I aced it right up until I dropped out of school. Set their heads spinning."

Alva shook her head. "He was a troubled boy then, but we got him back now, praise the Lord."

Henry got up and pulled at Adele's arm. "When the woman starts praising Jesus, it's time to get out of the way and down to business, or she'll have both of us down at the revival tent."

Ducking Alva's admonishments, they went into the living room, where an older man slept in a wheelchair.

"That's my mama's brother, Uncle Lamont," Henry whispered.

"The one you don't like?"

Henry nodded, a sneer on his lips. "Yeah. Uncle Lamont's got an attitude ever since he win the 'You Come a Long Way Baby' awards."

Following Nelson's manner of inquiry, Adele cocked her head.

"See, until the eighties, Lamont used to be a nigger cripple, now he's black and disabled. It's the role change thing? The man acts more like Ted-fucking-Turner than a brother now. Makes him hard to live with."

"What you sayin', boy?" Uncle Lamont stirred and opened his eyes with a theatrical groan. "You bad-talkin' me?" Seeing Adele, he nodded and touched his forehead after the fashion of a man tipping his hat to a lady. She returned a smile, instantly charmed.

Uncle Lamont stared at Henry in bleary-eyed reproach. "Have some respect, boy. I was pickin' cotton before you was born. I—"

Henry rolled his head. "Aw, man, the only cotton you ever picked was your BVDs outta the drawer."

"What you do say them things for?" Uncle Lamont asked, sitting up straighter. "Ain't you got no respect for this old disabled black man? And me here in this ol' wheelchair can't stand up to whup your black ass. Why, I ought—"

Henry grabbed her hand and dragged her away.

"Where you goin', boy?" Uncle Lamont said, hitting the armrest of the wheelchair for effect. "Ya'll git your ass over here and listen to what I gots to say."

Henry took her to a small room off the living room and

closed the door. It was sparsely furnished with a twin bed, a desk, and a chair. On top of the desk was a computer monitor Henry often referred to as his square-headed girlfriend.

"This be the learning cell." He sat on the bed and pointed to the desk chair—the only other available place to sit.

Settling on the zebra-striped cushion, she examined the room more closely, starting with the mini stereo system with dual headphones set into a recessed part of the wall. CDs, tapes, and a huge variety of books on subjects from the Civil War to haiku covered every square inch of space.

She scanned over one corner of his music—Mezz Mezzrow, Fats Waller, Bunk Johnson, Alberta Hunter, Vivaldi, Mozart, Pine Top Smith, Edith Piaf, Peggy Lee. She wondered how long it would take to listen to every tape and CD.

"What you want me to do, girl? It doesn't have nothing to do with the man, does it?"

"It doesn't." Adele took out her cell phone and a piece of paper. "I'm going to call a hotel in Paris, and I want you to ask to speak to the manager. Tell him you're interpreting for the police in San Francisco, and you need to know if a Mr. and Mrs. Raymond Clemmons stayed at his hotel on these dates. Find out for how long they stayed and if he knows anything about Mr. Clemmons being ill. If he says they didn't stay there, ask him if he knows where they went."

Henry's charm worked miracles in loosening the manager's tongue. Rude Parisian or not, the man spoke rapidly and with feeling. There were times in the conversation when he spoke in such a rage that Henry had to hold the phone away from his ear. Writing down a number and a notation above it in French, Henry hung up with the announcement that he and the dude were "cool."

"My man Monsieur Toulegant said La Femme Araignée— that be French for Spider Woman—and the old man hung around for two nights then cut out, but, see, they'd booked the room for two weeks, so Spider Bitch arranges to have two of her relatives take over the room. Except the relatives are Arabs." He pronounced it Ay-rabs.

"Is that what he was ranting about?" Adele asked.

Henry's head bobbed. "He hates them almost as much as he hates the Americans. Then the Arabs go and cause some kind of major shit while taking up residence. Seems an American dude goes to their room, and gets himself carried out the next morning and dumped into a taxi looking like he's dead. The two ragheads go back to the room, pack up a bunch of shit that belongs to the hotel, and split without paying the tab."

"What kind of shit?"

Henry shrugged. "Sheets, towels, mattress covers, blankets—that kind of shit. One of the cleanup women sees them heading out the back door with the stuff and says they were all covered with blood. When the owner catches an eyeful of that noise, he has himself a righteous fit. Right about at the same time he's adding up the missing towels, old lady Clemmons makes the mistake of calling the Arabs from Istanbul. Toulegant gets her on the line and threatens to report them to the gendarmes if they didn't pay for everything. The bitch hangs up on him, but he has one of them international callback ID things and gets the number of where they're parked, so he calls them back and threatens some more bad shit."

"Did they pay?"

"Every franc and centime got wired that night."

Adele slumped back against the chair. "Holy shit."

Henry handed her the paper on which he'd written the Istanbul number and had set about searching among the papers on his desk when he noticed her worried expression. He slipped a pair of headphones over her ears. Instantly, the sound of Paul Whiteman filled her head, the bass sending vibrations through her center.

When he found the papers he was looking for, he put them all inside a large manila folder and wrote on the tab: "MEDICAL ETHICS PAPER—BRAIN NOT INCLUDED."

"Three thousand words, Adele, in fourteen days," he said. "Pay up or I'll send Uncle Lamont to your house, and there ain't no way you want *that*. The old man will talk both your ears off, eat all your food, and stay for five years."

* * *

Mirek wasn't hard to find. The Beast pulled into the College of Marin parking lot and parked next to the Citroën Deux Chevaux. Mirek would be in the clinical lab, working with Ventilator Victor—the perpetually intubated dummy—and the respirator it was hooked into.

As soon as Adele entered the corridor, she heard the ear-splitting alarm of the ventilator. Mirek was hunched over the instrument panel, turning dials and flicking switches, all to no avail. The training screen above the ventilator read: WARNING: PATIENT NOT RECEIVING OXYGEN!

In the corner of the screen was a running stopwatch to let the students know how long the patient had been without oxygen. Adele wondered if at six minutes the machine was programmed to give the message: PATIENT BRAIN-DEAD. MORGUE WAGON REQUIRED.

Reaching over Mirek, she unhooked the tubing from the end of Victor's endotracheal tube and emptied the water that had pooled inside. At once, the alarm stopped and the screen read: OXYGEN DELIVERY 100%.

"You had the humidifier turned up?" Adele asked.

"Yes," Mirek answered, not terribly surprised to see her. "The test orders said that the humidity be up for ten minutes to make the secretions soft and liquid for the suctioning."

Adele nodded. "Good, but what you need to always remember is that steam condenses on the inside of the tubing and eventually fills it with water, which creates a plug. Always check for blocked ventilator tubing or a blocked endotracheal tube first."

"I will do this. Thank you." His eyebrows shot up. "Why you are here?"

She sat in the chair next to the hospital bed. "I came to ask you a favor."

Mirek bowed. "I am doing your service."

Adele smiled. "You are at my service," she corrected.

"Yes I am."

"How many languages do you speak?"

He held up a hand and began to count them off, rating his abilities as he did so: "English–not too good; French—okay;

Spanish and Italian—good; Polish and Czech—perfect; German—okay; Greek—bad; Turkish—so-so; Latin—good; Russian—not bad."

"Christ on a bike, how did you learn all those?"

Mirek frowned. "With my mind."

"No, I mean why do you know so many?"

"My father has many friends of Italy, Russia, France, Greece, and España. They come and live with us many times for long time. Instead of money, to pay my father, they teach us the languages. My mother comes from family of German and Turkish peoples and she teaches us her languages. Why do you ask me this?"

"I need you to make a call to Istanbul. Can you come by my house when you're done here?"

He bowed again. "I come now to service you."

The statement hung in the air like a curve ball. She smiled to herself, wondering if she should correct his errant phraseology, and let the statement stand as it was. There was no telling if he would ask for an explanation, and that was nothing she wanted to tackle.

After he'd eaten a veggie salad and a dozen onion pancakes with mushroom and shallot gravy, she made him a cup of hot milk with honey, nutmeg, and cardamom and served it with a plate of oatmeal cookies plumped up with cranberries and chunks of oranges. He ate like any twenty-two-year-old starving student might: strictly by inhalation, chewing optional.

She explained where and whom he was calling, and what she needed to know, encouraging him to take the initiative and find out as much information as he could. When he was finished, she dialed the number in Istanbul and let him loose.

The beginning of the conversation was stiff and formal to the point of being awkward, but then things changed and Mirek relaxed. Soon there was a lot of giggling, and then what she recognized as outright flirting. Fifteen minutes later, when his tone had become increasingly teasing and flirty, she pointed to her watch. "I asked you to find out some simple information, not clean out my entire life savings!" she whispered in his free ear. "Wind it up or I'll be paying off Pac Bell for the next ten years."

Five minutes later, Mirek hung up grinning. "Azzah was nice girl. Very pretty."

"How do you know if she was pretty?"

"We trade how we look. She likes my eyes."

"Oh great," Adele said, rolling her eyes. "I've just spent a fortune so you can have a phone date with a girl in Istanbul?"

"Ah." Mirek held up a forefinger and smiled. "But Azzah tells me much more than her father who is owning the hotel. He is very mean to everyone, but he was sleeping, so I am lucky to speak with her."

Adele got up and returned with another dozen cookies and a second glass of milk. "Okay, tell me everything she said and don't leave anything out."

"Azzah says the Clemmons peoples are most strange," he said, demolishing half a cookie in one bite. "They come to hotel. The man, Mr. Clemmons, goes right away in a car. Then the wife goes soon after in taxi. Three hours later he comes back to hotel alone but he is very sick and weak." He paused, drank off half the milk, and picked up another cookie. "Azzah must help him to his room. She says he goes away fat and comes back skinny. When she puts him in his bed, she sees blood on his shirt down here." Mirek grabbed his uniform shirt at waist level. "Azzah says he is in bed three days. When he walks again, he walks as if there is pain in his belly. Azzah offers to help, but the wife says many bad words to drive her away. The Clemmons peoples leave one week later. The wife goes out very much—sometimes all night. Azzah says she sees her once with men who are tourists."

"Does she know where Mr. Clemmons went?"

Mirek, chewing again, shook his head.

"Did she recognize the car or the driver?"

He cleared his mouth with the rest of the milk. "No, she says they are not from the local people."

Adele brought the gallon jug of milk back into the living room and let him pour his own. There were four cookies left on the plate.

"Azzah says one hotel manager of Paris calls her father to tell him the Clemmons are bad peoples. He says Clemmons brings many troubles. Azzah's father gets money . . ." He paused. "How do you say money is paid before?"

"He asked them for room payment in advance?"

"Yes. He tells them he wants no trouble, so Mr. Clemmons pays advance money and there is no troubles. That is all Azzah knows. This is good news?" He finished the last cookie, and carefully wiped the crumbs off his fingers onto the plate.

"This is good. Thank you, Mirek. I owe you one."

Puzzled, Mirek looked at her and then down at the empty plate. "Oh no, Adele, that is okay. No more cookies. They are very good, but I am full."

Adele pinched the smile off her face and nodded.

"I am sorry," he said turning sheepish, "that I talk for long time to the girl."

She patted his back. "Don't be. The information you got is worth every cookie."

He squinted one eye and cupped his hand around the match flame as he lit the cigarette. It was his favorite Marlboro man pose, one he practiced often. Flicking away the used match, he sucked in the smoke impatiently, turned on the car radio, turned it off. In the rearview mirror, he combed back his hair like the American James Dean and squinted again. He stared at himself for a long time, changing his expressions to match the American movie stars he liked.

When he tired of the game, he looked back at the house and took another drag. He wished Amar would give him the word soon on this one. He was sick of watching the fat whore. He was sick of staring at the stupid flowers painted on the house. He was sick of being the warm-up act for Amar and Fahad.

He took another hit off his cigarette, inhaling deeply. He didn't mind getting blood on his hands. He could bathe in the blood of his enemy and rejoice. That was what a good soldier did. He looked at himself again.

The Marlboro man would do that—get blood on his hands.

The hunger to return home was growing day by day. If they

had put him in charge, they would be done by now and ready
to go on with phase 2. There was so much time wasted waiting for the signals. It was making him crazy.

A young man and woman, wearing identical outfits and
headphones, jogged toward him. He stared at the woman,
then the man, and blew smoke out the window so they would
have to breathe it in as they passed.

The woman held a hand over her mouth and nose, and gave
him a bad look. He leered in return and in his native tongue
told her she was good only for sucking the anuses of dogs.

Out of the corner of his eye he saw the fat whore walk
past the window toward the front door. Flicking the cigarette
out the window, he watched carefully, wanting to keep his
record clear of any mistakes. Amar had made many. Fahad
and Kadeja had each made a few. If their leader could not see
from his perfect record that he was meant to be a commander,
he would threaten to leave the group.

He sat up when the whore came out the front door. She had
a drink in her hand as always, but instead of collecting the
newspaper and going inside, she was coming across the lawn.

Unsure of what she was doing, he hastily lit another cigarette. She stepped into the street, headed right for the car. She
waved at him.

Amar had been a fool to talk to her at the party. She must
think he was Amar. It was not the first time a woman had mistaken them for each other. Even their mother sometimes
made this mistake.

The whore was ten meters away, mouthing words, and
pointing to her glass. Wouldn't he like to come in and relax?

He looked around. If she got close enough she might even
recognize him as the telephone person and become confused,
then start asking questions. He thought of what Amar, or Fahad, or any man who understood American women might do.

He put the car in gear and rolled toward her. As he came
even with her, she was asking him to please come in for a little
nip. He kissed the air and smiled his best smile—the one he
gave the boys he liked. Then he told her in his own language

that he couldn't wait until he could cut through the fat of her throat. It would remind him of cutting the throats of the pigs.

He said something to her in Arabic that Daisy imagined was a love poem. She clapped and yelled out, "Bravo! Encore!"

Utterly charmed by his smile, she pleaded with him as he drove past her. "Oh, don't go away. Come back, my own sweet knight." She caught his air kisses and returned them. "Come in for a drink. It's the least I can do to repay your kindness at the party."

Still, he did not stop. When the car turned the corner, she stomped her foot and walked slowly back to the house. Perhaps, as he had told her at the party, it wasn't the right time. He promised that when the right time for them came, he would come to her door and together they would expose their hearts and souls.

She scratched at the raw flesh of her buttock, gazing at the beautiful painted daisies. She hoped she hadn't scared him off. She liked having him near her at night—even if it was outside in his car. And she could always dream about the night he would come to the door and expose her heart.

Nelson was despondent. Of late, his life had been a wealth of losses: first Bugs, then Mickey Rug, and now Helen. Roddy Rug was somewhat of a consolation, but it was still too new and stiff to take the sting away completely.

Adele was worried. He'd walked away from the onion pancakes, and now he was hiding under the bed when she had offered to take him on her run. Rather than chewing up the phone or working on shredding Roddy Rug, he spent his days staring forlornly out the bedroom window into the neighbor's yard.

Adele got on all fours until her head was level with his. She stared out the window, trying to see what he did. All she saw was the neighbor's backyard—the plum tree, Fluffy's pen, a collection of odd, broken toys, two kid's bikes, a green plastic picnic table, and five matching chairs.

Before she left for her run, she put in a call to Dr. Nutt and left a message saying Nelson was in crisis.

THIRTEEN

BY EIGHT, ADELE HAD GONE THROUGH HER USUAL day-off routine—grocery shopping, laundry, housecleaning, and outside grounds maintenance. By nine, she'd paid the bills, brought the rent check to her landlord, cleaned the Beast inside and out, and worked in a breakfast of yogurt, bananas, and strawberries. It was 10 A.M. before Nelson could be coaxed out from under the bed with the aid of a Big Veggie Dog Biscuit. Another got him on top of the bed so they sat face to muzzle.

"You have to snap out of this, Nelson. I need your help." Adele tacked a four-foot length of butcher paper on the wall at the end of her bed. Using a Magic Marker of blue persuasion, she divided the paper into several parts, and transferred the information from her notebook onto the makeshift storyboard. When she was finished, she rested her head against the dog and studied her notes. Forty minutes and three sheets of notations later, Nelson scratched at the kitchen door, wanting to be let out.

"Promise you won't go very far?" she asked before she let him go.

He responded with something that sounded very much like "Sure, sure."

There was something about the intensity of his eyes boring holes through the hand that held the doorknob she didn't trust. "Nelson? Stay in the yard. Promise?"

He wagged his tail, looked up without moving his head, and scratched the door again.

"Nelson, be good!" she said in the command voice. "Good Nelson. Stay in yard."

He whined and tore his eyes away from her hand long enough to say, "Yeah, yeah sure. Just open the doggone door!"

Against her better judgment she let him out, then stood watching for a while. After ceremoniously marking off the yard, he sniffed every blade of grass, then dropped low as the fur along the ridge of his back went up. Freezing after each step, one foot held aloft, tail steady, the black Lab turned into something more primitive as he stalked the thing behind the fig tree.

She moved to the bedroom window in order to see what merited such hostile attention. During the night, a dead branch had fallen. If she squinted and held her head at just the right angle, the tangle of branches and knobs of dried fruit looked like a giant crow.

Unmindful of Her sudden burst of Crazy Woman laughter, Nelson sprang forward to attack the deadly Thing.

"Have you heard from Harlan?" Adele asked the moment Tim answered.

"Not yet. What's up? You sound agitated."

"Can we call Onorato again?"

"How about running it by me first?"

"Okay, how about at your office?"

"When?"

She thought for minute, craning her neck to find Nelson. Just seconds before, he'd been by the fence of thick rosemary bushes that separated their yard from the neighbor's. She glanced back at the storyboard. A thousand facts and phrases were bumping into each other in every corner of her brain.

"How about now? I need some information or I'm going to go crazy—well, crazier, I mean."

When he didn't answer right away, she sighed. "Oh, for Buddha's sake, just say yes and go through your ethics list after the fact. It never does you any good anyway. I came up with a couple of things we could ask Onorato to check out."

He took off his tie and draped it on the coatrack. "Okay. Come on up and we'll wing it."

"I'm going to bring Nelson and let him hang out in the car. He's despondent, and I can't afford another front door or a new phone. God knows what else he'll find to chew. He's been eyeing the couch lately—makes me very nervous."

"See you here." He hung up and stared out the window. "Jesus," he said under his breath. "Adele Monsarrat is going to spill. Second time in two days. Will wonders never cease?"

She found the hole he'd dug between two of the older rosemary bushes.

"Nelson!" she yelled in her I'm-going-to-brain-you tone. She looked over the bushes into the neighbor's yard, which was carpeted by toys of every description. On the lawn near Fluffy's empty pen, sat five-year-old Jessica arduously changing a diaper on one of her dolls.

"Hey, Jess, did you see Nelson?" Adele called over the fence.

Jessica nodded and pointed toward the front of the house. "Nelsie ran through there."

She ran to the front yard and scanned the neighborhood in all four directions. He wouldn't go toward the railroad tracks. Ever since he'd been sprayed by a skunk living under the switch house, that whole area had been off-limits. He wouldn't dare go to Mrs. Coolidge's house—not since Queen Shredder discovered his nose. In the churchyard next door was a statue of a devilish-looking saint that terrified him into pulling his tail in between his legs. That meant Nelson was where he always went when he ran away from home: down at the Silver Peso Bar being fed corn nuts and beer by the locals.

She swore under her breath. Just what she needed: a depressed, drunk dog with the pukes. As she turned to run, she caught a glimpse of four black legs hiding behind the Beast.

"Nelson!" She meant to sound like she meant business, but couldn't hide the relief in her voice. "Come here!"

Nelson moved shyly, almost cautiously, out from behind the car.

"What are you doing?" she asked, suspiciously, walking toward him. "I called you. Come here!"

As if suddenly recognizing her, he bounded across the lawn, leapt into the air, and barked. *Let's play! Get the ball! Come on! Let's run!* The Insane and Frenetic Dog Vapors were upon him, leaving him without pride or sense.

Half-appalled, half-amused, she watched as he chased his tail, raced back and forth across the lawn, and leapt up from the lawn like a dolphin at Sea World doing tricks. When he tired, she knelt down and looked into the brown eyes that were as innocent as the devil is sweet.

Sticking to his mouth were tufts of white fur like that found on stuffed animals. "Nelson?" she said in her shame-on-you voice. "Did you tear up another of Jessica's stuffed toys?"

He whined in his *mea culpa, mea culpa* voice.

She sighed: she'd have to buy Jessie another stuffed toy. Maybe this time, she'd buy two or three—to save herself future trips to the toy store.

"Want to go for a ride?"

He panted, licked his chops, and barked so that it came out sounding like "Yep."

"Will you be good?" she asked, strapping him into his Doggie Stay safety seat.

He answered with his sweetest bipolar smile.

Common threads and motivators, Kitch said from the passenger seat as she took the entrance ramp onto Highway 101. *Think in terms of common threads, then go through the prime motivators: love, sex, power, money.*

"I doubt it's love. Too many different people involved. Ditto for sex. Even with the mutilation aspects—it's not consistent enough. Has to be power or money."

She checked her rearview mirror. Dead center, Nelson's huge black head was reflected. She was relieved to see he had a smile and was taking interest in the passing scenery.

The blare of a horn tore through her head and brought her eyes back to the road in front of her. She'd begun creeping into the right lane. To save face, she put on her blinker and pulled the rest of the way over.

With Nelson momentarily placated by Roddy Rug and two Jumbo Veggie Dog Biscuits, she found her way to Tim's office. Two mugs, a thermos, and a white bag filled with nonfat biscotti in hand, she followed him to the conference room. The long oval laminated table was littered with coffee-stained styrofoam cups with teeth marks along the rims, empty Coke cans, and a half-eaten sugared twist donut on a tissue-thin paper spotted with grease.

He gathered up the debris then laid out the file folders and binders of all the known victims. Next, he uncovered the department's storyboards on Zelda Fischer and Raymond Clemmons. She stood in awe at the size of the boards themselves—five feet tall and at least twenty feet long. Each case was done in sections: an Overall Timeline, which listed the progression of events from time of notification; the Victim's Timeline, which listed such things as when the victim was last seen, last meal, last phone call. Then there were Witnesses segments—who saw the victims and when; then the Suspects section, under which was a big, white blank; then there was a Question section, which included the names of the detectives who were assigned to find the answers to those questions. The next segment was Leads to Be Followed, and who was assigned to those, and at the bottom was Other Facts. Under this was Similars, and then the list of all the other victims Onorato had given them.

Humbled, Adele unrolled her storyboard and taped it to a column in the center of the room.

"Threads," she said, using a blank section of marker board on which to make her own notes. "We're looking for common threads."

Starting with the thirty-four-year-old found in Belvedere Lake in New York City, she listed each victim by date of murder, sex, age, location, types of wounds, and profession.

When she was done, they both stood across the conference table, staring at the board. Tim took the Magic Marker and went to the empty section they'd claimed as their own.

#1: 11 victims—4 male / 7 female

#2: Methodology—vertical slash to both carotid arteries / exsanguination

#2A: Weapon—serrated blade / at least three different knives / CA victims have identical irregularity specific to one serrated blade.

She took the marker out of his hand, stood back, studied both boards, and finally wrote:

#3: 4 of 7 females—missing one or both breasts. (Marin, NYC, LA X2)

5 out of 11 victims—scalped and part of face removed (NY, DC, Denver, Houston, Chicago)

4 out of 11 missing part of buttock (NY, LA X2, Houston)

1 male genitalia removed (Miami)

1 male decapitated, disemboweled—amputated hands (SF)

#4: California Victims—

Marin/Fischer—serrated blade + scalpel (mutilated breast)

SF/Clemmons—scalpel (decapitation, amputation of hands, removal of all major abdominal organs)

LA/actress—serrated blade + scalpel (amputation of feet, one breast, part of buttock, complete hysterectomy)

LA/new victim—serrated blade + scalpel (amputated breast, part of buttock)

"Except for the California victims," Tim said, "the killer used the same serrated blade for everything: mutilation, amputation, and to cut into the carotids. The combination of serrated blade and scalpel cuts is only in California. California also has the only victim who was beheaded and disemboweled, and the only victims who had what appears to be surgical-type procedures done or the amputation of limbs."

"Yeah," Adele laughed. "Just like everything else in California, we've got the weirdo and the rest of the country has the normal psycho serial killer."

Tim sat down in one of the uncomfortable chairs and pressed his hands together, resting his chin on them, his fingertips touching his mouth.

"So let's say the guy in California has a medical background," she said.

"Okay, so what else?" Tim looked back and forth between her storyboard and the department's. It both scared and pleased him that she actually kept a storyboard. It had to have been something old man Heslin had taught her.

On the board she wrote:

#5: All victims—overseas within six months of murder

Adele paced behind the conference table, tapping her notebook. "Something's hinky, Timothy. It's right in front of our faces but we're not seeing it."

Tim bit into a biscotti. "Whole thing is pretty hinky if you ask me, Adele."

"Yeah, but look at the similarity of mutilations. There's got to be something behind the high number of breasts and scalps. They aren't just mutilated: the flesh is taken, as if someone is harvesting the tissue, or keeping souvenirs."

"Souvenirs falls more within my range of experience, but maybe this is a medical harvesting operation."

She snorted. "Breasts, buttocks, scalps, and a penis? I don't think so."

"How about harvesting the tissue for illegal research? Cloning or something like that?" He looked at her. "You're the medical person here. What do you think it is?"

She brought her cup to her nose and inhaled the sweet scent of chamomile.

"It could be use of the tissue for something weird and illegal, but why go to all that trouble? There's plenty of available cadaver tissue to go around. It's not like breast or scalp tissue has some sort of miracle properties. And Fischer had a rash—" She stopped and pointed a finger at Tim. "Hey! Ask Onorato if any of the other women had breast implants, and how recent they were." To herself, she wrote a note to call Alan Bonnewitz.

"You know, those are all places on the body that aren't normally explored in an autopsy," Tim said, using the remainder of his biscotti as a pointer. "Scalp, buttocks, breasts, penis."

She made a notation in her notebook and went back to staring at the board.

He put the stub of biscotti between his teeth, took the marker, and wrote:

#6: Three victims (Marin, NY, DC) known to have a rash
    before death

"When I see rashes," Adele said, "I think of allergies."

"But not all of them had rashes as far as we know," Tim said.

"And not all people are allergic types. Take my mother and me: all you have to do is wave a tomato or a peanut under her nose, and she'll break out into a rash. Me? You can feed me tomatoes, shellfish, and peanuts and then roll me around on beds of poison oak, and I'll never get so much as a hive."

"That's good to know, Adele," Tim said, straight-faced.

She rolled her eyes and brushed past him. For a long time she stood with her back to him, tapping her pen and absently humming a tune she wasn't aware was playing in her head.

He watched her for a long time, wanting to wrap himself around her mind and take a walk inside to see how it was working. What he really wanted was to spend a lifetime with her, if only for the pleasure of watching how her mind worked every day.

"Unholy Christ on a freakin' bike!" she yelled so suddenly

that he jumped. She grabbed his hand, pumping it up and down in her excitement. "I got it! I got it! Look at this!"

She checked off the victims who'd had a breast removed. "Look at the ages: forty-two, thirty-four, twenty-eight, thirty. That's probably a pretty good cross-section of typical ages for breast implants. Now look at these." She put a check next to the scalping victims' names. "Fifty-nine, forty-eight, forty-six, fifty-two, forty-seven." She looked at him expectantly. "Do you see it? Do you see the possibility? Everything fits! Can you see it?"

He studied the board. "Midlife people," he said finally.

"Right! And what do men and women do in midlife?"

"Fall apart and have affairs?"

"They fall apart because the effects of aging are beginning to show. They aren't getting away with looking ten years younger anymore, so they panic. Midlife crisis freak-out. These are all fairly upwardly mobile people. Face-lifts. Neck-lifts. Hair transplants. Eye jobs. Boob jobs. Lip expanders."

Excited, she put a cross next to the Miami victim's name. "This guy is sixty-five and his genitalia was removed. What do guys that age have done?"

He raised his hands in a gesture of helplessness. "Electrolysis for ear and nose hairs?"

"Penile implants, Timothy. They can't achieve or maintain erections as easily, so they go out and get Viagra and a little something extra for it to work on."

"What about him?" Tim tapped Mr. Clemmons with his biscotti.

"The girl in the hotel in Istanbul said he—"

He held up a hand. "Wait a minute. You called someone in Turkey?"

She made her lips disappear and nodded, her eyes sparkling. "I had a friend call. Anyway, the girl said Clemmons left the hotel almost as soon as he arrived. She said he left fat and came back skinny a few hours later, then spent the rest of the week in his room in bed. There was blood soaking through his shirt."

"So what are you saying?"

"One of Clemmons's friends told me that Mrs. Clemmons was always on her husband's back about his paunch and how old and fat he was."

Tim shifted on his feet. She was looking at him like he was supposed to come up with the answer. He reached out and grabbed at the first thought going through. "Liposuction, or a tummy tuck?"

"Somebody give that boy a beer!" Adele said. "Clemmons had his abdomen cut open. Maybe the killer was cutting out the scars from a liposuction or a tummy tuck."

"What about the removal of the organs, or the feet and hands?"

She smacked her lips and sighed. "Why were surgical procedures done on any of these people? I don't know." She looked at her watch. "How soon can you call Onorato?"

"Let's give him until morning, in case we come up with more. I'll give him a call around seven our time and run it by him." He yawned, and stretched.

"Need a wake-up call?"

He shook his head. "Not unless you're offering to bring me hot coffee and sweet rolls in person." *And then stay for the rest of your life.*

"Not tomorrow. I'm going into work early. Everyone on Ward Eight is going neurotic, not to mention that my dog has jumped off the deep end."

"Ah, spring," Tim sighed. "When thoughts turn to love and neuroses."

She almost wished she'd found the vinyl piping on the back seat torn off and shredded. At least then she'd know Nelson was venting some of the negative emotions he seemed to be repressing.

His spirits picked up a bit during the ride home. His tongue hung out the side of his mouth as he watched the landscape fly by. Soon, the worried knot in his forehead eased. He seemed to be looking for a familiar landmark. She could hear him thinking: *PetClubPetClubPetClub. She's taking me to PetClubPetClubPetClub.*

In truth, it wasn't a bad idea. The store was close by, and
Nelson was smelling rank. He was going to need a bath soon,
and she'd run out of the natural doggie shampoo that made
him smell like fresh laundry.

"Oh what the hell," she said and checked her watch. The
Beast swerved into the next lane where a white van was a half
car length alongside her. The van's horn blared, making her
teeth go on edge. She pulled back into her own lane, and
looked over as the van came even, window to window. She
waved apologetically, then froze at the sight of the scars on
the driver's face and neck.

Conversely, as soon as he saw her, his lips parted in astonishment as his expression changed from one of annoyance to
one of incredulity. He looked so stunned, she felt like checking the top of her head to see if there might be something
crawling there that would cause such a look.

He hit his brakes and dropped quickly behind her.

She guessed it took all kinds to make up the potentially
deadly corridor that was Highway 101.

"We'll go to Pet Club, but only for ten minutes. Okay, Nelson?" She looked in the rearview mirror. "Nelson? Did you
hear me? I said—"

Her fingers gripped the wheel as she applied pressure to
the brakes. The van was speeding down the Madera Boulevard exit ramp. She'd managed to catch only a glimpse of
what was painted on the side of the vehicle, but there was no
mistake: it was the symbol Wanda and Opal had seen. Under
it were words and numbers, but the van was too far away and
angling out of her range of vision.

Tromping on the accelerator, she jockeyed around a slow
truck to the Paradise/Tamalpais Drive exit, only to screech to
a halt behind a line of cars that had barely cleared the highway. She looked around for a way to circumvent the line
when she noticed the blue flashing lights on the highway patrol car directly behind her.

She bit her lip, swore, then smiled and waved. The CHP officer did not return her greetings. He was busy talking into his
radio, more than likely running a check on her plate.

* * *

He didn't present her with a moving violation ticket, although at first she hadn't understood why—she had been doing eighty after all. When he saw her license and compared the picture with the face looking up at the underside of his chin, a cross between a smirk and a smile settled Mona Lisa–like around his mouth. He handed back her license.

"Do you know why I pulled you over, Adele?"

She disliked the fact he used her first name—as if he were some overbearing older brother. She would claim ignorance, she decided. If he pushed it, she'd say something casual like "Oh, *that*. It's these new shoes. I can't believe how heavy they are!"

"No idea," she said glancing at his name tag, "Bob, but I bet you're going to tell me."

"Would you step out of the vehicle, please?" His eyebrows were scrunched down, creating deep lines between his eyes.

"Why?" She bridled at the thought he was going to make her get out of the car and stand on display for all to see. *Hey! Isn't that Adele Monsarrat, the nurse who works Ward Eight? What a dork.*

"Get out of the car, please," he said, stepping away from the door.

His officiousness infuriated her. Cops: they were so like doctors in that arrogant, controlling way. "I'll get out of the car when you tell me why," she said firmly.

As if it hurt him to lean down, he rested a forearm on the window casing. "Ma'am. Are you aware of the fact that you have a dead animal hanging off the bumper of your car?"

Her mouth opened then closed. Obviously, the man was out of his mind. Automatically she locked her door. She pictured herself calling 911 for help, but realized that might be confusing for the dispatcher.

". . . we got a couple of calls about it," he was saying, watching her carefully for signs of violent behavior.

She finally sighed, opened the door, and got out. Not taking her eyes off him, she stepped to the back of the car, glanced over, did a double take and covered her mouth to stifle the scream.

Tucked securely inside the well of the bumper was the body of Fluffy, the neighbor's rabbit. Its head dangled in a macabre limp way next to the tailpipe.

Whoever was running the projectionist's booth of her mind put on the reel featuring the hole through the rosemary bushes and the empty pen and Jessica pointing and saying, "Nelsie ran through there." The next reel showed the murderer hiding behind the car, then acting crazy in the front yard to divert her attention, then it panned to a closeup of the tufts of white fluff stuck to his mouth.

Her imagination played unwanted scenes of Nelson finding the poor defenseless creature hopping innocently around its own backyard, and then clamping his jaws around the animal's neck, throwing it up into the air, and catching it on his fangs.

"Shades of Cujo." She sunk in at the middle and covered her mouth, wanting desperately to cry. All she could see were the expressions of horror on the children's faces when they found that their beloved Fluffy was dead—murdered by the heinous, vicious, twisted Nelsie. How could she explain to those innocent children that Nelson was clinically depressed and he didn't know he was hurting poor Fluffy—that he just got too rough while playing and didn't know any better?

The worst of it was, he did know better.

Nostrils flaring, she turned to look in the backseat. Nelson, guilty as sin itself, was looking out the rear window. Suddenly he seemed as evil a dog as she had ever known. A real homicidal maniac. A Norman Bates in a Labrador's coat. As vile a creature as had ever slept under or on her bed, or used her toilet.

"I'm afraid I can't let you drive around like that, ma'am," the officer said in a much kinder tone. It was obvious she was genuinely shaken by the way she was still biting the inside of her palm. "Do you want me to remove the body for you?"

"No," she said. "No. I'll take it home and give it a proper burial."

She searched around under the backseat and pulled out the old shoe box in which she kept odd ends of rope and twine. Dumping the rope, she walked around to the rear of the car and as gently as she could, disengaged the dead rabbit from the bumper and put it in the box. Only when she had covered it with an old sweater did she dare breathe through her nose.

". . . probably a prank by some kids," the officer was saying in a conciliatory tone. "I'm sorry. Are you sure. . . ?"

She narrowed her eyes at the butcher in the backseat. "No, thank you, officer; I'll manage." She got back inside the car, not trusting herself to say a word to the assassin behind her.

Slinking down, he ventured a soft "Let me explain" whine.

She snapped around in her seat. "Don't you dare give me that 'I'm innocent' bullshit!" she hissed, hysteria at the edges of her voice. "You've killed! This is serious. This means doggie reform school—solitary confinement level for dangerous dogs."

With a dejected groan, the dog slunk even lower, draping his jowls on the back of the seat.

When she passed Pet Club without so much as slowing, he didn't even whine.

The Blessed Virgin Mary was parked outside the duplex, wrapped in its robe of royal blue paint. Inside, the living room lights blazed.

Without looking at Nelson, she removed the makeshift coffin from the back of the car and headed toward the house. The moment she stepped onto the porch, Cynthia threw open the door, red-eyed and sniveling. The misery on her face was hard to ignore.

Instinctively, Adele put down the box holding Fluffy's corpse and pushed it into a corner of the porch with her foot. No telling *how* Cynthia might respond to something like that in her present unhinged state.

While the two women sat at the kitchen table, Nelson lay still in the corner of the kitchen. He accepted a biscuit from

Cynthia, listlessly chewed halfway through it, and dropped the rest into the toilet.

"So?" Adele asked when Cynthia was down to a sniffle or two. "What's up?"

"I've decided."

Adele waited, steeling herself not to react either way. Judge not, lest thee be judged. "Ayuhn?"

"I'm . . ." Cynthia began to hyperventilate. "I've decided that I'm going to have it."

"Have what?"

"It." Cynthia was pale, and her upper lip was suddenly dotted with beads of perspiration.

Adele quickly checked the immediate surrounds for anything sharp that might injure her when she finally keeled over.

"Let's put your head between your knees and take some deep breaths, sweetie."

In direct opposition, Cynthia stood and hit the table with the flat of her hand. "I'm going to have it, by God, and nobody can stop—"

The last thing Cynthia saw were the black and white tiles of the kitchen floor coming up rapidly to say hello to her face.

"I'll strap it on my back or something and take it wherever I have to go," Cynthia said, holding the ice pack to her forehead. The bump wouldn't be so bad that she couldn't hide it under her bangs.

"You might find that difficult when the child gets to be five or six," Adele said, careful to remove any hint of mirth from her voice.

"Then I'll buy it a stroller."

Adele nodded in total understanding. "You know, honey," she began in her Mr. Rogers voice, "I think it's wonderful that you've made a decision. But what bothers me a little is the way you keep referring to the baby as 'it.'"

"I can't say the B word, Del," Cynthia said, her eyes darting. "Don't make me say the B word."

"Okay, okay. No B word." Adele patted her on the back and rose from her chair. "Would you like to spend the night?"

"Yes, but I can't." Cynthia squared her shoulders. "I've got to be responsible now." She said this like a prisoner on her way to the gas chamber. "I need to go home and be there for Ryme. I need to learn how to be a committed, dutiful wife and mo—mo—mother for the next eighteen years."

She grabbed hold of the kitchen table and looked off toward the ceiling.

"Fuck. Eighteen years. They're putting me away for eighteen years! I'll be old by the time it's out of the house for good. My whole youth will have passed me by."

A thought struck her and she fell back into the chair. "My God," she whispered. "The PTA will have access to my phone number. I'll be one of the park women."

"Park women?"

"The women who go to the park with the strollers and sit and talk about spit-up, poopy diapers, breast milk, and ear infections?" She lowered her head, blubbering. "Oh dear God. My good silk blouses are going to have milky stains and spit-up blobber all over them."

Adele knelt next to her chair. "Cyn? Why don't you talk to Jeffrey Lavine? Let him help you through this decision. You sound a little conflicted and I—"

"A shrink?" Looking offended, Cynthia let out a short, shrill laugh. "You think I need a shrink?"

"I think you need someone to help guide you through your decision-making process. You're obviously—"

Cynthia stood abruptly. "I'm hungry again." A look of horror suddenly crossed her face and her hand flew to her mouth. "Jesus, it's like Rosemary's incubus! It's demanding meat. I got up at two this morning, went out to the kitchen, and cooked up a half pound of liver, and while I waited for it to cook, I ate two cold quarter-pounders."

"Come on," Adele said good-humoredly. "Get a grip, Cyn. You need protein. Pregnant women crave protein." She stared closely at her friend. "You're upset. How about if I call Jeff at home and maybe you two can have a little chat. I'll be right here in case—"

"I don't need a shrink, Adele. I'm not crazy."

"I know, Cyn, but I think you're riding the fence around left field a little bit too close."

She kept her mind off the business at hand by trying to re-create the details of the driver and the van. She couldn't remember the details of his build or what he'd been wearing, but that wasn't surprising—considering. The eyes had been dark and deep-set, although what took her full attention had been his skin.

The sides and lower half of his face and neck appeared to have been extensively scarred either by burns or perhaps by some childhood disease. It appeared that grafting had been attempted at some point, but had not gone well. She tried to visualize the printing on the side of the van, squeezing her memory for anything it could get.

There were two words, the first longer than the second. The last word was only three or four letters. The last two, she was fairly certain, were GS.

She turned off the spray nozzle and checked the limp, wet body of Fluffy for any trace of shampoo. Toweling him off, she lay him gently on top of the washing machine and plugged in the blow dryer.

She shook her head. "What the hell am I doing blow-drying a dead rabbit in my kitchen in the middle of the night?"

On top of her dryer, St. Francis of Assisi sat, legs crossed, manicuring his nails with a file. Around his feet hopped precious brown bunnies. *Ah, but I say unto thee, reflect upon the children's faces when thou tellest them their bunny was mauled unto death by yonder rabid pit bull of a mongrel.*

She glanced over at Nelson, who had not moved out of the small space between the refrigerator and the washer, and wondered if it was her fault her boy turned out so rotten to the core. She sneered at him and growled.

Nelson groaned.

When the dead animal's fur was restored, it looked much better. It looked so good, she would not have believed Fluffy was dead if she weren't so sure he really was.

Changing into what Cynthia called her sleuthing outfit—

black leggings, turtleneck, and gloves—she concealed the furry corpse inside a black sweatshirt and sneaked around to the backyard. Looking over the hedge of rosemary, she could see the family gathered around the television in the family room, their attention completely absorbed by the show.

She crouched down and slipped through a break in the rosemary hedges into their yard. Creeping over, she peered through the bottom of the window to see what show they'd found so captivating.

The corners of her mouth turned down. On the screen was one of those nature programs. It appeared to be about—she grimaced—rabbits.

Sneaking back into the yard, she placed Fluffy back in his pen and latched the door.

It's the kindest way, Adele, St. Francis said, floating a few feet above the hedges. *They'll think it died peacefully in its sleep. No one need ever know you're harboring a brutal murderer of innocents.*

"Oh great," she said under her breath, "Just call me Mrs. Gacy."

The phone was ringing when she came in from her gruesome task. Closing her eyes, she tried to get the vibes of the person waiting on the other end of the phone. "Dr. Ravens, Cynthia, or my mother," she said, and picked up the receiver.

"Mrs. Adele Monstrot? Er, Mantrasat? No. Ah, Mansasnot . . . ?"

"Hi, Haresh. It's Monsarrat, but don't worry about it. What's up?"

"Oh. Hello, Adele. I am so sorry, but American names are very hard to pronounce."

"Well, don't worry about it, Haresh. If I lived in India, I wouldn't be able to pronounce anybody's name either."

"Did you like the tea I gave to you?"

"Yes, thank you. It was very nice."

He didn't say anything for a second or two, then: "I remember something for you. It may not be so important, but you should know."

She waited, then realized he was waiting for her to acknowledge this. "Oh. Yes. What is it?"

"I told you Mrs. Clemmons wanted Raymond to go to her doctor?"

"Yes."

"I remember his name now."

Again there was silence in which she realized he needed prompting. "What was it?"

"I am stupid that I did not think of it before. It is so simple a name."

"Uh-huh." After a silence, she said, "Do you want me to guess?"

"You can guess his name?"

"No, no, Haresh, I'm only kidding. What is the name of Mrs. Clemmons's doctor?"

"Dr. English." He let out a shrill laugh. "It is such a funny name."

"Yeah," Adele sighed. "A laugh a minute."

A mouthful of gin helped the last of the antibiotics go down. "Cheers," Daisy said to her reflection, then continued to smear her face and neck with the bright blue goop that, according to the advertisement on the jar, would smooth the fine lines away and reclaim the youth that had fled some twenty years ago, along with her svelteness. Using the back of her hand, she patted the underside of her chins, and examined her profile from each side.

Tomorrow, she wouldn't let him get away. Tomorrow evening she would walk out the back door, go around the block, and surprise him from behind. She'd look so smashing, he wouldn't be able to resist. Lisa could touch up her hair and do her nails in the morning, and then she'd pick up the yellow platform heels at Nine West, and the yellow daisy print dress at bebe's.

Daisy picked up the plate of cucumber slices, ate one, and carried the rest to the bathroom. Stepping into the hot sudsy water infused with Epsom salts, she cautiously lowered her backside into the water. The second the water touched the itchy spot, she gasped, gritted her teeth, and lowered herself completely.

The cucumber slices felt cool on her eyelids. She would have to remember to throw another one into the Cuisinart to use on her bum, and then perhaps she might even throw on a layer of the blue goop. It certainly couldn't hurt.

Adele dialed the Silver Circle Gallery and snapped out her tooth guard. She didn't want Alan Bonnewitz to think she was a drunk besides being artistically challenged. He came on the line sounding tired and irritable. As soon as she told him who was calling, she could practically hear him roll his eyes.

"I have one quick question, Mr. Bonnewitz. You told me you didn't know the name of the physician who performed Ms. Fischer's breast augmentation, but I was wondering if maybe you might recall the name of the clinic or hospital where she had it done?"

"I don't," he said impatiently. "I told you that."

"Okay, then, how about the country and city where she had it done? And before you blow me off, let me remind you, Mr. Bonnewitz, that I am trying very hard to find the person who murdered her."

He huffed and clucked his tongue. "It was some beauty clinic in Paris where they specialize in cosmetic surgeries. That's all I know."

"No idea what the name of it might have been?"

He heaved a dramatic sigh. "I think it was the Parisian Beauty Clinic."

"I understand you're the executor of her estate?"

"Yes." His voice went to business.

"Then you have access to her accounts. There must have been a bill or a Visa statement—some documentation that had the name of the clinic on it."

"They demanded payment in cash," he said. "Zelda was thrilled because the bill was about a quarter of what she would have paid in the States. She said she'd paid more for lunches in San Francisco."

"Did they give her a card, or some way to contact the doctor or the clinic if she had problems?"

"She had a card. I saw it in her address book, but when I went through her stuff after the funeral, the card was gone."

"Do you remember anything on the card? Part of a name? A street address?"

He was no longer listening; he was giving directions to someone to get Holmby on the line and ask him where the check was.

"Was that all you wanted to know?" he asked in a rushed, obstinate tone when he came back on the line.

She measured her words carefully, letting them out between clenched teeth. "I said, do you remember what was on the card?"

"It was in San Francisco. Some doctor. I don't remember."

"Does the name Dr. Edward English ring any chimes?"

"Never heard of him."

"Okay, well, thanks for your time and if you think of the name of—"

Alan Bonnewitz wasn't listening. He was yelling for someone to call Holmby.

Surfing the Internet for answers was, Adele decided, only for those of abundant patience. After the better part of an hour, she was rewarded with the white and yellow pages for Paris, including pictures of the buildings, street maps, and directions to the nearest Metro station. The only things that were missing, she thought, were the aromas wafting out of the patisseries, the sounds of the Parisians insulting all non-Parisians, and any listing for the Parisian Beauty Clinic.

Adele held the bundle wrapped in a blue flannel receiving blanket and wondered if she should attempt breastfeeding. She remembered from obstetrics training that one had to have had a baby in order to have milk, but then thought it might have been something she dreamed.

She undid the buttons of her blouse and released her breast from the confines of her Jogbra. The moment it hit the air, it began to grow—rather like the pudding in Woody Allen's *Sleeper*. Within a second or two, she could no longer see the baby, and she worried whether the breast might smother it. She moved the bundle around to the top of the breast that was now heading out the front door and across the street. Throwing back the edges of the blanket, she was not surprised that the baby was Fluffy, the dead rabbit. It was the lagomorph's nose rings that threw her.

Baby Fluffy opened her mouth and yowled. The noise jerked her awake.

Eye level on the pillow, she was somewhat relieved to see that Nelson had not moved since he'd crawled up on the bed beside her and fallen asleep whining. She'd softened enough just before bed that she'd read him the latest copy of *Animal Times*, the *People Magazine* for pets, and then sang the words to "Old McDonald Had a Farm." By the time she got to the pig, he was sound asleep. By the time she got to the horse, she was snoring.

The horrible yowling noise came again, forcing her brain cells to fall into place. It wasn't yowling; it was the phone ringing. She looked at the clock and picked up the receiver at the same time the answering machine clicked into action. She waited for the outgoing message to finish.

"It's four-thirty," she said, her voice gravelly. "Are you sure you want to identify yourself, because I'll warn you that if this isn't Muhammad, Buddha, Jesus, Mary, or Joseph, you will—I repeat—you will regret this call."

"Adele Monsarrat?" someone asked. It sounded a lot like someone speaking through a wad of Kleenex.

"I believe I was when I went to bed a few hours ago."

"Ward Eight won't be needing your help today," the voice said.

Adele wiped the sleep drool off her chin and snapped out her tooth guard. "Ward Eight needs all the help it can get, pal. We're understaffed by five nurses for day shift. So, unless two-thirds of the patients died or were discharged on the swing shift, you obviously don't know what the hell you're talking about."

Adele sat up. "Say, is this Mr. Walton? Listen, I know you're still sore at me for giving you that double dose of milk of magnesia by mistake, but that's no reason for you to—"

"This is Ellis nursing office," the voice said menacingly. "Don't come in today. You aren't needed."

The recorder on the answering machine clicked and bleeped when the connection was broken. Nelson awoke with a snort and looked at her with an expression that clearly said, "Who the hell was that?"

She yawned and hopped out of bed. "Ellis has demanded I take the day off, Nelson. I'd ask you to go running with me, but frankly I'm afraid you might attack something."

The dog's ear twitched, though he did not raise his head from the pillow.

She stepped into a pair of black running shorts, ignoring the dried white rings of sweat cascading down from the waistband, found a pair of socks that almost stood up by themselves, and put them on.

Nelson whined and slid out of bed. He came over and dropped Roddy Rug on her shoes, his eyes pleading for forgiveness.

"All right," she said stiffly. "You can come, but I'm leaving another message with Dr. Nutt's answering service. We'll see if you can get an early appointment, and then maybe we'll see if you can keep your teeth to yourself at Pet Club."

"Pet Club" reverberated through his tiny brain, bounced off the sides and made some kind of connection to his pleasure center. All killer instincts instantly suppressed, he grabbed Roddy Rug and headed for the front door wagging his tail. The dog was back in business and ready to roll.

After they returned from running, Dr. Nutt called as she was stepping out of the shower to say he had a 7:15 opening and could she pick up a cup of coffee for him on her way— he needed something to fortify himself before dealing with Nelson.

She gave Nelson his leash to carry, to build up a sense of responsibility, and together they ventured outside. She had just put Nelson in the car when she heard Jessica screaming her name.

Bracing herself, Adele looked up and forced an unnatural smile. "Hi, Jessie, how are you?" *Found your dead rabbit yet?*

"Come here quick, Adele!" The urgency in the child's voice wrenched her heart. "Quick, come and see Fluffy!"

Before she could decline and lock herself in the car, Jessica had grabbed her hand and was pulling her toward the backyard.

"Listen, Jess, I can't come in right now. I've got to bring Nelson to the doctor." *To have his head examined.* "I'll come over later when . . ."

The sight of the whole family—still in their robes and slippers—gathered around Fluffy's cage almost undid her. She opened her mouth to spill it all and beg their mercy for a dog gone wrong, when she noticed that instead of shedding tears of grief, each member of the family looked bewildered.

"It's the damnedest thing, Adele," Frank said, shaking his head.

"Yeah," Derek, the ten-year-old piped up. "Fluffy croaked on Tuesday and we buried her right over there under the plum tree?"

Sue looked at her with stricken eyes. "She was in pretty bad shape when we buried her."

"Euew. She stinked," Jessica said, holding her nose.

Kyle, the youngest, mimicked his sister and shrieked, "Euew! P.U.!" then screamed with laughter.

"And this morning we found her all clean and pretty locked in her cage," Sue finished.

"Have you ever heard of such a thing, Adele?" Frank asked, pulling the children close. "You think it's one of those metaphysical animal stories? Animals rising from the dead?"

Jessica tugged at her sleeve to get her attention. "Mommy says he smells like baby shampoo. She's silly."

Adele didn't trust herself to open her mouth, so she shook her head and clucked her tongue, looking appropriately mystified. She glanced toward the Beast where Nelson's head could

be seen sticking up over the backseat and was suddenly over-
joyed. She'd take a grave robber over a bunny killer any day.

She bid them goodbye and suggested they might try crema-
tion, in case they had a restless spirit hanging around trying
to inhabit dead rabbits. She marched straight to the car and
crawled into the backseat to give her grave-robbing baby a
kiss between his eyes.

Nuzzling her neck, the dog stuck his nose in her ear and
gave it a lick.

Twenty minutes later she sat staring at the sign on Dr.
Nutt's waiting-room wall:

IF YOU ARE THE PARENTS OF A NEUROTIC OR PSYCHOTIC ANI-
MAL, YOU CAN STILL GO ON TO LEAD NORMAL LIVES. CALL
THE MENTALLY IMPAIRED PET HOT LINE AT: 1-800-PSYCHOS

She jotted down the number, trying to decide what she'd do
with the rest of the day. She would take Nelson to Pet Club
and let him schmooze with the other dogs for a while, then
she'd drop him off and give Cynthia a call at work.

Her cell phone bleated like some electronic lamb.

"Where the hell are you?" Cynthia whispered the moment
she answered.

"At Dr. Nutt's. Where are you?"

"At work just like you're supposed to be. Grace just dispatched Twin Cities PD to go to your house to see if you're
dead. Nursing Department has been calling since seven-
fifteen. I keep telling them the Beast probably stranded you
and you're walking. Mattie has been up here crowing that
you're going to be charged with everything from negligence
to killing firstborn sons. She's having the gallows built in the
side parking lot as I speak."

"No way," Adele said. "Nursing Office called me off this
morning."

"You were dreaming, girl. We're understaffed. Until you
get here, Skip and I are each carrying fifteen patients, six of
whom are acute care. Abby has ten and she's in charge. We'd

ask Grace to cover for you, but there aren't any patients we hate enough. How soon can you get here?"

"I can't interrupt Dr. Nutt," Adele said, looking at her watch. "It's a special hot tub and massage session. I guess I could get in there by nine."

"Well, what do you want me to tell them?" Cynthia asked. In the background Skip was whining to someone about his patient load. He sounded a lot like Nelson.

Adele sighed. "Tell Grace I'm on my way. I'll explain the rest later."

Telling Nelson that Pet Club was out and that she had to go to work after all was not easy. Which is why she took the coward's way out and waited until they drove past Pet Club to say something. As soon as they passed the store's driveway, he let out an angry "Hey! What the hell are you doing? Turn right! Turn right!" series of barks and draped his paw heavily over her shoulder.

"Listen, Nelson, I'm really sorry, but I've got to go to work. I promise we'll go next—"

His howl was so forcefully loud, she turned and looked just to make sure there wasn't someone plunging a rusty knife into his heart.

Mattie Noel was loaded for bear as she strode into Ward 8, smiling triumphantly. She threw open the door to the report room and bore down on Adele, who was at that moment pointing out the right ventricle on the plastic model of the heart that rested on her lap. Four of Ward 8's post-bypass-surgery patients sat around her.

"Out!" Mattie yelled, jerking her thumb in the direction of the door. "Turn in your time card and leave the hospital immediately! You've been suspended for real this time."

Ms. Laguna, a retired WAC, turned in her chair. "Excuse me. Can't you see the girl is in the middle of something here?"

"I don't see where this is any of your business," Mattie

sniffed, barely looking at the woman. "This nurse is being suspended for neglect of her patients. She's failed to—"

Mr. Klein stood, two blue-veined hands gripping his cane. "Don't you say anything against this young woman. She's not failed anything. She's a good nurse."

The supervisor's smile dropped. "Don't worry, I'll have one of the other nurses come in and finish whatever business she's started, but I'm afraid she's going to have to—"

"Oh, no, you don't!" spit Mrs. Foley, staring at the supervisor through fierce, rheumy eyes. The octogenarian grabbed her walker and hoisted her ninety pounds out of the chair. "If this nurse goes, I'll walk out right behind her and take a few of the other prisoners with me."

Mrs. Dietel raised a knobby, arthritic hand. "I'll go."

"Mrs. Noel, I'll meet with you in Grace's office after I give report in an hour," Adele said calmly. "Please ask Grace and a second person from nursing administration to be there, and if you can, bring someone who's familiar with everyone who works in Nursing Office, will you?"

Mrs. Noel's neck went splotchy as she pulled the clipboard tighter to her chest. There was something about the way she did it that reminded Adele of a turtle pulling into its shell.

"Why?" Mattie asked, craning forward a little. "Why do you want all those people there? You're out of here, Ardel. You're history. You have no—"

"I'd like to share a tape recording of an interesting conversation I had with someone in Nursing Office about four-thirty this morning," Adele said.

They all turned in unison and gave Mattie hard, beady-eyed stares. Splotches of red spread across her neck.

Mrs. Foley sidled up to the supervisor and gave her a crafty old lady look. "Sounds to me like you're about to be diddled, little woman."

Under the scrutiny of Queen Elizabeth (still waving), they listened to the tape from Adele's answering machine for the fifth time. Kate Costanza, Adele's union representative, shook her head and stood. "Frankly, I don't think there's anything to discuss. It's clear that someone in your nursing office made a mistake and called Ms. Monsarrat off."

"But who?" asked Josie Hubert, the director of nurses. Josie had large dark blue eyes, lots of thick auburn hair, and a wide, serious mouth. She carried her five feet eight inches very well. She looked at Grace. "Do you recognize that voice?"

Grace shook her head. "How about you, Mattie? Who was on in staffing last night?"

Oddly silent, Mattie sat in the corner, no longer splotchy, but solidly flushed. Dark sweat rings had formed under each arm. "I don't really know," she said, standing. She gave her skirt a sharp tug to straighten it.

"Well, who did you get a report from this morning?" Kate asked.

Mattie's eyes darted around the room like two trapped animals. "I didn't get a report this morning. No one was in the office. I figured things out on my own."

"But don't you have the scheduling sheet?" asked Josie. "Surely you must have seen the scheduling sheet from last night."

Mattie sidestepped to the door. "Can't find it," she said apologetically. "I think whoever worked nights must have accidentally taken it home on their clipboard."

"In any event, I believe Ms. Monsarrat is cleared of all charges?" Kate said.

Mattie Noel opened the office door, her face blank and gray without a trace of color, natural or otherwise.

"Hold on a minute, Mrs. Noel," Adele said. "I think you should stay for the rest of this."

Mattie stopped and slowly turned around.

"I thought that since I'm here and have three of the top nursing management people in one room, perhaps you'd like to discuss the matter of several disturbing memos that have recently come into my possession."

Mattie closed the door. "Well, I don't know." Her voice came out just as gray as her face. "I suppose I could stay for a *little* while."

"Oh, stay for the whole thing, Mattie," Adele said waving a hand, "You'll find this very stimulating."

With Mrs. Foley keeping watch, Henry and Adele slipped into her bathroom and closed the door behind them

"What you be up to now, girl?" Henry said. He sat down on the toilet.

"How's your French today, Henry?"

He did the African American male head roll. "It be mo' better den my English. What do you want to know for?"

She handed him her cell phone and a small writing tablet on which was written an international phone number. "I got a real challenge for you," she said. "It's going to be sort of like finding your way through the Paris sewer system in the dark."

He raised his eyebrows in question.

"I want you to locate the number and address for the Parisian Beauty Clinic. This is the number you dial to get to a live Parisian operator and see if they can give you any kind of a lead on an agency with a similar name—one that does cosmetic surgeries."

"Why don't you go online? They got yellow and white pages for France on there."

"Been there, done that," Adele said. "No luck."

"How you doing on that medical ethics paper?" he asked, not moving.

"Fine," she said quickly, pointing to the numbers. "Want me to dial for you?"

"Twelve days, Adele," he said, beginning to punch in the numbers. "Dat's all you got left, girl. Don't mess up."

After several disconnections and reconnections with the information service for Paris, then questions, exclamations, harsh words, laughter, and finally cajoling, his tone turned flirtatious and stayed that way for about ten minutes. Incredulous that the same thing could be happening twice, she was getting ready to crush his foot under hers when he began writing down numbers.

"Well?" she said, the second he disconnected.

"No such place," he said, ripping out the page with the phone number and putting it in his wallet.

"What?!"

"The operator tried six different ways to Sunday to find something even close to the name. She found one Paris Clinique de Beauté, but they only do up hair and facials and that shit. I asked her if there was a place with that name that did beauty surgeries like fake titties. She said there weren't any listings and that she'd never heard of such a place. She doubted it was even on the red list."

"Red list?"

"Like our unlisted numbers here in the States."

She pointed at the pad of paper. "Then what were those numbers you took down?"

"Them?" Henry smiled. "Well, let's just say whenever I find myself in Paris, I got myself a friend."

"Christ on a bike!" She snatched the pad out of his hand. "I'm paying for international dating services! My phone bill is going to be more than if I just hopped on a plane and went—"

He snapped the headphones—broadcasting some Guy Davis blues harmonica—over her ears and held them in place until she calmed down.

Adele came out of the stall and activated the motion sensor. At once, the automated voice, identical to Hal's in *2001*, filled the nurses' lounge: "Please return to the wash station and disinfect your hands before returning to work!" A management brainchild, the motion-triggered announcements had been installed in each of the nurses' lounges at a cost rumored to be over two million dollars. The nurses' main objection to the devices was that it insulted their intelligence and integrity, plus the money would have been better spent replacing some of the equipment that was over thirty years old. That Larry Millbanks's brother-in-law was the recipient of the contract to install the useless things also did not escape their notice.

Cynthia stood in front of the lounge mirror rebraiding her

hair. "Ryme has evening rounds, and the Virgin Mary is in the shop on sabbatical. I was wondering if you could come back about seven and give me a ride home?"

"No problem," Adele said, changing out of her uniform into her sleuthing outfit. She pulled on the black top, and for the hundredth time in the fifteen years they'd been friends, she studied Cynthia's reflection in the mirror. Wide green eyes, creamy skin, sensuous mouth, high cheekbones: it almost made Cynthia's sexual promiscuity understandable. The combination of a good-looking person, dysfunctional parenting, and low self-esteem could almost always be counted on to produce some aberrancy in sexual behavior.

Cynthia sprayed a halo mist of Paloma Picasso perfume over her head. "We could go to dinner," she continued. "I promise we don't have to eat at Jack in the Box. We can go to Good Earth if you want, or maybe an all-you-can-eat Italian place so I don't embarrass you. Then we could go to Baskin-Robbins for a few quarts of lemon-custard frozen yogurt?"

Adele's stomach tightened. She didn't want to say she had a date to meet Tim. Her reluctance to talk about Tim with Cynthia still lingered. "Ah, actually, I can give you a ride home, but I'm busy after that."

Cynthia was suddenly at attention. If she'd been a retriever, her tail would have been pointing. "Busy? Busy doing what . . . or should I say who?"

"Pfft." Adele waved a nonchalant hand. "Why does everything always have to come down to sex and romance with you? I'm just signing up for a cooking class at the college."

"And you didn't tell *me*?" Cynthia frowned. "What cooking class?"

"A vegetarian cooking class—nothing you'd be interested in, oh Ms. Eater of Three Pounds of Liver."

"A half pound," Cynthia said, searching through her purse. She pulled out an apple left over from her lunch and bit into it with enthusiasm.

Glad to have escaped the interrogation, Adele stuffed her scrub dress into the canvas sack printed with names of San

Francisco tourist attractions and closed her locker door. She came to stand next to Cynthia. "Did you tell Ryme yet?"

Cynthia shook her head. "No, but I think he suspects. I caught him looking over my monthly planner this morning. Then later he was so *attentive*—like I was an invalid or a mental defective. 'Let me take out the garbage, honey,' she mimicked. 'Don't strain yourself. Here, have another glass of milk, darling.' God, it was enough to send me searching for a rusty coat hanger."

Adele laughed and finished tying her shoes. "I still think you need to talk to Dr. Lavine about this, Cyn."

Cynthia held up a hand. "I don't have time to get into this right now. I have to go back to work." She finished the apple in two more bites. "Meet me in the ER lobby no later than seven-fifteen?"

"Beast willing, I will."

Gearing up for a little breaking and entering, Adele sat inside le Beast finishing off a small bag of stale popcorn. If being floated to unfamiliar wards was the downside of nursing, stakeouts were, for her, the downside of sleuthing. Most of the time she loved her car, but not enough to want to hang out in it for hours on end. Keeping one eye on the iron gate guarding the Clemmonses' building, she took out her cell phone and punched in Tim's number.

"Any news from either of the Fan Belt Inspectors yet?" Adele asked when he came on the line.

"I told Onorato what you came up with and asked him to check with the survivors of the other victims about any surgeries, but he hasn't gotten back to me yet. Haven't heard word one from Harlan."

"Can you call him and ask what's going on?"

"Cardinal rule, Adele: Don't bother the boys while they're working. Don't worry, he's just as enthused about finding out what's so special about that pacer as you are. He'll call when he's got something.

"We're still on for tonight, right?"

Adele paused, waiting for an empty school bus to go by.

"Seven-thirty at the College of Marin registration office. The Vegetarian Epicurean, Part One."

"Right. You still at work?"

She didn't answer. She was watching Mrs. Clemmons—uncharacteristically dressed in jeans, light jacket, and baseball cap with the Forty-Niners logo—come out the front door laughing. At the evil gnome iron gate, she turned and said something to the trim dark-haired man with her. Smiling, he opened the gate for her and let her by. They linked arms and walked right toward her.

Adele pulled down the visor and looked away, though not before she got a good look at him. He had to be ten years younger than Mrs. Clemmons.

"You there? Adele?"

"Yeah," she whispered.

"You at work? What's going on?"

"Well, I'm sort of at work," she said, tracking them in her rearview mirror. They got into a black Mercedes and pulled away from the curb. "I'm watching the Widow Clemmons grieve."

For all its menacing appearance, the gate lock was easy to pick. It was the security alarms on the front door that proved difficult. Security systems had been her forte since her early teens, when she'd worked for a home-and-business security company. The Clemmonses had gone to some expense to install one of the more complex systems. For ten minutes she worked on it before giving up and walking around to the back of the building.

At the foot of a narrow set of concrete steps was another iron gate, sans gnome, which was easier to pick than the one in front. The back door, the door that *should* have had the five-star system, was outfitted with a half-star system. Within fifty seconds, she had it disabled and was standing inside the kitchen fitting her hands into soft kid gloves.

After closing her eyes to listen, she moved cautiously but steadily through the house, scanning every drawer and cabinet. The commonplace nature of what she found—folders containing grocery coupons, greeting cards, recipes—triggered a rising sense that her hunch was wrong.

In the bedroom, an address book lay open on the bed. Most of it was written in Arabic. She knew better. She knew it was wrong on all counts, but she couldn't stop herself. Unzipping her fanny pack, she slipped the book inside.

Under the bed she found a storage box containing four leather-bound photo albums. About fifty loose photos lay scattered on top. She picked up a handful and rapidly scanned them. In the middle she found a four-by-six color glossy of Raymond Clemmons in red swim trunks, standing on a beach smiling broadly into the camera. There was a wide gap between his two front teeth that gave the face an almost boyish quality. He stood with his arms crossed self-consciously in front of him, as if to hide the paunch underneath.

Adele turned the photo over. It had been taken in Miami six months before. Tossing the photo back on the top of the others, she gave it a final glance then slowly picked it up again. His left arm was decorated with a tattoo of a blue heart with a red arrow shot through the middle. It was the tattoo Laila Clemmons had told Boxer was not there.

Opening the door to what she thought was an extra closet, she found an adjoining bedroom. The room was sparsely furnished with twin beds, a mammoth antique mahogany wardrobe, and a matching bedside table. The contents of the bedside drawer were as uninteresting as a small blue jar of Vicks Vapo-Rub and a travel packet of Kleenex. When she closed the drawer, however, the jar rolled and hit something at the back.

She pulled the drawer open. At the rear was a small picture frame. She stared at the photograph in the semidark, her heart rate picking up. It was a close-up of Mrs. Clemmons, her arm clasped around the shoulders of Kadeja Shakir. In the background was the unmistakable shape of the Arc de Triomphe. Kadeja, unlike Mrs. Clemmons, was not smiling. Rather, her eyes held an expression of disdain.

Adele returned the frame to the bedside table, then wandered toward the back door as her internal alarm system sounded that she needed to vacate the premises ASAP. As she stepped outside, a thought came to her that sent her sprinting back to the bedside table. She took out the photo. The penlight trained specifically on Mrs. Clemmons, Adele studied her neck. The black scarf obscured part of the square gold pendant, but not enough that the symbol couldn't be made out.

The sound of voices and laughter drifted up from the front foyer, putting an end to that line of thought. Panic held her motionless for a second until, jamming the photo between the pages of the address book, she stepped inside the wardrobe. A brief thought came to her that the sleuthing business was going to give her a heart attack at a young age.

Mrs. Clemmons and her male companion were speaking both Arabic and English. Close by, a door opened and closed. They were in the bedroom, eight feet away, discussing where they would go for dinner. He wanted Chinese. She wanted grilled seafood. He teased her about eating so much fish and how some day a fish might eat her. She replied in Arabic, using the name Raymond in her comment. They both laughed. It didn't take much to imagine the joke.

She said she was going to take a shower. He invited himself to shower with her. They laughed again—a more intimate type of laughter that suggested they were comfortable with the banter, and had been for a long time. There was the sound of water running and then her voice coming through the echo chamber of the bathroom, telling him there was a clean robe in the guest room wardrobe.

Adele stopped breathing, and for a moment her mind went blurry. On instinct, she pushed herself back to the very corner of the wardrobe and crouched. That was when she saw the plaid flannel robe hanging over her.

I promise, she prayed in her head, *I promise on the life of my dog and my mother and Cynthia and Timothy that I will never get myself into such a tight situation again.*

Another part of her brain had just enough time to say, *Oh yeah, right,* when footfalls approached and stopped in front of the door. Frantic, her eyes fell upon the dark piece of fabric near her hand. She threw it over her head as the door opened, and a hand and arm reached in, took the robe by the shoulder, and yanked it off its hanger. The hem fluttered around her head, pulling the piece of fabric off her.

Heart skipping beats, she flattened herself against the wall of the wardrobe, making herself as small and invisible as possible. She wondered how it would feel to have her carotids cut and decided it couldn't be nearly as bad as how it was going to feel to bleed to death.

"You can have grilled fish at the Blue Dragon," he said, already in the other room. She let out her breath and pulled back the dark-colored garment that lay on the floor just outside the closet door. In the dim light coming from the other room, she saw it was a silk blouse. On an impulse that was distinctly female, she checked the label: Marc Jacobs—of course.

She stepped out of the wardrobe and crept soundlessly to the door. Under the sound of the shower, came the familiar sounds of lovemaking. Peering through the crack into the master bedroom, she could see their clothes littering the bed and floor in a trail all the way to the bathroom. Clouds of steam billowed into the room.

The moment she hit the sidewalk, she ran like a crazy woman until she got to the Beast and locked herself in.

She opted for Tim's voicemail rather than dialing his cell phone directly. The outgoing message was of those institutional say-your-name-here types.

"Hey! I'm headed north, about midspan on the Golden Gate. I've—"

A car honked and she pulled the Beast back into her lane. Even at the strictly enforced forty-five miles per hour limit, the bridge was not a place where one wanted to swerve into other lanes, unless one wanted to have a fatal head-on. "I've got something important. I'm on my way right now to pick up Cyn at the hospital and give her a ride home. Traffic is heavy, so I might be a few minutes late getting to the registration office. We need to talk to Onorato and Harlan, like immediately.

I've got a couple more things that Harlan might be interested in seeing. See ya."

It hit her like a bolt of lightning just as she was about to take the Lucky Drive exit ramp.

"Rugs," she whispered, seeing the white van clearly in her mind. UGS: the last word under the symbol had to have been rugs. What was the word before it? New and used? She shook her head. Persian? Oriental?

She unfolded the phone again and called the San Rafael library. Martha Monsarrat answered. Just the sound of her mother's voice seemed to put all things into perspective.

"Hello, darling. How are you feeling, and how's my grand-dog? Is he still having problems?"

"I'm fine. Nelson is, well, physically fine. The jury is still deliberating on the mental part. Listen, Ma. If you aren't busy, could you check all the Bay Area phone books under carpet and rug dealers? I need you to check the ads for one that has a logo that looks like a tilde, with a circle inside a circle at each curve."

"A circle inside a circle," Martha said, then "Isn't Nelson's Rod Stewart rug working out?"

"Yes, Ma, it's working out fine. I'm just following a lead on something I'm working on. I'll call you back in a half hour?"

"Nothing dangerous, I hope."

"Everything's dangerous these days, Ma." Adele sighed. "Shelving books is dangerous, grocery shopping is—"

"I got the message, dear, no need to expand," her mother said. "It's the dinner hour, so we're slow. I could probably do it right now. Do you want me to check on the Web for you as well?"

Adele smiled, reflecting on how things had changed. As little as twenty-five years before, a daughter called her mother to search for a certain cookie recipe. Now they called to ask them to search the Web.

"That would be great, Mom. I'll call you back in a while."

She folded the phone and worked it into her purse, pleased that she hadn't swerved out of her lane once.

* * *

Daisy moaned and bit down on a corner of the pink satin pillow. Lying on her stomach, she worked a stainless steel spatula over her backside. The blue goop, which had hardened to the consistency of cement, refused to budge. Underneath it waged a war of pain and itch. Throwing the spatula across the room, she rolled onto her side, popped two more Valium and three Darvocet, and took a long nip from the half-empty bottle of Beefeaters. "Bloody hell!" she said, pushing to her feet. Weaving slightly, she went into the bedroom and dialed her mother's number.

"For God's sake, Daisy, use your head," her mother said, irritated at being awakened at one in the morning let alone having to listen to her daughter go on ad nauseam about the problem with her bum. "Soak the damned stuff off."

"Righto, Mum. I'll go have a soak straightaway. Thanks ever."

Bottle firmly in hand, Daisy filled the tub and set the jets to high. Easing herself down, she positioned the raw spot in front of the strongest jet and let it go to town.

Bits of blue goop appeared in the swirling bubbles, going round then down, then surfacing, and getting pulled down into the pretty pink water.

She sobered at once. Pink water? In a yellow tub?

Turning off the jets, she lumbered wet and naked to the mirror. Her lips formed a perfect pink O at the sight of blood oozing down her leg to the floor.

Saad lit his thirty-fifth Marlboro of the day and continued with his letter to his mother.

America is very rich and clean. Every person owns a machine for washing clothes, and all the streets have a place to put garbage. Garbage is taken away twice a week! There is special machine built into the kitchen sink that will eat garbage as well. Every house has many bathtubs and toilets, and the kitchens are like in a palace.

It is law that all the children must go to school. Tell my sister that even the girls must have a full education—even college—but the dress of the women in America is shameful, especially the unmarried women. The food is sold in one store called a supermarket. They eat much food and are fat like the Germans.

Amar is prospering in his medical studies. He will be a fine surgeon. He says there is no tuberculosis here, and the children do not suffer from whooping cough or measles because all children have vaccinations when they are born. Fahad says nothing, but I do not think he likes what he is doing . . .

A car horn caused Saad to look up just as a yellow taxi pulled up in front of the American woman's house. Immediately, he threw the pad of paper into the backseat and started the car. If he lost sight of her so close to her time, Amar would kill him.

A minute later, she appeared. She walked down the porch steps, stumbled, fell, picked herself up, and drunkenly tottered toward the taxi.

He unzipped the cell phone and hit one button on the keypad. Before it could ring a second time, someone answered.

Saad spoke hurriedly, then waited for instructions.

Adele chose to sit in the ER waiting room, where she'd not only have a full view of the ER lobby but be in the thick of the action as it came down. Kitty-corner to her, a young man in his late teens or early twenties sat with a woman he called Mom. Adele could see the week-old row of blue 5.0 Prolene stitches ready to be cut and plucked at the top of his forehead.

Next to mom was a fiftyish woman with what appeared to be a roll of toilet paper wrapped around her right index finger, and directly across from her were two women, one holding the other. The one being held had a piece of too-short gauze wrapped around her right forearm, where blood was seeping through.

"Is that hair on your hand, Jeremy?" the mother asked the

youth with the stitches. Her expression was one of those maternal shock/wonder combo deals.

The unconcerned young man looked at his hand then at his mother's expression. "Yeah? So? Everybody has hair there."

"Well, I don't!" his mother exclaimed.

"Well, all the women I date do." Jeremy had not yet advanced beyond his mother-defiance developmental stage.

"Maybe that's the problem with your love life, dear," his mother said dryly, patting his arm. "Next time try someone a bit more evolved."

Under the guise of looking at her watch, Adele scrutinized her own hand for hair and found none. Bored, she got up and walked to the house phone at the switchboard operator's station and dialed the library again.

"I'm sorry, sweetheart, but I couldn't locate anything like you described," her mother told her when she came on the line. "However, we did have ourselves a good laugh over some of the photos used in the ads. There were some rather interesting-looking rug merchants in the area. There was one proprietor from Ali Baba and the Forty Rugs who looked like a—"

The rest of her mother's statement was lost as her internal Richter Scale registered the low rumble—that first telltale omen of an earthquake. She bid her mother a hurried goodbye as the phone was jolted off the narrow shelf and fell onto the tiles.

Turning first to the lobby, she shouted at the waiting patients to take cover, then ran for the pneumatic doors leading to the ambulance bay. She had never believed in the old safety standard of standing in a doorway during a quake; she'd seen too many photographs of postquake buildings where nothing was left standing except the rubble and the bodies under all those collapsed door frames. She preferred to take her chances in the open, watching both the sky for falling electrical lines and debris and the ground for fissures.

Adele waited out two small aftershocks, then went back inside to find the lobby deserted. A brief search found her former waiting room companions lined up under the double-wide doorway of the gift shop, happily chatting among themselves.

It was yet another example to prove her theory that there was nothing like an earthquake to break the ice.

"It's over," she informed them, and took her old seat. The others did the same. She looked at her watch again, not surprised that Cynthia was late, and picked up a ragtag book that had been left by the volunteers. She read the flap copy and put it down. It was a book from that generation of literature when practically every female author wrote novels the plots of which revolved around a woman writer living in a secluded, out-of-the-way cabin in the woods of Vermont or some other too-cold or too-hot place.

Out of curiosity, she picked it up again. She had turned to the back cover to look at the author photo when the lights flickered. Her head snapped up. The lobby TV, which had been on without the sound, suddenly blared and began changing channels by itself.

A woman with the platinum ringlets so fashionable during the 1940s in Miami, came out of the ER, a discharge form flapping in her hand. Her progression toward the exit door was marked by electrical chaos: hallway lights flickered and went out then came back on, the elevators chimed, and the switchboard operator yelped, stood, and flung away her headset.

At the automatic exit door, she engaged in a tag-me-if-you-can game. She'd start through, the doors would close, she'd pull back, the doors would open, she'd try again, and the doors would again try to crush her.

Giggling like a child, she finally rushed the partially opened door, making it halfway through before it closed and caught the back of her pink-and-yellow-striped caftan. With a tug, she pulled it through and stepped into a waiting taxi.

Adele sprinted to the door that now refused to open at all. The taxi pulled away and sped down the hospital driveway. As soon as it was out of sight, the door opened.

In the crowd of ER professionals who rushed in and out of treatment rooms, Adele managed to find one familiar face.

Brenda waved from the utility sink where she was emptying an emesis basin. "Hey, what's up, Del?"

"A woman just left here—platinum ringlets, pink and yellow stripes?"

Brenda laughed. "Oh, you mean Shirley Temple in a tent?"

"What was she in for?"

"She's got a rash on her butt that looks like the Grand Canyon at sunset. It was—"

Adele cut her off. "I need her name and address STAT."

Brenda pulled back. "Jesus. What'd she do? Kill somebody?"

"No," Adele said, "but I think somebody is going to try it on her."

Like a set of square lips, the pneumatic doors opened and spit Adele out into the waiting room, where Cynthia sat eating a cup of frozen yogurt, deeply absorbed in a copy of *Town and Country*.

"We gotta go now, Cyn," Adele said, tugging at her sleeve.

"Why is it," Cynthia asked without looking up, "that ninety percent of all the brides in *Town and Country* are blond?"

"Rich men prefer blondes because their mothers are blondes, and lots of rich men are in love with their mothers. Come on."

Cynthia read the expression on her friend's face as she was pulled toward the parking lot by the front of her scrub top. "What is it? What's going on? Does this mean I'm going to miss my dinner?"

"I'll tell you the whole story in the car. We've got a housecall to make in Sleepy Hollow, but I'll stop by Señor Taco Homeboy on the way—I hear they have killer fries."

Cynthia finished her second Burrito el Grande Dandy and was beginning on her third Rio Grande Coke and Super Fries, as Adele punched in the number Brenda had given her. On the sixth ring, a Betty Boop–like voice answered in a British accent.

Daisy hung up. "Extraordinary," she said to the fresh bottle of gin. "Bloody extraordinary." Here she was, just moments

after arriving home, and two home visit nurses had already
been dispatched to check on her.

She poured herself a glass of gin, took two more of the
antihistamines the doctor had prescribed, and downed them.
For good measure, she fished out a third and washed it down
with the rest of the glass: if one was good, three was better.

The clock in the hall chimed eight times. She took out a
plate and filled it with the chocolate truffles she'd purchased
that afternoon. Nurses were partial to sweets—everyone
knew that.

Perhaps, she thought, there was time for a quick bath before they arrived.

Daisy filled her glass again and padded to the bathroom,
dropping articles of clothing as she went. She'd be up and
presentable before they came round.

Saad tapped the pine-tree-shaped air freshener hanging
from the rearview mirror without taking his eyes off the dash-
board clock. It was almost time. Amar wanted her before anything else had a chance to go wrong. They could not afford a
second failure, not now—not so soon after the last one.

Settling back behind the wheel, he flicked the last of his
cigarette out the window and pushed in the car lighter. As always, the excitement of the game rendered him a little nervous, just enough to make him more vigilant.

The tip of his tongue found the end of the cigarette, and
using only his lips, he pulled it out of the pack. This one was
going to be easy, not like the young one in Los Angeles. He
had not liked that one. The young whore had been strong and
fought him. She did not die fast, and had spat in his face and
called him a fucker.

He had had two dreams about her, and that bothered him
almost as much as Amar having taken chances to drive the
length of California with parts of the body in the car. He did
not like it that his brother took things too far sometimes. It
put the operation in jeopardy.

The car lighter clicked. He pulled it out and studied the
small round circles of orange. As they faded, he held the

end of the Marlboro against it and inhaled the smoke deep into his lungs. He imagined himself to be Al Capone or John Dillinger.

He narrowed his eyes into mean slits and checked the look in the mirror. With this one, he would go around to the back of the house, where he would be invisible. He would put on his gloves and the covers for his shoes and hair, careful to leave nothing exposed. Inside, he would kill the lights and make his way to the bedroom where the pig would be on the bed sleeping off the drink and pills. Or maybe in the tub, which was even better. He'd cut her before she could react.

It was a good method they taught him—quick and easy. He laughed. Like frozen TV dinners, it was American to be quick and easy, even in killing.

The sound of a motor close by caused him to slide down in the seat. A station wagon slowed and parked in front of the whore's house. The two women stepped out of the car. His phone rang once, then stopped.

FOURTEEN

THE YELLOW HOUSE WITH THE BRIGHT PINK AND yellow Peter Max daisies painted across the front came into view. Both Cynthia and Adele stared at the mural in silence.

"It's an interesting statement," Cynthia said finally.

"Very." Adele placed the Colt and the cell phone inside the overflowing purse and got out of the car. "I have a feeling this will be a singular experience in evolutionary throwback home decoration, so pay attention."

They had to search for the doorbell. Cynthia eventually found it in the dark center of a painted pink daisy. They rang several times, knocked, then pounded.

"She said she'd be here," Adele said. "She sounded glad we were coming."

Cynthia was already heading down the driveway at the side of the house.

"Maybe she's in the back," she said. "Painting more flowers."

The scream of the tea kettle could be heard, shrill and unnerving through the back door. They took turns knocking until Adele's gut took charge.

Stepping inside, she turned the gas off under the kettle. "Mrs. Rothschild? Hellllloooo? Daisy Rothschild?"

Cynthia ventured into the hallway where she had to force herself to ignore a dish of assorted chocolate truffles on the side table. As she turned away, she noticed the pink-and-yellow-striped dress on the floor. Following the trail of clothes, the two nurses entered the master bedroom.

Cynthia stooped to pick up the latex girdle and turned it over in her hand.

"What is it?" she whispered.

Studying the article, Adele fingered the four stocking hooks and shook her head. "I think it's what they used to call a girdle. It's a pre-pantyhose torture device for women."

"You mean, like a hair shirt?"

Adele nodded. "Mrs. Rothschild?" she called through the partially opened door and over the noise of the Jacuzzi jets. "Your home visit nurses are here from Ellis Hospital. Are you okay?"

When there was no response, Adele walked boldly into the bathroom. In the tub, the ringleted blond head of Daisy Rothschild bobbed facedown in the foam of bubbles spilling over the rim and across the floor.

They shifted into critical care mode without missing a beat. Cynthia pulled back Daisy's head and wiped away the bubbles clinging to her face, while Adele's fingers probed for a carotid pulse. The woman resembled a large foam-beaked bird with hair that had been sculpted into a permanent architectural creation.

"She's breathing," Adele said, and the surge of adrenaline subsided.

Cynthia picked the two prescription bottles from the top of the toilet tank and checked the labels. The larger of the two contained a prescription antihistamine, the smaller a strong pain medication. She counted out the remaining pills in each.

"She's taken four of each since she got home—three times the normal dose."

Adele held up the half-empty bottle of gin. "I guess her interpretation of 'take with plenty of liquids' was pretty literal. Why don't you go into the kitchen and see if you can find some tea or instant coffee and put that hot water to use. I'll stay in here and run cold water over her until she wakes up."

Amar answered on the first ring. It was clear he was angry at being disturbed a second time, especially since he'd already issued precise orders.

"The nurse," Saad said hurriedly. "The meddler. She is in the house with the fat one. What are we to do?"

Amar leaned back in his chair drumming his fingers on the desk. "You will bring her with the fat one to the warehouse. Do it now—we will meet you there."

"There is another woman with the meddler. She is dressed like a nurse. What about her?"

Saad's lack of ability to think for himself irritated Amar. His brain had gone soft from watching too many American movies.

"Kill her." He paused; his irritation escalated. "No mistakes this time, young brother. You left the Negro woman alive and it cost us. This time you will use more than your fists. Cut her and then make sure she is dead, or I will send you home to Mama in shame."

Daisy didn't wake up until her body started to shiver. Adding ice cubes to the cold water had been Cynthia's idea, and even though Adele thought the method cruel and unusual, it had worked.

Introducing themselves, they helped her out of the tub, toweled her awake, and then slipped the striped caftan over her head. To say the woman was Rubensesque would have been kind. Though she had a pretty face and enormous hazel eyes, Daisy Rothschild needed to make Jenny Craig and Richard Simmons her closest friends.

Three cups of instant coffee and hot milk later, Daisy was finally able to look at them without seeing four fuzzy images.

"How do you feel?" Adele asked.

"Terrific!" Daisy propped herself up in a corner of the couch. "I daresay, I should, after you two saved my life. How shall I ever repay you for your kindness?"

Adele turned to look at Cynthia. "You first."

"May I have a piece of fruit and some of those tea biscuits in the kitchen? I'm famished."

In a cascade of waving, fluttering hands, Daisy told her she could have anything she liked, and to please feel free to raid the larder. Cynthia was already in the kitchen, while Daisy was still going on about the lovely seeded rye and the nice bit of roast beef in the fridge, when Adele interrupted.

"Mrs. Rothschild, I don't want to alarm you, but I need to ask you some questions that have to do with your safety."

"That sounds ominous."

"Yes, well I'm wondering if . . ."

"Ooh. I know!" Daisy sat up, her curls bouncing like the springs in an old mattress. "You must have seen him on your way in. You're worried about that lovely chap outside. I assure you, he's perfectly safe. Did you see him? Isn't he the most beautiful thing you've ever—?"

"What chap outside?"

"Oh, this divine man who's been courting me." She giggled. "He's quite old-fashioned, really. Reminds me of how the Spaniards serenade the women they love standing under their windows. He's been waiting afar all these—"

"You've met him?" Adele asked, surprised. "When was the last time you saw him?"

Daisy looked surprised. "Well, yes, I've met him briefly at a party on Friday, but he'd been watching me from his car for over a week. As for the last I saw him, I suppose you could say when I came back from hospital just an hour ago. I'd intended on asking him in for a drink this evening."

She leaned forward and spoke in a lowered tone. "Isn't it romantic? And he's so polite. At this party the other night, he—"

"What kind of car does he drive?"

"Oh. Well, it's an American car. What you Yanks call a boat." A concerned expression crossed Daisy's face. "Is something wrong? Why are you—?"

"Mrs. Rothschild—Daisy—have you recently been abroad?"

"Well, yes. I went to London to visit my mother, but I returned over a month ago and I—"

"Did you have a surgery of some sort while you were there?"

Daisy's hand automatically went to her breast, panic in her eyes. "Yes. A biopsy of my . . . Why do you ask? Have you been told something about it? Did the tests indicate cancer or—?"

"No, no. Nothing like that. I was mainly interested in the doctor who did your breast biopsy in London."

"Dr. Wilson and his nurse. Nurse Murphy."

"What do you remember about the biopsy?"

Daisy blinked as she thought about it. "It was a thoroughly awkward, bloody awful experience. The office was south of the river in Lambeth." Daisy blew her bangs off her forehead. "It isn't a very respectable section of London. I thought it odd at the time, because Dr. Knowles—he's my regular doctor—is quite exacting about his office. He gets his knickers all in a twist if the magazines are out of order in his reception office. Dr. Wilson and Nurse Murphy said he'd been detained and they had to perform the biopsy for him. Then, about a week ago, Mum called Dr. Knowles to ask about the rash, and he knew nothing about the surgery. He said he'd never assigned anyone to ring me up for a biopsy. I'm sure he thought Mum had gone quite off her rail."

"What about Dr. Wilson? Had you seen him before?"

"Horrid man." Daisy shuddered. "Wouldn't even help me to the WC after the surgery. He warned me that if anything went wrong, I had to see Dr. English and no one else. It was more like he was threatening me."

Adele took out her notebook. "Can you recall anything else about them or that day?"

"They both had accents, and I believe it was Nurse Murphy who actually performed the surgery. I was quite perturbed that they didn't seem to be interested in my breast at all, but in my bum. It was strange, really. They both wore a lot of jewelry. Nurse Murphy had a gold Rolex and several large diamonds—real ones, not those bloody awful zirconium things. He wore two or three rings."

Adele turned to the sketch in her notebook and held it up. "Did any of the rings have this symbol on it?"

"Yes!" Daisy said, clapping her hands as though she'd won a prize. "That was it!"

Adele put away the notebook and pulled out the photograph of Laila Clemmons and Kadeja.

"Recognize anyone here?"

Daisy's pencil-thin, semicircular eyebrows rose. "Well,

damn my bloody soul," she said, pointing at Mrs. Clemmons. "It's Nurse Murphy."

A slow smile rearranged Adele's mouth as she nodded and moved casually toward the windows that overlooked the street at the front of the house. Through a slat in the vertical blinds, she searched for a vehicle that fit Daisy's description. The street was lined with parked cars, but the only one that came close to fitting into the "boat" category was the Beast.

She was closing the blinds when a tiny spot of orange caught her eye. His outline, hidden in the shadows of the shrubs, was scarcely visible. Had it not been for the glowing end of his cigarette, she would have missed him altogether.

In the last narrow bit of space before the slats closed, she saw him stand and start toward the house.

Unhooking her fanny pack, she stuffed it down the cushions of the couch, picked up her purse off the floor, and ran for the kitchen.

The Rothschild kitchen was indeed a cornucopia. Bent over the crisper, Cynthia was sorting through the lettuce and tomatoes for a sweet onion when a sudden pain ripped through her lower abdomen to her back. It was so abrupt it took her breath away, then passed as unexpectedly as it came.

Giving up on the onion, she added a few slices of cucumber, slapped a slice of seeded rye over the slab of roast beef, and fit the end of the man-sized sandwich into her mouth. Her teeth were cutting through the layer of lettuce and cucumber when Adele came into the kitchen wearing an alarmed expression. At the same instant, the front door crashed open, followed by Daisy's screams.

Adele shoved her purse at Cynthia and pushed her out the back door. "Run like hell. Call nine-one-one for the police then call Tim. I'll hold this guy here as long as I can. Go!"

Sandwich held firmly in her mouth, Cynthia knew better than to question. Clutching the purse to her chest, she turned and fled.

In the driveway alongside the house was a gray Buick LeSabre. She threw Adele's purse under the hedges of daisies, and knelt beside the car. At once, a second wave of cramps caused her to clench her teeth. When the episode passed, she raised up just enough to see through an opening in the curtains. In the dining room outside the kitchen, she could barely make out Adele standing sideways to the window, hands resting on the top of her head like a prisoner.

Aiming a gun at her was a man wearing a Harley Davidson jacket and a pair of Dockers. A heavy gold chain hung around his neck, gaudy enough to be part of a Mr. T starter kit. The blue bandanna was tied around his head like the homeboys in the Mission district. In one hand, he held the ends of a rope looped tightly around Daisy's neck. A second loop was pulled across her mouth.

The man stared at Adele with cold, flat eyes, and made a motion with the barrel of his gun. He demanded she put her gun on the table.

Adele reached around with one hand and pulled the Colt from the waistband of her jeans. She slid it toward him.

"Where is the other woman?" he asked, picking up her gun and sticking it into the front of his pants.

"She walked down to Sir Francis Drake to pick up a pizza," Adele said, nodding once toward the back door. "She'll be back in about twenty minutes."

The man seemed irritated and confused by this news. After a minute of silent deliberation, he waved his gun. "Out the door now," he said. "Move slow. If you make one mistake or scream, I kill you both."

With the barrel of his gun pressed against the back of her head, Adele moved slowly toward the door. He dragged Daisy by the rope. On the steps leading to the backyard, Daisy stumbled and fell to her knees. He staggered slightly, then jerked the rope so tight, her head snapped back.

Instead of crumbling into a weeping heap, Daisy kicked at him, missed, and tried again. With his gun he slammed the side of her head hard enough to daze her.

Despite the corkscrew curls, Cynthia decided Daisy's inner fabric was a hell of a lot tougher than anyone might suspect.

*   *   *

The first thing Adele saw was an inch of her purse strap sticking out from under a hedge of daisies next to the car. Next to it, like an afterthought, was a roast beef sandwich with a large bite missing.

The man opened the trunk. "You in first," he said, waving the Glock at Adele.

"I can't," she said, praying that Cynthia hadn't left the cell phone behind. "I'm claustrophobic. How about if I ride in front with you?"

He jammed the gun against her forehead, his eyes wild. "Get in, or I'll kill you now. It makes no difference."

Keeping an eye on the finger depressing the trigger, Adele crawled sideways into the trunk. He bent Daisy over the lip then shoved her the rest of the way in. Adele slid out from underneath her as the lid came down.

The last thing Adele saw before the lid shut was the smallest blur of a blue scrub top as it disappeared down behind the Beast.

Tim checked his watch with the Seth Thomas on the wall of the registration office for the third time in ten minutes and walked outside. The night was clear and warm, the kind of weather that made for smooth commute traffic.

Adele would have called him if there'd been a problem with traffic or if the car had broken down. He frowned and watched the crush of young students scanning the sandwich boards where the lists of classes were posted. Two gangly boys with several ear and eyebrow piercings apiece rushed to one board, scanned it, went to the next, and said, "Fuck, man! Full!" simultaneously.

A third teen at one of the other boards laughed, and in a voice caught in the between stages of changing, said, "Fucking afternoon classes all taken, man. We're fucked. Don't think I can even remember how to get up before noon."

Tim went back into the registration office. He could call her on the cell, but decided it seemed too desperate. He'd wait for another twenty minutes, then register for her. Pushing down the bad feeling starting in the lower forty of his gut, he began to pace.

The Beast had never liked her. Probably, Cynthia thought, because it instinctively knew how much she hated it. Knowing Adele's fondness for the piece of mechanical junk, she'd kept her true feelings to herself, offering to drive most of the time, just to limit her exposure to Satan's own mechanical familiar.

She bit her lip, trying not to hyperventilate as the Buick rolled down the driveway and sped away. As soon as it turned the corner, she got in behind the Beast's wheel and sighed in relief at finding the keys on the floor.

Her hands shook as she tried to fit the key in the ignition. "You'd better start, you worthless piece of shit," she hissed desperately. "Because if you don't, I'll see to it you die the worst death any car has ever known."

Just to scare her, the Beast sputtered, choked, backfired, and, after a slight hesitation, reluctantly lurched forward. Asserting her control, she pressed the pedal to the floor and instinctively turned onto Sir Francis Drake Boulevard, heading south toward Highway 101.

A Buick was one of a half dozen cars she could recognize at a distance. Her mother had been partial to Buicks. And although she would never admit it, she herself had learned how to drive in one in a dusty trailer park in the Nevada desert.

Within a mile she caught sight of the Buick's taillights. Careful to stay behind minivans and sports utility vehicles—of which there was no shortage—she did brave a few moments of close proximity, in order to read his license number through the windows of a BMW and a Mercedes. Only when she slowed for the tollbooths on the last third of the Golden Gate did she feel confident enough to dial Tim's number.

She felt for Adele's purse and let the panic settle in her stomach before starting to cry. The purse, the phone, the sandwich—were right where she'd thrown them when Daisy and Adele were herded out of the house.

Fifteen cars from the booth, she had to make up her mind

what to do. She could alert the toll taker to call the CHP, but that idea crashed abruptly as she imagined the whole scene beginning to end: First, trying to explain to the toll taker that she was trailing a car driven by a kidnapper, and that her best friend and a fat woman were in the trunk. Then, even if the toll taker didn't try to have her arrested and actually sent the CHP to check it out, what would the kidnapper do?

What if he panicked and led them on a high-speed chase that ended when the car hit an embankment and burst into flames? Or, what if the CHP—not exactly known for their high IQs—began shooting, and bullets penetrated the trunk?

No. Cynthia squared her shoulders and sat taller behind the wheel. She'd wait until they landed somewhere and Adele was out of the trunk before trying to alert someone.

She maneuvered the Beast up a car, suddenly glad for all the years she'd trailed boyfriends who she suspected were cheating on her. At the tollbooth she removed three singles from her uniform pocket, thanking herself for deciding against a third dish of frozen yogurt at lunch.

The Buick took the Lombard exit and proceeded to the Civic Center where it then headed east toward China Basin. The traffic began thinning out until there were only two cars separating them. She turned off her lights and hung back even farther. As soon as he turned onto Townsend, he slowed to a crawl, as if he wasn't quite sure where he was going.

Cynthia looked around, biting her thumbnail. On one side of Townsend were the Caltrain tracks; on the other was an endless row of warehouses, some old and out of plumb, as if they'd been there since before the 1906 quake and were standing on the sheer strength of the termites holding hands within their walls.

There was nothing else around, no trees or shrubs, not even a blade of grass pushing its way through the cracks in the street. The buildings all seemed to melt into each other, only occasionally broken by a driveway or a work yard. Graffiti crowded every unprotected surface with violent images and words. Two of the largest took her attention. Done in red, black, and white, it was at least five feet tall and depicted a white man hanging by the neck, his body torn and bleeding. In another, a white woman with a knife through her eye was being gang-raped.

Cynthia shivered and another surge of pain, stronger this time, tore through her lower abdomen. *I've pulled a muscle,* she thought. *It's nothing more than that.* Something inside her released, and a warm ooze began between her legs. Automatically she squeezed her thighs together, as if to hold back what she could not stop. She gripped the wheel, waiting for it to pass, concentrating on not being seen. If he pulled into a warehouse yard, she'd have no cover.

The thought had no sooner registered than he slowed and turned in to one of the yards. She pulled over to the side, not daring to touch her brakes until his taillights disappeared from view. She drove past and parked around the next corner.

The red painted curb and the pain in her belly both went ignored as she got out and hurried back to where she'd seen him turn. An automatic fence on rollers barred entry to the warehouse yard. She couldn't see the car itself, but the glow of the taillights was reflecting off the buildings to her right. Finding no less daunting entrance, she heaved herself up and began to climb the fence. From the looks of the area, it was sheer good fortune there were no barbed-wire coils at the top.

She had scaled higher, more dangerous fences. During the years she'd obsessed over a train of misogynistic men, she'd once climbed up the side of a house built on cliffs a hundred feet above jagged rocks just to peek inside the bedroom of the current flame who'd sworn on his mother's life that he was home alone. Of course he wasn't—none of them ever were.

Soundlessly, she dropped to the blacktop, nursed another wave of cramps, then headed for the red glow of the car's brake lights.

The ride in the trunk had not been smooth. However, the situation, coupled with the close, pitch-black quarters, did give the two captives an opportunity to become quite familiar with each other in a short time. Rather than screaming or becoming hysterical over a situation in which most women would have gone mad, Daisy remained relatively unruffled.

They worked together identifying audible landmarks, which, when coupled with distance and time traveled, gave them a pretty good idea of where they were. The fog horn of the Golden Gate, the tollbooth, then the steep upward climb— Gough Street hill—the leveling off at Washington Street, and then the steep downhill. Minutes later, the car stopped and bits of highbrow conversations filtered in. Michael Tilson Thomas's name was mentioned, and a young girl's voice rose above the others to proclaim that Mozart was the Jerry Garcia of his time.

"He's at the stoplight at Van Ness and Grove," Daisy said. "The symphony must be letting out."

For a time there was only traffic noise and then a rhythmic, hollow *ka-klank, ka-klank* from overhead that had them stumped. A minute later, they heard a train and Adele knew exactly where they were.

"We just passed under the freeway on Fourth Street," Adele said. "This has to be Townsend by the Caltrain depot. That's probably the last commuter train pulling out."

Adele pictured the area in her mind. It was well populated with warehouses. Thomas Penn's description of a large room lined with carpet rolls and Onorato's information about the young victim in L.A. being found in an abandoned warehouse left little doubt about where they were going. She was glad Daisy couldn't see her face.

Running her hands over as much of the interior of the trunk as she could, she was working on pulling off the flimsy cover over the rear panel when they came to a stop. The sound of a gate rolling back sent Adele's adrenals into hyperpump.

"He's going to open the trunk," she said, working her body around, so that her feet were closest to the opening of the trunk. "Lie on your stomach or your side if you can. Turn your face away so he can't see it and stay still."

Daisy turned over and pressed her face against the side of the trunk.

"If he's alone, play dead, and I'll try to get a kick at him. If there's more than one, do what they want, but look for a moment to distract them. And if you get half a chance, run like hell."

"When I was in upper sixth, I was quite good at PE, you know," Daisy said, lifting her head briefly.

Adele was still trying to figure out how to respond when the car stopped and the motor was cut. A second passed before they heard the thunk of the trunk release and the lid sprang up a couple of inches. Through the crack, Adele could see two corrugated metal doors.

The driver got out, but did not close his door. Adele pulled her legs up, and drew even farther toward the back of the trunk.

"Play dead," Adele whispered. "I'll . . ."

The trunk opened. The barrel of the Glock was aimed between her eyes. "You," he said. "Get out."

Adele did not move. "I think she's dead," she said, tilting her head at Daisy. "She stopped breathing about ten minutes ago."

His eyes automatically went to Daisy. In that instant, she kicked at the hand that held the gun. One foot connected with his wrist, the other with his ribs.

He spun backward, losing his grip on the Glock. It fell and slid a few feet away. Before he could retrieve it, Adele was out of the trunk and running as fast as she'd ever run in her life.

Twice he'd tried her home number and left messages. Her cell phone went unanswered as well. Tim drove to Adele's house and checked around for himself, looking in the windows and talking to Nelson through the front door. He debated whether or not to use the spare key she kept hidden under the frame of the bay windows, and decided that was taking things too far. He imagined how that might look should she suddenly show up and find him looking in her closets.

He was looking through the side door window, hands cupped around his eyes, when two Twin Cities uniforms approached.

"What's up, guys?" he said, shoving his hands into the pockets of his raincoat.

Officer Lauterbach laughed. "A neighbor called in on a suspicious person. We won't tell her just how suspicious you really are, Ritmann."

Tim rolled his eyes. He'd forgotten about Mrs. Coolidge being under special assignment from Adele to report any suspicious activity around her house to the police. He looked across the street. The two round circles of her binoculars set permanently between the slats of her front blinds flashed in the light from the streetlamp. He waved and blew her a kiss. Instantly, the blind snapped closed.

"Yeah, well, Adele was supposed to meet me, and didn't. Didn't call either. Thought I'd swing by to see if she's okay."

"Oh sure, Ritmann," Officer Rabe snickered. "You're the only cop I know who'd go peeping in his girlfriend's windows when you know there isn't anybody home. Big thrill."

"Everybody's a comedian," Tim said, shaking his head. "But seriously, folks, do me a favor and if you see her on the beat, tell her I'm brokenhearted and to call ASAP. Thanks for checking up anyway."

The two cops snickered all the way to their patrol unit.

Tim drove past Ellis Hospital, got to the first intersection, and did an illegal U-turn with Santo and Johnny's "Sleepwalk" blaring on the civilian radio. What the hell, he thought, unconsciously moving his fingers to match the chords, he'd check the ER in case she somehow got hung up waiting for Cynthia, who'd never been on time in her life.

Cynthia closed her eyes, waited for the pain to pass, then opened them in time to see the driver stagger back from the trunk and Adele running like a madwoman. Taking advantage of the distraction, she crouched and made her way rapidly toward the stacks of crates. She found a narrow opening between two rows of crates and squeezed in, her hipbones pressed tight against the wood slats.

The driver retrieved his gun and was pointing it down into the trunk, barking in Arabic. He grabbed a fistful of Daisy's hair and yanked her off the floor of the trunk. His hatred was almost palpable as he grew more impatient with her slow, heavy movements.

Before Daisy could put one in front of the other, the driver grabbed her by the neck and began hitting her with his fist. Instinctively, she tucked her head into her chest so that most of the blows landed on her shoulders and upper arms.

As she fell, he jerked her head up and hit her in the face. Daisy fell back, hitting her head on the bumper as she went down. He kicked at her then stopped as two men in suits came running out of the shadows, shouting.

The man who wore a beige suit resembled the driver, although his features were more refined and he was of a larger build. The taller, more slender of the two men had something wrong with his face. At first she thought he was wearing a mask. Squinting, she realized it was his skin. Leathery and scarred, it appeared to have been badly burned. He took a handkerchief from his pocket and dabbed at his mouth. His attitude was different from that of the other two, as if he found what they were doing distasteful or beneath him.

It was easy to surmise the man in the beige suit was the one in command by the way he spoke and moved without hesitation or fear. He barked something at the driver, then viciously slapped him across the face with enough force to knock him down. He kicked the cowering man until the scarred man pulled him off.

The driver got to his feet, stumbled, and shook his head. Blood was streaming from his nose. More angry words were exchanged between the two men until Beige Suit was on the driver again, using his fists. The driver threw one arm over his head to protect himself; with the other arm, he pointed in the direction Adele had gone. Beige Suit shouted and immediately the scarred man and the bleeding driver dragged Daisy into the warehouse.

For several minutes, Beige Suit stood alone. His face crumpled and then recomposed itself into an evil smile that corrupted the handsomeness of it. He pulled a pistol from his shoulder holster and turned in several directions, listening carefully.

Sick with fear, Cynthia recoiled into the shadows, waiting until his footsteps faded.

Brenda was big and slender at the same time. Big bones, but not much meat, he thought. She was looking at him now through dark eyes made much darker with eyeliner and mascara.

She snapped her gum artfully and shook her head. "Not really sure where they went." She pulled her ponytail to the crown of her head. It brought the end of the chestnut-colored tail to her waist. "But they took off like bats out of hell."

"They?" Tim asked, holding the courteous smile.

"Adele and Cynthia. Adele came in all hyper about one of the patients we treated and discharged." She gestured slightly with her head to indicate a pile of charts that had been set aside in a box marked TO BE REVIEWED.

"Tell me about the patient," Tim said.

Gum still snapping, she considered his question with concentration worthy of a complicated math problem. "Is this like, official business? That's patient confidentiality and I can't just break—"

"It's not official," he said evenly. "But I could make it that way."

She went to a short hallway on the far side of what she had referred to as the Central Intelligence Area—that area meant for medical personnel only—and leaned against the wall. "Adele wanted to know about a patient we'd just discharged. I gave her the chart; she freaked out and wrote down the lady's phone number and address. I asked her why she was so interested, and she said something like she thought somebody was going to try and kill her." Brenda uncrossed her arms and snickered. "I didn't take it seriously. I mean, she's a Ward Eight nurse, and you know Monsarrat—she's one of the 'out there' people."

He debated for two seconds about asking exactly what she

meant, and decided he'd ask when there was more time. "What did you treat the woman for?"

The nurse hiked up one side of her mouth. "She had a rash on her butt that was infected as hell." Brenda shrugged. "She'd had some surgery in England recently—probably something she got off the sheets. Hospital sheets carry all sorts of bugs and parasites, you know."

"I didn't know," Tim said, feeling suddenly itchy. "But I'll make sure to keep it in mind next time I come to a hospital."

Brenda thought some more. "You know, there was this other weird thing that kept happening? All the lights and the monitors kept going on and off while she was here? It was freaky as hell."

Tim smiled one of his full-strength lady-killer smiles. "I want her address and phone number." He gave a meaningful stare. "Stat, please."

Brenda took a minute to think about it, the gum cracking every third chew. Finally she pushed herself languidly off the wall and found the chart, though she insisted he take it into the back room to copy the phone number and the Sleepy Hollow address—which, to his amazement, just happened to be in his jurisdiction.

Not two seconds before the men passed, Adele pulled herself onto the loading dock of the warehouse and rolled behind a stack of wooden pallets. As soon as they were out of hearing range, she got to her feet and ducked inside. Throughout the darkened room, she could make out the general outlines of large square shapes.

She waited for her eyes to acclimate, feeling her way cautiously across the vast space. Surely there would be an office or a phone in such a large building. Within a few feet, she realized the shapes were pallets, filled four and five feet high with Persian and other oriental rugs. Against the opposite wall were rolls of carpet.

At the back of the warehouse, partially obscured by several tiers of pallets, she found the kind of wooden door that might have been found in a house built at the end of the nineteenth century.

She opened the door a crack and looked in. The room was flooded with light from a surgical lamp which hung from the ceiling. Her mouth went dry, and for a moment she wanted to run. What had once been an office had been transformed into an operating room. A steel operating table covered with a blue surgical drape stood in the center. Around it, trays of surgical instruments and packages of dressings lay neatly arranged on slender, gleaming instrument tables. Operating lamps on extension arms were placed at each end. In the center of the newly tiled floor was a drain hole. Nearby hung a garden hose with a pressure nozzle.

Noiselessly, she went in and opened the first of the cabinets that lined the walls. Inside were stacks of surgical drapes, boxes of disposable scalpels and latex gloves, and more trays of instruments. The door to the fourth cabinet stuck. Using both hands, she worked the swollen wood until it jerked open.

A pair of brown eyes set in a grayish-white face stared out at her from a large glass specimen jar. Crying out, she jumped back, knocking over the steel waste bucket. It rolled across the tile floor, the noise echoing off the walls.

The head belonged to a man whose photograph she kept in her purse. Raymond Clemmons looked like the veteran of several anatomy classes. One eye had been partially enucleated, the layers of tissue around the mouth carefully peeled back. The top plate of the skull was gone, exposing the dome of the brain.

In a similar jar on the shelf above floated a pair of hands, amputated above the wrists. Next to it was a jar holding a foot, and next to that a jar containing a uterus, fallopian tubes, and ovaries.

Next to that was a square of Styrofoam to which was pinned a tattoo of a blue heart shot through the middle by a red arrow.

"Good evening, Nurse Adele," the man at the door said. "I see you have found your own way."

Adele stifled the scream that had risen to her throat and fell into a crouch. As she scuttled backward into the corner, the bucket again got in her way. She fell on her back.

The man who had introduced himself at Rulli's as Pierre Pandett stood over her aiming a gun at her head. Behind him, their captor and the scarred driver of the white van were supporting Daisy.

Pierre removed the jar holding the head and held it to the light, turning it around as if to show off all views.

Daisy gasped and let a cry escape.

"Why?" Adele whispered.

"Why not?" he said. "Why allow a perfectly good specimen to go to waste? I have learned twenty different surgical procedures on him so far, and I haven't even begun. He is much more useful dead than he was alive."

"That's why you kill these people? So you can practice your surgical skills?"

He put the jar back onto the shelf. "I have killed no one. That is my brother's doing. I am only the harvester of goods, shall we say."

She thought through the parade of victims. "What are you saying? That you harvest organs and tissue from the people you murder for trade?"

He put away the jar and closed the cabinet door clucking his tongue in contempt. "Organs and tissue for trade? Such a messy business." He gave her a hard look. "Money for the reuse of organs is insignificant. My work will have consequences greater than you can imagine. It will change the course of history. The practicing of my surgical skills reflects only my belief that nothing should go to waste."

It was surreal: the naked bulbs on the walls, the girlie calendar, and the wooden pallets holding hundreds of rugs. Following the hum of voices, Cynthia crept along the wall toward the rear of the warehouse. She saw the door, but didn't dare go near. She could hear Adele's voice. From the tone it was clear she was pissed off. It was nowhere near how pissed off she was going to be when she realized help was not on its way.

She waited for the cramping to pass before going back outside to the Buick.

Tim stared at the daisies painted across the front of the house, murallike, and rang the bell for a fifth time. The fact that the door was open a couple of inches had him excited. He pushed it open another foot.

Silence.

Unholstering his Beretta .38-caliber automatic, he opened the door the rest of the way. The thought of calling a Code 2 backup zipped through his mind and exited as he began his building search—department policy violation be damned. Two minutes' delay wouldn't hurt anybody.

He moved through the house so fast, he almost missed the black canvas fanny pack stuffed down between the couch cushions. The familiar blue triangle logo stitched to the outside flap started his heart pounding. He removed an address book with Arabic markings and a photo of two women he didn't recognize. He pushed the items back into the pack and pulled the strap over his shoulder.

In the kitchen he felt the top of the range. One burner was still warm. The back door was unlocked, as was the single-car garage set back from the house. Inside was parked a new silver Mercedes with a cold motor. Holstering the Beretta, he walked down the driveway and stooped over the roast beef sandwich.

He hooked the strap of the purse with his pen and pulled it out from under the daisy bushes. The sight of the myriad odds and ends caused him to groan. Like the fanny pack, the contents were familiar. The driver's license and the fake ID clinched it. The roast beef sandwich, however, remained a mystery.

He stowed Adele's purse and pack on the floor of his car and radioed dispatch to request the closest available backup Code 2. Across the street, the houses looked deserted, but the house bordering the driveway was lit up.

He rang the doorbell. From inside, a TV blared—a cop show from the sound of it.

A wiry man, maybe in his early sixties, answered the door with a bag of Doritos in one hand and a remote control in the other. A smear of cheese-yellow powder clung to the corner of his mouth.

Tim held up his ID. "I'm looking for your neighbor, Mrs. Rothschild. Have you seen her this evening?"

The man nodded and craned his neck to look next door. "She came home about seven-fifteen tonight. I noticed 'cause she was in a taxi." He started to pull out another chip, stopped, and offered the bag to Tim. "The only time she takes a taxi is when she's either too drunk to drive or her car is in the shop. Is she okay?"

"I don't know. I found her front door open, and thought I'd check with the neighbors. Did you see her go out again, or if she had any visitors? Hear anything unusual?"

The man paused and shook his head. "No, but then again, I can't say I've been watching too close." He paused again. "Now, there was that fella in the Buick for the last week or so. Daisy was chummy with him. He was over there tonight. First time I've seen him parked in the driveway, though."

Tim's heart rate picked up again as a dull ache began deep in his gut. "A Buick?" He took out his notebook. "Can I get your name, sir?"

"Landor. Jim Landor. Is Mrs. Rothschild in trouble of some kind?"

"Not that I know of, Mr. Landor. Do you think you could tell me what you remember about the Buick and this—fella?"

Mr. Landor dropped the chip back into the bag. "It was a gray LeSabre. The fella driving was one of those Saddam Hussein types."

"You mean someone of Arab descent?"

"That's right. He was about thirty, I'd say. Couldn't tell you for sure what he looked like. He's been parking outside Daisy's house every night for the last week and a half. Just sitting there smoking cigarettes. One after the other. The guy is going to end up with lung cancer. My wife, God rest her soul, died from smoking. She wouldn't listen to me, though. Said the tobacco companies wouldn't sell cigarettes if they were harmful to folks. I told her that was a bunch of hooey."

"You said he was here tonight, in her driveway?"

"Yes. I think he was picking something up, because I saw the trunk was open."

"You didn't by any chance get his license number, or the year of the car?"

"I think it was a ninety-four or a ninety-five. Good shape. Didn't pay any attention to the plate, although if I had to say, I'd say it was California—would have noticed if it wasn't."

The sounds of sirens, squealing brakes, and a collision came from inside the house. Mr. Landor aimed the remote backwards over his shoulder and pressed the mute button. At once it was quiet.

"See any other unfamiliar cars parked out front?"

Mr. Landor licked his lips, found the cheese powder, and went after it with the tip of his tongue. "No, none that I noticed."

"Do you know who this guy was?" Tim asked. "Was he dating Mrs. Rothschild?"

"Daisy is a nice gal, God bless her, but kind of a lost soul, if you know what I mean." Mr. Landor seemed embarrassed. "We try to mind our own business on this block, but when the kid first showed up outside her house, Mrs. Conway—that's the neighbor lady lives on the other side of Daisy—and I said something to her one morning about him. We didn't know if he was bothering her or not. For all we knew, he could have been a stalker. But Daisy told everybody on the block not to worry—she said he was courting her and he was shy."

He made a dismissive wave with the remote control hand. "I dunno, I try to mind my own business. People got funny ways."

"Did you notice a 1978 Pontiac station wagon parked anywhere near here tonight? Pale yellow with wood paneling? It's got a vanity plate that says Le Beast?"

He shook his head again. "I didn't. Sorry, young man. This is a pretty boring neighborhood, I'm afraid."

Tim nodded, wishing to hell it were the truth.

* * *

The makeshift operating room was cold. Adele involuntarily shivered and crossed her arms in an effort to warm herself. It dawned on her that none of the men had taken precautions to disguise themselves. This did not bode well: it meant they did not mean to leave her or Daisy alive. They freely used their true names. The man who'd introduced himself as Pierre Pandett was Amar, the driver was his brother Saad, and the scarred man was Fahad.

Amar covered the steel table with a plastic sheet, pulled on an apron, and opened a box of latex gloves. "This evening you will act as my scrub nurse." He switched on the overhead surgical lamp. "You will assist without hysterics—do you understand?"

"Why are you doing this?" she asked, her eyes narrowed.

He did not answer but motioned to his brother, who promptly dragged Daisy to the surgical table. Saad forced her head down, lifted his trouser leg, and pulled a serrated knife from a leather sheath. Crudely carved into the black bone handle was the symbol of the wavy line flanked by the double circles.

Adele stepped forward, arms outstretched, as if to stop his hand. Fahad pinioned her and pulled her back, his arms around her neck like a steel band. The driver raised his knife, gazing at Daisy with a faraway look. Adele thought it was probably the same way he must have looked at all the other people he had killed. Immobilized with terror, she could not look away. He brought the knife down through the layers of Daisy's clothing once, then again. The caftan, a rubber girdle, a pair of pink panties, and a hot-pink satin brassiere fell to the concrete floor in pieces. Standing naked, save for her terrycloth slippers, Daisy did not try to cover herself, but instead glared at Amar. "You bastard! I should have known. The lot of you are mad."

Fahad said something in Arabic, and the men laughed. On cue from Amar, Saad grabbed both of Daisy's ankles and flipped her facedown onto the table, binding her to it with a length of nylon clothesline. The cord cut into her flesh. Amar wrapped duct tape over her mouth and around her head, so it too was anchored.

"You will help now," Amar said, pointing to a spot on the other side of the table. Fahad pushed her forward. Amar set a pile of gauze on the back of Daisy's thighs and handed Adele a long hemostat. With a purple surgical marker, he outlined the circle of inflammation on the outer quadrant of Daisy's left buttock, then pulled one of the two instrument tables closer and indicated she should do the same. On her table lay a leather attaché case.

"Open the case and take out two specimen cups and the bottle of sterile saline. Fill each cup halfway."

Adele did as she was told while he chose a scalpel from the instrument tray.

"Your job is to keep the site sponged so I can see what I am doing." He indicated the gauze sponges lying in the crevice of Daisy's thighs.

"Tell me why you are killing people," she said, unable to stop her voice from quivering.

"I told you," he said, leaning over Daisy's buttock to concentrate on the area within the purple circle. "I have killed no one. I am a surgeon." He held the scalpel poised over the area.

Adele suddenly realized what he meant to do. "You can't be serious. You're not going to cut her without some kind of local anesthetic?" She looked at him disbelieving. "You can't do that."

Daisy did not react immediately to the first incision. With the second, he cut an elliptical shape around the inflamed area. The moment the thin line of blood came to the surface, Daisy's body began shaking violently as her eyes rolled back. A strangled, unearthly series of screams and guttural noises came from her throat and nose. Under the tape, her face was bloodless.

"Please stop!" Adele begged, outraged by the calculated cruelty. "Please, give her something! Numb the area with some Xylocaine or put her out!"

"She will become unconscious soon," Amar said confidently. "Sponge now."

Adele's hands were shaking so badly she had trouble picking up the wad of gauze with the hemostats.

Concentrating on the discolored tissue, Amar methodically cut away layer after layer of skin and fat, probing, letting the pieces fall to the floor. Adele felt sick as Daisy continued to pull in air in long, sonorous gasps. She prayed the woman would have a vasovagal response to the pain and pass out.

Amar probed through a mound of yellow adipose tissue, snapped at her to sponge, and made an even deeper cut. Daisy's body convulsed several times, then all muscle twitches ceased as she went unconscious.

"So much fat," he murmured. "A country of obesity. In my country, there are no fat people, only starvation." He pointed to an area. "Keep up with the sponging!"

She pulled away the blood-soaked wad of gauze and saw the small square of iridescent black at the same time he did. With extreme care, he picked the chip out of the tissue and held it under the lamp. Pointing to one of the specimen cups, he indicated she was to bring it close. After rinsing the square free of blood he studied it with a magnifying glass. "Your future," he said in a mocking tone, holding it out to her.

"And what is that supposed to mean?"

"It is beyond your comprehension." He dropped the chip into the cup of saline and screwed the lid into place. With the surgical pen he wrote "SF—#117" on the side and handed it to Fahad.

Fahad took the cup to a well-lit worktable in her line of vision. She watched as he carefully removed the chip from the saline and placed it on the platform of a large microscope.

"Pay attention to sponging," Amar shouted. His impatience was underscored by the force with which he sliced through the tissue.

Her eyes snapped back to the surgical site. Using the last of the gauze, she sponged a large amount of blood from the hole. Daisy's pulse was rapid but steady. "I need more sponges."

"In the lower cabinet behind me. Don't take any more than you need."

As she opened the cabinet, she glanced over Fahad's shoulder. He removed the chip from the microscope and snapped it inside a device the size and shape of a handheld computer with a keypad along one side. A cable connected the keypad to a laptop on the worktable. Fahad began pressing keys and the computer screen flickered to life.

"What are you doing?" Amar yelled. "You need to sponge now."

She grabbed a handful of sponges and returned to the table. "You're implanting these chips into Americans traveling abroad. I want to know what they are."

Amar's eyes jerked to her, then to Fahad. A moment later, he waved the scalpel. "Who told you this nonsense?"

"No one," she spoke derisively. "You've left a trail a mile wide. You'd have to be a baboon not to figure it out. I want to know what they are and why you're planting them inside humans. Why don't you put them in luggage or computers? It would seem a lot easier and safer than having to track these people down and kill them."

There was a long silence before Fahad turned from the computer screen. "This is very simple." He spoke in an even, reasonable voice. The British accent, though slight, could not be missed. "You must first consider the psychology of the host being completely unaware they are the means of transportation. In the past, we have found that no matter how controlled one of our members might be, there is always the awareness that they are in possession of something of great importance. Naturally, this produces an underlying fear and nervousness that can be detected by those trained to recognize such characteristics no matter how subtle."

Adele sponged out the cavity, which was going deeper into Daisy's hip. She tried to remember what major vessels or nerves were in the area.

"Then there is the safety of the chip itself to consider," Fahad continued. "Any carrier such as a portable cassette player, a radio, luggage, computer, can be lost, damaged, or stolen. Short of a catastrophic accident wherein the host body is badly battered or burned, the chip is perfectly safe."

"But what are they that you must kill for them?"

Amar straightened, his face red with frustration. *"Iskot!"* he yelled, turning to Fahad. "Shut up and do what you have been told. You don't have enough to do that you must let your mouth run? Why bother with her questions? She has caused us an important loss."

Fahad smiled indulgently and shook his head. "Calm down, Amar. She has intelligence. She outwitted us all—she deserves answers." He shrugged. "And what does it matter now?"

Amar turned back to the bloody hole he was creating and commanded her to sponge.

"You must forgive Amar," Fahad said, with a vaguely regretful expression. "He takes everyone else's mistakes personally.

"These chips hold information—do you know microchips?"

She nodded once, not daring to speak for fear of rousing Amar's anger.

"These chips are much smaller. They carry much information and can be programmed to do many different things. Among other tasks, these chips can be triggered by an outside signal to release certain chemicals inside the body. Most people will react to these chemicals with a pronounced rash, much in the same manner this woman has. The inflammation indicates the exact location of the chip. You can see how this might save time, especially for those less skilled than Amar. Unfortunately," he went on, "the chemicals sometimes release on their own as the nanochip naturally migrates toward the skin surface."

"That's how you find them," she said softly. "But what exactly are these chips ultimately programmed to do?"

Fahad paused, playing with his pen. He glanced at Amar then back at her and shrugged. "Like Amar said, they will change the course of history."

For a second, Adele was afraid he would not continue, but after a few seconds, he began again. "These are multiuse chips that hold certain coded information which—how shall I put this—allows for infiltration into high-security areas. What is more important is that we are in the process of developing a chip that also carries a self-replicating microorganism."

"You mean like the nanoprobes in *Star Trek*?" she asked.

Behind her, Saad snickered. Fahad gave her a blank stare. *"Star Trek?"* he repeated.

"Never mind," she said quickly. "What does the microorganism do?"

"It is . . ." He paused, looking for a delicate way to state his case. ". . . harmful when taken into the body." He shrugged again and shook his head. "It does not matter—so far this part of the technology has failed."

"But why so many?" Adele asked.

Fahad raised his eyebrows and smiled as though the effort hurt him. "Ah, well, this technology is relatively new. The scientists' attempts are crude at best. Many things go wrong. These chips are very small. They operate at the molecular level, so that if even one atom is out of place, the chips fail. We have lost others, and still others have been damaged. It took us almost a year to find the right protective coating for it. So you see, for each region there must be many."

"And the symbol of your group?" She wanted to get as many questions in before Amar stopped them. "What does it signify?"

"That is hard to explain," he said. "It involves several concepts about the Muslim mind and his relationship with God that the Americans do not readily understand. The circles are a symbol of power in the divine realm. For the sake of brevity, I would say the symbol means the changing tides of power under the hand of God." He shrugged. "Of course, there is much more to it than this, but it is not of interest to you."

"Where do Kadeja Shakir and Laila Clemmons fit into the group?"

At the mention of the names, a tense jolt went through the room. Amar whirled on Fahad, yelling in Arabic. His neck veins were distended with the force of his voice.

Fahad reverted to his flat expression and turned to the screen without another word.

Amar gave her a straight, hard stare. "Silence!"

Adele lowered her eyes and kept silent. Five minutes later she saw the black square hidden under a globe of fat. Gently, she pushed aside the yellow tissue with her hemostats, allowing him to extract the plastic fragment and repeat the same procedures as he had with the first chip.

Fahad checked the chip under his microscope and then in the handheld unit. Seemingly satisfied with what he saw, he said a few words to Amar, who removed the plastic apron.

Adele's eyes went to the scalpels then back to the three men. Hooking her foot around the leg of the instrument table, she knocked it over, but the confusion she hoped for did not come. It barely fazed them.

Amar told her to back away and gave orders to Saad. Her hope of getting her hands on a scalpel departed, as Saad gathered all the instruments, including the long hemostat she still held.

The three men were in motion, each precisely organized in his task—but then again, she thought, they'd done it before. Saad cut the ropes while Fahad carefully arranged the two specimen cups and the small device in the attaché. Amar emptied the bloody gauze sponges and tissue into a plastic bag, and wiped each instrument down with an alcohol solution.

She took the chance of packing the gouge in Daisy's hip with the remainder of the gauze, and managed to slap a length of adhesive tape over the wound. She had barely let go of the tape when the Glock was shoved against her sternum and she was pushed against the wall.

Fahad and Amar took the corners of the plastic sheet on which Daisy lay and hauled her off the table. There was a considerable amount of grunting from both men as they carried her. Amar strained under his load. The sheet slipped out of his hands, and in frustration he kicked the lump inside.

Fahad lay a hand on his arm. "Get ahold of yourself. It is only a means to an end. They will all be dead soon."

Saad moved the Glock from her chest around to the back of her head and pushed her forward. She resisted. Her options had narrowed down to the most hackneyed of ploys.

"I have to go to the bathroom," she announced.

They paid no attention, though Amar said something that caused the other two to laugh.

She refused to move. "I told you I have to go to the—"

Saad roughly pushed her. "No one cares," he said belligerently. "Shut up and go in your pants."

After Tim gave them a report of events, Deputies Rodham and Banesworth ran the check for alarms or emergency cards on file for the Rothschild residence and found none. They secured the house, leaving a note for Daisy to contact Detective Ritmann.

Tim called dispatch to put out a BOL, a "Be On the Lookout" report, for Adele and the Pontiac. He added an officer safety warning just in case whoever was with her wasn't friendly.

"You going to need a follow-up report on my assist?" Officer Rodham asked.

"Yeah," Tim said, the radio still in his hand. "I already drew a suspicious circumstance case number from Communications. Just submit it to my attention."

"You okay, Ritmann?" Banesworth asked. "You're looking peaked, pal."

Tim took a drink of bottled water and smiled. "Nice to know you care, but I'm okay—nothing a week in Cabo San Lucas wouldn't cure."

As soon as the unit pulled around the corner, Tim took out his cell phone. It was good to have friends in high places, he thought as he waited to speak to Jeb Gonzales, dispatcher at San Francisco PD Operations Center.

"Hey, Anglo," Jeb laughed when he came on the line. "Whatsamatter, you got to go looking for trouble in other counties now? Don't have enough of your own?"

"I need a favor, Jeb," Tim said, no levity in his voice. He was more than anxious.

"As long as it don't got nothin' to do with women. My old lady gets very jealous. I don't do no double dates no more."

"Me either," Tim said and smiled a little. "I need you to put out an immediate APB BOL on a vehicle with a referral to contact me. If the vehicle is found, nothing is to be touched before they call. You should probably put an officer safety warning on that as well."

"This personal, or part of a case?"

"Both. I've got a lady friend who the bad guys think has some important information of theirs. I was supposed to meet her tonight and she never showed up. I found her purse sitting in somebody's driveway with her cell phone inside, but no sign of her. Highly unlike this lady."

Jeb whistled. "Okay, okay, man. I got you. I'll put it out there right now. Give me the information and I'll see what I can do."

After a frenzied search of the front seat, Cynthia found a manila envelope under the litter of empty Coke cans and McDonald wrappers. The photos of random bathrooms and kitchens and living rooms made no sense to her except perhaps that they'd been used in casing people's homes. She'd almost given up finding anything useful when her hand found a cell phone lying under the black plastic tarp in the backseat. Keeping an eye out from over the top of the seat, Cynthia dialed, praying to no deity in particular that the battery was still working.

She almost couldn't believe it when the voice at the other end said, "San Francisco Emergency." She opened her mouth to respond as Adele emerged from the warehouse, a pistol held to the back of her head. The other two men followed carrying a bloodied sheet. Hanging over one end, Daisy's head flopped from side to side; she appeared to be either unconscious or dead.

Survival instinct snapped Nurse O'Neil out of her stupor.

Before she could move on her own, Adele was picked up and thrown into the trunk with Daisy. She'd just managed to disentangle her legs from the bloodied sheet when the trunk was slammed shut, leaving them in total darkness. Adele moved over to pull off the duct tape still wrapped around Daisy's mouth.

"Daisy? Can you hear me? Wake up!"

To her relief, Daisy mumbled incoherently.

Adele felt for her pulse. "Daisy! Wake up!"

"Sleepy," the woman said in a jumbled, confused tone. "I'm cold. My bum hurts . . ."

"You need to wake up, Daisy," Adele said, already running her fingers over the rear panel cover, looking for a loose section. She found a flap and pulled.

As Saad's rage grew, the harder his hands shook. He tried to light the cigarette with the glowing end of the old one, and dropped both in his lap. Jumping up, he brushed at the burning ashes and swerved into the next lane. The blast of horns sent him into a fury of shouts and gestures.

He saw the burn hole in his new Dockers and burst into a new salvo of curses. He'd just put a new cigarette between his lips when the low thud came from the back of the car. His foot automatically lifted off the pedal.

Listening carefully, it came again and then again. The dark-haired woman was trying to kick their way out. She could kick all she wanted: it would not open. American cars were like tanks.

He turned up the radio to cover the sound. Elvis, his favorite singer—the greatest singer of all time—vocally hiccuped and jerked his way through "Blue Suede Shoes." Relaxing a little, he sped up. Perhaps Fahad and Amar were right about changing methods of killing. It might throw off the people who were trying to track them. The car would be traced to the owner, who was away and did not even know it was missing from the garage. He inhaled deeply. It would not be a quick death like the others, but it would be just as certain.

Cynthia realized too late that the putrid smell was coming from the tarp that covered her. A rip in the black plastic afforded her a good view of the opening between the seats. She could just make out the outline of the man's right shoulder and arm. His hand was tapping the steering wheel as he sang along to "American Pie" in perfect English. He knew all the words.

Inch by inch, she raised her hand to her face to shield it from the tarp. Her fingers found a thick slime smeared onto her cheek and neck. She didn't need to see it to know it was old blood. The smell alone was enough. She gagged in silence until tears ran down her face. Close to vomiting, she forced herself to focus on the pain in her knees. The way they felt now, she was sure she had knelt directly on several broken bottles. She clutched her stomach and breathed through her mouth.

With a blare of horns, the car suddenly swerved so that she had to grab the backseat to steady herself. The plastic tarp crackled and slid partially off, exposing the side of her that was closest to him. Her eyes darted to his, relieved to see that his attention was focused to his left. He was bellowing in Arabic out the window and giving someone the finger.

Seizing the instant, she pulled the tarp back over herself as carefully as she could. That was when she heard the first thump. It was distant enough that at first she couldn't locate its origin. It came again, and she pinpointed the noise as coming from the trunk. The driver heard it as well and slowed the car. There were three more thuds in quick succession.

She held her breath, afraid that he would stop and do something to Adele. But then again she supposed there was nothing he could do as long as he was on the open road. Unless he was completely insane, he wasn't going to pull over, get out, and shoot off a couple of rounds into his trunk.

Timothy hung up and leaned back in his chair to think. What Harlan Jacquot told him sounded straight out of a Tom Clancy novel. He picked up the phone again and pressed the two numbers for his secretary.

"Jane, I need you to round up the dicks ASAP."

Jane, a small, sixtyish woman with delicate bones and pure white hair, laughed. "You want all of 'em, or just yours?"

He looked at his watch. "Just mine plus Robinson." Tim sighed. "Try to get David Takamoto on a conference line. He'll be at home. If he's not, try his cell phone."

"You want the coffee machine set up in the conference room?" She didn't really have to ask. Having been with him since he was a youngster at the DA's office, she knew his moods and needs better than he did.

"Yeah, and if there's any more of those oatmeal cookies, bring 'em. I haven't eaten since lunch. And Jane? Thanks for staying late."

"It forces me to catch up on the paperwork, Timothy."

He disconnected and dialed Adele's home number, leaving another message for her to call him immediately. He looked at her purse and thought about the sandwich with the bite missing and then Brenda saying that Adele and Cynthia had left the ER lobby in a rush—*as if they had a plane to catch.*

In a desperate moment, he dialed Cynthia's home number. He made no secret that he was fond of Cynthia—as a friend. Considering that he'd never maintained friendly ties with any ex-lover before her, especially one who had dumped him, he supposed he might appear as a threat to her present live-in.

Tim cleared his throat. If the guy answered, he'd be straight—tell him right out who he was and that he wanted to speak to Cynthia.

When Rymesteade Dhery answered, Tim started to hang up, changed his mind, and asked for Cynthia in a business-like tone. He ended up sounding officious.

"No," Rymesteade said. "I actually expected her to be home when I got here, but she isn't and she hasn't called. May I tell her who called?"

Tim grimaced. "Ah, Tim Ritmann. I was actually looking for—"

"Oh yeah. Hi, Tim. You're the seventh guy back—the detective."

"The seventh guy back?"

Ryme laughed. "That's how I keep all her exes straight. No offense."

"You mean there were six guys in between you and me?"

"Uh-huh. I've actually met one that was ninety-third back from me."

Tim was stunned. "You're kidding. Was he human enough to be standing upright?"

"I don't know." Ryme laughed. "But he was one of the ones who didn't speak English."

"Yeah, but were his ears low on his neck?"

They both chuckled. "Say, listen, I'm actually looking for Adele. You know where they went?"

"Can't help you there," Rymesteade said. "Cyn has a tendency to disappear sometimes, and I never question it. Well, I mean, I don't have to tell *you* that."

"I guess not. But listen, if she comes in, or if Adele shows up there, would you have her call me?"

"Sure," Ryme said, then added, "Is anything wrong?"

"I don't know," Tim said. No sense making the guy worry before he knew for sure there really was something to worry about. And besides, if he could go a few more hours anxiety-free, why not let him? "Adele was supposed to meet me this evening, and she never showed. I know she was picking Cynthia up at Ellis to give her a ride home, but she should've been back by now."

"It's probably Adele's car," Ryme said, completely unconcerned. "You know how it cuts out on her all the time."

"I'm sure it's something like that. Well, sorry to bother you. Thanks."

"Anytime."

Tim reached into his desk drawer and pulled out the family-sized bottle of Mylanta. He took a mouthful of the mint-flavored chalk, grimaced, and flicked on his computer.

Jane placed several files on the corner of his desk. She saw the chalky residue flaking at the corners of his mouth. He was worried: the lines between his eyes were deeper than usual.

"I've put out a BOL on Adele and her vehicle with a referral to me. I thought just in case she got into something she couldn't handle, I'd be notified right away."

"You're not her mother or her keeper, Timothy," Jane said.

He lowered the bottle, wiped away the antacid mustache, and nodded. "I know, but I've got this lousy feeling in the pit of my stomach that she's in trouble."

"That's your ulcer, Timothy. Ms. Monsarrat can handle herself."

Johnny "Piston" Depardo wiped his nose on his sleeve and stuck a finger black with grease into his ear. He liked listening to Garth Brooks cranked up to full volume. The only problem being that the bass vibrated the tiny hairs in his ears, making them itch like crazy. He found that the engine grease helped slick them down.

He took his time smoking the unfiltered Camel down till it burned his fingers, then, grabbing on to the door handle, he swung himself out of the truck cab and jumped down onto the pavement.

At five foot one and a hundred forty pounds, he hadn't been able to make it as an interstate trucker. Not so much because the companies didn't want any midget driving their eighteen-wheelers, but because of his temper. The first trucker who'd called him Shorty was still wearing his balls as a bow tie.

He may have been the smallest tow-truck driver in San Francisco, but as the owner of six tow trucks and a million-dollar business, he didn't much give a shit anymore. He had everything he wanted: a good-looking squeeze to do him twice a day, an expensive car and house, Forty-Niner season tickets, and employees who feared him.

The nose of the 1978 Pontiac wagon was pointed in the wrong direction, its hood ornament pressed against the pole of the no parking sign. Probably some drunken asshole, he thought as he unhooked his halogen flashlight from his belt. He hoped the asshole was inside sleeping it off; scaring the shit out of some drunk might be just the thing to start off his night with a chuckle.

He frowned at the orderly neatness of the backseat, then checked the cargo space: also clean and neat. He tucked his light under his chin and slid his slim-jim down behind the belt molding. As he jimmied the connecting rods inside the door shell, the light fell across the dark red smears on the driver's seat. He aimed the light directly on the seat. In the center, where the depression was the deepest, was a thick smudge of blood.

Johnny climbed up into the cab and got on his radio. Six attempts to raise his dispatcher without a response was enough to send his blood pressure out of the ballpark. The stupid bastard was watching the TV again. He was going to have to remember to get rid of the idiot box.

"Hey, cocksucker!" he yelled loud enough that his voice cracked.

"Yes, Mr. Depardo?"

"Turn off the fuckin' boob tube and call the fuckin' PD. I'm at the corner of Townsend and Seventh. Tell 'em I've got a station wagon here that looks like the Valentine's Day massacre took place inside."

"Oh wow. They had a massacre down there?"

"You fuckin' moron. Just call the fuckin' cops, will ya? And turn off that fuckin' box or you're gonna be wearin' my shoes up your ass on your way out the door."

"Daisy!" Adele shook the woman hard.

The woman's breath quickened and she moaned.

"Can you talk?"

"Are we still in the boot?" Her voice was weak. Adele could barely hear her over the noise of the car.

"Yes. Are you okay? Can you stay awake?"

"I—yes. Are they going to kill us?"

"I think they're going to give it their best shot. I need you to help me disable the taillights. Do you think you can?"

"Well, I suppose, but wait a minute." Daisy reached up and ran her hand along the underside of the quarter panel. "Mr. Rothschild's mother owned a Lincoln Town Car before she went stark raving mad. In that car there was a cable in this area that used to stick. Mr. Rothschild would fix it, but it always broke again. Perhaps this car will have one as well."

"What's the cable for?"

"It opens the little door to the fuel filler hole." Daisy grunted softly with her efforts. "If I can find it, I can make it pop open.

Someone's bound to notice. The police tag automobiles for open gas hatches, don't they?"

"Anything is worth a try," Adele told her, seriously doubting that San Francisco cops gave a damn about an open fuel door, although, if someone behind them saw the hatch suddenly spring open, it might raise suspicions.

"Must not be a common feature," Adele said after a minute of searching. "This is a Buick. Not all American cars are made alike. Pull the panel cover off the taillight assembly on your side. I want to try playing with the wires—maybe try to send an SOS. Do you know Morse code?"

"I learned it when I was in the Blue Birds."

"Can you move enough to get to it?"

Grunting, Daisy turned over onto her belly and pushed herself up against the back of the trunk. With Adele's help, she inched around, until her head was next to the taillight.

They both pulled at the tangle of wires. Both sets popped and went out at once. Adele was attempting to reconnect two of her wires when the car slowed, made a left turn, and continued on at about fifteen miles an hour. Traffic noise ceased.

"He's pulled off," Daisy said.

"Yeah," Adele said gravely, letting go of the taillight wires and turning her attention to the unit housing the lock. "Let's hope it's the Palace Hotel instead of the cemetery."

The spasms of pain persisted, growing in strength and duration until she thought she was going to pass out. Her scrub pants were sticking to the blood on her thighs.

The car slowed, turned, and continued on for a mile or more at a crawl. The driver had ceased talking to himself and was strangely quiet. Her hand tightened around a beer bottle as she peered out the hole in the plastic. This time she could see the steering wheel and the panels below it. They were traveling at fifteen miles an hour, there were 89,207 miles on the odometer, and the gas tank was half full.

She thought he might be searching for an address or a landmark although she couldn't hear any traffic or see any streetlights. They might be in a quiet neighborhood where he was planning to let them go—or, a more frightening thought, in an out-of-the-way place where he intended to kill them. It wasn't Golden Gate Park—they'd traveled too far for that— but it might have been one farther out on the west side of the city. Possibly McLaren or Lake Merced?

They had gone about a mile when the car turned right, went a few more yards, and stopped. She peered out and saw nothing except black sky. The car rolled and went off the smooth pavement to a bumpy surface. She thought there was a slight downhill, then, a minute later, a bumpy incline. The car leveled off, angled down sharply, and came to a complete stop.

The glove compartment opened, followed by the sound of things being thrown into a plastic shopping bag. In an instant he turned, his arm coming toward the tarp. She stopped breathing.

He picked up the manila envelope, stuck it in the plastic bag, and then began searching for something else. The cell phone, she thought, praying that it had not fallen on the floor.

She breathed out when she saw him turn around and drop the phone into the bag. A chilling breeze and the smell of exhaust signaled that the two front windows were being rolled down. The door opened and the car squeaked as he got out. She managed a glimpse outside. Beyond a clump of shrubs, she thought she saw lights reflecting off water.

He came back to the car dragging something heavy. The door was shoved open to its limit, followed by a loud thud as a large rock landed on the driver's side floor. The rock was lifted onto the gas pedal. In response, the motor strained at a high-pitched scream. Almost immediately his arm came through the opened window, a long forked branch in his hand. He set it against the gear shift lever and withdrew.

She heard rather than saw the branch as it was pushed, wood clacking against plastic. He lost his grip, and the stick slipped off the gear lever. He cursed and reset it.

The car lurched forward, tires squealing. She pushed herself up, willing her numb legs to get her to the front seat. Her hand reached for the gear shift. The impact threw her into the back of the driver's seat and then into the windshield as if she were a rag doll.

The last thing she heard was silence being destroyed by Adele's screams.

Daisy yelled something, but Adele couldn't hear the words over the racing engine—not that she could have answered: her mouth was dry and her throat tight. In a true panic, she concentrated on kicking at the trunk latch until she was sure she'd broken every bone in her foot.

With Daisy pawing at her back, she turned just as the car lurched forward. She kicked once, then again, and felt something give. At the same moment they were thrown violently back. The car tilted at a sharp angle, then straightened out.

Only when water began seeping in did Adele scream for help.

Tim stood next to the storyboard. "Okay, let me go over this from the top, and then I'll fill you in on the latest from the FBI."

He walked around the oval table and sat down next to Hermonicus Robinson. Using the laser pointer on his key chain, he started at the top. Five minutes into his monologue, invisible hands pulled him from his chair. Gasping for breath, he clawed at the buttons of his collar. The rest of the men looked at him curiously, then at each other.

"You okay, boss?" Enrico Cini started out of his chair. "What's the matter?"

Tim waved them away and lurched for the door. It was the oddest feeling, his inability to get his breath. He wondered if this was the air hunger his doctor said might happen from time to time.

Out in the hallway, he was going for the water cooler when Jane hurried over.

"Timothy. SFPD dispatch is on the line. I think you'd better . . ." She paused, seeing his face set on the brink of panic. "What's wrong? Are you sick? Talk!"

"Water," Tim said, pointing to the cooler.

She got him a cup of water, waited while he drank it, then got him another, chasing him down the hall to his office.

He picked up the line. "Detective Sergeant Ritmann."

"It's Jeb, boss. We just got a call from a tow company. He's located a vehicle at Townsend and Seventh with the plate: Lincoln Edward Boy Edward Adam Sam Tom, registered to one Adele Monsarrat of Larkspur."

Tim could barely respond. He couldn't have been more surprised if it had been a conference call from Jesus Christ, the twelve disciples, *and* Andy Warhol.

"We can't seem to locate the registered owner in the area and we can't raise her by landwire."

Jeb paused. "I know you don't want to hear this, man, but the officer at the scene found some blood in the vehicle. He requested us to check with your office on the off chance your department may be working a case involving the registered owner."

Tim's hands shook as he drank off the rest of the Mylanta. He had to remain professional. "She's involved in the investigation on a case I'm working," he said so casually he could barely believe it was his own voice. "I'm pretty concerned, Jeb. Why don't you ask the beat officer to secure the vehicle there and I'll respond. Could you also request an inspector to meet me there?"

"Will do. What's your ETA to the scene?"

Tim looked at his watch then at Cini and Chernin, who were standing in the doorway behind Jane. "Thirty minutes tops."

He grabbed his coat jacket and cell phone. "I've got to go," Tim said, rushing past them.

"I'll drive," Enrico volunteered.

"No, I'm okay, I can—"

"Screw you. I'm going too," Chernin said and herded them down the hallway.

Impatient, Saad looked at his watch again. Amar told him to stay until after the car had been under the surface for ten minutes. He told him he would kill him or, worse, ship him back in disgrace if anything went wrong. Still, that the car did not sink like a rock fascinated him.

"American cars," he said under his breath. "They are the best."

He checked the time again and then stared back at the car. It was another useless waste of his time. The Americans had a good name for it: busywork. Something to keep the children occupied. He kicked angrily at the sand. The car was sinking, he could see that, but not as fast as it should. The front went in first, but then the car leveled out; the trunk stayed afloat. He thought about disobeying and leaving it to go down in its own time, but then a brief fear crossed his mind that the car might be hung up on a rock or part of a fallen tree. If the car did not go all the way under, he would be expected to go into the water to try to sink it. The very idea of being surrounded by all that black water made him sick. His terror of the water was his one weakness. As a child of the desert, he had had no reason to learn to swim.

The muffled sound of the women screaming drilled through him. He inhaled deeply, spilled ash down the front of his Harley Davidson jacket, and cursed. Taking two final drags, he flicked the tail end of the cigarette into the water, picked up the plastic bag holding his personal things, and began to climb up the hill to the cement bridge.

He didn't want to hear the women's screams. They reminded him too much of the bombings; they made everything too personal, too real.

What harm could there be if he left? The car was sinking slowly, but still sinking. The women were as good as dead, and Amar would never know.

Cynthia was dreaming about the time when she was ten years old and her mother had taken her and run away from her father. They'd driven the Buick to Arkansas and found themselves a shack near Toad Suck Lake for fifty dollars a month. It was August, and the heat and humidity had put her into a stupor as she floated on the plastic air mattress that often served as her bed when her mother brought back men from the bars.

In the dream, Cynthia woke up as the sun was cooling. Her mother was no longer on the shore, but neither was anyone else. The boats were in, and as she looked around, she realized she had drifted to the middle of the lake. The air mattress was smaller and half submerged in the chilly water as it slowly deflated from the small hole made by the prongs of her diamond ring—the one that made her finger green.

Holding on to the fully inflated headrest, she paddled toward the beach. Ten yards away, she saw the alligators. Five, ten, fifteen of them—all heading for her, slithering so fast that they were on her, gnawing on her legs and belly, before she could take another breath.

She came to consciousness with a gasp, surrounded by the icy water rushing in around her. Out the smashed rear window, she could see that the top of the trunk was still an inch or two above water. There was no sound other than the water rushing into the cabin. Grasping the rearview mirror, she pulled herself up and began a search for the glove compartment. The realization that Adele could already be dead panicked her.

"Adele!" she screamed. "Adele, hold on." Her fingers were growing as numb as the rest of her body as they stumbled and groped the inside walls of the glove compartment.

The car tipped forward, plunging her deeper into the cold water. She willed her hands to work faster, moving in circles. She kept her eyes on the window, judging how long she had before she had to get out. Listing to the left, the car bobbed and threw her off balance. She grabbed at the steering wheel, pushed herself back, and reached into the glove compartment again. Her fingers grazed the button on the left of the compartment door. Eyes closed, she pressed it, letting a strangled cry escape at the muffled sound of the trunk release.

She gripped the top of the window and pulled herself out of the car and into the water, kicking with legs she no longer felt. The trunk was completely submerged. Her hand brushed over two icy fingers that had found their way through the one-inch crack and were frantically clawing at the latch.

Filling her lungs with air, she went underwater, pushed the fingers away and fit her own fingers inside. The latch was bent slightly, trapping the lid. After she had worked it for a few seconds, it began to give. She surfaced for air then went down again, keeping at it until her lungs burned and she felt dizzy.

More fingers came through the crack and clutched at her wrist. Scenes from *Titanic*—which she watched by peeking out from between her fingers—whirled through her mind. Drowning, the amorphous "they" said, was supposed to be an easy, almost pleasant death. There was a euphoria that overcame the panic, "they" said, making drowning seem like a really good high off some major killer weed.

Bullfuck, her mind yelled. Death was death, and it sucked. Period.

Cynthia gave one final pull, hardly believing it when the latch released and the crack widened.

As they passed under the first arch of the Golden Gate Bridge, Tim finished explaining the highlights of the case to Inspector Americo Bettoni from his cell phone.

Already on the scene, Bettoni, his lips pursed around prominent front teeth, looked into the cabin of the Pontiac. "Blood on the driver's seat, but nothing on the handles or the windows—nowhere else. Just the seat."

"What else is around there?" Tim asked.

"Nothing," Bettoni said, swinging his flashlight around as if to make his point. "Townsend is mostly warehouses, and they're locked up at night. Nothing goes on down here after six P.M. Once in a while we get couples screwin' in a car, or a drunk who gets inside and sleeps in one of the warehouses. Maybe a tourist gets lost and we gotta go in and give them an escort out, but otherwise it's dead. Even the gangs don't come in here."

"Well, there's someone down there tonight, Americo, and I'm going to find her wherever she is."

* * *

Cynthia grabbed hair in one hand and flesh in the other and pulled the load to the surface. Behind her she felt a push of water as Adele broke the surface with a gasp. Desperately, she pulled in air until she vomited and then began to cough.

The shore was less than fifteen feet away. Confused, Daisy fought them until Cynthia locked her in a swimmer's save hold. With Adele pushing, they got the naked woman onto the sandy shore where they collapsed. For a few minutes the three of them lay shivering with the letdown of adrenaline.

"You okay?" Cynthia whispered when she was able to speak.

Adele nodded. "We're alive. Because of you. Where were you? How did you—?"

Drained of strength, Cynthia broke down and cried in earnest.

Adele crawled over and held her until she stopped, then checked on Daisy. As far as she could tell, Daisy seemed okay despite her injuries and some considerable pain.

She cleared a small hiding space inside a thick growth of bushes and lined the ground with two paper grocery bags she found along the bank. The plastic shopping bag she found went to cover Daisy's open wound.

"I'll get help," she said. "Stay completely out of sight in the bushes and don't make a sound. Don't come out for anything until you see the lights from an ambulance or a cop car."

It wasn't until they moved Daisy to the shelter of the shrubs that Adele saw the blood on Cynthia's pants. In the dark, her face looked gray.

Adele maneuvered Cynthia's feet up into some branches. "Lay flat with your feet up, and keep close together for warmth. I'll be back with help."

Daisy moved closer to Cynthia. She shifted around, slipping her large fleshy arm under the shivering woman's head. Cynthia closed her eyes and nodded.

Adele climbed the hill to the bridge and looked across to the opposite shore. Through the fog she saw regular dots of light and some large buildings. Despite the the horrors of the night, she smiled. While she was a student at San Francisco State, she'd run here hundreds of times.

"Lake Merced," she whispered, and started across the footbridge in the direction of the streetlights that lined Lake Merced Boulevard. At the end of the bridge she came to three concrete abutments. In the misty light coming from a streetlight a good distance away, Saad hurried in and out of shadows. From his halting movements she could tell he was unsure of which way to go.

She crossed the clearing, staying close to the trees, but she lost sight of him when he cut suddenly to the right and disappeared over a tree-studded rise. She heard him curse then realized he was running back toward her. Ducking into the shadows of the trees, she fell flat, cautiously crawling backward under a cluster of thick bushes.

He was close enough that she could hear him breathing. She held her breath and lowered her face, listening for him to pass, terrified that he had seen her. Something warm fell onto the backs of her legs and made its way cautiously over her rump and up her back.

A squirrel or a baby raccoon, she thought, as her mind veered away from the possibility it could be a rat. Except it wasn't vibrating the way rats did, and the footpads were too far apart. No sooner had she felt some relief that it might be only a baby raccoon than Marlin Perkins materialized next to her.

But, he reminded her, adjusting his safari hat, *while raccoons may be regarded as the cute little rascals of the wild kingdom, one must not lose sight of the fact that raccoons can be healthy carriers of rabies. Don't let those cute faces fool you—they have sharp teeth and claws and can tear apart a full-grown housecat inside of twenty seconds.*

Her attention was diverted from the thing crawling around her back by Saad, now standing less than ten feet from her head. He seemed uncertain of where to go.

Crooks always take the path of least resistance, said Kitch, relaxing next to Marlin. *If there's a steep hill to climb, you can bet a scumball won't be on it.*

She pushed back another foot deeper into the brush. The

thing moved up to her neck, where it set about sniffing close to her ear. It was doing something with its paws in her hair.

Saad retraced his steps back toward the bridge. Raising her eyes, she watched him pass, her stomach bouncing into her throat as she realized he was headed back to the car.

"Sergeant Ritmann?" Americo Bettoni held his flashlight on the dark red spots.

Tim knelt down and stared at the blood on the concrete. "How fast can your lab run this?" he asked Bettoni. He knew both Cynthia's and Adele's types.

"As fast as we can get it there."

Tim nodded and turned to face the small side door to the warehouse. The wood around the frame was sagging badly, and the paint had peeled off long ago. "You have a way to get inside?" he asked over his shoulder.

"No, but we can have Dispatch find the owner's number through our emergency file."

"Could you get that in motion too?"

He waited until Bettoni was out of the immediate area before looking around for something to smash the lock. Ten feet away, lying next to a metal barrel, a two-foot length of lead pipe provided the perfect tool. The rusted lock took one good hit and gave way.

The Beretta pointed at the ceiling, Tim slipped inside the warehouse, listened, then flicked on the lights. Decay, dampness, and another odor that was more than unpleasant assailed his nostrils. Within a second, his olfactory memory had retrieved the file and sent it to his brain: old blood.

A rat scampered across the floor carrying something red and yellow in its mouth. Tim lunged, jabbing at it with the pipe. Choosing survival over food, the rat dropped its treasure and ran.

Without touching the object, Tim studied it carefully. He'd seen enough fresh cadavers to recognize the bloody tissue as human.

*   *   *

His lungs were on fire as he slowed to a walk. Each breath was an effort. He found his cigarettes, put one between his lips, and pulled out his lighter. His thumb stopped just as he was about to press the flame release. With the police so close, the light could attract attention.

How could Amar have made such a mistake and sent him to such a dangerous place? How could he have put him in such jeopardy? Was he being tested?

Saad sat on his haunches and lit the cigarette anyway, shielding the flame inside cupped hands. If Amar saw him shaking like a woman, he would never let him forget it. He needed to calm down and think of what to do.

Amar would never have made a mistake like this—not Amar, not unless he meant for him to be caught.

Saad's breath came faster. *No, Amar would not turn on his own brother.* He looked across the water narrowing his eyes. Would he? Did he not say that he would sacrifice his own son for the cause if he had to? Had he not said they were all expendable for the cause?

Saad spit on the glowing end of the cigarette and began walking, his hands thrust into his pockets. After a moment, he broke into a run.

Adele watched as he abruptly changed course yet again, running away from where the women waited for her. She counted to ten after he was out of sight, and grabbed hold of the thing that had sunk its needle claws into her neck. She was about to fling it away when a piteous mewl stayed her hand.

All that showed through the dark were pink gums and tiny white teeth. She brought it close to her face. A black kitten clung to her for dear life as it simultaneously purred and cried. She tucked it under her jersey and ran up the hill Saad had just come down. She'd gone no more than a few yards, when she became aware of a presence to her right. Slowly, she turned.

Towering over her in the mist, backlit by a streetlamp, stood a fifteen-foot penguin, his beak pointed to the sky.

* * *

Officers Chere Levitt and Bob Ulrich sat perfectly still, staring out the window.

"Jesus Christ!" Officer Levitt said, raising her eyes to the headliner. "We can't keep doing this night after night, Bob. We're going to get caught. If the chief ever gets wind of this, I'm going to end up being suspended. I—"

"Shhh!" Officer Ulrich did not lower the special night binoculars. "Patience, Levitt. Learn some patience. Nobody's going to miss us if we're off the beat for an hour."

Chere Levitt slumped in her seat and rolled down the window. "Somebody is going to catch on," she said after a minute. "You don't have to worry—I do. What you don't seem to understand, Bob, is that I'm a female officer. That means I'm subjected to a more rigid standard than the male officers. I'm the one who's going to take the heat if somebody finds out that you're using on-duty time to engage in personal activities."

Officer Ulrich searched the lower branches of a scrub oak, then moved the binoculars slightly to the left to search the tree next to it.

"Lang already asked if we were having an affair," Chere persisted.

"Lang's a perverted fuck," Bob Ulrich said, not blinking. "He thinks everybody is screwing everybody."

Chere looked out the window and sighed. "How much longer do we have to do this?"

Bob adjusted the focus on the binoculars as he ran them over the branches of the sycamore tree. "He's here, Levitt. I know he is."

Officer Levitt leaned out the window and took a deep breath. She unclipped a barrette holding back a clump of blond hair and adjusted a strand that didn't need adjusting.

"Jesus," she said again, then turned her body around to face him. "What the fuck is so goddamned special about an owl that I've gotta lose my job over it? Go to the goddamned zoo, why don't you? Take your kids. Come out here on your night off, but shit, Ulrich, let's get back to the beat, okay?"

Officer Ulrich sighed and lowered the binoculars. "He's here," he said sadly. "I don't know why I can't find him."

She slapped her hand over her mouth before she could scream. She'd forgotten about the penguin. Made of granite and steel, the fifteen-foot Benjamino Bufano statue stood at the top of a hill, praying to the sky. She recalled that not far on the other side of the penguin was a small parking lot off Lake Merced Boulevard. Once she was on the main street, she'd be able to summon help.

Taking the rest of the hill at a run, she reached the statue, passed it, and flew down the other side.

"We've been from one end of this place to the other for the last month," Officer Levitt griped; she couldn't let it rest. "The stupid bird ain't here, Bob. I'm telling you: go to the zoo."

Bob Ulrich put away the binoculars with care and started the patrol car. The second he switched on the headlights, they both let out a cry of surprise.

"Whoa!" breathed Officer Levitt. "Check out that eight hundred coming our way!"

In the glare, the disheveled woman, dressed all in black, came from behind the penguin running toward the car. With one hand she shielded her eyes, in the other, she held some sort of squirming, black animal.

Both officers, who had long ago reached their wacko limit, had the same thought at the same time: it was another one of those drugged-out Haight Street Satan worshipers.

Tim pressed the heels of his hands to his temples and stared at the brown and white terrazzo floor of Americo Bettoni's office. He traced the thin inlay of a brass star with his eyes. The blood in the car was Cynthia's, but the blood from the tissue sample was the same type as Adele's.

"It could be anybody," Inspector Bettoni said. "O positive is the most common blood type. You know that."

"With her car parked a block away?" Tim rubbed the back of his neck. "I don't think so."

Unable to come up with anything to say, the inspector was glad when his phone rang a second later. He listened for a minute then covered the mouthpiece. "They've found Ms. Monsarrat," he said hurriedly. "She flagged down a patrol unit in a parking lot out at Lake Merced. They've requested paramedics for two other citizens out there."

Tim's cell phone rang. He almost broke a finger getting it out and open.

"Tim? It's Adele. I'm okay. They're patching me through the police radio. Can you hear me okay?"

At the first sound of her voice, he had to stand and turn away from Bettoni so the man wouldn't see his eyes.

"Tim? You there?"

"Oh God," he choked. "Adele. You okay?" He walked into the hallway. "We found your car with blood all over the seat. Is Cyn okay? What happened?"

"I'm in the back of a patrol car at the south end of the footbridge over Lake Merced. The ambulances just got here." She stroked the small body curled up under her sweatshirt, vibrating against her belly. "Cynthia's . . ." She hesitated. ". . . going to be okay. We were with another woman who was hurt pretty bad. The paramedics are here. Can you come out? I mean, are you—?"

"We'll be right there," he said. "Hang tight."

"Tim?"

He brought the phone back to his ear. "What?"

"What's going to happen now?"

"A San Francisco cop and I will come to the scene. Then we'll bring you back to their office. We'll want to tape an interview. Are you okay with that?"

"If I can get a hot cup of tea and a blanket I am." She snapped her fingers. "Oh yeah, and could you bring a can of cat food?"

"Cat food?"

"I picked up a hitchhiker."

"Okay," he said, not entirely sure what she was talking

about. "Cat food, hot tea, and a blanket. I'll see you there." He lowered his voice. "I am glad you're okay, lady. I thought you'd bought it this time for sure."

Despite the wet clothes and a headache, Adele smiled. "Not me," she said. "I'm too mean to buy it."

"Don't be so sure," he said. "Harlan called and gave me the scoop. The bureau wants to talk to you. You have no idea how bad these guys really are."

The lights from the patrol car and the ambulances flashed red and blue off the shrubs. Through the crush of bodies surrounding Cynthia and Daisy, she saw that IVs had been started and that both women were being transferred to stretchers.

"Trust me, Timothy, when I tell you that I know from firsthand experience exactly who and what we're dealing with."

Other than the belly bulging with the entire can of Kitty King kidney bits, the kitten's appearance was astonishing. Chocolate brown fur made it unique enough, but the huge gold eyes were so pronounced, it reminded her of E.T. In an interrogation room inside the Hall of Justice, it purred contentedly while washing itself on Adele's lap. She stroked the soft sable fur with one hand, while the other held the blanket tight around herself. She spoke into the tape recorder microphone, relating everything that happened, from the moment she saw Daisy's pink and yellow caftan in the ER lobby until she found Officers Ulrich and Levitt.

After each had asked the questions that seemed most appropriate, Inspector Bettoni popped the tape out of the recorder and wrote her name, the date, and time on the cassette. "Okay, Ms. Monsarrat. I thank you for your patience and going through this again for me. You'll probably want to go home and get a hot shower and a meal."

"May I have my car back?"

Tim and the inspector looked at one another.

"I'm afraid we're going to have to hang on to it for the night," Bettoni began. "It's been taken to our impound yard for evidence processing. The evidence techs will go over it first thing in the morning. You'll be able to claim it when they're finished. I'm sure Detective Ritmann will give you a ride home."

"Sure enough." Tim looked at Adele, their eyes catching for a split second.

Americo saw the look—and the connection—and was not surprised. The woman was exceptional in ways that would hold a man's interest. A flicker of envy brought him to his feet.

"Thank you, Sergeant," he said, shaking hands with Tim. "I'll be in touch with you tomorrow."

Alone with her, Tim longed to be able to touch her, to erase the horrors of her day. "How about if I buy you a nice hot meal, or do you want to go home and just get some sleep? I'll give you a back rub. Whatever you want."

Adele kept her eyes on the sleeping sable kitten. When she spoke it was in a low but clear voice. "First I want to call Pacific Medical Center and see how Cynthia and Daisy are doing, then I want to go home and introduce Nelson to his new brother, take a long hot shower, open a bottle of wine, and while we cook dinner, I want you to tell me what's going to happen now."

He opened his mouth to respond, but she stopped him.

"I also want to know what Harlan and Onorato had to say, and everything else you know."

Again, he opened his mouth, and again, she held up a hand.

"And then, I need to sleep for a thousand years."

FIFTEEN

NELSON SAT CLEAR OF THE FRONT DOOR, BARELY able to contain his smile. Somehow, in that anthropomorphic-metaphysical realm of those things unexplainable, the dog knew his sibling, in some form, was coming.

After he'd nudged Her arm away from her sweatshirt and the thing had found its way to the floor, Nelson sniffed at the wriggling package. The kitten hissed and drew back. Nelson dismissed the small rudeness as a function of the cat's youth. Being a proper big brother, he gently took it by the scruff of its neck to meet Roddy Rug and the food bowls.

"We need to come up with a name for a meal served at two in the morning." Adele added sherry to the marinade of soy sauce, garlic, and fresh lemon and rotated the soaking strips of portobello mushroom.

The aroma of sautéing garlic cloves, scallions, and roasted red peppers was making his mouth water to the point where he had to keep swallowing. "Well," he said, splashing white wine into the pan and stirring the mixture. "It's too early for baker's breakfast and too late for midnight supper. How about supfast."

Adele snorted and placed the wineglasses on the table. She allowed the cabernet sauvignon to take a few short breaths then poured them each a healthy glass. She popped an oil-cured olive into his mouth.

"It's such a romantic time to be eating a meal." She pushed in next to him to add the meaty portobello strips and stir in a pint of her homemade roasted vegetable stock. "We could call it dreamer's repast, or bon vivant binge."

His arm brushed against hers and at once went around her waist. Everything else around them stopped.

A soft sound, halfway between a moan and a gasp, escaped her. The most intimate and arousing touch for her had always been on her lips and waist. She swallowed and without moving let her body lean against him. The hard muscles of his thighs and the strength of his arm seemed to paralyze her. Eyes closed, her head fell back and her lips parted slightly. His smell, the sheer maleness of him, brought an image of his hands sliding over her waist and down her hips while making love.

He dared to look at her hair hanging halfway down her back. Still damp, it held the scent of her perfume. His eyes went to her neck—delicate and long—then to the outline of her breasts under the silk robe. When he looked back, he found the golden eyes settled on his lips.

"Adele," he whispered—or thought he did. His hand moved to the small of her back and pressed her body into him. The robe slipped off one shoulder, revealing the smooth white hollow of her collarbone. His head dipped and his lips brushed down over her neck. Under his hands, her back arched.

Later, she would liken their kiss to the image of someone being sucked into the raging center of a huge fireball. Time or perception of anything outside themselves did not exist.

Adele was sure she was losing consciousness when a sensation began at the base of her throat and spread to her chest and head. It was strangely like the panic she'd felt inside the trunk of the Buick as the water rushed in.

It's too fast, too hot, too consuming, she managed to think. *The passion will devour us until we're nothing more than our passion. It has to go slower, until we are as strong as this . . .*

She blinked, shook back the hair from her face, and slipped out of his hands. It took an effort, but she managed to smile. "I have to finish slicing the tomatoes and mozzarella. Will you put the ramekins of crushed red pepper and olive oil on the table? Oh, and check the bread. If the crust is crispy and the—"

He reached for her again. "Adele." His voice was low and tremulous. He was still not returned from the kiss.

She dared not look at him, forcing her feet to continue in the direction of the sink. "Maybe you could stick a couple of plates in the oven and—"

"Adele." He moved close. "What went on inside you just now? Why did you stop yourself?"

She arranged slices of buffalo mozzarella and tomato in a flower design, sprinkled fresh basil leaves over it, and turned. "Because I want this relationship to be as good and as much as I think it can be, Timothy. I want us to last for a long time. I—I want you, but I want to take it slower."

His arms recaptured her. His eyes did not leave hers. "I know everything you just said is true, but it's hard to hold back. You're going to have to help me out there." He ran his fingers through his hair. "See, there have been a lot of women. Most of them came and went; a few stayed until we got sick of each other. I've never wanted anyone to stay for very long. It always went from bed to bicker very fast."

"You're different. I'm interested and excited about having a simple conversation with you. I love the fact we can go to a movie and have the same reaction, or the way we can sit in a room full of people and know exactly what the other is thinking. I love who you are, Adele."

Emotions welled, lumped inside her throat until she had to break away. She sliced an orange until she could get her throat to work. "There's another component to this that you should know," she began hesitantly.

He stroked her hair once. "Okay."

"I'm afraid. No, wait. I'm terrified of this—of us."

He watched her spoon pulp from the orange into the food processor, saying nothing.

"I'm afraid of losing you, and, afraid of being smothered and losing myself in you—in us. I need to get my boundaries fixed a little better. Time will help that." She poured nonfat yogurt and vegetable-based gelatin on top of the orange pulp and turned the processor on high, making conversation impossible.

While he waited, it came to him that the ultimate challenge was not to draw her into his life, but to give her the safety to be fully herself. Could he make her feel alive and free, all without boring her silly? She would never respond to pressure, but to natural order and humor—to letting things fall where they were supposed to. That was easy enough, he thought, because he was sure of where things were supposed to fall. It was all a matter of waiting for her to realize he was up to the task.

When she was finished, she turned to him. "Do you understand?"

He nodded and reached for her again. She leaned into him, anticipating his touch, when Nelson, paws going faster than his body, ran in from the hallway and slid across the kitchen floor. It was a direct hit against the backs of Tim's knees, knocking him off balance. Trailing behind, batting at the feathers of his tail, the kitten slid into Nelson. Without missing a beat, it jumped onto the dog's back, and the two took off, rider holding on with tiny claws.

Spell broken, Adele spooned the fluffy yogurt mixture into thin shells of crushed almonds and caramel and put them in the freezer.

"Bring me up to speed on what Corey and Harlan gave you," she said, dropping pasta into the boiling water.

Tim sighed, and refilled their wineglasses. "Compared to what you've got for them, it's lame or old news."

"Oh, give it to me anyway." Idly, she stirred the pasta until it went soft enough to slip all the way under.

"Onorato's people went over the medical files and spoke to family members again after I told him your plastic surgery theory." He lifted the lid to the sauce and inhaled. "I think he was a little leery of that idea initially, so when the reports started coming in to confirm it, he was more than a little surprised that they'd all had surgery overseas within a few months of their murders. Breast surgeries, hair transplants, face lifts—"

"Pacemaker."

Tim removed the loaf of hot sourdough from the oven and

placed it on the breadboard. "That little piece of plastic certainly got the bureau's attention."

"And?"

"It's some amazing technology," he said. "They ran it through a logic analyzer which showed the chip to contain codes for gaining access to the main water treatment plant for San Francisco."

Adele stopped stirring the sauce. "What about the self-replicating microorganism Fahad mentioned?"

"In the second phase of the investigation, they used an electron microscope and found evidence of microbes." He dipped a slice of hot sourdough into a saucer of garlic olive oil and bit into it. There was something about the movement of his jaw when he chewed that caused her stomach and nether regions to roll and slide.

"Nanobots," she said, deliberately looking away. "Hollis talked about them. I always thought they were more sci-fi than actuality."

"The computer boys said the microbes weren't functional, so I guess the group's scientists aren't as sophisticated as they'd like to be."

"Yet," Adele said. "Fahad said there were problems with the chips, but just the fact they're working on it and using Americans as guinea pigs is enough to scare me into buying bottled water for the rest of my life."

A few minutes later, she ladled sauce over the plates of naked linguini. Tim raised his glass. "To good food, a beautiful woman, and nanobots."

"And to the newest member of the family," she said, picking up the tiny brown body sitting on her foot. The kitten made its way to her left shoulder and hung his paws over the top sitting in the cradle of her elbow. At her side, Nelson fretted, his eyes fixed on the cat. She held the end of the cat's tail over her upper lip to create a Charlie Chaplin mustache and rolled her eyes until Nelson barked his disapproval. The sound of Tim's breathing coming hard and raspy stopped the forkful of linguini on its way to her mouth.

Tim's eyes were glazed over. "Jesus!" he said slumping back in his chair. "Jesus!"

She tasted the pasta, thinking she'd mistaken soap powder for salt. The rich flavor of the mushroom had been brought out and framed by subtle undertones of sherry and butter.

"What's wrong?" she asked. "You look like you're having a coronary."

"Nothing's wrong," he said, shaking his head. "I think my taste buds just had an orgasm."

She smiled and they continued to eat in silence until she arrived at the pick-and-graze phase of her meal.

"Did Harlan happen to mention anything about how the nanobots are supposed to work?" she asked.

He refilled his fork with a strip of portobello. "I'd rather you have him explain the details, because a lot of the technical stuff was way over my head. The general idea is that this chip is dumped into the water supply and through some sort of triggering device, the microbes are released and activated. The elements in the water help them multiply like otters, and bingo—seventy percent of the population is dead." Tim wiped his mouth and took another piece of sourdough. "Did Fahad say anything about the rashes?"

"Well, supposedly they can trigger the chip to release chemicals with some outside device. The chemicals cause the rash which makes it easy to find in the body. But once in a while the chips work their way to the surface of the body and trigger themselves." Wearing the cat over her shoulder, Adele removed the desserts from the freezer and a carton of low-fat cream—one of those strange food oxymorons—from the fridge. "The rash pinpoints the location of the chip for the harvester and thus saves time. Amar's custom of practicing his surgical talents on the victims isn't the norm. I got the impression the surgical touch isn't appreciated by all."

"But if these nanobots are so deadly that they can kill millions of people, why wouldn't it kill the host after it was triggered?"

Adele put the cat down and plugged in a hand mixer. "It must be something in the blood that renders the stuff harmless."

"Like what?"

"Don't know. Maybe the concentrations of certain electrolytes like sodium or potassium?" She shrugged. "Maybe water is the only medium the organism is meant to replicate in."

She whipped the cream into a stiff cloud, then quickly checked the living room. The kitten lay a safe distance from Nelson, grooming his nails. Nelson lay with Roddy Rug, studying the cat's every move, as if trying to understand the ways and temperament of his new companion.

"What did you do with the address book and the photograph I took from the Clemmons house?" Adele asked.

"Dropped them at the bureau office in San Rafael. Onorato is on his way out from D.C. as we chew. I've e-mailed to tell him they're there and waiting for him."

"When does he want to talk to me?"

"I would imagine first thing after he hooks up with San Francisco and San Rafael agents."

She plopped a dollop of whipped cream on top of the desserts, yawned, and checked her watch: three-thirty, time to get up and run. Her body instantly sent a refusal to her brain: NO WAY.

When she turned around, her eyes locked directly on his.

He watched her intently, still not wanting to accept that she wasn't ready for him—for them. After a minute, she ran her fingers through her hair.

"Please tell me you aren't working Ward Eight today." He speared the last slice of portobello mushroom.

"Oh, yes, I am. I'm committed for four hours this morning. It's an administrative day—I told Grace I'd set up the scheduling for evaluations. I figure I'll be out in two hours. I'll bus it over to the city, pick up the Beast, check on Cynthia and Daisy, come back, take the new child into the vet, and then talk to Harlan and Onorato."

"I doubt Onorato will let you get that far into your day without talking to him."

"Then he's going to have to find me first." She added a thin slice of orange to the top of the whipped cream and placed the dessert before him. "It's a recipe I made up for Cynthia's birthday last year," she said, and poured them each a cup of chamomile tea.

He took a tentative bite, moaned, and finished the dessert in the time it took her to sit down.

"Christ on a bike," she said, horrified at the empty bowl. "Did you have a chance to taste or chew?"

He popped the last piece of almond-caramel shell into his mouth, pretending to think. He shook his head. "I didn't get the essence of the flavors. I think I'd better try again."

She pushed her dessert over to him. "Be my guest. I'm more tired than hungry."

"Forget the classes, Adele," he said, dipping his spoon into the whipped mixture. "You don't need them."

"Yes I do. I really don't know very much about the culinary art. This," she said, waving her hand over the table, "is throw-it-together-in-a-pot stuff. When you're a vegetarian and don't have much time, you learn to make the most of simple things."

"I can just see it now," he said. *"The Adele Monsarrat Cookbook: Meatless Cooking for Those Living on the Edge; Broccoli for the Soul."*

"I'm going to tuck my children and myself in for a couple of hours," she said, filling the sink with hot soapy water. "Let the dishes soak—I'll get them in the morning."

"How about if I pick you up at Ellis about eight-thirty?"

She cocked her head, eyes squinted, trying to remember if they'd made a date. "What for?"

"To escort you over to the Hall of Justice so you can pick up your car. I told Inspector Bettino I'd bring over copies of the case files."

"What a liar you are." She laughed. "You'll rob me of the pleasure of taking the bus, but I think I can handle it just this once."

"Go on to bed, and I'll let myself out when I'm done licking the crumbs off the table."

She looked around the kitchen and decided she didn't have the wherewithal to cope with anything, even if it was simply sweeping the floor. "Deal," she said and shuffled into the hall.

Halfway to her bedroom, she stopped and went back to the kitchen. Without a word, she leaned over and kissed him on the cheek.

"Thank you for being there, Timothy," she whispered in his ear. "Thank you for being my friend. I—" She stopped her tongue a second before "love you" came out.

She awoke in a panic, remembered she had provided the cat with a litter box, and was drifting off to sleep when the phone rang. Her hands pawed the side table until she found the phone. "What time is it?" she asked, her voice low and muzzy.

"Five thirty-nine," Cynthia replied. "I figured you'd be up and running by now with a police escort."

"And I thought you'd sleep for a week with all the drugs you'd demand be pumped into your IV." Her fingers turned the switch on the lamp. She squinted under the assault of light. "How are you?"

"Actually," Cynthia began slowly, her voice flat, "I'm home. Depressed, but okay physically. The doctor said I'd probably been in the process of miscarrying for two days. Last night brought on the finishing touches."

"Oh, Cyn, I am so sorry," Adele said, feeling a mixture of true regret and relief. "Is there anything I can do? How about if I take a cab over?"

Cynthia was softly weeping. "No. I feel empty and numb at the same time? I know it's all hormones talking, but it's like there's this wall and I can't get through to how I really feel."

Adele searched the room for her robe, and found it under Nelson. She yanked it rapidly out from under him, the way a magician might pull a tablecloth off a table filled with dishes. Neither the dog nor the kitten curled against his belly so much as twitched a hair. "You sure you don't want me to come over and sit with you for a while before I go to work?"

"No. I'm going into work."

Adele stopped in the middle of slipping on her shoes. "Christ on a freakin' bike, Cyn, don't be ridiculous. You are *not* going to work. You've just—"

"Yeah, I *am* going to work, Adele, and don't give me any shit about it or I'll hang up. I'm fine. It's like having a heavy period. And besides, if I stay home, I'll only get more depressed. I need to keep busy."

"Listen, Cyn, be reasonable. You need rest. Where's Ryme? Why don't the two of you—"

"Ryme's gone," Cynthia said quickly. There was an edge of defiance to her voice. "I asked him to pack up his stuff and leave as soon as we got home."

"Why?" Adele was astounded. "Why would you do that? Ryme's a nice guy. He adores you." She stopped. "He must know you were pregnant."

"They told him when he got to the hospital." Cynthia snorted. "What a joke. As soon as they discovered my significant other was a medical deity, they practically wet themselves trying to be nice and accommodating. Before he arrived, they were about as unhappy a crew of assholes as you could get. Nasty, nasty people."

"Didn't you tell them you were a nurse?" Adele grabbed her clothes and made her way to the bathroom.

"Sure. Why else would they be such jerks?"

Adele snapped the floss out from between her two front teeth. "So how did Ryme react—before you kicked him out?"

"Rollercoastian," Cynthia said. "He was relieved, then sad, then angry, then he felt betrayed, then he was neutral, then he was logical, then he was ecstatic that I'd been pregnant, then he'd go back to being sad. I don't know, it was all so freakin' weird, I didn't want to deal with it. I don't think he believed me when I finally told him to get out. I had to get . . . well, a little nasty myself. I said some things that . . ." She began to cry again.

Adele held the phone to her ear with her shoulder as she slipped into a pair of black slacks. "How about if I come over and we'll take a taxi to work together from there? We can call Tina's new squeeze and get the Ward Eight rates."

"I've got a ride already. That cute guy from the lab."

The hand that worked the toothbrush stopped. Adele closed her eyes and sighed. "You called the lab tech for a ride to work? You've just lost a baby, and a man who cared deeply for you. How can you—?"

"Stuff the Catholic nun repressed sexuality guilt trip routine, Del," Cynthia said, the angry defiance returning to her voice. "I need to break this guy in as my transition man right away. Don't let the sheets get cold, as my mother always used to say. Anyway, I'm due for a good, no-ties fuck. Use them and lose them. I should have dumped Ryme after the first three weeks. I was dumb. I should have—" Cynthia broke down again. "Want to hear the sickest thing?"

Adele remained silent, the lump growing in her throat. Dealing with the emotional pain of people she loved just about killed her.

"Last night? The guy in the car? I'm in the backseat, scared to death, looking at him, knowing that he's going to kill us, but somewhere in this little dark, mega-sick corner of my mind, I'm wondering what it would be like to screw him. Then the cop who came to the hospital to ask me questions? I started coming on to him. Right there in the hospital. I've just lost my baby, and I asked him how old he was and if he was single. He looked at me like I was some kind of bottom-feeding scum."

Adele closed her eyes. "Cynthia, you've had a big loss. You're hurting. You're looking for any panacea you can find. Some people take drugs, some drink, some do religion—you do sex. Call Jeff Lavine and get some help getting through this. If you want, I'll call him and make sure you get in to see him today."

"I can't. I'm working."

"How about after work?"

During the silence, Adele braided her hair. When she got to the end, Cynthia sighed. "Okay, but I'm afraid," she said.

"Of what?"

"That I'll try and seduce him."

"You aren't afraid that you'll try to seduce him," Adele said. "You're more afraid that he'll let you." She tied her shoes. "Jeff's good. He knows all the tricks and games. He won't let you."

"I don't want to change, Adele. I like my life like this."

"Old habits are comfortable. Face it: you're miserable.
Maybe it's time to break in a few new rules of conduct."

Her jaw unhinged when she entered the kitchen. It was
spotless. The dishes had been washed and put away, and the
tiled counters gleamed. On closer inspection of the kitchen
table, she realized he'd not only wiped it off, but oiled and
polished it as well. Even the kitchen floor had been swept and
damp-mopped. The kitchen smelled of eucalyptus oil.

She filled a bowl with the leftover pasta and sauce, sprinkled
it liberally with vegetarian kibbles, cottage cheese, and two
raw eggs, then set it down for Nelson. Into a smaller bowl, she
mixed Nelson's veggie kibbles with cottage cheese and added
an egg.

The brown kitten sniffed, turned eyes the same color as
hers to the heavens, and mewled. "Where's the meat?" it
seemed to say.

"Vegetarian household, pal."

The kitten meowed again. It had a definite worried look
around the eyes.

"Try it. You'll like it," Adele encouraged.

The cat sat down and stared at her.

With an unmistakable air of maternal authority, Nelson
looked over, assessed the situation, nudged the kitten close to
the bowl, then pushed its head down into the mess.

The cat pulled back sneezing and shaking his head. He
licked at the smear of egg yolk and cottage cheese, watching
Nelson scarf down his breakfast. After a few more cautious
sniffs, he mewled in resignation and began to eat.

Adele was almost finished with the evaluation schedules
when Cynthia came out of report. Normally conscientious
about her appearance, she wore a wrinkled scrub dress with a
scruffy, shrunken sweater that was too short in the back. Pre-
dictably pale and hollow-eyed, there was a flat quality to her
gaze, as though her spirit was gone and wasn't expected back
any time soon. Even Grace, who pretty much lived in her of-

fice since being reprimanded by the union, said she looked ghastly.

"Good to see you've found a sweater to match those pill balls," Adele joked.

Cynthia shrugged.

"Jeff can see you at seven-thirty tonight in his Mill Valley office," Adele said. "Think you can get down there in time?"

Cynthia nodded.

"Want me to take you?"

"No. My mechanic is going to deliver the Virgin Mary here this afternoon."

Adele was shocked. Marin mechanics weren't kindly, home-delivery type fellows; they were more the strong, silent maniac types one might find along a freeway in Los Angeles. In other words, a mechanic delivering a car from the repair shop was rather like a physician making a home visit: nonexistent.

She opened her mouth to ask Cynthia how she had managed to talk one of them into such a thing, and thought better of it.

"Listen, how about if you tell Grace you want to go home sick, and I'll come over and we can just hang out and talk?" Adele asked, herding Cynthia toward the kitchen. "We'll have a good old-fashioned girls' day—crimp our hair, get pedicures and a massage. What do you say? My treat."

At the entry to the kitchen both nurses stopped and gawked at the unbelievable: Tina lip-locked with Mikie McCourty the cabby. Except for their efforts at breathing, not a sound could be heard.

Tina motioned them away. When they didn't move, she broke suction, and turned on them, hands on hips. "So like take a picture why dontcha? Lasts longer."

Cynthia burst into tears and took off in the direction of the nurses' lounge.

Adele turned on Tina. "Hey, save that for the back of the cab, will you?"

"Jeez," Tina said, holding up her hands in a gesture of defiant guilt, "what'd I say wrong?"

* * *

Adele nodded lots of shrink nods and uttered "uh-huhs" and "I understands" while she let Cynthia do a preshrink visit run-through of complaints and dysfunctions. When Cynthia was at the hiccuping stage of tears, Adele offered to take over her shift.

Cynthia waved it off: "Can't. I need the money. I've got a shrink to pay and I've gone from a Volvo- to a Volkswagen-income household."

"I'll give you the money," Adele said. "Just please go home and rest. You look terrible, and this can't be good for your body."

Cynthia stubbornly shook her head. "No. If I go home I'll be miserable. I'll . . ." She stopped and stared.

Adele took Cynthia's hands in hers. "You'll what, sweetie? Cyn, you really shouldn't be alone right now."

"No, but you should," Cynthia said, standing abruptly and giving her eyes a quick swipe with the Kleenex. "These suits look like they're here for you."

Adele turned. Two men in dark suits stood by the door.

Cynthia brushed past them then turned back to Adele. A corner of her mouth turned up and a light came into her eyes. "I'll wait for you, Del," she said wistfully, "No matter how many years they put you away for, I'll be on the outside waiting. Don't forget me with all those hot prison babes around. See ya."

"Ms. Cynthia O'Neil?" It was the taller of the two men who spoke.

Cynthia stopped. "Uh, yeah?"

"I'm Special Agent Corey Onorato and this is Agent Groat. We're with the FBI. We'd like to have a little chat with both you and Ms. Monsarrat."

Special Agent in Charge Corey Onorato was a big man, at least six four and well over two hundred pounds. "Beefy" was the word that most often came to people's minds. He and San Rafael agent Doug Groat were about the same age, though they were as different as Mutt and Jeff.

Onorato had thick blond hair and a broad Slavic face. His

smile was friendly, which surprised her; it always surprised her when men this big were friendly, almost as if sullenness should come with the territory. Agent Groat's thin black hair was greased and combed straight back over a white scalp. It drew attention to his nose, which, on the thin, pinched face, looked especially large and pointed. His muddy brown eyes were in constant motion, so that he gave the impression of a caged animal.

Corey Onorato had already heard about "the nurse" from the local agents and Detective Sergeant Ritmann. He'd formed a mental picture of what she looked like after he spoke with her at Ritmann's office. With the exception of the light gold eyes, he'd not been far off.

"We tried reaching you at home," he said. "We also tried your mobile phone, but weren't able to get through. Sergeant Ritmann said we'd find you here."

"Okay," Adele said. "So what now?"

"We checked with your supervisor—she told us you were off duty," Doug Groat said in a deep, resonant voice that be-lied his size. "We'd like you to come with us to our office in San Rafael."

"Right now?"

Agent Onorato smiled. "And do not pass go."

The room was sixties office style: pale mustard walls, non-descript wall-to-wall institutional carpeting, laminated fruit-wood rectangular table, uncomfortable metal folding chairs, and overhead fluorescent lighting that hummed in that distant, high-pitched way.

On the upside, the decaf coffee was great, and they'd bent over backwards to make her comfortable. They'd stopped by her house so she could pick up her storyboard and feed the kitten again. While they were there, Agent Groat took Nelson for a pee walk in the backyard, while Agent Onorato took a look at the loose latch on her side door and recommended a new one. She got the feeling that if she'd asked one of them for a foot rub, they might actually have complied without hesitation.

With the aid of her storyboard and notebook, she told them every detail of every event that had taken place since the day she'd admitted Mr. Penn—even the part about sitting inside an antique wardrobe holding a Marc Jacobs original over her head while listening to Mrs. Clemmons screwing in the shower.

The only interruption was Agent Groat asking who Marc Jacobs was.

Two and a half hours later, Special Agent Onorato turned off the tape recorder and asked if she needed to use the bathroom. The moment the door closed behind her, the two men looked at each other, with identical astonished expressions.

"Holy shit," Douglas Groat whispered, chuckling without humor. "Do you believe this broad? Think we ought to check her for testicles?"

Corey Onorato slid a hand over his face, elbow resting on his belly. His shoulders began to shake. The laughter he'd been holding surfaced and filled the room. "She's a wild woman," he said, wiping away tears. "Call J. Edgar and let's sign her up. We can use her as our next secret weapon. Man, talk about moxie? This chick's—"

The door opened, and all laughter and snorting abruptly stopped. They greeted her with stone faces.

"Okay," she said, "now it's my turn."

They looked at her blankly.

She crossed her arms over her chest. "You didn't really think I was just going to give you all the goodies and not get something in return?"

"What did you have in mind, Ms. Monsarrat?" Corey asked.

She opened her notebook and fished a pen out of her purse. "Since I've done a lot of your legwork for you, and have come this"—she held her thumb and forefinger a sixteenth of an inch apart—"close to being killed by these guys, I think I at least deserve to know who they are, don't you?"

She aborted the pregnant pause with her next question: "So, who are these psychos?"

Groat looked away, deferring to Agent Onorato.

Corey turned a couple of pages in the folder lying on the table before him, the amusement fading from his face. "They're an anti-American terrorist group known as Black Tide. They're bankrolled by a private party close to the Osama bin Laden camp. They're a small operation, but extremely sophisticated. These aren't the bomb-toting, rifle-carrying religious fanatics you see on the news. We're talking about a unique group of radicals: intellectuals and scientists who've been brought together to develop new methods of destroying large numbers of humans."

"Techno-terrorists."

He nodded. "Right."

"What about Laila Clemmons and Kadeja Shakir? Where are they and what part did they play in this?"

"We don't know where they are yet, and as far as where they fit in in the group, let's just say they do."

"Let's not just say they do, Mr. Onorato," she said, her voice taking on a severe tone. "Let's share the details."

There was a slight bobble in Corey Onorato's demeanor. He looked at Doug Groat, who looked down at his lap, shaking his head.

"I can't tell you that, Ms. Monsarrat," said Special Agent Onorato.

She waited, not taking her eyes off his for a second. "Sure you can, Mr. Onorato. Try it. One word at a time."

"It's top-secret information," Onorato argued, though he wore the expression of someone swimming upstream against a strong current.

"Everything I told you is top secret. The information that Fahad Al-Yassari gave me—whether the Bureau likes it or not—gives me insight into the whole operation. How can anything you tell me be more top secret than that? All I want from you is enough information to tie up a few of the loose details."

Onorato didn't take his eyes off hers. After a moment he nodded. "Okay. Shakir and Laila Clemmons are cogs in the Black Tide wheel. We assume there are three, maybe four camps of Tide members who are working within the United

States. You've run into the faction assigned to the Pacific Coast.

"Fahad Al-Yassari is a computer operations expert. He was born into a wealthy Iraqi family and educated at Oxford. Later, he was known to be in Afghanistan around the time the United States was firing Cruise missiles at suspected terrorist camps run by bin Laden."

"Is that how he was burned?"

The agent nodded. "As far as we know.

"Saad is the younger of the Askeri brothers and he's eager to prove himself a worthy member of the group. We suspect he's the one doing the actual murders. Amar is in charge of West Coast operations. In his own country, he was a surgical intern. Because he is a capable leader, they allow his surgical eccentricities."

"And Mrs. Clemmons?" Adele asked.

"Laila Clemmons a.k.a. Laila Al-Yassari: Fahad's wife. She married Clemmons a few years ago as a cover—not to mention all the benefits of having a wealthy American as a husband. From what we know, Clemmons believed that the three men were his wife's brothers. I would imagine she badgered him into putting up the cash for the warehouse and the rug business, which, of course, the group used as a front for their other operations—no pun intended.

"Originally, Laila trained as a nurse in Saudi Arabia and worked in an American hospital there. Unlike most women in terrorist groups, she was a major player in organizing the medical operations overseas. She found not only the doctors, but the victims as well. We're hoping that the address book you found will give us some key names. Some of the physicians and nurses involved are paid to let Laila know of potential carriers. If the carrier lives in or near a U.S. target city, they are operated on, usually at a much lower cost to make the deal even more enticing, and told they must see a particular 'partner' doctor when they get home."

Agent Onorato pointed the pen at her. "I wanted to commend you on your catching the plastic surgery angle. That was good."

"Thanks. So what if the carrier refuses to see the doctor ιey recommend and sees their own doctors once they get ome?"

"It doesn't matter. No physician is going to be looking for omputer chips. Mostly, they either do as they are told and are illed and the chips harvested, or they don't, and they're illed and the chips harvested—like Mrs. Rothschild. When ιe group started losing chips to malfunctions, and having in- ιidents like Mr. Penn's pacemaker being 'found,' you can be- ιeve they got a lot more aggressive about tracking and etting to their carriers sooner."

"Thus the surveillance on Mr. Penn and Daisy," Adele said.

"Right. I can imagine how pissed off they were when you ιuck your nose in and walked away with Penn's pacemaker. 'm surprised they didn't kill you at his house."

"Why did they murder Raymond Clemmons?" she asked. 'Seems to me that was like shooting themselves in the foot."

"Not at all. He was probably starting to suspect something ιnd was causing problems by pulling the purse strings too ight."

He came to her end of the table and sat on the edge. "In ιght of the group's mission, human life means little to these ιeople. There's a strong cohesion within the group. This is 'amily—they'll do anything for family."

"What about Kadeja?"

Agent Onorato tapped his pen on the palm of his hand. 'Kadeja Shakir is the daughter of Laila Clemmons—father ιnknown. She, like her mother, trained as a nurse in Saudi. She signed on as a per diem person with the Ellis nursing staff as soon as she was told there were three carriers return- ιng to Marin.

"We suspect some of their people infiltrate the major hos- ιitals around the target cities. On five of the victims we found ιhat their hospital's medical data on them was missing or in- ιomplete. People with ties to Black Tide worked in three of those hospitals."

Agent Groat gathered up his papers, gave Corey a look that said, "Enough already," and turned to Adele. "Tomorrow we'll need you to come in and read over the transcripts of the tape make corrections if needed, and then sign them."

She opened her mouth.

"Yes, you may have a copy of your own," Groat said, study ing her as if he were about to tell her she was fired. "However we must insist that while we appreciate what you've done up to this point to help the case, this is serious business, and we ask you to please refrain from any further involvement And I assume I don't need to tell you that all of this is strictly confidential?"

Adele bit her tongue.

"Are you aware that you are still in personal danger?' Corey Onorato asked.

"It isn't the first time," she said.

"From what you and Sergeant Ritmann have told us," said Groat, "I don't doubt that for a second, but the fact is, you're a witness and we'll need your testimony in the future. We're going to offer you some alternatives and then insist you take one. You can let the bureau put you up someplace we consider safe, or, you can stay with a friend or a relative outside this area." He hesitated. "Or the bureau can offer you the company of agents who'll be with you twenty-four hours a day."

"Like a shadow," Corey Onorato said, grinning. He was thinking about the poor saps who'd have to keep up with her. It'd be like being in the academy again.

Adele thought his smile had a sadistic quality to it. She resisted the whole idea of a guard, yet at the same time it made sense. "Do I have time to think this over?"

"Not much," they said in unison.

"And," Doug Groat continued, "if you don't accept our agents, we would need to be able to reach you at any time day or night. We'll provide you with a cell phone, but you must keep it with you at all times."

"What about work?"

They shook their heads. "Probably best not to," said Groat. "Not unless you want to take us up on our offer of constant company."

"But I have to work," Adele said petulantly. "I can't just hang around. You're kidding about this, right?"

"Ms. Monsarrat," Agent Groat said in a funereal tone, "the bureau never kids anybody about anything."

They were approaching the Golden Gate Bridge just as the sun melted through the fog. It looked for all the world like a large, radiant grapefruit in the sky. Adele's mood changed on a dime from introspective and morose to supremely happy— on the edge of giddiness. Riding the wave, she leaned over and kissed Tim on the cheek.

"Have I ever told you how glad I am that you're my friend?" she said in a voice that hit the lower registers.

Tim processed the carefree kiss and the simple statement of fact into something arduous and complex. He worked it over in his mind like a difficult *New York Times* crossword puzzle, until in the end he became so overloaded with possible interpretations that he said nothing.

Adele raised her hands over her head and sighed happily, looking over the mouth of the Bay to the Faralon Islands. "Glorious day, isn't it, Timothy? Don't you just love this city?"

He glanced at her then back at the road, wondering what she'd meant. Was it a glorious day because they were together? What did she mean by "don't you just love this city?" What was the subtext? Was she trying to tell him something? Or maybe she was trying to tell him she wanted more and that . . .

"I've got such a craving for vanilla frozen yogurt," she said, suddenly. "Let's stop and get one on the way."

"Sure," he said, hitting the switch that routed his train of thinking from one track to another. But who could blame him? He'd cleaned the kitchen until almost five, then gone home and climbed into a cold shower. After that, sleep never came, chased away by the double whammy of worry for her safety and his lust, which lingered in his groin like a disturbed hornet's nest.

Careful not to snag her IV line, Daisy attempted to re-coil her hair while Adele watched in mild fascination.

"I give up," Daisy said finally. Around her right eye, the flesh was puffy and blue. One side of her bottom lip was badly swollen, but she had no problem talking. "I reckon I'm about the most dreadful lot you've run across in a long while."

"No," Adele said. "Actually I've already dealt with several other dreadful lots just this morning. You're relatively normal compared to them."

Daisy giggled and sat up in bed with some difficulty. Adele could see she was in pain. "The plastic surgeon said I'd have a dent in my bum, but I guess it can afford to have a few dents." She looked at Adele. "Did the FBI agents visit you, too?"

Adele nodded. "Ayuhn. They must have gotten to you before the breakfast trays."

"I don't believe it was even six A.M. before they came. At first I thought it was those dreadful men, come back to finish me off." Her eyes filled. "They said it was a good thing I didn't call that Dr. English, and that if I'd gone to see him, they probably would have killed me then. My head might be in a jar on someone's shelf." Daisy closed her eyes and shuddered. "Can you imagine? Me? Carrying around a couple of terrorist computer chips in my bum? Mum will have a good laugh over that one."

"Daisy," Adele said, "do you still have the card that they gave you in London? The one with Dr. English's address and phone number?"

She nodded. "I found it about a week ago when the rash first got infected. I meant to ring him up, but I thought I'd try curing it on my own first."

"Is there a chance you could recall his number or address?"

Daisy studied her nails, chipped and broken from tearing at the trunk latch. "There wasn't a phone number on the card—it was handwritten on the back. I believe the street was Sutter, but I can't remember the number. I'm terrible with numbers."

Adele nodded. "Do you know where this card is right now?"

Daisy waved a hand. "In my bedroom somewhere. I'd have to look."

"Would you mind if I went over and looked around for it? Like today?"

"Well, I—of course." Daisy looked stricken. "Do you think this Dr. English is—is the man last night who—"

"That's my guess."

Nelson and Adele sat on the bench in the exam room, paw in hand, looking very much like concerned parents of a newborn. "Burmese?" Adele said. "You mean like Siamese?"

Dr. Pratt shook her head. She was a lively, petite woman. Around her eyes was a permanent, determined squint, as though life were something that had to be taken by the horns and dealt with rather than enjoyed.

"Burmese are a breed all their own. They're called 'people cats' because their personality is such that they bond with one person—"

Nelson whined.

"With one person or," she said, nodding to Nelson, "one animal for their whole lives." Dr. Pratt ran her hands over the small sable-brown body, dwarfing the animal even more. Flattening the kitten's ears to its head, she examined the alienlike eyes. Adele was amazed at how much the animal resembled Yoda, the diminutive *Star Wars* Jedi master.

"These cats can't be without that main person—or animal—for long or they'll go into a depression, and eventually will fail to thrive. It's a characteristic that distinguishes them from the rest of the feline empire." Dr. Pratt seemed to reconsider, then added, "That and their little baseball heads."

Adele craned her head forward. "Pardon? Their little baseball what?"

Dr. Pratt laughed. "Baseball heads. Unless they're being used as studs, Burmese don't grow to be very large and that includes the skull." The veterinarian held down the kitten's ears again while it squirmed to free them. "Their heads are characteristically round and small—they always remind me of baseballs."

Glancing over at Nelson, whose head was canted and whose face bore that vacant, walnut-sized-brain stare, Adele panicked. "Are you trying to tell me that these cats aren't very bright? I don't know if I could handle another mental special-needs animal."

"Oh no, no, no." Dr. Pratt held up her hand. "To the contrary—if there hasn't been too much inbreeding in their line, Burmese are particularly clever animals."

"Is he healthy?" Adele asked, picking at a piece of dead skin around her thumb.

Dr. Pratt nodded. "All his tests are negative, and I've given him his shots for now. We've scheduled him a month from today for neutering. He's going to make a great pet." She picked up the kitten and nuzzled it. Nelson growled and jumped to the floor.

"How old is he?" Adele asked.

"I'd guess about eight to ten weeks. He probably wandered away from somebody . . . maybe a breeder's yard, although I'd doubt that. These fluff balls can fetch anywhere from six hundred to two thousand dollars apiece. Most owners don't let them out of their sight. Have you put an ad in the *Chronicle*?"

Adele gave Nelson a sideways glance, hoping he wouldn't understand what was being said. "Yes, and reported him to San Francisco SPCA. No claims have been made so far, but it's only been ten hours. We've got our fingers and toes crossed."

The vet picked up the file and looked it over, then snapped her fingers. "Oh. There's something else you should take into consideration. You can get away with having a vegetarian dog, but it won't work with a cat. I've never seen a vegetarian feline in fifteen years of practice. Not that they won't eat strange things—I've got a salad-eating cat, a strawberry fanatic cat, one who adores potato chips, and another who prefers corn pudding to liver, but those are quirks. When it comes to chowing down, these animals want meat."

Nelson whined.

Adele sighed. "Okay. As long as I don't have to fry up slabs of meat or touch any dead animal parts."

Dr. Pratt laughed. "You won't have to touch any dead flesh.

We'll start him out right with a balanced diet for kittens." The veterinarian glanced at the file again. "What have you decided on for a name?"

"No idea," Adele said.

"Great name," Dr. Pratt replied and handed her the bill.

"Hey."

It had become their signature opening instead of "hi," "hello," or the ever popular "yo."

"Hey yourself. Where are you?"

Adele crawled out from under Daisy's bed and searched the floor with her eyes. "Oh, you know. Just around."

There was silence while he considered pushing to know where "just around" was. He dropped it for the moment. He knew the FBI would have her on a tight leash.

"Well, Enrico Cini, my master paper chaser, has done it again," Tim said, barely containing his satisfaction.

"Obviously you're either referring to the fact he's dropped another inch off his height and is now a candidate for Barnum and Bailey, or he's spawned yet another child—this must be number seven or eight."

"Your fondness for the man overwhelms me, but, no, Cini dug up records on the warehouse over on Townsend, and you'll never guess who the owner and CEO of Persian Rugs, Limited was."

"Raymond Clemmons," Adele said.

He swiveled around in his chair and looked out the window toward the Santa Venetia hills as a flock of seagulls passed over the Civic Center pond. "I don't even want to know how you knew that." He sounded depressed.

"You know what the worst part of it is?" Adele asked.

"That the guy was cut up in his own warehouse?"

"Yeah. Talk about adding insult to injury."

"Uh-huh. And, are you ready for this?"

Adele sat down on the bed. "Shoot."

"Not only were Fahad Al-Yassari and Saad and Amar Askeri his employees, Al-Yassari was Mrs. Clemmons's husband."

Not wanting to blow his thunder by telling him this was old

news, she faked an excited "Whoa!" and lay back on the pink taffeta quilt covering Daisy's bed. She bolted back into a sitting position, choking on the heavy scent of Attar of Roses.

When she was able, she asked, "Have you gotten any word on whether or not they found Mrs. Clemmons or Kadeja?"

"No. I think you can safely bet they won't be back any time soon. My guess is they're out there in the Big Somewhere along with the three men who tried to kill you last night. So, where are you?" His voice took on enough of an edge to let her know he wanted a straight answer.

"Daisy's house. She asked me to pick up some things for her."

"That's a secured area, Adele."

"Yeah, and?" There was a hint of acrimony in her voice.

He sighed the sigh of a man backing away from the edge. "Never mind."

She found the card behind the bedside table, wedged between the baseboard and the wall. The number had a San Francisco prefix, although it was not the same number given to Mr. Penn. She imagined there was a different one for each victim.

Not giving it a second thought, she dialed the number, then jerked the receiver away from her ear as those three, irritating, overly loud, and discordant tones blasted. Halfway through the standard "We're sorry, you have reached a number which has been disconnected. Please check the number and try again" message, she hung up. The FBI would be checking phone records. She supposed she should call the Men in Black and give them the number.

She lay back down and went over her safety options once more. Staying with Tim would be too much like throwing a match into the gasoline of her emotional health, period. Harlan Jacquot had surprised her by leaving a message offering his guest room, and while it seemed like the ideal choice, she didn't want to impose on someone she barely knew. Raven, she knew, would be more than willing to have her stay with him, but that, too, carried its own set of liabilities.

Then there was the consideration that no matter where she went, she carried with her a certain risk. She imagined herself walking in someone's front door, bags in hand and saying, *"Oh and by the way, there's a chance a bunch of terrorists might break in and kill us all, but I* will *supply my own towels and sheets."*

The deciding factors, however, were Nelson and the new baby. She didn't want to uproot them, especially so soon after the kitten's arrival.

She got up and walked through the house to the kitchen. On the counter, a lone caraway seed was mixed in with some bread crumbs. Pressing the tip of her finger against it, she put it in her mouth and chewed thoughtfully.

"Well," she said, hoisting her purse to her shoulder, "I guess I'd better go home and prepare the kids for guests. Let's just hope nobody is allergic to fur."

SIXTEEN

AFTER ONLY A FEW DAYS OF SHARING HER SHADOW with Olivia Light, Adele had come to think of the agent as an extra body part, like a tail, or as a mute Siamese twin. All her apprehensions about the woman having animal allergies, being a smoker of cigars, or—the worst—a nonstop talker— were unfounded. Olivia Light was sort of there and sort of not, like a shadow.

In appearance, she was amorphous. She could have been one of those people who sat with the potted plants at parties and later you could never quite remember what she looked like. Her personality either was on sabbatical, had been killed during FBI training, or had never been there at all. Adele was betting on the latter.

Adele was convinced nothing short of an injection of PCP would get a reaction out of the woman. Nothing fazed her except bananas, for which she had a passion. Once, Adele thought she'd seen a flash of excitement in the woman's eyes as she peeled one for breakfast. Whenever she was on duty, she came with at least two bunches tucked into a string bag. By the time she went off watch, every one had been consumed.

Conversation was out of the question. Agent Light's responses were limited to single words and four-word sentences. Nelson, the kitten (who reduced everyone else to baby talk), Adele's running, and even Ward 8 chaos, including a Code Blue, elicited the same, monotone response: "Uhn."

Adele was aware the woman was only doing her job, but couldn't they have chosen an agent who was alive? She was sure that if she ever saw Agent Light naked, she'd find a switch in the middle of the woman's back with a brass plate underneath that read: Property of Automatons R Us—Please return if found wandering or repeating phrases.

Mrs. Coolidge, of course, did not believe for one moment that Olivia Light was Adele's second cousin from Oklahoma. By the end of the third day of binocular surveillance, Deena Mae had begun spreading rumors that Adele had turned over a new leaf and gone lesbo. And oh, what a shame: she had been such a nice girl with so much going for her, and tsk-tsk, wasn't it *too tragic* just when the romance with that nice young man with the red hair seemed to be back on again, and perhaps someone should look into having the dog taken out of that perverse atmosphere, and—yadda yadda yadda.

One thing for sure, Adele could now claim that she knew exactly what the president felt being surrounded by the secret service twenty-four hours a day. The only time Adele was released from Agent Light's scrutiny was when she was sleeping, in the bathroom, or with the other agents or Timothy.

When Agent Light was off duty, Agents Aristi or Skaehill took over watch. Adele found them easier to take. They took her to run on deserted roads outside Marin, and preferred to hang out in Ward 8's waiting room, checking on her once an hour rather than being in her face every minute, reeking of banana breath.

All in all she knew she was fortunate to have the freedom rather than being virtually in custody like Daisy, protected under strict FBI terms in some podunk motel room: no running, no work, no visitors, limited monitored phone calls, but as many romance novels as she could read. She'd told Corey Onorato she'd rather be dead.

Against his better judgment, Agent Onorato agreed to let her work, although, in return, she had to agree to work under an assumed name. She had not been allowed to drive or leave the house alone.

Under the circumstances, Adele knew they were being more than fair to her and she really didn't want to complain— but the bananas were getting to her.

* * *

Seeing a movie then going to the Coffee Roastery in Mill Valley for coffee and biscotti was a treat Adele looked forward to with as much excitement as winning the lottery. In order to give her and Agent Light a break from each other (although Adele was sure that her shadow switched to the "off " mode the moment she walked out of the house), Tim made the arrangements. She was so desperate to get out, she actually enjoyed the Disney feature-length cartoon he'd chosen for them to see.

In a far dark corner of the Roastery, Adele sipped her decaf and brushed her hands free of biscotti crumbs. "You're not telling me something important, and it's killing you," she said, breaking the silence.

Tim shook his head and picked at a thread in the burlap sack of coffee beans they were using as seats. "How the hell did you come up with that?"

"I know you," she said simply and sipped her decaf latte. "You can run, Timothy, but you cannot hide."

In truth, he had been debating whether or not to tell her. He couldn't predict how she'd react, but if he *didn't* tell her, he knew exactly what her reaction would be.

"Corey Onorato called," he began. "They've tracked down a surgeon in Berlin—a plastic surgeon who implanted some of the chips for Black Tide."

Adele's calm response totally belied the excitement she felt: "Oh? What else did he say?"

Tim finished his coffee. "An upper-level member of the group approached the surgeon a year ago and told her if she didn't cooperate, they'd kill her family. To prove their point, they kidnapped her two children and threatened to cut them up piece by piece until she agreed to work with them. The doctor said she'd implanted twenty of the things in twelve people, each time with a gun held to her head. Most of the time the patients were already anesthetized by the time she got into the room, but about a month ago, the doctor decided to find out exactly who these patients were. With the help of an assistant, she managed to get the name and address of one of the people she was operating on."

He paused, looking at her and then back at the pulled thread, which had left a line of small gaps in the burlap. "It seems San Francisco has a resident with brand-new breast implants. The FBI was waiting for her when she got home from work last Monday. She was most cooperative."

Adele stared. "Holy shit," she whispered eventually.

He smiled and sipped the black espresso. "Onorato is thinking of throwing a little party."

"A party?"

"Yeah. A sting setup."

"When?"

"Day after tomorrow. They're briefing a female agent from the San Jose office as we speak."

At the mention of the female agent, Adele's face fell, a billboard for disappointment. He realized the only reason he'd put off telling her was because he hadn't wanted to see that look. He hurried on, almost running his words together. He pulled at the thread again, winding it around his finger until the tip turned purplish red.

"Onorato wants to net as many of these people as he can, as quietly as he can. They've got an appointment set with Dr. English. The woman called and said she had a rash at the incision site and that—"

"I can't believe Onorato didn't tell me," Adele said, staring off as if she was going to cry. "I gave him all that information, and he never even mentioned it?"

She pulled herself up from the bag of coffee beans. "Son of a bitch!" she said under her breath and headed to the exit without a backward glance.

"Adele, this is a bureau operation," Tim said when he caught up with her. "He can't tell anybody except those who are—"

She turned on him at the doorway, furious. "I'm not just anybody. I had as much to do with the breaking of this case as anyone. If I were some ding-dong I'd understand, but I'm— I'm . . ."

Adele rapidly crossed Miller Avenue, remembered on the

other side that Tim's car was parked in front of the Sweet-water, and retraced her footsteps, much to the aggravation of the drivers waiting to turn.

Tim caught up with her outside Two Neat, and gently steered her inside the card shop. "Adele, he couldn't tell you, and I sure as hell shouldn't have told you."

She picked a card out of the wall rack and stared at it without seeing. When she looked at him, the gold eyes were undecipherable. "You don't get it, Timothy, because you're on the other side of the wall. You're all so brainwashed by the boys' club bureaucratic bullshit that none of you ever look beyond it for what might be better answers. You've already got all the answers—they're in the Boy Scout's handbook they give you in the academy. And God forbid that any of you get creative or color outside the lines on your own!"

He took the card out of her hands before she crunched it. "So what are you saying, Adele? That we should just turn over FBI or police cases to you because you're clever and know how to shoot a gun?" He forced a laugh, aware that his neck and face were probably crimson by now. "It ain't gonna happen, babe. You're still a civilian. That's the part *you* don't get. If you wanted to play cops and robbers, you should have become a cop. I've told you that a thousand times."

She pulled the card back and looked at it. The cover was a black-and-white snapshot, circa the early 1950s, of two homely middle-aged women in bathing suits lying next to a pool.

"My becoming a cop or not has nothing to do with this, Tim. I've already dealt with these people, I know what they're like. I wouldn't have to be briefed about much except the woman's name and what she looks like. I already know what to expect from these assholes."

"Bingo, Adele," he said, taking the card back. "Key words: you've already dealt with them. They know you. They'd recognize you in a heartbeat. Gold eyes. Taller than the Empire State building? Jesus, get beyond that keyhole vision of yours, will you?"

The storm inside her was blowing over. "The Empire State building?" she snorted. After a pause, she put a hand on her hip. "I was in the drama department at San Francisco State. I know how to do my own makeup. I've got a closet full of disguises, wigs, colored contacts—you name it. Just show me a photograph of this woman and I'll look so much like her in forty-five minutes, her own mother wouldn't know the difference. I can mimic any accent. Tell me the region of the country she's from originally, and I can—"

"Adele." He shook his head and opened the card. "It ain't gonna happen, so get used to it and move on."

Inside the card were three lines that looked like they were typed on someone's old Underwood: *"The gals were left alone while Gary and Ron went to the boat show. They loved their husbands . . . and everyone else's too—for they were whores."*

Adele snorted and laughed until she wheezed. Tim frowned, reading it again. "I don't get it," he said, checking the photo on the front of the card.

She pointed at him. "You're right about that much anyway."

Over the course of a night, the animals had a tendency to migrate in a pattern. The cat started out in the far left corner of the bedroom. By eleven, he'd curled up next to Nelson under the bed. At 1 A.M., he moved up onto the bed, settling between Adele's feet, and at 2, he crept to her armpit. By 3 he was in his final destination: draped over her forehead looking like a coonskin cap, his tail curled around her nose.

Shortly thereafter, Nelson left his station under the bed and climbed under the covers on the left side, settling his head on the pillow and one paw on the cat's rump.

When Adele's internal alarm went off at three-thirty, the animals were a snoring nest of limbs and fur under which she was firmly pinned. Her hand snaked around to find the penlight she'd put under her pillow. She pushed the kitten's tail away from her nose and took in a deep, clearing breath before she pushed herself up.

It was Tuesday. She couldn't give a concrete reason for wanting the day off other than her sixth sense had nagged her into it. If pushed, she would have found tucked into a curve of her cerebral cortex an idea that maybe Tim or Corey Onorato might call and allow her to sit in one of the unmarked units parked somewhere within a mile radius of the office building where the sting operation was to take place.

Finding someone to take her shift proved harder than pulling scales off an indignant armadillo. She was already developing a list of excuses for not going to work *(Hi, Mrs. Noel? I can't come into work today because my stigmata started acting up right after the voices told me to clean all the guns)* when Linda came through at the last minute. Nelson and the kitten watched with some interest as She dressed for Her run, then silently knocked the screen out of the bedroom window.

At the cost of running without brushing her teeth first, she simply could not face running with Agent Light again. The silent whining and the not-so-silent huffing and puffing was distracting. She needed to concentrate on how she was going to talk Onorato into letting her at least be near the action.

Dropping to the walkway at the side of the house, she crawled through the bushes into her neighbor's yard and pushed the Beast away from the house before starting the engine.

"Houston, we have a problem," the voice said the moment Detective Sergeant Ritmann answered his cell phone.

"Hey, Special Agent in Charge. What's up?"

Onorato paused. "How'd you know who—?"

"I've got a photographic memory for voices," Tim said, leaning back in his chair. "What's the problem?"

Onorato sighed. "The operation is falling. This is a heads-up to you that I don't think we're going to be able to go in. The agent we had just got herself creamed in a hit-and-run on Highway Two-Eighty down by Stanford. They're taking her to surgery now."

"Was it accidental?"

"We're checking, but CHP says it happens all the time down there. I doubt there could be any connection since only six people know this is even happening. The problem is, there isn't another female agent that's even close in size, let alone trying to brief her for this in," he looked at his watch, "less than five and a half hours."

On the other side of Tim's desk, Jane went over the list of things he'd given her to do. She circled one and put a question mark next to it.

Tim paused, biting his thumbnail. "There may be a way so that we don't have to let this die in the water."

"I'm all ears."

"Adele. Think about it: she's close in size and she already knows the background on this. Give her a photograph of the subject and she could look real close. Shit," Tim laughed, "I'll bet you could give her a picture of your dog and she'd do a good enough job to fool the vet."

The silence from the other end of the line was a good sign. It meant Onorato was running it over in his brain.

"Corey, it's better than letting the ship sink, isn't it?"

Onorato didn't answer right away. He was thinking about his interview with her. He knew agents working in the field who couldn't hold a candle to her—and if it meant saving the operation . . .

"You think she'd agree to it? She's already had one close call."

"Are you kidding?" Tim said. "The only reason she might give you a hard time is because she's so pissed off that you didn't ask her in the first place. She's barely talking to me, and I was just the messenger."

Onorato looked across the room where Agent Groat was working at the computer. "Tell you what, let me put this in the think tank and we'll kick it around for a little. Maybe you could alert Ms. Monsarrat as to what's going on?"

"Will do," Tim said, his smile so broad that it almost interfered with his speech.

Jane was frowning, shaking her head.

"What?" he asked as soon as he disconnected.

"No comment," Jane said stiffly, and ruffled the papers on her lap. "However, I do have a question about the last item here on your list. What do you need with a hairnet, Timothy?"

"Ah," he said. "The first cooking class is tonight. My mother told me I'd need a hairnet."

"What for?"

He thought about it for a minute. "Don't you know?"

She shook her head. "No. The last time I saw hairnets being used was in nineteen fifty-seven in a cafeteria in Bakersfield. We thought it was odd then."

"Oh. Well, cross it off." He picked up the desk phone receiver. Jane didn't move. He gave her a questioning look.

"I don't understand, Timothy," Jane said, clipping the pen to her sweater, "why you'd even consider subjecting that poor woman to any more danger. Don't you think Adele has been through enough with this case?"

"Enough is not in her vocabulary, Jane." He punched in Adele's number. "And if I didn't 'subject' her, as you put it, I'd be banished from the kingdom forever."

Adele was on a crusade. Short of physically torturing Agent Light, she was determined to get some sort of human reaction out of her. When the rubber replica of a tarantula, complete with hairy legs and beady eyes, strategically placed in a bunch of the agent's bananas failed to earn so much as a gasp, Adele knew she'd have to stretch. It was during her run that it came to her. She'd come around a bend in Yolanda Trail and tripped over something that looked like a long white bone. It turned out to be a branch, but it had been enough to unlock the warped closet of her mind and pull out a couple of ideas that were hanging pressed and ready to go.

She called Timothy as she was pulling away from Ross Commons.

"So, what do you think?" he said before she'd even said hello.

"Think about what?"

"Didn't you get my message?"

"No. I escaped out the bedroom window about four this morning and went running. I ended up watching the sun come up. I'm heading home from Ross now. I just called to check the latest news on the operation."

"Maybe I should wait until you're parked. I don't want you going up over any curbs."

Pulse and respiratory rate rocketing through the roof, Adele sailed through a stop sign, never seeing it. "I'm perfectly capable of driving safely while receiving news of any sort. Dribble and shoot."

"The lady agent who was going to be in the setup was involved in a hit-and-run accident this morning down on Two-Eighty and is now in surgery. They had her primed, everything is set, they've got people in place all through the building. The appointment is for two o'clock."

Adele looked at her watch and her accelerator foot took on lead. "So what are you leading up to?"

"Onorato called me a few minutes ago and I told them you wanted to do this. He said they were going to knock the idea around and call you."

The Beast squealed around a corner, through two more stop signs, and onto Magnolia Avenue. "What's the likelihood of them actually calling?"

"Better than good," Tim told her. "Think about it. They're in the middle of the final prep. All the units are set, including San Francisco plainclothes people. Don't forget, Onorato has recruited lots of bodies for this operation. If you're going to crunch these people, you need to overwhelm them with numbers. The more time slips by, the more likely the targets are to vanish."

She cut the motor a half a block away from the house and rolled the rest of the way. The blinds were still closed in the bay window, which meant Agent Light was probably still asleep.

"Okay, so what should I do now?" She crouched and ran along the side of the house and around the back to her bedroom window.

"Get a bunch of your disguises together with your makeup and wigs. They should be calling you within the next forty minutes."

"Are you going to be there?"

"You kidding? I wouldn't miss seeing Adele Monsarrat in action for the world."

* * *

"You mean the bitch with the balls?" San Rafael agent Schoon sat with his feet up on the table, pushing the front legs of his chair off the ground.

Onorato nodded. "Bottom line is that this lady has the moxie to do it. You wouldn't believe some of the shit she's done already."

Doug Groat hadn't said much, and when he had, it had been brief and conflicted. Now, they waited for him to put in his vote. He leaned forward, his hands palm down on the table. He seemed cautiously uneasy. "The real bottom line is that we're going to lose this operation and these assholes are going to be gone with the wind. It's been five days since they dumped the car. San Francisco coroner's office reported two calls yesterday inquiring about possible bodies found in Lake Merced. They're wondering why it hasn't shown up in the papers. If these guys haven't figured out that both women are still alive by now, they will shortly. Once they know that, they'll dig in so deep, we'll never find them again."

Groat tapped the table thoughtfully with the sides of his thumbs. "We're here with at least fifty bodies in on this. The operation is set up and ready to fire. If we don't run with it today, we're fucked. Ms. Monsarrat, civilian or not, already knows about the situation and has some," he coughed and looked even more pained, "skills in dealing with these types of situations."

"Ritmann swears she's great at disguise," added Onorato.

Agent Schoon let down his chair. "So, if she's willing to come in on the operation, go with her. She sounds a little risky but better than losing the whole show."

"It's just that she seems . . ." Groat tapped his fingers on the table and screwed up his face. "I don't know—overeager? I don't trust civilians when they're that zealous; they lose their cool and screw up. She could be dangerous."

"I disagree," Onorato said, his fingers gripping the back of his chair. "This woman is as confident as they come. All you have to do is look at how she handled the kidnap and attempted murder situation."

"Yes," Groat warned, "but she also got herself and Rit-mann shot not too long ago on another case. Lost the shooter on top of that. She's cocky and that's dangerous."

Corey checked his watch. "That was a whole different ball of wax, Doug." His face hardened. "We haven't much time, gentlemen. I say we give Ms. Monsarrat a call."

"Fine with me," Schoon said, letting down the front legs of his chair.

They looked at Doug Groat.

"Okay," he said finally, throwing up his hands. "Let's get her in here and see if she can do the magic tricks."

She placed the three cardboard boxes on the antique oak dresser in the small foyer by the front door. Agent Light, none the worse for not knowing that Adele had slipped out the back window, bit into a half-peeled banana and watched without comment.

"Don't you want to know what I'm doing?" Adele asked. It was her intent to elicit some kind of a response from the agent if she had to eat a live chinchilla to do it.

"Uhn?" Agent Light said staring at Adele, studying her, though her thoughts were wandering.

"Detective Ritmann called to say Agent Onorato might use me in the operation this afternoon."

Olivia Light kept on chewing without so much as a blink.

"He's going to be calling here in a minute. I thought I'd put together a few disguises—you know, in case."

"Uh-huh."

"Do you think they'd let me carry my gun?"

Olivia hesitated, frowned, shook her head, and kept on chewing. "Uhn."

Adele stared at the woman and sat down looking grave. "Olivia, this is none of my business, but aren't you worried about eating bananas?"

Olivia stopped chewing, looked at the half-eaten banana and then at her. "What's wrong with bananas?"

Adele detected a quarter note of indignation. It was a

start. "Oh, you know—that whole business about the South African bone worms."

Olivia resumed chewing, but Adele noted she was inspecting her banana. "What bone worms?"

"We've had about sixty-five patients admitted with it so far this week, but we only lost forty-one, so things are improving."

Agent Light swallowed hard. "Lost forty-one?" she asked. "You mean they—?"

"Uh-huh," Adele said. "It's got the scientists stumped. All they know so far is that the worms originate in the feces of the Umfolozi blue-tail monkey. Transference of the larvae takes place when the monkeys handle the bananas. The larvae bore through the peels and get into the banana core where they multiply by the trillions. Then, of course, the bananas are harvested and sent to America, and we eat them and the larvae get transferred into the host bodies and . . ." Adele shuddered. "Well, you know the rest."

Olivia put down the banana. "Uhn, what rest?"

"The bone bore part," Adele said. "You know—how they bore their way through the bones to get to the marrow? They say as few as seven hundred can eat through the femur of an adult male inside of two days. And, my God, once they're loose in the bloodstream? Ugh! There goes all the cartilage as well."

Agent Light got up abruptly and washed her hands and face at the sink. When she sat down again, she was pale. "What happens then?"

"Ever seen a human being without a skeleton?" Adele asked. "I had one expire on me the other morning—had to scoop the body out of the bed—what a mess."

It was while Agent Light was out back dumping her bananas in the garbage that the phone rang.

Hands folded, thumbs worrying each other, Adele waited for Special Agent in Charge Onorato to come up with the Ellsworth file.

He found the folder, opened it and began reciting. "Your

name is Beth Ellsworth. Your birthday is June ninth. You're thirty-seven, unmarried. You graduated Berkeley ten years ago with an MBA. You lived the first eighteen years of your life in Atlanta, Georgia, then seven years in Berkeley, and for the last twelve you've lived in Modesto. You smoke a pack of Winstons a day to keep your weight down." He left off to dig in his jacket pocket and brought out a half a pack of the cigarettes. He handed them to her across the table.

"You work as a sales rep for . . ." He smiled. "This is perfect: Hewlett-Packard medical equipment division selling cardiac monitors. You had breast implants inserted one month ago today. You paid five hundred dollars for them."

"How many cc's?" Adele asked.

"Three hundred," he said, giving no indication of how impressed he was that she'd thought to ask. "You live alone, and you travel a lot. HP sent you to Berlin a month ago for a world conference on the latest in medical equipment. You were also given a week's vacation. During the conference, you met a German woman in the bar of your hotel who introduced herself as Dr. Ritter, a plastic surgeon. During the course of conversation you told her you'd always wanted implants, and she offered to do them for five hundred dollars and a promise that follow-up could be done in San Francisco free of charge by one Dr. English.

"You called the number you were given last Tuesday and told the woman who answered that you were having redness and itching of your right breast and right buttock. You have an appointment with Dr. English at two."

He slid a packet of eight-by-ten glossy photos over to her side of the table. "Think you can get close to this?"

Adele studied the real Beth Ellsworth carefully, mentally inventoried what she had in common with her, and nodded. Rounded cheeks, short strawberry blond hair, freckles, light blue eyes. In several of the photos the woman wore large gold hoop earrings and bright red lipstick. Her choice of clothing was consistent with what Adele and Cynthia called Jaunty Trampwear: high-heeled ankle boots, tight jeans, and sexy, short-waisted jackets or blouses tied under her breasts. In several of the photos she wore a baseball cap slung backwards.

"Tim said you'd be wiring me?"

From his inside pocket he brought out a clear plastic box. Set into the foam was a pair of dangling earrings: black shiny disks hanging from delicate silver chains. He examined the back of each one, and held one out, pointing to a tiny silver dot on the back. "This is a wireless mike. Try not to knock it around too much."

He opened his briefcase and took out a ball cap wrapped in tissue paper. Woven on the front was an intricate design of ocean waves and a dolphin juggling five balls of different colors. "We also have you fixed up with a miniature camera we call a lipstick cam," he said. He turned the cap inside out and pulled up a flap to reveal a small compartment holding a thin tube. The lens was pushed up against one of the round pieces of colored see-through mesh that made up the juggled balls.

"I'll be watching the video monitor and listening in the entire time. All the backup people will be listening in as well. After we know you're in the building, Groat and I will be right on your tail. We'll make base in an office on the first floor right below you watching everything on the screen and listening to every word. There'll be people covering the rest of the building inside and out." He pushed his chair back with a squeak. "We'll set up a couple of signals that you'll give at specific times. As soon as you give the second signal, lie low and stay put until after the bust."

Without another word, he led her to a room that had a round wall mirror with makeup lights around it. There were several chairs and a low counter. Her three boxes had been placed at one end of the counter.

"How long do I have?"

"Frankly, Ms. Monsarrat," Onorato said, "we're seriously hurting for time, so the sooner you can do your thing, the sooner we can get this operation rolling."

The second she was alone, anxiety snakes began slithering around her stomach and up her esophagus. She was playing in the big leagues against people who would just as soon slit her throat as look at her. Her life would depend in part on how good her disguise was.

She opened the boxes, pulled out a couple of outfits, and hung them on the portable clothes rack set up at the end of the room. Sliding the photographs into the mirror clips, she studied them while pinning her hair close to her head and pulling on a stocking cap.

A shoebox marked FILLERS contained a dozen or more samples of thin silicone gel pads that she'd picked up at a medical supplies trade fair. She chose two without advertising on them to fill out her cheeks. A heavy application of fair foundation over face, neck, and chest created the background for sprinkles of freckles. Next, she lightened her lashes and brows with a coating of glycerin and powder, and finished with blue eyeshadow and bright red lipstick. The strawberry blond shag wig went on next, then she inserted the light blue contact lenses. With the aid of a Wonderbra and the silicone enhancers Cynthia had given her, cleavage spilled out from the opening of the plaid flannel shirt that was tied under her breasts. A pair of tight black jeans and black heels finished the look.

Adele pressed on the last inch-long dragon-lady fire-engine-red fingernail, turned her back to the mirror, and closed her eyes. When she turned again, the image staring at her from the mirror so closely resembled Beth Ellsworth, it startled her. Watching herself carefully, Adele rehearsed the woman's smile and the way she held her shoulders and hands. "Hi, do you come here often?" she asked the woman in the mirror, changing her normally low voice to a higher register, and her unplaceable accent to Georgia Peachian.

Adele shifted to her left. "Only during sting operations. It's a strange place, don't you think?"

"Uh-huh." She turned to her right. "What's your name?"

"Beth Ellsworth, and yours?"

"Beth Ellsworth. Isn't that quaint?"

"Hey, nice cleavage you've got there, Beth, even though they are hanging a little uneven . . ."

Handling her phony augmented breasts the same way she'd

seen Dawn Joy handle hers—that is to say, like priceless mu-
seum pieces—Adele adjusted them so they were level. "So,
what do you do for a living and where did you come from?"

"I'm a—" Adele had to think for a second. "—a medical
equipment rep for HP. I moved to Modesto from Atlanta almost twelve years ago."

"I'm thirty-seven. How about you?"

"The same. When's your birthday?"

"The same as yours! June ninth—I'm a Gemini."

"Well, shut my mouth, a double personality! Are you
married?"

"Nope."

"Me either. Where'd you have your udders done?"

"Berlin by Dr. Ritter. And you?"

"The same." She practiced the smile in the photos. "Would
you like some lung cancer?"

Adele gave an exaggerated smile that bordered on a grimace and pulled out the half-empty package of Winstons from
her blouse pocket. Using the stage method of lighting a cigarette without inhaling, she lit up then walked back and forth in
front of the mirror, working on the slight slump of the shoulders. On the last turn, she sailed through the door and down
the hallway past Agents Onorato and Groat. At the end of the
hall she turned and took a convincing drag on her cigarette.

"Excuse me, but do y'all know where I could find Ms.
Monsarrat?"

Both men gaped.

"Well?" Adele said in Beth Ellsworth's voice and accent.
"What do y'all think?"

The agents looked at each other then back at her. Doug
Groat crossed his arms and shook his head, pinching in the
corners of his smile. "Okay, you win."

Onorato, in an uncharacteristic moment of frivolity, let out
a long low whistle and made the thumbs-up sign.

"The trigger or bust signal . . ." Agent Groat paused and
fought back a smile. ". . . no pun intended, is your parachute.
Usually we have a couple of standard phrases we use here.

'It's Miller time' is one and the other is . . ." He blushed. "Nothing you'd be wanting to repeat to anyone, so why don't you come up with a phrase."

"Actually," Onorato said, "I want two signals."

Groat looked at him, interested.

"The first one I want you to give just before they examine you—or, when you feel things getting tight. Say, 'Before we go any further, I have to use the bathroom.' "

"Before we go any further, I have to use the bathroom," Groat and Adele repeated in unison.

"Once you're locked in the bathroom, I want another signal," Onorato said. "As soon as we hear that, we come in."

"How about if I start singing 'Zip-a-Dee-Doo-Dah'?" Adele asked, slipping on the minicorder earring.

"It's original," Onorato said.

"This is the one thing you absolutely cannot screw up on," Groat said. "Use those exact words. If you say, 'I have to pee' or 'I gotta use the potty'—we won't take the alert. It has to be exactly 'Before we go any further, I have to use the bathroom.' And make sure you've got the right song. If you start singing the theme to *Gone with the Wind*, we won't know what the hell is up."

"You will be driving Ms. Ellsworth's Honda Civic hatchback to the appointment," Onorato said. "Can you handle a stick shift?"

Adele gave him a look, not bothering to grace the question with an answer.

"Doug and I will be right behind you. Take the route we discussed, and when you get to the Army Street address, we'll have an agent in a red Plymouth Voyager parked in front of the building. As soon as they see you, they'll pull out. You pull into that spot, then go in the front door of the building. Take the stairs to the second floor and turn left. Two-twelve is about halfway down the hall on your left.

"And remember: as soon as you give the signal, stay in the bathroom and keep the door locked. Don't come out until I give you the okay. Okay?"

Adele nodded. "Can I carry my gun in my purse?"

"No!" the two men said in unison. "It's too much of a liability," said Groat. "We wouldn't even let one of our own agents carry in a gun."

"What happens if something goes wrong?" Adele asked.

"Like what?" Groat asked.

"Like if they recognize me, or if they try to kill me outright, without any preliminaries."

"In that case," said Corey, "I'd suggest you keep your wits about you, think fast, and sing at the top of your lungs."

Her bowels locked up and bucked a few times about midspan of the Golden Gate—right around the same time her legs started shaking. "What the hell am I doing?"

Shit, Adele, this isn't anything you haven't done before, Skip Langdon said from the backseat.

Quite so, dear, said Miss Marple, patting her hand. *You've been in tighter spots than this. Why, look at just last week. The FBI won't let anything happen to you. Take some deep breaths and let them out. Why don't you chant something soothing like "I won't worry. I will pull this off smoothly."*

Adele tried it a few times, then glanced in the rearview mirror, hoping that the agents couldn't see her talking to herself. For as nervous as she was, she didn't want them reconsidering their decision at the last minute, thinking she was off her tracks.

The toll taker resembled someone who was really bummed out over the outcome of his sex-change operation. As Adele rolled up, she/he grumbled and yanked the three dollars from her hand.

"How do you do?" Adele gave a bright, genuine smile. "My name is Beth Ellsworth and I think your surgery came out beautifully. Don't y'all worry now. It'll get better as soon as the hormones kick in."

To jettison the physical nervousness, she sped down the Park Presidio exit and practiced singing "Zip-a-Dee-Doo-Dah" at the top of her lungs.

* * *

Three cars behind the blue Honda, Agents Onorato and Groat listened to Adele chatting and singing to herself with almost as much enjoyment as they had listened to her talking to her alter ego in the changing room.

Groat looked at Onorato, doubt pinching his features. "And you really believe this woman is mentally stable?"

"Hell no," chuckled Onorato. "Considering what she's about to do, mental stability is the last fucking thing she needs."

Adele turned onto Army Street and slowed, ostensibly to look for parking. In the middle of the block, a man approached a red Voyager, got in, and pulled out. The Honda slipped into the vacated space. Taking another deep breath, she checked herself in the mirror, and exhaled.

"I won't worry," she whispered. "I will pull this off smoothly."

A walking-a-tightrope-over-the-Grand Canyon-without-a-safety-net feeling washed over her, knocked her around for a few seconds, then subsided and dried up. She hunched her shoulders forward and marched up the steps and into the building.

On the other side of the revolving door she spotted Tim dressed in the khaki-colored work uniform of an elevator maintenance service person. Staring straight ahead, she stepped in front of him, paused long enough to check her watch, and walked in the direction of the stairs.

In the blue Ford parked in the lot across the street, Onorato put down the binoculars and spoke into his radio. "Okay everybody, she's inside the building." He covered his mike and turned to Groat, chuckling. "Ritmann looked right at her and never saw her."

Adele hesitated at the office door, took her last deep breath, and walked into the empty waiting room. Behind the counter, dressed in a white lab coat, Laila Clemmons raised her eyebrows inquiringly, as if she were not expected. The gesture momentarily unsettled her.

"Hi, I'm Beth Ellsworth. I have an appointment with Dr. English at two?"

Mrs. Clemmons gave her a warm smile and came around the counter. She wore a name tag that read L. DANIELS, R.N. "Oh yes, Ms. Ellsworth, we've been waiting for you. I'm afraid we have to move to another office. The carpet cleaners are coming this afternoon, so Dr. English will see you downstairs in room one-fourteen instead."

Adele was mentally chanting like crazy, trying not to panic. "We're moving to room one-fourteen—you mean room one-fourteen downstairs?" she repeated clearly.

Mrs. Clemmons nodded and ushered her back into the hallway. A woman in a lab coat and a man with a briefcase passed them. Next to the elevators, on a wooden bench, sat an older man with a cane. Adele wondered how many of them were agents. "Okay," she said, overly loud and cheerful. "Off we go to room one-fourteen, then."

Still flushed about the neck and cheeks, Timothy Ritmann stood next to Onorato watching the small TV screen that was showing images of the hallway. Laila Clemmons, a man with a briefcase, and an old guy sitting in front of the elevators were plainly visible.

The knowledge that Adele had stood less than twenty-four inches from him and he had not recognized her first embarrassed, then pleased him. She would never let him live it down, no matter how many times he beat her at Scrabble.

Corey spoke into his mike: "You heard the lady, everybody. They're shifting to room one-fourteen. Everybody go to plan two. Who do we have down here right now?"

He put a finger to his earpiece and listened for a minute, then asked, "Can we buy a couple of minutes by holding the elevator?" He waited. "Well, okay, but see what you can do. Hubert and Martin, keep your positions near two-twelve. I want it covered just in case they decide to play musical offices."

Mrs. Clemmons pressed the down button as Adele started for the stairwell. The prospect of being alone with Mrs.

Clemmons in an elevator made her break out into a sweat. "I'm claustrophobic," Adele called over her shoulder. "I'll take the stairs and meet you down there."

Mrs. Clemmons's expression turned disapproving. "You should really come with me so you don't get lost. Surely you can stand it for a few seconds, huh?"

Adele felt the situation through and changed course. If she insisted on taking the stairs, it might cause suspicion. She smiled and shrugged good-naturedly. "You're right. I should try to get over it one of these days."

When the elevator arrived, the old man with the cane got to his feet with difficulty and hobbled in slow motion after them, shouting, "Hold that car!" in a voice as feeble as his legs.

Adele saw the hearing aid tucked into his left ear and decided he was an agent purposely trying to delay the car, "buying seconds" as Kitch used to say.

"We going down?" the man asked Mrs. Clemmons as soon as the door closed.

Laila Clemmons gave a curt nod.

"Are you going to the lobby or the first floor?" he asked.

"We are going to the first floor." Mrs. Clemmons deliberately moved a step away from him. "Are you going to the lobby?"

"What'd you say?" the old man said, holding his ear. "I don't hear so good."

"Are you going to the lobby?" Mrs. Clemmons repeated impatiently.

"Eh?" The man stepped closer, stumbled over his own cane, and grabbed for Adele's arm. As he did so, he pressed his fingers into her flesh twice in what she interpreted as a deliberate signal.

In an instant, all her apprehensions disappeared. Miss Marple was right: the FBI was behind her all the way, even in the elevator. She guessed they'd have agents covering her from every angle.

He righted himself with his cane. "Lobby! I want the lobby!"

Mrs. Clemmons pressed the button for the lobby just as the

door opened on to the first floor. As it did, the old man stepped in front of them, got his cane tip stuck in the crack between the elevator and the floor, and wrestled with it, successfully blocking Mrs. Clemmons's way.

"This is not the lobby!" Mrs. Clemmons shouted in a shrill, raised voice, trying to push around him. The rubber tip came free of the crack and swung out between Mrs. Clemmons's ankles. He jerked it back toward himself, causing her to trip and stumble into him.

"What are you doing?" She shoved him away. The elevator doors started to close, hit her in the back, and knocked her into him for a second time.

"I declare!" Adele said, stepping around them. "I think it would have been a whole lot faster if we'd taken the stairs."

Mrs. Clemmons disentangled herself from the old man again and practically leapt into the hall. "This way," she said, walking in front of Adele.

Without windows at each end, the first floor hall was much darker than the second floor. Several of the fluorescent lights were broken, and the tiles were a dark brown. Room one-fourteen turned out to be at the end of the hall next to the freight elevator.

Of course, Adele thought. *Freight elevators and dumb-waiters—the best methods for body disposal.*

Onorato laughed despite the intensity of the situation and pressed his earpiece.

"Isn't the old guy one of yours?" Tim asked.

Onorato shook his head. "About the only one in there who isn't, but he did a superb job."

Nurse Daniels handed Adele a patient gown. "When did you have this done?"

"One month ago today," Adele recited, laying on the Georgia accent. "Dr. Ritter said if I had any problems I should see Dr. English right away."

"And how long has it been since you noticed the rash?"

"Well, like I told you last Tuesday when I made the appointment, it's not really a rash, but it itches right"—Adele held her right breast like a melon and shifted it higher— "right around here and here." She pointed in the general direction of her nipple then patted the outer quadrant of her right buttock.

Laila Clemmons frowned and shook her head. "That doesn't sound good. We might have to treat you for an infection."

"You mean with antibiotics?"

"Yes. We will give you a shot and send you home with pills to take. Please remove your clothes and I will have Dr. English and his assistant come in to examine you."

"His assistant?" Adele asked. "Why does he need an assistant? I thought this was just going to be an examination."

"It is, of course, but Dr. English sometimes has an intern come from University of California to assist him with the patients. You won't mind, will you?"

"Well, I . . ."

Somewhere close by, a door closed. "Hurry now," the woman said. "The doctor is here and he does not like to be behind in his schedule. He has many patients to see this afternoon."

Adele took the johnny and slipped off her shoes. Without thinking, she began humming the old Joe Cocker tune "You Can Leave Your Hat On" as she shuffled to the dressing room.

Recognizing the tune at once, Corey laughed. "It takes a special woman who can have a sense of humor in the face of danger," he said, slipping into his jacket. "It's almost time to go." At the door he turned to Timothy. "You okay with this, Ritmann?"

"Why wouldn't I be?" Tim's light blue gaze frosted over.

Agent Onorato shook his head. "Don't take it personally, Tim, but you've got some kind of emotional investment in this woman."

"I'm fine with this, Corey. I'm the one who volunteered her, remember?"

"Okay," Onorato said and turned his attention back to the screen.

* * *

She sat on the cold exam table and poufed up the gown so that the loss of three cup sizes wouldn't be so noticeable. If any of them said anything about the baseball cap, she'd just say she had to wear it at all times for religious reasons.

Nurse Daniels stepped into the room and, without looking at her, began setting up a tray of instruments just out of her range of vision. Adele heard the cracking of a medicine vial and glanced around in time to see Laila pierce the rubber top of the vial with a syringe and draw up some clear liquid.

Pavulon, she thought. *Curare. They'll paralyze me first then kill me . . . try to kill me.* "Is that the antibiotics you're drawing up?" Adele said, wanting to announce to whoever was listening that they were getting ready to rock and roll.

Before the woman could answer, Amar came in wearing a pristine white lab coat. He looked her over—sizing her up, she thought, for usable parts. From the way he was looking at her throat, she wondered if he was going to practice up on his thoracotomies.

"You are having problems with the new implants?" He reached for the ties at the back of her gown.

She pulled away. "Yes, I'm itching a lot around the outside of my right breast and also on my buttock where Dr. Ritter gave me the shot. Say, listen, before we go on, I need to —I need to . . ."

Overwhelming panic caused her breath to pull up short and stop. She'd forgotten the words of the signal.

"It was a long drive, I have to pee?"

No.

"I have to go to the bathroom now?"

No.

"What I mean is, well, I . . ." she began.

Was it "must" or "have to"?

". . . you know, use the bathroom?"

Odd expressions crossed both their faces as they stared at her. She wracked her brain for the words, but all she could remember was what Agent Groat said about using exact words for the signals.

*　*　*

"She forgot the trigger signal," Onorato said. The tension in his voice was building.

"Shit!" Groat said. "I say we give her three more minutes and go in."

Onorato shook his head. "She's not stupid, Doug. I think she saw Askeri, momentarily panicked, and forgot the words. She wouldn't be the first person who fucked up on a signal."

"Shhh." Groat held up a hand. "Listen."

"I'm sorry," Adele said. "I lost my train of thought there for a second. What I was going to say was that before we go any further, I—"

Was it "must" or "have to"?

". . . have to use the bathroom."

Amar gave her a disgusted look. "Can't you hold it?"

Adele shook her head, looking sweet and innocently flustered. "I'm sorry. I had two cups of coffee before I left the house and it was a long drive. Traffic was backed up forever and, well, you know what that can do to a girl's bladder."

Amar threw up his hands and shot Laila a look so derisive and full of condescension, Adele wanted to congratulate him on achieving the state of medical deityhood.

"Hurry," Laila snapped. "The doctor does not like to be kept waiting."

Adele hopped off the table holding the gown closed in the back and took two steps toward the door.

From behind, Laila grabbed her shoulders. Adele's arms shot up then out as she dropped into a protective crouch.

Onorato was speaking into his radio, watching the video screen. "Okay. The minute the skinny lady sings 'Zip-a-Dee-Doo-Dah,' go in. I don't want any civilians hurt. I want at least . . ."

He went silent and pressed the earpiece farther into his ear. "What the shit is this?"

Both grossly unhappy, Groat and Onorato bent toward the snowy screen and listened to the buzz of nothingness.

* * *

Laila Clemmons and Amar stared at her. The surprise on their faces dissolved into suspicion.

"God!" Adele said, clutching her gown. "Please don't *ever* do that again! I—" she said, lowering her eyes, "I was once raped by a man who grabbed me from behind like that. I guess I'm still jumpy."

"Oh, I am so sorry!" Laila said, a note of genuine apology in her voice. She stepped forward to help Adele to her feet and stepped squarely on the baseball cap. "I was just going to guide you to the bathroom. It is two doors past the dressing room on the right."

Adele picked up the cap without a hint of the alarm burning in her temples and casually padded down the cold linoleum floor to the bathroom. Laila followed close behind.

She closed the door with a smile, imagining the woman would stay outside with her ear pressed to the door. Filling a Dixie cup with water, she held it seat level and poured it slowly back into the toilet. She mentally counted out the right amount of time, then flushed. While the water ran, she examined the lipstick cam inside the cap and began singing: "Zip-a-dee-doo-dah, zip-a-dee-ay. My oh my, what a wonderful day . . ." Her fingers walked to her right earring, did a dance around the end of the silver chain where the mike was supposed to be—and wasn't. She stopped singing. If there was anything left in her adrenals, it dumped every drop into her system. She pulled the earring from her ear and gaped, unable to believe the mike was gone.

Frantically, she searched the gown and the floor of the bathroom. *The toilet? Christ on a bike, did it fall into the toilet and get flushed?*

Her voice quivered. To cover it, she sang louder.

"Plenty of sunshine coming my . . ."

Out in the hall, she could hear Amar and Laila whispering angrily in Arabic. From the cadence of their sentences, she imagined that Amar was telling Laila that something did not feel right and they needed to get on with it—break down the door and kill the American whore.

She waited, looking at her watch and trying to think.

Fifteen seconds later, Laila Clemmons banged on the bathroom door. "Ms. Ellsworth? You need to come out now, we must get on with this. Doctor is waiting."

Adele opened the door and gave her murderers a pleasant smile.

"What the fuck is going on?" Tim asked, his eyes darting back and forth from the blank monitor to the agents' faces.

Onorato stared at the screen, his jaw working. "I can't hear anything."

"Something's gone haywire," Groat said.

"Shit!" Onorato said after a few seconds. "What the fuck happened?"

"Fuck it, Corey, I say we go in now," Groat said.

"Two more minutes," Onorato said, looking at his watch.

"Two more minutes, Onorato," Timothy said, his eyes turned to ice, "and she could be dead."

On the way to the exam table, her eyes swept the room, specifically the area where she fell into her crouch. Under a metal cabinet, she saw the black disk and mentally sighed in relief. She sent a prayer to Buddha that it was still working.

Stepping up, she clapped her hands and broke into song. "Zip-a-dee-doo-dah!" she sang as loud as she dared. "And a zip-a-dee-ay! My, oh my, what a beautiful day!"

Amar put a hand on her shoulder. "Have you gone mad? Be quiet!" he hissed as he untied her gown again. "This is an office, not a karaoke bar!"

Behind her, Adele could feel Nurse Daniels standing close, waiting to give her her eternal "antibiotic."

Amar tugged at her gown. Before it could fall away from her breasts, she grabbed it. "I'm sorry," Adele said, getting up again. "This was a mistake. I—I'm very modest and I would rather not—"

Nurse Daniels stepped in front of her, holding the syringe. "I need to give your antibiotics now. If you would please . . ."

The woman's eyes went wide as they stared at Adele's throat. Automatically, Adele's hand followed the gaze. Her

fingers touched her garnet pendant, the one that Mrs. Clemmons had admired—the one she forgot to remove in her
haste.

Projected on her mind screen, Kitch sat in his swivel chair,
concern etched into the lines of his frown. *You've done it
again, Adele. You forgot that it's the little fuckups that get you
killed.*

Laila yanked off her wig. Both she and Amar stared in
stunned disbelief then Laila screamed something in Arabic.
In an instant Saad burst into the room and rushed toward her,
knife at the ready.

"Kill her!" Laila hissed. "Kill her now!"

Adele was, for the umpteenth time, grateful for having married a Green Beret who insisted on teaching her everything
he knew. If she survived, she promised she'd send Gavin a
thank-you card and perhaps a pair of size 12 pumps and some
queen-sized black pantyhose to go with his black miniskirts.

She pulled her legs up and kicked before they knew what
she was doing. Her right foot caught Amar in the neck, the
left hit Laila's shoulder, spinning her around in a complete
circle. Saad made a grab for her leg and jerked her off the
table. The raw metal edge of the step gouged the thin flesh
over her vertebrae. The shock of pain took her breath away as
she rolled off to the floor.

Standing over her, Saad raised the knife above her throat. It
was his smile, snide and confident, that caused her to react as
violently as she did. With an indignant scream, she brought
her knee up and caught him square in the testicles. He gasped
and collapsed in on himself, but did not drop the knife.

With her other foot she kicked again, connecting with his
abdomen and knocking him over. In a movement that was
both awkward and ineffectual, Amar lunged. Adele rolled, hit
the wall, and slid to the cabinet. Her hand closed around the
disk and brought it to her mouth. It was, she felt, an appropriate time to scream loud enough for people on the next block
to hear.

"ZIP-A-DEE-FUCKING-DOO-DAH . . ."

Six FBI agents in full assault gear burst into the room,

guns drawn, shouting for everyone to get down on the floor.
Within seconds, Amar, Saad, and Laila were flipped onto
their stomachs and handcuffed. From out in the hall came the
sound of doors slamming and shouts. Above the melee Fahad
Al-Yassari demanded he be told what was going on.

On her feet, Adele sidestepped into the hall.

Corey Onorato stood ten feet away, a 9 mm Glock held in
one hand. His other arm shot out, a finger pointed at her like a
knife. "Freeze right there!" he shouted. "Don't fucking move
until I tell you to." He turned his attention back to the room in
front of him.

When he finally moved toward her, she could see from his
narrowed, steely eyes that he was in no mood for anything
nice and friendly.

"What the fuck happened, Monsarrat?" His voice, like his
expression, was icy.

Words poured out. "Laila grabbed me from behind as I was
walking to the bathroom. I dropped, the cap came off, and she
stepped on it. The mike must have come off at the same time
and rolled under the cabinet. I didn't realize it until I got into
the bathroom. They were right on me the whole time. I stalled
as long as I could then went back to the exam room." Sheep-
ishly she added, "You didn't hear me singing?"

The agent looked at her then let out a breath. "Shit. You
gave us all heart attacks."

"That's a nurse for you," Adele said dryly. "Always trying
to drum up a little extra business."

SEVENTEEN

GRACE CATHEDRAL WAS EMPTY SAVE FOR AN EL-derly woman bent over her rosary in the front pew. Cynthia had instigated the trip, calling it a holy pilgrimage made in the wake of her grief. Since her last appointment with Jeffrey Lavine, her miscarriage had become "The Tragedy," and the lost fetus "Little Ernesto."

In the back of the cathedral, at the base of the baptismal font, Adele removed her shoes in preparation for walking the Char-tres Labyrinth—a large floor tapestry into which was woven an intricate labyrinth in the lightest shades of gray-lavender.

They entered the path at the beginning, each bent on shed-ding extraneous thoughts and feelings that might inhibit the meditative journey.

"Jeffrey called it 'multiple partnorgasms,'" Cynthia said, breaking the silence after only six minutes. She had a knack for beginning conversations in the middle of a thought.

Adele kept her eyes on her feet and continued to take the jour-ney one step at a time. She'd been meditating on her father and the day he taught her how to ride a bicycle. "Partnorgasms?"

"Yeah. He said that the stress of losing Little Ernesto trig-gered a psyche regression involving the willingness to let myself love and be loved, and mostly to trust that attachments would last and I wouldn't be hurt. When The Tragedy hap-pened, all my hopes of having a normal life crumbled and I returned to acting out by having multiple sexual partners and telling Ryme to leave."

"Psychobabble," Adele said. "What'd he really say?"

"Loosely translated, it means that somewhere early on I

learned that it was a whole lot more fun and much safer just to go for gratification as long as I'm in control."

"Are you going to stick with the therapy?"

Cynthia took a tight turn too fast and wobbled. Adele reached out and steadied her.

"Nah. I think I've got it. I mean, I feel better now. I think if I can just learn the positive hair sign, I'll be okay."

"What the hell is the positive hair sign?"

"Oh, well, Jeff told me that in shrink school, the students learn that if the hair on the back of their neck stands up while they're interviewing somebody, then they know that person is a super bad psychotic dude or dudette. I've got to learn that trick. It might come in handy when I pick my men." Cynthia sighed. "In any case, I can't afford to keep going—you know, with managed care, and the insurance only paying twenty dollars a visit."

"No one works through something like this in four sessions. I'm sure it feels like you have, but it's all cognitive at this point. Ask Jeff if you can work out a trade. Offer to answer his phones or wash his car or something."

"I don't know." Cynthia teared up. "Every time I go to him, everything hurts all over again. It isn't something I love doing, you know?"

Adele reached over and pushed back a few strands of hair that had fallen across Cynthia's face. "Do you know why I love you, Cynthia?"

The younger woman wiped her face on her sleeve and stared at Adele for several moments. "Yes, because I'm a stray with bizarre thought patterns that are actually farther out in left field than yours."

"I love you," Adele resumed, "because you are so vulnerable and strong at the same time. And, because when you live, you live big. You love big, you enjoy big, you hurt big—everything is to the limit. It takes courage to do that." Timothy crossed her mind. "I wish I were that brave."

Cynthia snorted. "Oh, right. You go after the most dangerous people in the world without twisting an underarm hair, and you think you're not brave?"

"That's a different kind of bravery," Adele said, walking again. "Have you seen Ryme?"

"Yeah. No. Well, sort of. We've been talking on the phone. He's staying with Dr. Ravens until I—we decide what we want to do. I miss him, but I'm still not sure I want to live with him again. Anyway, Jeff said restraint might be the best thing right now."

In silence, they covered a few more turns of the maze. Adele's thoughts again drifted back to her father and a memory of his wheezy laughter over her lame, homemade knock-knock jokes.

"Ryme said Dr. Ravens likes you a lot," Cynthia said without preamble.

"That sounds like something a child would say."

"His exact words were that Ravens would like to get to know you." Cynthia hesitated. "And he said something else about you mowing his lawn? You interested?"

"I wouldn't mind getting to know him." Adele said, "He seems interesting, but . . ."

Cynthia stopped. "God, I'll bet you two would make great-looking babies. And, you know, I think you'd balance each other. I mean, you're both smart with an inclination toward all that woo-woo spiritual stuff, and he's so—"

"Stop," Adele warned. "Don't even go there. That's not the kind of interest I'm talking about. I'd like to get to know him as a person, and that's all."

"Okay, okay." Cynthia hunched her shoulders. "Sorry. I just want you to get married and have children so I can live a normal life vicariously—but big."

They went on walking, sometimes paralleling each other, sometimes yards apart. Adele was reliving a memory of her father: The day he died, he'd been reading aloud from one of her fairytale books. She was lying on the floor next to his chair, letting her imagination project the vivid scenes onto the ceiling. He'd stopped in the middle of sentence, and when Adele looked up, he was wearing the most pained expression, as if he'd been given the saddest news in the world—which, of course, he had.

"What did you name the kitten?" Cynthia asked.

Adele gave a one-shouldered shrug. "We're not a hundred

percent sure yet. Some days he's Pumpkin, others he's the Buddha Man. Nelson wants to name him Wayne."

Cynthia stared thoughtfully at the back of Adele's head, considering the psychiatric implications of Adele's alleged communication with Nelson. "Why Wayne?"

Adele shrugged. "He says he likes it."

"Oh." Cynthia let that sink in, then, "Have you heard from Daisy since the British Heavyweight Championships took place on Ward Eight?"

They paused to laugh. After her release from Pacific Medical Center, but before her motel incarceration, Daisy had stopped in at Ward 8 to say hello. The moment Daisy stepped foot on the ward and she and Grace got a load of each other, their lips had curled back to reveal their fangs. Nasty words had shot back and forth like so many clay pigeons at a skeet shoot.

By the time Adele and Skip broke up the verbal battle, both women had regressed to slinging such Britishisms as "Up your duff," and "fat slag" and "bloody slapper" and something about a "wanker"—not that any of the Americans would admit to knowing what that meant.

"I went by her house after work yesterday," Adele said. "She was moaning and groaning about being lonely and bored, so I told her I thought she had too much time on her hands and that she needed to volunteer somewhere where she could be of use. I should have kept my mouth shut. Now she wants to be a volunteer in ER. I got the feeling she equated it to signing up for the Women's Voluntary Service."

"Oh God," Cynthia groaned. "They'll have to hide the rubbing alcohol."

"Yeah, not to mention the male patients. I tried to steer her to some singles events: line dancing, British singles support groups, Clueless Women/Dumb Choices workshops—whatever works."

The path was growing tighter as they drew closer to the middle.

"What's the latest on the Black Tide people?" Cynthia asked.

"Kadeja still hasn't been apprehended, and the rest are being held at San Francisco City Jail until after the grand jury indictment. None of them have spilled a word. All they'll say is that whatever they've done was for the good of their people."

They reached the center of the labyrinth. For a time they both stared at their toes: Adele's, long, narrow, and callused; Cynthia's two full sizes wider and the nails painted pearlescent green. It seemed to sum up who they were as individuals.

"I think you need some shiny green nail polish in your life, Adele," Cynthia said, then added in the same breath, "How's Timothy?"

Adele's breath eased out in a long stream. "We've graduated from nontoxic cookware to sauté. Next we'll be learning about combinations of spices and useful kitchen gadgets."

Cynthia gave Adele's arm a playful pinch. "Evasion does not become you, Del. Now take me, for instance—I use evasion as a seduction tool. Men love it."

Adele rolled her eyes. "Your idea of evasion, Cyn, is not to unzip the guy's fly and grab his balls until after you've slept with him four or five times."

At the front of the church, the older woman was genuflecting and having a hard time getting her joints to obey. The crack of her knee echoed throughout the cathedral.

"This is the way I see it," Adele said without introduction, "the path to the center of the labyrinth is the way of our life from birth to present. The center is the present and who we are at this moment. The way back is for the contemplation of the rest of our lives until we're at the end—which, of course, is actually the beginning, because as soon as we die, we're spit back into the world to do the turns all over again, only with more of our soul present."

"Jeez," Cynthia said in a monotone. "I think I'll go hang myself. All that spitting and turning—it's too depressing."

The woman approached them, still clutching her rosary beads. Up close, she appeared to be in her late sixties. Her graying hair was pulled back into a braided bun at the nape of her neck. She had one of those long-suffering faces so common to Catholics who believed, hook, line, and sinker, in guilt and everlasting damnation: say five Hail Marys and leave 20 percent of your income at the door on your way out.

"This does not belong in the house of God," the woman said, pointing at the rug. "It belongs in a playground."

"This is an Episcopal church," Adele said, trying to remember how comforting a severely strict, narrow-viewed religion was to some. "This is where God comes on Her days off to relax and maybe act like a kid Herself."

"Look at it this way," Cynthia piped up when the woman failed to grasp the concept. "It's tiring taking care of all those requests. Day in, day out: Oh God, I need a new car; oh God, let me have a good bowel movement; oh God, please don't let them blow up the world; oh God, please make Monica Lewinsky disappear. You know what I'm saying? This poor bastard— and, I mean that in the literal sense, of course—has to work Herself to the bone just to . . ."

The woman's face was turning stony.

"Everybody has to get their God fix in a different way, you know?" Adele offered gently. "God is supposed to be in everything: this nice rug here, your prayer beads, my dog. All things living and not have an element of the divine."

She paused as a young couple with a baby walked by and smiled shyly. The baby waved, its chubby fingers opening and closing in the way of children.

"See?" Adele said, waving back. "Here's God now."

Ward 8 was, for the time being, back to normal, which is to say it had returned to chaos. The administration's desire for an increase in annual compensation and perks for themselves had resulted in a 15 percent cutback of the nursing staff and increased patient loads for the nurses who'd survived the cuts. Mortality rates were beginning to climb again, although the facts had been withheld from the public.

The head nurses were told to continue the witch-hunt, firing staff at the least infraction of the rules. And since the rules had been set in a time of safe and thorough care—a time that would never come again—rules were broken a lot.

Thomas Edison Penn and Walter Minka were both readmitted on the same day. Five days later, they were both discharged—Mr. Penn to his mood-lit mansion and his aged chicken, Walter to the care of the Hospice.

Flame Desire, a.k.a. Dawn Joy, also made a brief reappearance in ER. Dr. Murray called off resuscitation attempts three minutes after she arrived with a self-inflicted gunshot wound to the head.

Contrary to human nature, love and lust had not softened Tina as they all hoped it might. If anything, the woman was more irascible than ever. Abby thought it might have something to do with Tina's hormones—those fuel pellets for PMS and other nasty behaviors—having been stirred up and needing time to level out. Skip disagreed, saying Tina would never have allowed anything so tritely human as hormones to rule her one way or the other. Tina, he was convinced, had a stainless-steel pump for a heart and toxic waste for blood. No one gave him an argument on that.

Skip's theory was in evidence as Tina stood in the doorway of 806, hands on hips. "You hard a hearing or something, Monsarrat?"

Adele lifted the bell off the patient's chest and pulled out one earpiece of her stethoscope. "Sorry? I couldn't hear you. I've been—"

Tina closed her eyes and sighed dramatically. "I been buzzing the intercom for the last ten minutes. Get yourself a freakin' hearing aid, willya?"

"Ah, Tina, Mr. Supré here needs a—"

"What? You can't listen to the guy's heart with one earpiece? You need two ears to hear lub-dub? I gotta interrupt the flow of *my* work to come down here and personally deliver messages to you?"

Adele bit her tongue and reached for the top sheet that was resting across Mr. Supré's ankles. Slowly, she brought it to his shoulders, paused to close his eyes, and pulled the sheet the rest of the way over his face.

"I'm sorry, Tina," Adele said in exaggerated saccharine tones. "I was tied up comforting Mr. Supré as he expired. I'm sure if he'd known that it was going to interfere with your work flow, he'd have waited until you were off duty to die."

The monitor tech rolled her head. "Oh, great. Now I've got a freakin' stiff on the ward." Hesitantly, she stepped into the room, inching closer to the bed. "So, like, what happened to him?"

Curiosity, the killer of cats, had momentarily tamed the she-lion.

"He died," Adele answered dryly, tying on the toe tag.

"I know, smartass. Why didn't you call a code?"

"He didn't want one."

Tina lifted the sheet away from the man's face and studied it from several angles. "Why not? He looks kind of young."

"He was, but he wanted to exit peacefully and with as much dignity as possible. Doesn't happen much anymore."

"He had brain cancer, right?"

"Right," Adele said, washing her hands. Out of the corner of her eye, she watched Tina study the dead man. The sharp barbs of the tech's demeanor seemed to have dropped away and her face was touched with something like compassion.

"So, like, where's his wife and kids?"

Adele shrugged. "In a plane headed for Oakland airport. No one thought it was going to happen this quick."

"You mean, the guy died alone? Without his wife or . . ." Tina swallowed.

"He wasn't alone," Adele said and looked away from the sight of Tina misting over. "I held him and talked to him all the way. That's why I didn't hear the intercom."

"Oh."

It was the softest word she'd ever heard come out of Tina's mouth. "What was the message you wanted to give me?"

Shaking herself free of the millstone of human emotion, Tina dropped the soft voice, and turned on her heel. "Call Ritmann. The jerk sounded like he had a scorpion attached to his balls. Said it was important. Got all huffy when I told him to stuff it."

A large hand came down on each of her shoulders while the strong thumbs dug deep into her trapezius muscles. Adele spun around.

Hands still poised where her shoulders had been, Henry

Williams's eyebrows shot up and disappeared under the peach-colored bandanna wrapped around his forehead. "Shit, girl, you one jumpy honky."

Adele stood, rubbing her sternum, trying to ease out the spasm of pain in the vicinity of her heart. "Christ on a bike, Henry, you're going to give me a heart attack someday."

"Then you be just like all my other girlfriends. They all say the same thing afterward."

She wrinkled her eyebrows. "I thought you were celibate while you're in school."

"I was, but the chains of enslavement have done fallen away and I have been liberated by that fine honky tradition called spring break. Man's got to clean out the pipes sometimes, Adele, or his brain don't work right. Gets all backed up. Shit, I was just about to lose my mind with all them fine young sisters giving me the eye, talking to me with those fine bodies wriggling all around. Even Uncle Lamont was startin' to look good."

"So, how did you do?" she asked, sitting on a corner of the nurses' desk.

"Not bad," Henry said. "Started with Sarah on Monday night, last night was Keesha. Tonight I've got Martina, and tomorrow—"

"I meant how did you do in school, Henry," Adele said. "What kind of grades are you getting?"

"Oh, that. I got all A's and one B. I would have pulled all A's, 'cept for your euthanasia paper giving me a C minus."

"C minus?" Adele was offended. "I spent hours on that paper. It deserved at least a B plus."

"Yeah, well, the man thought it was unrealistic to propose that medical folk in the hospital sometimes give dyin' folks a little help and then keep it to themselves."

"What's unrealistic about the truth?"

Henry rolled his head. "You and me know that, but this dude, he has to say it ain't the way it is 'cause he be the medical ethics king—he don't want nobody knowin' nothing 'bout the real truth. If that news got out, next thing you know, the newspapers be sayin' old Dr. Smith over there at San Francisco State is feeding radical ideas to them young minds—

teaching them medical students how to kill their suffering patients in the name of humanity. Then you'd have a riot of all
the right-wingers and the Christian Coalition, and then the
Kevorkian folks will want to get in on it and then the politi-
cians and all the conservative AMA assholes would be deny-
ing everything. Then all them rich Republican backers gonna
be taking their monetary support away from the college faster
than a baby pulls his fingers out of a fire. Shit, girl, we'd have
ourselves a righteous down-home campus riot."

Adele put her hands in her pockets and slouched against
the wall as she regarded Henry with a defiant what-else-is-
new expression. "C minus, huh?" she said, shaking her head.

"Don't worry 'bout that, sister." Henry slid the earphones
down and untied his bandanna, using it to wipe his face. "Uncle Lamont read it and he thinks you're a fine writer. Matter a
fact, he wants to talk to you 'bout writing the story of his life.
He thinks you and him could make it a best-seller."

Adele gave him a wry smile. "Tell him I don't have a phone."

Henry flinched reflexively. "Oops."

"You didn't give him my number!" Adele said, staring at
him in outraged disbelief.

He raised his eyebrows in a sheepish grimace. "Oh, well."

She opened her mouth, but before the blast could clear her
vocal cords, he slipped a little Sir Miles Davis over her ears
and held it there.

"Hey," Adele said at the sound of his voice. "I heard you
called."

"What is the proper psychological term for the woman
who answers your phones up there?" Timothy asked, sounding irritated.

"Now, now. Tina is a bit misguided, but we all have our
crosses to bear. You have Detective Cini, we have Tina."

"You sitting down?"

Adele sat down and rolled her chair out of earshot of Cynthia and Skip. "Shoot."

He took a long swig of Mylanta. "You are never going to
guess what just happened over at the city jail."

EIGHTEEN

THE BREAKFAST TRAYS RATTLED ON THE STEEL cart as the wheels rolled over the automatic door grate. Paddy Kelly waited for the door to lock behind him. In twenty-nine years, no prisoner of his had ever escaped and he wasn't about to blow his record now—not this close to retirement.

He lifted the cover and checked the dish: scrambled eggs, sausage, two slices of buttered toast, coffee, orange juice, sliced banana, grape jelly, and milk. Paddy sighed, removed the jelly, and slid the tray through the slot to the gaunt, hollow-eyed prisoner.

Morning cigarette dangling from his bottom lip, Jenks took the tray with a polite nod and sat down on his bunk. The pale, thin man seemed to be all legs and bony knees.

"Damn kitchen never gonna get the diabetics straight," Paddy said, picking two individual serving containers of no-sugar spread from the bag of extra condiments. He set them on the tray slot.

Taking off his glasses, Paddy polished them using his handkerchief with the embroidered blue monogram in one corner.

"Gonna kill me someday, Paddy," Jenks said, trading his cigarette for a mouth full of eggs. He chewed for a minute, opened one of the jam packets, and smiled. "Oh, I love that apple butter. Thanks, Paddy."

Paddy nodded, but rather than moving on, he lingered, wanting to talk. He'd taken a liking to Robert Jenkins. On the days when things were quiet, he'd stand outside Jenks's cell to chew the fat. Over the course of seven months they found they had a lot in common. Both had been the babies of large

462

families, each adored his mother and hated his old man. Both had been married to saints, and both had been widowed. Neither had children. They shared a passion for fishing and a secret desire that someday, when Jenks was finally released and Paddy was retired, they might go to Florida and do a little fishing.

When it came right down to it, Paddy didn't see much difference between them. Robert Jenkins was awaiting sentencing before going to prison for murdering a man who had broken into his house, killed his dog, and tried to rob him. He himself had killed fifty men who had robbed and killed their neighbors during a war, and been given a medal. It didn't seem fair.

"How'd the new ones do last night?" Paddy asked, taking time to adjust his glasses. He had to be careful not to linger too long; the other prisoners complained if the coffee was cold.

Jenks stirred his coffee; his heavy brows drew close together and kissed. "Quiet as dead groupers. Tried to yap with the one down there a couple a times, but I guess he didn't feel like talking. Not even a 'hello, Jack, go fuck yourself.' "

"Might be a blessing, Jenks." Paddy spoke almost apologetically. "They could've been a couple of them talkers that keep you awake all night." He chuckled. "Hell, for all we know, they could be save-the-fish environmental radical types."

In a rare smile, Jenks showed the gap between his two front teeth. "Maybe they're all part of some religious fanatic thing."

"You might be right about that. I heard from night shift that all of 'em are on some kind of no-talking strike." Paddy pushed the cart forward a few inches. The rubber wheels squeaked against the tile floor.

"Hey, Paddy," Jenks called out in a low, conspiratorial tone. He put his tray aside and went to the door. Paddy stepped back close to Jenks's cell.

"Is it true what they're saying about these guys being terrorists planning to kill all of San Francisco by poisoning the water supply?" Jenks's weathered hands gripped the bars.

"That's what they're saying."

"Was it true the woman was the brains of the operation?"

Paddy had a brief glimpse of her the day before: black hair, big dark eyes, strong legs and ass. Attractive in the way dark women are. "Oh, I don't know, Jenks. You never know who's who with them people."

"Do you know who they were working for?"

Jenks's question caused a certain uneasy feeling in Paddy's gut, though he couldn't have said why. It might have been the memory of the old "Loose lips sink ships" motto his old man was always throwing around. "Don't know. They're not talking."

"Well, find out, wouldya?" Jenks blinked rapidly several times and lowered his voice to a whisper. "I'll be straight with ya, Paddy: they're giving everybody the heebie-jeebies the way they're always staring at people." Jenks hesitated. "Might be a good idea to get the pricks into the segregation tier before something happens to them."

"All right, Jenks." He nodded solemnly, rolling toward the next cell. "I'll pass the word along to the chief." Paddy's glance was brief but telling: he was a man who meant what he said.

He delivered the trays, calling each man's name as he slid them through the slot into waiting hands.

"Kemper?"

Through the bars came all kinds of hands. Young, old, black, white, broken, strong.

"Jaffe?"

There were times when he'd get caught up in those hands— trying to imagine them pulling triggers, or plunging knives into flesh, collapsing windpipes.

"Parker?"

It was hard to imagine they'd all somehow created that much violence.

"Askeri?"

Before he even craned his neck to get a better look into the darkened cell, Paddy's belly began to ache with apprehension. "Askeri? You awake?"

Amar Askeri was lying in the fetal position. Part of the blanket had slipped off the cot, revealing one of prisoner's bare legs. There was something awful about the leg, Paddy thought. Something about the color of his skin.

"Hey! Askeri! Wake up! Chow time."

The prisoner didn't move. From where he stood, Paddy couldn't see the man's face, but he knew he was dead. He'd sensed the same immutable stillness the morning he'd found Joyce in her sewing room, the embroidery hoop still in her hands.

Taking out his cell phone, he tapped in Sergeant Paluzzi's extension.

"Paluzzi."

"It's Paddy Kelly." The ache from Paddy's stomach was spreading to his chest. "We have a problem down here on C. Askeri—one of the new prisoners? He's not responding to verbal commands. I don't know, but I think . . ." He lowered his voice. "I think he's dead."

Paul Paluzzi swore and covered the mouthpiece. When he came back on the line he sounded weary. "Okay, I'll send an extraction team down. Don't go anywhere."

Paddy disconnected and moved toward the opposite end of the tier.

Tom Jackson saw him leaving and looked back at the breakfast cart. "Hey, man! Where you goin'? I want my breakfast. You get back here and give me my breakfast!"

The other men, alerted by Jackson's shouts, all came to their cell doors and looked out as far as they could. Seeing Paddy hurrying away from the cart, they joined in the ruckus.

Paddy Kelly wasn't hearing them; he was listening to the voice of panic in his gut. Outside cell 1265, he banged against the bars with his baton. "Hey! Al-Yassari. You okay? You awake?"

When there was no reply from the form under the blanket, Paddy moved quickly to the last cell. "Askeri?" He hit the cell bars. "Askeri! Goddamn your ass, answer up!"

Like the other two, the younger Askeri brother remained motionless under his gray blanket.

The red light over the automatic door flashed three times.

Five officers ran onto the tier. Sergeant Paluzzi hurried in be-hind them. At the appearance of the sergeant, the prisoners settled down. Their shouts turned to whispers as speculations flowed like mercury from one cell to the next.

Paddy stood next to Paluzzi and watched as three men cau-tiously entered the cell and handcuffed the obviously dead man—one of the many useless policies the brass couldn't shake.

"We're going to need two more extraction teams for the brother and Al-Yassari," Paddy said.

Paluzzi stared at him. "Shit," he said after a few seconds, the features of his face squeezing together in a way that re-minded Paddy of someone with painful hemorrhoids.

Not one to let the grass grow under his feet, Paddy had al-ready worked the situation to be a positive: there were now three empty cells, and the government had been saved a few million dollars in trial costs. He would have liked to share this revelation with the sergeant, but didn't think Paluzzi would see it quite that way—Paluzzi was young and still needed to prove he could part the Red Sea with his dick.

Officer Davis Sewell stepped outside the cell to make room for the gurney. "I'm betting on cyanide poisoning," he said with calm authority.

"How the hell would you know, Sewell?" asked Paluzzi. "Who elected you medical examiner?"

"I used to be an orderly at San Francisco General ER." Sewell hitched up his pants. "I seen guys croak on cyanide before."

"And what makes you so sure that's what this is?" All traces of sarcasm were gone from Paluzzi's voice.

" 'Cause I know what I'm looking for," Sewell said.

"Where the hell did he get the cyanide?" Paluzzi asked, watching the men lift the body onto the gurney. "We shook him down the regular way. He didn't have nothing except the skin he was born with when he came in here."

"It was inside a hollowed-out false molar," Sewell replied. They both looked at him.

"I looked in his mouth. You learn to do that when you work

ER. Third time I've seen it. The first was a Jewish guy who survived the Holocaust. The last one was one of them skin-head Heil Hitler types."

As the gurney passed, Paddy was relieved to see they'd covered the man's leg with the blanket.

There wasn't a sound from any of the prisoners who were staring through the bars of their cells; all eyes were on the gurney. Paddy wondered what their reactions would be when the same scene was repeated twice more. Celebration or depression—he could never tell what it was going to be.

Tom Jackson watched solemnly as Paddy and the sergeant moved toward Al-Yassari's cell. "Hey, man, what about break-fast?" The fire had gone out of his tone completely.

"Shit, man," said Hutchinson in the next cell. "What the hell you think the sucker died from? That kitchen gonna poison us one at a time."

"Yeah," said someone from a cell farther down. "Didn't you never notice the eggs taste real funny sometimes?"

There was generalized laughter, though it was kept low and in check.

"How about I give the rest of the men their breakfasts, Sarge?" Paddy asked. Giving out cold coffee was one thing, but giving a man cold food first thing in the morning didn't seem humane.

Paluzzi nodded. It looked to Paddy as though he'd aged ten years in five minutes. "Sure. Just hurry it up."

By the time the trays were passed, the team returned for the second extraction. They were lifting the body onto the gurney when Paluzzi's cell phone buzzed. Paddy watched the man's face change. When he hung up, he looked like bad news itself.

"That was the third floor," the sergeant said, his face stunned. "The woman is gone."

"Gone?" Paddy didn't make the connection right away. "You mean, she got out?"

Heading for the automatic door, Paluzzi didn't bother to answer.

"Jesus," Jenks said, his hands dangling outside the bars. "They got them all."

"Who?" Paddy asked mildly, shifting his eyes slowly, as if it were an effort to move at all. "Who got them?"

"The rest of the fucking terrorists," Jenks said, surprised Paddy had to ask. "They can't have anybody in captivity. They might talk."

Paddy made a mental note to stop by the store on his way home and buy plenty of bottled water.

"What you think, Paddy? Is it bad?"

Paddy's eyes followed Paluzzi's retreating back. "Yeah, Jenks, it's bad, and it ain't over yet."

Forty-three-year-old Shelly Curry could hardly believe Sausalito office space was at such a premium that physicians were being forced to rent in the Sausalito Industrial Building. The monster-sized wooden structure had a long and varied history, most of it shady. The outside stairs were full of rotting boards. She hoped there wouldn't be an earthquake. The place was barely holding together as it was: one good shake, and the building would collapse like a house of cards. It would take them weeks to find the bodies.

Reluctantly, she followed the up arrows painted on the walls (each one blatantly phallic), directing her to the third floor. A building of its size without elevators seemed ludicrous. By the second flight, she was out of breath. She hoped Dr. Lincoln didn't have many elderly patients. People had probably had heart attacks and died on the very stairs she was climbing.

Another assault of itching caused her to dig her nails into the side of her breast. She prayed the rash wasn't going to be a big deal. She didn't want anything to go wrong with the new implants—not since Woody had finally taken notice.

She looked down at them standing up firm under the blue lambswool sweater. She liked them—liked the way they caught men's attention, liked the fact that she hadn't been without a date since she had them done. And, there was Woody. Mr. Gorgeous. Mr. Unavailable—until now.

Shelly shook her head. Who would have thought a little bit of silicone and plastic could have changed her life so drastically? If she had known, she would have had them done years ago. Really, she thought, it was the best thing she'd ever done for herself in her life, that and the Caribbean singles cruise. If it hadn't been for the cruise, she never would have met Dr. Cleveland, who had sent her to Dr. Lincoln, who agreed to do them for one thousand dollars—five thousand less than anyone else.

At the third floor the long hall was empty in both directions. The nurse said to turn left and it was the seventh door on the right.

One, two, three, four . . .

Shelly grabbed her breast again, scratching vigorously as she went. The itch and burning were worse than if she'd had fire ants crawling inside her bra. She had not slept for days and the circles under her eyes were getting darker. When she looked at herself in the mirror, she thought she was starting to look like the survivor of some major disaster.

. . . five, six, seven.

A piece of notebook paper with the number seven written in black was tacked to the door. It fluttered as she pushed the door open.

The shabby condition of the waiting room made her step back into the hall. Her instincts her told her to run, go to another doctor—a doctor someone had heard of before—a doctor who had an office in a normal office building

The itch claimed her attention again, and she dug at the side of her breast until she was sure she'd broken the skin.

No, she thought. She was being silly. And besides, the sooner the problem was cleared up, the sooner she could take the next big step with Woody. Moving back inside the office, she smiled at the dark-haired woman behind the desk and gave her name. The sight of the crisp white nurse's uniform and the woman's sympathetic smile pulled the story out of her like a confession: the rash and the itching and how it was driving her insane so that she couldn't sleep or eat.

She was on the brink of tears when the nurse put a comfort ing arm around her shoulder. Grateful to find someone who understood, Shelly couldn't stop the flow of words. She'd been so worried. And you see there was this man, Woody, and she liked him so much, and—well, it was all because the surgery had changed her life, and she didn't want anything to screw up her newfound happiness. And do you think the doctor can help?

Eyes full of concern, voice soothing, odd smile at the corners of her mouth, the nurse led her to an exam room telling her not to worry—she was *sure* the doctor could make the trouble all go away.